ANGLE OF ATTACK

"White starts things off with a terrific bang . . . Fast-paced and intelligent."
— *San Francisco Chronicle*

"The plot is as carefully assembled as a computer program."
— *The New York Times Book Review*

THE FLIGHT FROM WINTER'S SHADOW

"The flying sequences soar. The action in the skies as a small plane tries to evade a great new weapon [is] both frightening and exhilarating."
— *The Ocala Star-Banner*

"Impressive . . . Dramatic cockpit action and excellent high-country hide-and-seek in the Sierra Nevadas . . . White's conclusion will leave readers with a chill."
— *Publishers Weekly*

THE SWORD OF ORION

Robin A. White

FAWCETT CREST • NEW YORK

A Fawcett Crest Book
Published by Ballantine Books
Copyright © 1993 by Robin A. White

Library of Congress Catalog Card Number: 92-30136

ISBN 0-449-28709-2

This edition published by arrangement with Crown Publishers, Inc. CROWN is a trademark of Crown Publishers, Inc.

Manufactured in the United States of America

First Ballantine Books Edition: August 1995

10 9 8 7 6 5 4 3 2 1

Dedication

In aviation, most journeys begin with a line on a map. This book started the same way: with a mysterious course connecting a naval air station in Japan with Afghanistan. I found the marked-up chart, GNC-13, in the seat pocket of a U.S. Navy P-3 Orion. I wondered, out loud, what a Navy subhunter might find of interest in Kabul. Although its pilot was generous enough to let me keep the chart, he offered no explanations. *The Sword of Orion* was launched.

A great many people helped transform that line into a story: Afghan *mujahedin*, American naval aviators, Russian nuclear disarmament specialists. Most of them would prefer to remain anonymous. The subject of nuclear safeguards, Permissive Action Links, and lost hydrogen bombs is particularly sensitive. To all these people, my thanks.

But above all, my appreciation and my respect go to Knox and Kitty. *Honest prose; nerves of steel.* They found a single, tentative line wandering over unknown terrain and turned it to a destination.

1
—
THE WAR STEEDS

NAZIPHA HID UNDER THE STONE ARCHWAY OF A RUINED HOUSE and watched her city die. The predawn sky above Kabul was streaked with brilliant tracer fire as the victorious *mujahedin* of the Coalition fired straight up in celebration. A dazzling display of reds, greens, yellows, streamed across the stars. The occasional illumination shell burst in hard magnesium glare, floating to earth under a swaying parachute like a party favor. But the young Kabuli woman knew it wasn't all for show.

Like scavengers fighting over bleached bones, rival guerrilla bands battled one another at the perimeter of the ancient city. Some of the army had gone over to the rebels. Others fought on in the name of men already dead. Dressed in the same muddy fatigues, firing identical weapons at one another, men died screaming the same holy words. To the south and west, the ruins of Kabul were backlit by the flash of artillery and strobing impacts of heavy 122-mm rockets. The crump of the shells vibrated in Nazipha's chest like the thunder of an approaching storm. A rattle of spent shells fell from the sky, and she pressed herself deeper under the stone arch.

Somewhere out in that raging firestorm was her younger brother. Her only brother, now. Somehow, before the coming day was through, she would bring him back to Kabul. Alive.

She turned to face east. The sky held the earliest promise of dawn. They were late. She slung a heavy canvas rucksack over her shoulder. Inside it was the ransom that would release her younger brother from his kidnappers. Inside was a treasure more valuable than gold or silver: the keys to power. When the time came, she'd hand it over to the man most responsible for the carnage this night, a Moslem fanatic named Gulbuddin Hekmatyar. He wanted to turn Afghanistan into an Iranian-style Islamic republic; Kabul into the new capital of *Dar al Islam*, the House of Islam. Not that he cared much for religion; the only faith Hekmatyar truly understood was power. It no longer mattered to her. Nazipha was beyond politics. A cousin had made it to the Philippines by way of Pakistan, India, and Hong Kong. She and her brother would find him and leave this feast of bones behind.

She listened, waiting. Above the crack of rifle fire and the hammering of machine guns, the low moan of *"Allahu akbar"*—God is great!—rose from the direction of the presidential palace. Another storm of spent Kalashnikov rounds pelted the muddy streets and spattered against the broken masonry behind her. They fell like a copper rain, like hard tears.

She pulled up the sleeve of her dark green battle jacket to check the time, but then, against the incessant *pop pop pop* of AKs, she heard the one sound she'd been waiting for. She looked down the muddy street. *At last!*

Nazipha ran from beneath the sheltering stone as a wheezy Toyota pickup truck careened around the corner, its engine clattering, the one working headlight pointed off at a crazy angle. The yellow beam flashed across her. The truck's brakes squealed and the light went to high beam, blinding her in its one-eyed focus.

She held up the rucksack, in part to shade her eyes, in part to confirm her identity. The truck slewed to a stop directly beside her. Its windshield was shot out, jagged with glass shards. The door was flung wide.

A man wearing the PLO–style *kaffiyeh* of the radical *Hezb Islami*, the Party of Islam, leaned over and eyed her from behind the folds of the striped bandanna. His face was hidden. His dark eyes seemed black. An AK assault rifle with double ammunition clips was wedged on the floor by his feet. "I thought you were a boy."

Nazipha was dressed like one in jeans, black boots, and battle jacket. She held up the heavy satchel once again.

"Get in."

The seat was covered with glass. The driver's hands were bleeding. She felt the prick of needle-sharp slivers through her jeans as she jumped in. Before the door was closed, the driver clutched into first and moved off.

"He won't like your outfit," the driver said.

"Who won't?"

"The Baluchi. It's not womanly. Too much like a *mujahed*." He paused when she didn't reply. "I am Naim."

"Nazipha."

She didn't speak again as they took the empty streets north, then west. The flash of artillery fire and the thunder of exploding rounds grew brighter, louder. Closer. The driver kept his speed up, rounding corners fast enough to lift wheels from the mud as they went. Nazipha was about to ask whether this was wise when the anemic headlight beam swept over a running figure carrying a rifle. Then another. Suddenly, there were six. They all wore the uniform of the old Afghan Army.

"Uzbek devils!" The driver stomped the brake pedal to the floor, pumping it. But the mud was slippery. He swung the wheel and threw the battered Toyota into reverse as the first shot slammed into the wooden planks overhead. A second thumped into the body of the truck. "Get down!" He shoved Nazipha to the floor and snatched the AK from his feet, leveling it on the dashboard.

Suddenly, from behind a rubble mound, a brilliant spotlight lanced out from atop a hidden Army truck. It flashed directly at them, filling the battered Toyota's cab with a glare of almost liquid intensity. There was no warning. No ultimatum to surrender. After fourteen years of war, such niceties were no longer observed. Before the driver could squeeze off a round, a heavy machine gun erupted from behind the dazzling spotlight, raking the small truck with 12.7-mm fire.

It was as if the weapon had a direct link with all the ammunition factories in the world. Nothing could silence it. The hammering went on and on, ripping the truck apart. The world was filled with a deafening roar. Nazipha's blood pounded in her ears. She screamed, *"Brother!"* Still the fire went on. A spray of blood and bone, hot and sticky, spattered her forehead with enough velocity to sting. She glanced up and saw the driver's torso buck under the horrendous impact of the heavy slugs.

A bullet tumbled through the engine compartment and plucked at her jacket. Another struck the stock of the driver's Kalashnikov and split it with a dry snap like broken bone. Nazipha closed her eyes. She had failed. Failed. She would die with that one searing thought branded on the blackness behind her tightly shut eyes. *Failed.*

A tremendous *boom* stopped the machine gun. A cascade of automatic fire flattened the militiamen, strewing them like broken dolls. A voice called out for mercy in the name of God and was answered by a single sharp *crack*. Nazipha opened her eyes. Someone yanked open the door.

"She's not here!"

"Find it then!"

Hands pulled her out of the ruined truck. The shattered corpse of her driver followed her out. She fell to the ground. A hand yanked down the zipper of her bloodied jacket and brushed across the swell of her breasts. Someone laughed. "It *is* a woman!" More laughter, hard-edged and dangerous, echoed in her ears.

Not this, she silently prayed. *Please. Not this*.

A voice, filled with authority, stopped the laughing.

"Bring her!"

Arms scooped her up from the street. Another *mujahed* grabbed the canvas rucksack. Both wore the *kaffiyeh* head-gear of the Party of Islam. Hekmatyar's men.

Carried along like driftwood before a flood, Nazipha found herself tossed into the open back of yet another truck, a larger, Soviet-made diesel. This one was filled with armed men. They all carried RPG-7 rocket grenades on their backs like so many Roman spears. The driver's blood seeped through her shirt, through her jeans, cold now. *Naim,* she thought. He'd been a man a moment ago. Something hard was stuck in the smooth skin of her cheek. She touched it and pulled out a sliver. Was it wood or bone?

The engine turned over, over, then caught in a heavy cloud of smoke. They began to roll west once again, labor-ing uphill all the way.

"Where are we going?"

None of the fighters bothered to answer as the burdened truck ground its way steadily higher, higher. She could see the sky beyond them. Tracers still scored it, but they were not so bright against the swelling light of the new day. The engine lugged slower and slower as they climbed up narrow, winding curves in bottom gear. Suddenly, the old truck began to accelerate over more level ground. She sat upright and peered through the legs of the swaying fighters. Where were they? Then she knew. She could see in the dawn light the poles, the narrow death banners hanging limply. The stones. The flowers and the small crumpled photographs pinned to the base of each pole.

This was Tappe Shohada. The fifteen-hundred-foot hill that overlooked all of Kabul. They had brought her to the Cemetery of the Martyrs.

The truck slowed to a stop. The engine died. The thump and crash of battle seemed distant now. The same voice barked another order, and the *mujahedin* leaped down to the muddy ground. Nazipha was left alone in the back of the truck. She turned and saw a figure stand apart from the armed men. He wore the black *sayid* robe of a high priest, a mullah. The hood of his cloak was drawn tight over his head. A snow white beard streamed over his chest. Even in the dim light of dawn, he wore sunglasses. One of the *mujahedin* held out Nazipha's canvas satchel to him for inspection. He nodded.

"Where is my brother?" she called out to the mullah.

"Bring her proper clothes," he ordered.

A heavy, tentlike *chador* was thrust at her. She eased down to the muddy ground, her knees still shaking, and took it, stripping gladly out of the sticky battle jacket. She wiped off as much of the blood on her face as the rough weave would hold and put the *chador* over her head. It was warm and dry.

The wool smelled of dust, and the view out was now limited to the small woven screen directly before her eyes. She heard the sound of approaching engines and turned to find its source. It wasn't coming from the road. She looked up. A few tracers still lit the heavens. She turned again. The sound came from the sky.

A clattering Mi-8 Hip transport helicopter climbed up over the far side of the summit, tipped its blunt nose in their direction, and came straight for them. The blast of its rotors set the death banners flapping wildly all across the cemetery. The whine of its jet engines was joined by a new sound, deeper and more powerful. A second craft, this one a predatory Mi-24 Gorbach gunship, rose straight up the slope like a stalking beast moving in for the kill. It nodded its cannon-studded nose first left, then right, as though sniffing for a target.

Twenty heavily armed fighters stood, watching both helicopters approach. Not one ran for cover. The first craft drew near and began to descend as the gunship circled protectively overhead.

Nazipha sensed another presence. She spun, the viewing screen in her cloak like blinders. The black-robed mullah was standing next to her. She felt the pinch of his hand around her thin arm. A crab's touch. The helicopter's twin two-thousand-horsepower turbines screamed. "Where is my brother?"

"I promise you will join him."

The troopship bounced down hard. Even before it settled on its skids, the side door was thrown open. The priest grabbed her *chador* and pushed her toward the waiting helicopter. "Get in!" A hot hurricane of kerosene wind blasted across the graveyard. Twenty others in the assault squad leaped by them and into the Hip. Nazipha struggled under the cumbersome *chador* to put her boot onto the helicopter's step.

The mullah was already inside, gazing straight down at her. Through the net of her eyescreen, she saw that his sunglasses were not dark, but mirrored. They picked up the bloody tint of the coming dawn and beamed it straight at her eyes.

She felt a shudder of revulsion. His hooded black robe and mirrored glasses gave him the look of a giant insect. She got one foot onto a metal step. An iron band closed around her arm as the black-robed man hauled her up and inside. She was pushed by someone into a canvas sling seat. Her boots struck another canvas bag under her seat. The hatch slid closed and the jets began to howl. The mullah pulled out a black automatic pistol from beneath his robe and pounded on the cockpit bulkhead.

The engines swelled into a roar, the cabin shifted, and they were airborne, beating north toward the high Hindu Kush; the Killer of Hindus. As they shot through the first pass overlooking Kabul, the gunship joined up with them, keeping station off to the Hip's right and slightly above.

Nazipha watched warily as the robed mullah put on a headset and plugged into the helicopter's intercom. Her arm still hurt from where he had grabbed her. Who was he? What had her driver said? *The Baluchi.* She saw him speak into the headset's boom microphone, but the din of the twin turbines drowned out his words.

They climbed to the top of the northern mountains, racing the sun into the sky. It flashed red, then gold, then searing yellow. The peaks rose below them as they shot through a notch in an immense wall of granite. The crest reared up, then fell away. Suddenly, the helicopter took a sickening lurch and nosed over. Nazipha grabbed the metal rails of her seat. She'd flown before; many times, in fact. But always in a safe, comfortable seat and not in a canvas sling with twenty armed men and a priest. A hand grenade came loose from a strap and rolled to her feet. She drew in her breath with a hiss, waiting for the thing to explode. But the fighters only laughed at their prank.

She leaned back to look out the porthole. The northern flanks of the mountains were covered in deep drifts of snow. How far were they going? The shadow of the Mi-8 was a swelling black fleck against the snow. It grew larger, larger as they dropped lower. Suddenly, the snow turned dirty brown, then gray, then disappeared behind them. Where on earth . . . ?

The Baluchi leaned over her. "Look!" he shouted in her ear. His breath was foul and acrid.

Nazipha saw the terrain unroll below them. They were flying low, close to the dun earth, the sparse, stunted vegetation streaking by in brown blurs. Suddenly, the land dropped away below them, even though the helicopter had not gained altitude. The ground turned a darker brown; a line of trees swept by. *Trees!* Then she saw why: a roiling river white with the milk of glaciers flashed below. *The Amu Darya!* The Mother of Rivers.

On one side lay Afghanistan. On the far bank was the homeland of the enemy; once the Soviet Union, now the Independent Republic of Tajikistan. Dry ground appeared once again. The escorting Mi-24 gunship peeled off, nosed over, and pulled swiftly ahead. It would all be over. Soon.

The sun was barely above the mountains, and already a cloud of fine ocher dust coated every soldier and vehicle of Missile Battery Alfa. "What a shit hole," said its commanding colonel. He stepped out from beneath a tent of knotted camouflage and surveyed the four MAZ trucks, each with an intermediate-range nuclear missile on its launch rail. They were parked at the center of a defensive circle of mobile guns. Each launch vehicle was attended by a service van, within which the real purpose of Alfa lay hidden: 150-kiloton fusion warheads plus the command and control devices necessary for their release, arming, and launch.

After years of wandering like a high-tech nomad all over Kazakhstan, Alfa, like all the other nuclear forces of the former Soviet Union, was coming home. *But why this way?* the colonel wondered as he felt the heat of the day build. The other mobile missile units had been withdrawn to Russia by rail from Alma-Ata; that made sense. He had been directed overland to Dushanbe. And that did not make sense. Why the hell was he hauling nuclear missiles across Tajikistan? There were riots in Dushanbe nearly every day. Religious fanatics killing Communists; Communists shooting democrats. Why the devil was he being ordered into the middle of *that* mess?

He turned and faced south to Afghanistan. The mountains of what they called the Devil's Nest were a brooding presence on the undulating horizon. A snowy slash of white against lapis blue. They were altogether too close for his liking.

He listened to the faint crackle of his command radio, heard the shouts as a group of his men played soccer in the morning cool. There had been no message from Moscow for days. Their last pay packets had arrived three months back. The last food truck they'd met contained dehydrated meals stamped CONSUME BEFORE 1965.

He retreated into the shade of his tent and pulled out a camp chair and sat down to fill out the day's duty schedule. It was so quiet he could hear the rattle of stones as they broke free from the hundred-meter talus slope behind Alfa's temporary emplacement. Not even a fly buzzed. He thought of Moscow. Real food. Women. He had nearly nodded off when he heard a sound that was at once familiar and unexpected. He checked his watch, then listened again. *A helicopter?*

* * *

The pilot circled the gunship behind a ridge in a line of low, shattered mountains. Below him the terrain was nearly identical to that on the far side of the Mother of Rivers. But it was not the same. The dead land beneath the gunship's armored belly was the home of the invaders. No matter that it called itself independent. Had the thieving Tajiks been independent when the Russian tanks rolled through?

He gripped the cyclic with fierce exultation, listening to the powerful shout of two Isotov TV-3 jet engines a few feet above him. He twisted in more power from the turbines, and the surge of energy seemed to flow right through him. The gunship was a good machine, one of the most recent. The *shouravi* had been fools to give it to the Afghan Air Force.

He banked the gunship hard right and aimed for a break in the ridgeline. In the dry valley beyond that pass was his target. Below him in the forward cockpit, the pilot could see the nervous flicking of his gunner's head. His radio suddenly crackled and an excited voice shouted in Pashtun, the language of the mountains. The pilot nodded. He rolled out of his turn, leveled the gunship, and picked up speed. The pass swept nearer. "Get ready," he said to his gunner.

The pilot's radio crackled again. *"Allahu akbar!"* With that, he rolled in full power to the two Isotovs and pushed over into the attack run, the rotor blades slashing overhead in a high-speed buzz.

There! He saw the circle of dark vehicles against a fan of scree spilling off the flank of a low hill. The pilot forced his jaw to unclench. The Mi-24 swept down out of the sun on Missile Battery Alfa like a hawk diving on prey. He keyed the intercom to his gunner. "Now!"

The 30-mm cannon erupted. The gunner walked the shells through man and machine, scribing a line of death across the circle of Russian vehicles. Clouds of yellow dust rose first, followed by puffs of white, then black, smoke.

"Get the guns!" the pilot shouted. Trucks could not shoot back. He saw men running, the line of dust thrown skyward by his gunner's fire marching through them, flattening them as they ran for their weapons. Most never made it five steps. But a few were luckier.

One of the ZSUs suddenly swung his way, its radar nodding up and down frantically. "The gun!" the pilot shouted, but it was already too late.

The ZSU seemed to explode as its multibarrel cannon brought the gunship under fire. The pilot heard the whizzing of shells as he threw the cyclic over to escape.

The stream of shells corrected even faster. The pilot saw them draw near, nearer; the tracers merged with his flight path as he tensed his stomach against them, as though by force of his will he might deflect death away from its ballistic path.

The gunship was slapped aside as the first shells struck, then an endless roll of thunder echoed through it as it smashed into a solid wall of high explosive.

The windshield disintegrated right in front of the pilot's face as lights flashed on his instrument panel, then went dark. The ZSU was right off the nose, firing round after round. With a last push, the pilot shoved the cyclic full forward. The wrecked gunship fell toward the ZSU's flaming barrels. "The Faith!" the pilot screamed. "The Faith!"

The Mi-8 troopship lurched and slewed as it dropped nearer to the ground. They were flying nap of the earth, streaking low over the hills at high speed. The Baluchi unclipped his safety belt and fell against the cabin's wall as the Hip snaked its way up a dry ravine, rolled over a ridgeline, and dived down the shallow slope beyond. He looked down at the hurtling terrain. "Get ready!" he shouted back to the twenty *mujahedin*. He glanced at Nazipha. "You, too!"

She pulled up the hem of the stifling *chador*. The canvas satchel lay hidden beneath heavy folds of dark fabric. She opened the bag to reveal an exquisite Japanese oscilloscope and battery pack. She pushed aside the padding and pulled the coding box out, moved the thumbwheel on its bare aluminum one click. She checked that the wire bundle was still secure and nodded at the Baluchi.

"It will all be for nothing if you fail," he warned her. "Your life depends on it." He turned away, then back. "And your brother's." The Baluchi glanced outside again as the Hip suddenly reared in midair, killing nearly all its forward speed, then dropped straight down like a falling elevator.

The Baluchi stumbled over to the sliding hatch. He threw the lock lever open. The slipstream caught the door and slammed it aft in its tracks. The cabin immediately filled with the stench of burning tires and the sharp, familiar odor of cordite.

The Mi-8's engines screamed as it clawed to a hover a foot above the killing ground. A sharp *tick* came from overhead and a small, bright hole appeared in the roof like a lamp suddenly switched on. A second report came from the cockpit, followed an instant later by a scream. The helicopter bounced down hard, once, twice, settling on both skids.

The Baluchi threw his arm across Nazipha's chest to keep her in her seat and yelled, *"Boro! Boro! Boro!"*

Twenty fighters of the *Hezb Islami* leaped to the ground firing. They had come down in the center of a circle of vehicles. Some were burning; others served to protect the surviving Russian security troops. Fire erupted from the shelter of wrecked trucks, raking the ground around the troopship. One, two, then all twenty machine guns returned fire. The

Russians began falling back toward the dry slope beyond the encampment.

A Kalashnikov caught the tire of a burning Ural truck. It exploded, sending the Russian behind it flying through the air. A long whoosh ended in a terrific explosion as a rocket found a fuel tank, sending men and machinery up in a boil of filthy fire and smoke. Two *mujahedin* were cut down by a machine gun fired from behind an overturned table in a camouflaged tent. Another RPG-7 rocket silenced it. A string of firecracker reports terminated in a low, rumbling detonation as another RPG round struck, silencing the last of the Russian rear guard. It was no longer a battle. Now it was a deadly footrace.

Gunfire came from the slope beyond. Afghan fighters used to breathing the diamond air of the high country were loping in easy pursuit of the Russians scrabbling up the hot, dry gravel. It was no contest. Each race ended in the single, sharp crack of an assault rifle and the blossoming of a red flower upon the thirsty dust.

Nazipha watched in horror as a prone Russian held out his hands in surrender, then sagged. The sound of the shot came a second later.

"Come!" The Baluchi all but threw her from the idling helicopter. "Over there! Bring your sack and hurry!" He herded her in the direction of an untouched support vehicle immediately behind the number four SS-12M launcher.

The ambushers had been careful. Two Russians lay flat to the road, alive, their arms behind their heads. A *mujahed* prodded first one neck, then the other, with the hot muzzle of his AKM machine gun.

The Baluchi looked up at the locked rear doors of the armored support van. A tall whip antenna waved lazily from its dust-covered roof. He nodded at Nazipha. "Little bird," he said, "you speak their foul tongue. If you wish to join your brother, tell the two unbelievers they must open the doors."

Nazipha stepped forward. "Both of you," she began in accentless Russian. After ten years, the words tasted strange to her. "Listen to me. Listen to me very carefully. I know you can open the back of this truck. You must do so. Believe me. You will be killed if you do not."

"Fuck your mother!" screamed one of the Russians. His collar blazes identified him as part of the KGB guard contingent. His uniform was covered with patches and poorly sewn repairs. Nazipha looked up at the Baluchi. He needed no translation.

"The unbeliever cannot hear his own words," said the black-robed mullah. "Now, let the voice of God speak the truth." An AKM barked and the blond head bounced once and exploded.

The other Russian all but begged for the honor of opening the missile support truck's armored doors. Under the muzzles of five AKs, he scrambled to his feet and began punching numbers into the coded lock. His hands shook so badly he missed the first time, then the second.

The Baluchi shouted. A gun barrel was thrust into the Russian's buttocks. His scream made the fighters howl with laughter.

The Russian's eyes were wild with fear. They flicked first to Nazipha, then to the Baluchi, then to the muzzles of the AKMs pointed at him. He looked up the slope behind the encampment. The fleetest soldier slept in a puddle of his own gore not fifty meters uphill. The Russian entered the last number in the door lock and twisted the handle. "Please. I just want to go home. Please." He pulled the handle and the door swung on its heavy hinges. "Don't—"

"*Nyet!*" screamed a man from within the darkened truck. Alfa's political officer opened up on them with an RPK light machine gun, his motions professional and deliberate. He fired quick, accurate bursts, mowing down three *mujahedin* and the cooperative Russian like dry wheat, moving from one target to the next.

Nazipha saw the flaming circle of the RPK's muzzle swing her way. Her boots were only just moving. It was too late.

The roar of the RPK stopped. Nazipha's ears rang, but she was still standing. She looked up and saw the *zampolit*'s boots, a cloud of cordite slowly rising.

"Sometimes," said the Baluchi, "even God must be helped a little." There was a smoking hole in his black robe, three bright copper cartridge jackets at his feet. The mullah opened his robe wide enough for her to see the heavy pistol hidden in its folds. He jumped up into the van and held out his hand to pull Nazipha after him.

It was dark inside, dark and stifling. "I can't see in this damned thing!" She reached overhead and pulled off the *chador*, throwing it into a heap. Her shirt was plastered stiff with dried blood.

The Baluchi stopped and framed a protest, then thought better of it.

She felt her way along the wall. Large metal boxes, each the size and shape of a coffin, were locked into a steel rack. Small annunciator lights flashed from status boards above each one.

She reached up and touched one of the row of lights. Nine red eyes glowed back at her. Yes. It was as she had been told. Nazipha snapped on a flashlight and focused it on the dull gray metal of the warhead container. A label stamped into the lid announced that inside lay one KHYs-14, a 150-kiloton fusion weapon eleven months from rotation at the Troitsk enrichment facility. *Should I?* She hesitated, feeling the Baluchi's breath on her neck. *I can still pretend to—*

"Do it!" the Baluchi ordered her, his voice low and full of menace. "In your brother's name! Do it!"

She opened the green rucksack and removed a tangle of wires, the beautiful Japanese oscilloscope, and a small aluminum box. It was a simple little device. Nothing her teachers at Moscow Polytechnic would have been much impressed with. But here, this morning, it was worth a life. Her brother's. And an empire.

She untangled the wires spilling from the oscilloscope, clamping one to the cable feeding the warhead container and another to what was clearly a grounding strap. She threw the switch on the scope, and a wavy line began to undulate across the small screen.

"Well?" the Baluchi demanded.

She ignored him, concentrating instead on the rise and fall of the signal on the oscilloscope's screen. "The beat of the guardian's heart." It was a clock signal leaking out from the bomb's safing circuitry. A nine-digit code kept the wrath of heaven from unauthorized hands. Three numbers were known to the local commander and three more to STAVKA, the Russian High Command. The last three were known only to Boris Yeltsin.

In times of emergency, Moscow could transmit a single coded burst to each and every nuclear-tipped missile within receiving range. It would open the weapons' locks. But even more important, it permitted the final arming to take place. It was crude but reliable.

She clamped the wire from her coding box to the antenna feed terminal on the side of the warhead container and snapped on the power. A second wavy line appeared on her scope, completely out of phase with the one generated by the warhead's safeguard circuit. She carefully tuned the clock frequency of her Unique Signal Device to match the timing gate of the weapon. When they matched, she drew in her breath, dried her finger of sweat, and sent the first nine-digit code.

Nothing happened. The display panel was still lit with a row of red lights. She turned the tiny thumbwheel that altered her signal to the next combination. Again, nothing. A third time yielded the same results. She found her sweat had dried to a salt sheen on her brow. She tried a fourth; a fifth. Was there something wrong with the circuit? She clicked the thumbwheel again.

"Well?"

"Maybe we should break it free now, then later, when there's more time—"

"A woman should never have been trusted!" the Baluchi exploded. "Men have died—"

Her finger advanced the switch another click. Suddenly, nine red lights on the status board suddenly blinked as though in surprise. In the small windows beneath each light, numbers began to flash too quickly to read.

"Is it free?" The Baluchi was breathing fast again. A murmur came from a small group of fighters who waited, watching them from behind. The mullah tugged at the massive gray bomb container. It didn't so much as shake. "It does not—" His words were cut off as the final red lights turned green. A new tone sounded as the jaws of the warhead lock sprang open with a reptilian snap.

Nazipha sat back and breathed deeply, rocking on her heels. *Brother. I have done this for you.* Only then did she realize that she had been holding her breath. The sudden air made her dizzy. She'd done it. A live hydrogen bomb.

"There's no time to sleep!" The Baluchi turned around and grabbed one of the fighters. "Help me get it down to the ground!"

The warhead container was fitted with rollers, making it a simple job of maneuvering it back to the rear doors. It glided with an eerie, pneumatic smoothness across the van's deck. Five *mujahedin* struggled it to the ground and pushed it toward the waiting helicopter. The Baluchi turned to one of the men: "Take care of the truck. Leave nothing for the *shouravi*. Burn it and be quick. We will not wait for long."

The Hip's copilot was waiting in the main hatch. Nazipha watched as the heavy container was hoisted up onto the chopper's deck. She stood back, looking to the circle of destruction, as the rotor blades began to stir, faster, faster.

"Get in," said the Baluchi as the fires in the helicopter's engines took hold.

"Where is Ghulam?" she asked as she stood next to the Baluchi inside the cabin. The Hip's blades were already moving too fast to see. The surviving *mujahedin* leaped aboard.

"I will take you to him now."

The helicopter shot straight up and spun around to the south, throwing Nazipha into a corner of the cabin. It tilted nose down and accelerated, climbing hard and fast for the safety of the border and for the mountains beyond. The Baluchi moved close to her once more. She couldn't read his eyes from behind the mirrored glasses, but something, something was wrong. She could see it in the looks of the *mujahedin* sitting all around her. She could smell it. She glanced at one of the fighters. He quickly looked away. The mullah stood over her now. "Where . . . where is he?" she asked. "Where did you take him?"

"To the Cave," said the priest, toying with her as the helicopter climbed.

"What cave? Where is he now?"

"Read your *Qur'an*, whore. The Cave of the Sleepers. Where the righteous await the call of destiny."

"Keep your religion, priest," she shot back. "I only want my brother."

"You are already near him." The Baluchi reached between Nazipha's legs and pulled out a small canvas bundle that had been stashed under her seat. He yanked open the string that kept the bag closed and upended it, spilling its contents to the deck.

At first she thought they were enormous blue spiders. Then she saw the ring. She knew it well. She'd brought it back to him from Moscow. They were hands. Her brother's hands. Blue. White tendons. Bone. Blood dried to black.

"There." The Baluchi smiled. The fighters looked away.

"My . . . you have killed him!" Her ears popped as they climbed higher and higher.

The black-robed priest moved closer to her. The 9-mm appeared from the folds of his robe, its muzzle a hole pointed at her heart. "Whore," he said, "you opened your legs for the *shouravi*. You don't deserve the honor of death."

She could see two reflections of her face in his mirrored glasses. She glanced at the muzzle of the pistol, then at the warhead, then at the other men. "Help me!" The *mujahedin* looked stonily away from her. She looked beyond the Baluchi's robe at the blue sky in the Hip's porthole. They were high and still climbing. Nazipha shivered. It was getting cold. She could smell the snow in the air. "Help me." Her words came out as a whisper, drowned by the shriek of the turbines. "Help me."

Suddenly, the mullah reached back and threw open the sliding hatch. A fierce wind rampaged through the cabin. A sea of snowy teeth was framed in the open doorway, white daggers thrust deep into the dark blue sky. The Baluchi's arm shot out from beneath the black *sayid* robe and snatched a fistful of her bloody shirt. He pulled her to the edge.

She tried to scream but nothing found its way beyond her throat. Her feet teetered at the door's sharp metal rim. The wind cut like a blade too fine to feel. There was nothing below her but space, a skim of ice too thin to hold the smallest step without giving way, falling, falling.

The Baluchi's mirrored sunglasses reflected the utter emptiness of the Afghan sky. "Little bird," he whispered in her ear, the hard, cold circle of the pistol in her side, "fly."

Nazipha caught one final glimpse of the dull gray box before she tumbled out. One instant the cabin, the Baluchi, the helicopter, was there; the next there was nothing but a dark shape scuttling against the blue sky, the sun flashing on, then off, on then off, as she spun in her fall. Her legs found their way under her, her feet involuntarily bicycling.

The snowfield rushed up to meet her with the measured pace of a tidal wave. It grew larger, slowly at first, then faster as she fell, nearer, nearer, then blinding in its speed.

In the instant before the white wave broke over her, a billion, billion rainbow sparks flashed from the dry crystals, and then she plunged through the sun-rotted crust and into billows and billows of dry, ancient snow.

2
THE RESURRECTION

YASNEVO WAS JUST FIFTEEN KILOMETERS SOUTHWEST OF MOS-
cow, but few Russians knew it existed. The insiders called
it the *les*, or forest, for the stands of birches surrounding the
International Intelligence Directorate. Before the coup, it
had been known more simply as the headquarters of the
Committee for State Security: the KGB.

The main building rose twenty stories above the forest.
Its basement was rooted fully half as deep. On the lowest
floor, beneath the shooting ranges, beneath rooms stuffed
full of tapes, paper secrets, and the meticulous minutiae so
beloved by police states, beneath absolutely everything,
Capt. Aleksandr Belenko occupied an office.

Dozens of men once worked at the Southwest Asia desk.
The ones upstairs called them crabs, dwellers of the murky
bottom. Now only one crab was left. They'd all been
caught, one by one, yanked to the surface by the tightening
noose of a disappearing budget. Belenko felt the tickle of
the net, too. He hadn't been paid in three weeks.

If the men upstairs regarded Belenko as a bottom
dweller, Belenko looked up at the storms sweeping the surface and was glad for his place of quiet refuge. His subma-

rine. His time capsule. He'd been stuck in it now for four long years, safe, unbothered, as all hell broke loose upstairs. Empires had crumbled, most notably his own. Nations dissolved. Wars flashed into flame from long-smoldering coals. But down in the Yasnevo basement, the storms were all but imperceptible. Remote. Only the steadily diminishing payroll gave evidence to the chaos enveloping Russia.

The click and wheeze of Belenko's slow-heating samovar marked the time. Eventually he would have to surface. To find his way. Eventually, even a submarine runs out of air.

And then what? *Maybe I'll sell Persian carpets.* He had a small collection, a good one. A gorgeous red Kirman was hung on one of his cinder-block walls. It would sell for a lot, if it came to that. He imagined himself sitting with his carpets, a spidery souk dealer, waiting for the unwary tourist to fall into his web. Crabs and spiders; dwellers of the margins. He checked his watch. It was eleven-twenty.

Belenko carefully refolded the morning's *Jomhuri Islami*, placing it atop the *Teheran Times*. He took a pad of paper, a pen, and began translating. He was under no pressure. No deadline. No one had asked why he was translating Persian news. No one had asked for a briefing in months. They left him alone. The last Southwest Asia crab at the bottom of the sea. Forgotten. Belenko knew there were worse places to be. Far worse. He put the papers aside and glanced at a small framed photograph on his neat desktop.

In it, four men stood before an enormous sandstone boulder. Snowcapped peaks studded the horizon. Tanned dark by the high sun and with muscles sculpted by walking up mountains, the four were dressed in loose-fitting *shalwar kameez* outfits and *patou* overblankets: the uniform of the Afghan *mujahedin*. Except for the black beret each one wore, they were picture-perfect examples of the well-dressed guerrilla. The beret gave them away as members of

OSNAZ, the *Osobogo Naznacheniya*: the KGB's own Special Operations forces. A group so elite the Kremlin itself was not permitted to know its numbers or its names.

The brains of a scholar, the arms of a soldier, was their motto. Not that it had helped any of them. Belenko held the group portrait close. Three of the four men were dead. One by accident, one by loving war too well, another with a needle full of heroin in his arm. Only the last one, the one with one dark eyebrow and one as white as the snowcapped mountains, had survived, by burrowing himself deep into the mud at the bottom of Yasnevo. It was Belenko's own face staring back from across the years.

He held the photo with a reverential touch. *Ten years.* Could it really be so long ago? He'd been a member of the most elite Soviet fighting force. The only one the Afghan rebels truly feared. Fluent in Dari, in Pashto, in the ways of mountain warfare and the chapters of the holy *Qur'an*, they'd made the American Green Berets seem like a schoolboy rabble. OSNAZ had been the Soviet Union's best chance of winning an unwinnable war. Now the war was lost. The empire, too. Belenko knew the two facts were related. He placed the photograph back on his desk and hunted for a cigarette in the bottom desk drawer.

He found the last box of Primas, ripped open the lid, and lit one. The foul smoke was comforting, familiar. It had body. History. He sucked it down, feeling it attack his throat. Primas were grudging. They delivered, but not without protest. Not without bite. Giving and unyielding. In other words, Primas were very Russian. Like Belenko.

A click came from the old samovar he had rescued from a bombed Afghan teahouse. He watched the first tendrils of steam rise. The samovar was so covered with green tarnish that very little of the original copper plating showed through. A patch had been polished out in its base, revealing a Cyrillic inscription: TULSKAYA FABRIKA, ZOLOTAYA MEDAL, 1887. Belenko listened as the samovar perked softly, mimicking the low, conspiratorial voices of men.

Suddenly, without any warning, without so much as a knock, the door swung open on its creaky hinges.

"Sasha?"

Belenko shot straight in his chair.

"Hah. So it's true," said the man in the doorway. His broad shoulders spanning the opening, Pavel I. Markelov bulled his way in and shut the door behind him. "Captain Aleksandr Sergeivich Belenko of the OSNAZ. In the end, a deskman." The man looked around the small room disdainfully.

"Pavel Ivanovich?" A Russian thumb of a nose angled up from a broad, flat face. He wore blue jeans and a navy blazer, expensive imported ones Belenko noted, and a white sweater that accentuated his gut. And on his feet were slippers, not shoes. Belenko thought the American word for them was apt: *loafers*.

Markelov's pale eyes were the color of ball bearings, swiveling, examining. His face was both fleshy and frozen. Giving and unyielding. In other words, very Russian. "Frankly, I expected better than this. All this time."

Belenko forced his expression to remain calm, though his heart raced. He reminded himself that once, not very long ago, Markelov had been a very dangerous man. Belenko put on his glasses. "Ten years," he said. A stamp on a closed file.

"History," said Pavel Markelov with a shrug. Five years Belenko's junior, he'd once been the Kabul *rezident*, the KGB's number one man in Afghanistan. Now, in his expensive Western outfit, he looked ten years younger. Markelov chuckled at the perking samovar, the thick Kirman hanging from the opposite wall. "Still a romantic. I bet you have your beret hidden in your desk. Yes?"

Belenko's left hand involuntarily started to reach for it in the bottom drawer.

"Fuck your mother. I'm right!" Markelov grinned. "So. Working with a pen suits you better than a rifle?" He reached into his suit jacket and pulled out a box of American Marlboros. There were ads all over Moscow now: MARLBORO, THE CIGARETTE WITH BLAT. "Care for one?"

"I smoke Primas."

"They'll kill you."

"They're cheap."

Markelov wrinkled his nose. "Such a Russian. Always ready to be deceived."

"It's good to be able to count on something these days." Belenko examined Markelov's face as he relit his foul cigarette. Markelov's red hair had thinned to a few strands artfully combed across his forehead. His blazer had a crest, an insignia that Belenko didn't recognize. The style was cut too close to flatter. Markelov seemed ready to burst a seam. His expression seemed ready to burst, too. But into what?

"Aren't you glad to see me?" asked Markelov.

Belenko switched to Dari, the language of Kabul. "Forgive my manners." He nodded at the bubbling samovar. "I am the dust at your door. Tea?"

Markelov sniffed the steam. "Frankly, no. You have nothing stronger?" His Russian sounded harsh and guttural after the smooth Dari.

"A poor man sees heaven with a cup of tea."

"Fuck your mother." Markelov wrinkled his nose again, then he slowly, sadly, shook his head. "You still sound like one of them. Tea. Carpets." He nodded at the Kirman. "Nice. Expensive." Markelov smacked his thick lips. "Listen, Sasha, I haven't come for *bazaari* talk. Forgive my bluntness. But I'm here on business."

"After ten years? What kind of business?"

Markelov reached once more into his blazer and placed a small, gilt-edged card on Belenko's desk. It read, *P. I. Markelov, Associate Director, International MAYAK Corporation, LTD.* It bore a Geneva address.

Belenko looked up from the card. "An interesting name, MAYAK. A lighthouse beckoning Russia to the future?"

"Absolutely. As for Geneva, the women are cold or crazy. Or both. But things work there. Everything is in order. That I like."

"You would."

Markelov raised an eyebrow. "You think we don't need some here in Moscow?"

"We were talking about Geneva."

"Yes. Well, unfortunately," said Markelov, "order is breaking down everywhere. Who can stop it?"

"You?"

"I wish. Moscow. Kiev. Dushanbe. Alma-Ata. Frankly, it's all going to hell. Five years from now, we'll *wish* we had only a few places like Yugoslavia to sweat over. There is no glue. Nothing to keep the whole fucking thing from exploding. Am I right?"

"There's Islam."

Markelov smiled. "That," he said, "is very astute. In fact, it's why I have come." He yanked out a chair and sat down. "You know, you were hard to find. Upstairs they don't even know what you do. Or where. They call you—"

"Crabs."

"Yes." Markelov glanced around the tiny room. "Frankly, it's like a tomb down here."

"The Southwest Asia department has been thinned."

"Liquidated is more like it. It's not like this where I

work. We have two people to an office, we're so crowded. Computers. Fax machines. Everything. Money no object. MAYAK brings capital and technology together. It's a model of what Russia can be."

"In Geneva?"

"Very funny. I work for the future, Sasha. The future. The whole playing field is wide open. Not like before. Not like during the years of stagnation. MAYAK began when some far-seeing men saw the tidal wave coming. They were experts in many fields. Why throw away a generation of the best minds in Russia? That's what could have happened. Chaos. The West picking our bones for peanuts. So they moved themselves to high ground and set up the company. MAYAK. To preserve what is best. To rebuild."

"I see. But what exactly do you do?"

"Speaking generally, coordination with the West. Our knowledge has been quite valuable to them."

Belenko stared at the unfamiliar crest on Markelov's blazer.

"Ralph Lauren Polo," said Markelov proudly.

"Nice. Expensive," Belenko mocked. "So what knowledge does MAYAK coordinate?"

"This and that. Whatever pays. For example, we have helped Western concerns develop Russian markets."

"The only markets I know are empty."

"Not *physical* markets." Markelov laughed. "Market studies. Surveys. Perhaps you've heard of the piece we did for that big New York ad agency? Frankly, it was brilliant."

"I don't seem to recall it," said Belenko, wondering how he could get Markelov to leave him in peace. Wasn't it almost time for lunch?

"It's the key to selling in Russia." Markelov leaned over Belenko's desk, his elbows on the pile of Iranian newspapers. "You see, all Russians can be divided into five psychological profiles. *Kuptsi* are the merchants. The narrow-minded bastards who look to the West and say, *no thanks*. They must be shown the goods. Advertising works on them only so far."

"I wonder why."

"Cossacks are fiercely Russian, but they are also ambitious for status. Status means Western products."

"Ralph Lauren Polo."

"For example. *Students* want everything Western, but only on the cheap. *Russian souls* never make a decision unless someone else does, first. They expect to be deceived." Markelov snorted. "You are like that." He nodded at the acrid Prima. "You would rather poison yourself with a Russian product than use something foreign. True?"

"They actually pay you for this?"

"They pay plenty. Information has always been valuable. It's just like the KGB."

"With blue jeans. And the last category? You said there were five."

Markelov brightened. "People like myself. *Businessmen* are the new entrepreneurs. Successful. Wealthy. The ones who will guide the nation through difficult, uncharted waters."

"I thought you left the Service," said Belenko.

Even Markelov saw the spike of irony sticking through Belenko's words. "Very funny. But listen," he said, standing up and perching on the edge of Belenko's desk, "that's not why I'm here. You see, Sasha, I'd like to recruit you. We have a slot. Frankly, you can't say no."

An alarm rang in Belenko's head. "I don't do market studies."

"Of course you don't. We do many other things now. MAYAK is big business, Sasha. Global. We have offices in Moscow. In Kiev. Geneva, as you see. Even New York.

Self-supporting. Profit-making. In the black. Capitalized to three hundred and fifty million."

"That's a lot of rubles."

"*Dollars.* Backed up by a ton of Norilsk platinum. Silver. Gold, too. Whatever we need. Money talks and nobody walks. We have to be well capitalized in our new venture."

"Which is?"

Markelov's face both opened and shut. "Nuclear disposal is becoming quite an important market. Reactor wastes. Chemical sludges. A real witch's brew. And munitions, of course. Destroying atomic warheads is a growth industry. The biggest of them all. That's where you come in."

"Sorry. I have a job."

Markelov chuckled and reached into his breast pocket. He pulled out an envelope, limp with sweat. "I shouldn't do this, but frankly, you should know. Read."

At least he still sweats like a Russian, thought Belenko as he ripped the wet paper. Inside it was a copy of an internal memo from Grisha Azov, his boss.

"We're hiring Azov to staff the new Tokyo office. It's already set. And your little desk with Southwest Asia is no more," Markelov said simply. "Tell me, Sasha. Have you ever waited in an unemployment line? It's worse than waiting for a meat ration. Hunger is one thing, but uselessness . . ." Markelov watched Belenko's face. "I can't see it for Captain Belenko of the OSNAZ. Can you?"

Belenko tossed the damp envelope down. "So what could such a giant company need from me?" He stood up and walked to the perking samovar. He filled two glass teacups, handing one to the former KGB man.

"Some consulting for a very special contract. Perform as well as I know you can, and there's a permanent place at MAYAK. Who knows? Maybe even Geneva. Think."

"Who knows?"

"I argued in your favor for it. You're our man. There's work for you, Sasha—big work. It's a dangerous time for the world. You can help."

"Tell me."

"I will. But first you tell me. Do you believe in ghosts?" Markelov drained his cup, keeping his blue-gray eyes on Belenko.

Belenko sat back down. "Only if they have been thoroughly rehabilitated."

"Not these. You see, some ghosts have come out of the rocks. MAYAK wants you to find them and put them back underground where they belong. Rehabilitate them, yes. But with what our friends in Washington call extreme prejudice."

"Friends? What rocks?" Belenko took another sip from his steaming glass.

"Our old ground. *Your* old ground. Afghanistan." Markelov cleared his throat and looked around Belenko's office. He stood up from his perch on Belenko's desk and walked to the Kirman. He fingered the intricate knotting. "How much did the rug cost?"

"Carpet," Belenko corrected. "It was a gift."

Markelov ran his fingers across the brilliantly hued Kirman. "I remember when you used to say that Afghanistan was a rug with a million knots." He turned. "Well, my friend, some of the ones you tied have come loose. MAYAK has the contract to help put it right. We're working both sides on this one. Breaking new ground. The Americans are shitting in their pants. They see Yugoslavia, you know, the Serbs and the Croats?"

"I know."

"And then they look at the whole southern tier of the old Soviet Union. And more. You know what they're calling it? The Islamic Arc. From West Africa all the way to India.

Fuck your mother. Maybe as far as Indonesia. But instead of Slavs killing one another, they see millions and millions of black-assed Moslems. It's a tinderbox. A hundred sharp splinters sticking into their thumb. It could make Afghanistan look like a May Day parade. Except that it won't be a localized affair. It could spread. A worldwide war. A jihad. And that is very bad."

"For business?"

"I worry about your attitude, Sasha. Down here so long. You need some fresh air. Some new perspective. And MAYAK will pay you for it. Pay you well. Think of it as on-the-job training."

"Reeducation used to be free," said Belenko. But he was also interested. "Why did the Americans hire MAYAK? Why not work with the legitimate organs of the Russian government?"

"What organs? Yeltsin? They debate for weeks the color of a flag. Months on who sits where. You think *they* can take the necessary steps? Please. Washington is working with us because they know we value results. Just like they do."

Belenko nodded. "Then what has happened in Afghanistan?"

Markelov looked away, at the ceiling, at the samovar. His ball-bearing eyes rolling, restless. "A theft."

Belenko smiled. It was like saying there were food lines in Moscow.

"I'm not talking about goats, Sasha." His voice lowered until Belenko could hardly hear. He put his hand on Belenko's shoulder. His breath was minty, cloying. "Some of your old friends got together and conducted a cross-border raid. They hit a missile battery out in the middle of nowhere. *Behind* the middle of nowhere. They left quite a mess, and they took something back with them. Something nobody would want them to have."

Belenko's eyebrows bunched together, one black, one white. The alarm bell was deafening now. What had Markelov said was MAYAK's new specialty? Atomic munitions?

"They came, they blew some sleeping rocket troops to hell, and they left with a hydrogen bomb," Markelov said, watching Belenko's face for his reaction. "Not a big one, you understand, but then, these things are relative. We want that warhead back in safe hands. So does Washington. Fast. Otherwise . . ." He let his words trail off.

Belenko understood. *The wrath of God,* he thought, *given to those who still believe in it.* His eyes sharpened to tight focus. "How did they get over the border?"

"Goatherds flying gunships represent something of a new wrinkle in banditry. Rifles, of course. Rockets? Everybody has them. Even Stingers. But not gunships, Sasha. This was well planned. Well organized. And it involves certain aspects of a more technical nature. Frankly speaking, you may be partly responsible."

"What?"

"It's true. Do you remember a student at Kabul University? She was there when you first went in as a language instructor. Recruiting local talent, weren't you?"

"She?"

"Except that she recruited you." Markelov watched Belenko's face closely now. His gaze flashed like a scalpel in the operating room lights. "Still don't recall? I wonder. She made quite an impression on you then. So much so that you arranged to have her sent out of the country when the Red Army went in. You had her sent to Moscow. Now do you remember?"

A voice whispered to Belenko. Sweet and feminine. He

saw a cloud of fragrant steam escape from the old samovar. "There were many students at the university who left for Moscow."

"Not like this one. Think, Sasha. She took a double degree at Moscow Polytechnic. Electronics and computers. *Own the children and seize the future,*" he said, mimicking Lenin's words. "You still don't recall her?"

"It's been a long time." It was true, and it was a lie.

"Apparently too long." Markelov looked disappointed. "I'll tell you what I know"—he paused—"but first listen. A message was received in both Moscow and Washington. It's from a little black bastard named Hekmatyar."

"Gulbuddin Hekmatyar?"

"You see? You already know. Yes. The same. Seven guerrilla groups became two: the six of the Coalition and Hekmatyar. His gang of hooligans were cut out of the deal when Kabul fell. They think it highly unfair. You know that elections are scheduled in three weeks?"

"I do. About the woman. The student. Was she—"

"I see your memory becomes sharper even as we speak, yes? About the elections. Forget them. There won't be any unless we recover the weapon. The *Hezb Islami* issued an ultimatum: no Western support for the Coalition. Evacuate the city of all armed forces. Cancel the elections, or else."

"It sounds like something Hekmatyar would do." Belenko's brain was firing raggedly. An engine coughing to life in deepest winter. Oil a syrupy sludge. Only one spark was bright, a blue arc flashing. Could she really be alive? Or was this all a ploy to get him to work for MAYAK? The former KGB man would certainly know what the mention of her name would do. He looked up at Markelov. If this was a game, then two could play it. "I'm confused, Pavel. If you know who did it, why not go in and get him? He has a headquarters."

"Khadir?" Markelov laughed bitterly. "Think. It's in the middle of Afghanistan. We could send the entire Red Army into those mountains. Half would get lost. The other half would shoot one another. No. Perhaps if there were still an OSNAZ. But now, we'd never find a fucking thing. Not in three weeks. Not in three years."

"Yes." Belenko did know. That made sense.

"I knew you'd understand." Markelov enjoyed jigging the lure just out of the crab's reach. A little closer, then up. A twitch. A dangle. "Now Hekmatyar wants back in. And he claims to have the means. I don't need to tell you what would happen if he took over Kabul now. Riding a hydrogen bomb. The tinderbox. The Islamic Arc. Kaboom!"

Belenko's heart was beating fast now. He breathed in deeply, maintaining a stoic face. He would not let Markelov know. Never. He covered himself with the shell of an analyst. "Yes. It could be dangerous. Iran, Afghanistan, probably Pakistan, would fall. Then north."

"North is right. Azerbaijan. Tajikistan. The Kazakhs, too. A knife at our throat, Sasha. A scimitar."

Belenko nodded. The former Soviet republics were already simmering with religious hatred. It would be the dream of the fanatics come true. An enormous Islamic republic. A festering wound that would infect the whole of central Asia. And maybe more. Surely more. *With a bomb* . . .

Markelov dangled the bait above Belenko. Out of reach. In sight. "You can see why Moscow is very concerned." Twitch. Dangle.

Belenko looked up. "Yes."

"And so is Washington. I knew you'd understand." Markelov let the line out again. Closer. "The money's good. Better than whatever they used to pay you to sit down here." He reached once more into his jacket and pulled out another envelope. It was damp like the first. "I'm prepared to offer an advance. Swiss francs."

Belenko smiled. He felt like strangling this ex-KGB man in blue jeans. "Sorry, Pavel. I wish I could help, but you need somebody with recent in-country experience. It's been ten years. I wouldn't know my way around anymore."

"Sasha . . ."

"I mean it." He didn't.

"You're far too modest. You know how they think, how they operate. You made contact with the leaders when they still had goat shit between their toes. Including this woodchip Hekmatyar. And don't forget the woman. This student."

"Whoever it was, it was long ago."

"What's changed? You even managed to penetrate them." Markelov let out the last bit of line. It was time. "Now. We do know a few things. Perhaps this will help you remember. A casualty was brought into Kabul from a rural clinic. You know. *Médecins sans Frontières*. Those French bastards who patched up the *mujahedin* so they can go back out and kill Russians?"

"One of the raiding party?"

"You are very sharp, Sasha. Probably. And Allah Himself was watching over her. I shouldn't hold out on a colleague. Her name was Nazipha Popol."

The name hung in the air, turning slowly round and round.

"Yes," said Belenko.

"The mind is a strange machine. It can be totally blank, then something, a color, even a smell, can trigger everything. Don't you agree?"

"Yes."

Markelov saw Belenko gulp down the bait. "I think, and MAYAK thinks, she had something to do with the raid. The weapon was not just stolen. No. It is much worse than that."

Belenko's eyes locked with Markelov's. "How?"

"The release code was used. Nine digits. Only that kulak Yeltsin knows them all. And for once, he's innocent."

"You mean . . ."

"The bomb went out armed. I don't need to tell you that sophisticated means are necessary to release the weapons from storage. And arm them. Of course, an expert in Soviet electronics, in computers, someone like this might not have much difficulty. You begin to see?"

"She would never do it. Never."

"Perhaps. But then again, as you said, it's been a long time. People change. Ten years. Who knows? You yourself barely remember her. How do you know what she has become?"

"I do. People don't change that much."

Markelov shrugged. "Look at it this way, Sasha," he said jovially. He had him. He knew it. "You owe it to the world, yes? Who sent her to learn at the Polytechnic?"

"I did."

"Frankly, I always thought it was a mistake to bring those cannibals out of their mountains to civilization. But that's the past. MAYAK is the guardian of the future. You can join us. You can put things right. And be paid well for your troubles. How can you say no?"

"How do you know she was involved? You have proof?"

"Proof?" Markelov tossed the pay envelope containing the Swiss check to Belenko. "No. Not yet. Proof is what you will provide." He smiled. Giving and unyielding. "Think it over, Sasha," he said as he walked to the door. "I'll be upstairs. I can book you on a flight tomorrow morning. Think."

Belenko listened to Markelov's steps echo down the

empty corridor outside his office. The samovar whistled, hot now. He heard the grating slide of the elevator door open, then close. Only then did he open the bottom drawer of his desk.

He reached down deep. There, at the back, behind the empty carton of Primas, his hand brushed against coarse fabric. He pulled out the black beret and held it up to the light. An archaeological treasure from the bottom of the sea. He flipped it around and out tumbled a small photograph, a small square. A portrait snipped out from a larger group pose.

The woman's face was beautiful and noble, an exotic blend of dark Tajik mixed with the green-eyed racial remnants of Alexander's Greek legion. It was the face of a goddess.

It was Nazipha Popol.

Twenty hours later, Belenko wedged a thin pillow against an airliner's plastic porthole. At just past nine in the morning, it already felt like a very long day. He watched the second hand as it counted out the minutes, feeling his wariness grow with each kilometer passing beneath the IL-72's wing. He was the only passenger on board. *Money talks, nobody walks.* It had been chartered by the International MAYAK Corporation, Ltd.

The Ilyushin covered the 1,800 miles from Moscow's Sheremetyevo airport to Dushanbe in just over four hours; fortunately, there was no shooting going on that day. Islamic fanatics were gaining strength here, too. They'd chased out the president and taken his palace before the Russian garrison ejected them. The Thin Red Line. But they'd be back, of course. They always came back. Like ghosts.

From Dushanbe to Khorog was only two hundred miles

farther. The chartered military transport took a circuitous path along the border, not straight across the northward bulge of Afghanistan. Who knew what was down in those shadowed valleys? You could buy a Stinger missile for a thousand dollars in almost any bazaar.

The STOL transport followed the milky white Oxus River all the way to the remote village of Khorog, finally landing at a gravel airstrip. Filled with glacial melt and powdered rock, the Oxus ran cold and strong here. At its mouth in the diseased Aral Sea, it was nothing more than a choking sewer reeking with every poison the ingenious Soviet agriculturalists had devised.

As the engines spooled down, Belenko stood up and gathered his duffel bag and coat from the seat beside him. He patted the inside pocket of the long green overcoat for the reassuring piece of black cloth he had carefully carried. The old beret, his talisman, was there.

A heavily armed Mi-8 helicopter waited for him at Khorog, its blades shifting nervously in the wind off the hills. Overhead, two Mi-24 Gorbach gunships circled protectively. Had MAYAK arranged for all of this, too?

Belenko strapped into the troopship, noting that each of the side doors held a swinging Gatling gun manned by a worried-looking Russian sergeant.

They lifted off in a cloud of choking ocher dust and beat northeast, following the Oxus to where a tributary joined it from the north. The three helicopters turned their backs on Afghanistan and headed for the remains of Missile Battery Alfa.

The terrain below turned brown and sere as they found their way through the blasted crags and rock-strewn plains. At a nameless valley, the helicopter swung due north and began to descend. The two gunships broke off, circling. Out the window, against a backdrop of a low ramp of broken rock, Belenko saw the remains of the missile battery. It looked like a giant's sandbox with toy vehicles carelessly strewn about, some on their sides, others upright but burned black. The helicopter landed in the center of the ruined circle.

Why were they here? he wondered once again. Routing an atomic missile battery through such dangerous country made no more sense than dangling a bone in front of the nose of a wolf. What did they expect?

A UAZ-469 jeep roared up to Belenko as he stepped down from the chopper. The young Border Guards officer had a Tajik Republic badge sewn across his old Red Army insignia. He kept casting nervous glances up at the mountains, as though behind each rock an ambush lay waiting. "Captain Belenko?" he asked as the rotors spun down overhead. The dust was choking. The officer examined Belenko's civilian outfit.

"I used to be," Belenko said, nodding. "Where is it?"

"This way."

An R-105M radio squawked in the backseat as they passed the blackened, twisted metal that had once been Battery Alfa. Belenko saw the shredded vehicles, the pools of spilled oil on the dust. Blood, he knew from practical experience, was absorbed by the land and made invisible far more quickly than oil.

The jeep slowed as they passed a row of dark green rubber bags. They were inflated like flat, square balloons in the heat. Next to them, abuzz with flies and stacked like cordwood, lay a heap of dirty, bloody rags. Belenko looked closer and saw that they were the earthly remains of several *mujahedin* warriors. "Stop!"

The Border Guards officer wrinkled his nose. "Here?"

"Here."

The UAZ jeep slowed to a stop. Belenko hopped out and

walked to the tangled pile of bodies. The smell was as familiar to him as the four jaunty men in the photograph on his desk. *Three, four. Five at least,* he thought as he counted limbs frozen in death, dark and sinewy, powerful enough to climb mountains before breakfast and never complain. Then he noticed a peculiar pattern on one piece of cloth. The PLO-style bandanna was an unmistakable signature. This raid had been conducted by the *Hezb Islami.* The Party of Islam. Markelov had spoken that much truth.

He checked the others. They were the same. But why would Nazipha, an urbane, well-educated woman of Kabul, help men such as these? It didn't make sense.

"Find anything?" the Border Guards officer asked as Belenko got back into the jeep.

"Something."

Passing the ruins of a helicopter that had smashed headlong into one of Battery Alfa's tanks, they came to the burned shell of a missile support van. According to his briefing, four atomic warheads had been locked away inside. Now, the armored doors gaped open like a rifled safe. The jeep stopped and was almost instantly covered by a dust cloud of its own making. The engine died.

It was getting too hot for Belenko's green overcoat. "Let's take a look," he said as he stepped out of the jeep.

He walked to the charred missile support van. The unmistakable aroma of roasted meat wafted from within. He pulled out a Prima and got it lit.

"The *zampolit* took three of them right here," said the captain. "We found him inside. The heat . . ."

"Shot?"

"The fire was intense."

A man with a long-probed Geiger counter emerged from the hulk. He switched it to a higher sensitivity level and swept the van's entry. "It's clean. No breaches."

"The other weapons?" asked Belenko.

"Safe," said the man with the radiation probe.

"Safe." Like the size of a nuclear weapon, safe was a relative measure. Belenko gripped the handhold and pulled himself up to the rear of the van. "Light." The captain thrust a powerful flashlight into his hand. He snapped it on.

A rocket battery sent to wander a dangerous border. An air assault complete with helicopter gunships. Men dressed in the colors of the *Hezb Islami*, the Islamic fundamentalist outfit commanded by Gulbuddin Hekmatyar. And Nazipha. He knew she was smart enough to pull it off. But why would she?

He pushed aside a tangle of blackened wires and moved farther inside. The dead air concentrated the burned smell. Despite himself, the odor made his saliva run. Belenko nearly gagged. He sucked down hard on the smoke and focused the beam on a heavy gray box clamped to the warhead rack. Belenko ran a finger over the soot. Underneath, the metal gleamed, impervious to mere fire. *One.* He shifted the beam. *Two. Three.* The third warhead container was firmly locked in its cradle.

He reached up and caught the broken stub of the van's communications cable. He fingered the charred end. *Not broken. Unscrewed.* He turned the flashlight onto the empty spot where the fourth 150-kiloton hydrogen warhead had once been secured. The steel jaws were wide open. Only a specific nine-digit code could do this. Whatever else was mysterious about the attack, this much Belenko knew: the weapon had gone out the back door of the van armed.

"Well? Is it not as we reported?" the Tajik captain asked.

"Exactly so," said Belenko as he turned south to face the high wall of the Afghan Hindu Kush. The Killer of Hindus. Plumes of snow rose from their peaks like great question marks against the dark blue sky. "How quickly can you arrange a flight to Kabul?"

The Tajik shook his head. "Impossible. It isn't safe for us to go there. Even Air India can't land now. No one can."

Belenko thought of Markelov. The gilded calling card. The fat coffers of the company he worked for. What had he said? *Money talks, nobody walks.* He faced the young officer. "There you might be wrong," said Belenko.

3

—

THOSE WHO ARE SENT FORTH

COMDR. RICHARD DONOVAN SURVEYED THE REMAINS OF HIS office. A pile of sealed boxes stood in one corner, marked for his new posting at NAS Barbers Point on Oahu. The cartons swallowed nearly everything he had accumulated in his three years in Japan. Only one remained to be filled and taped. When it was done, he and the United States Navy would turn Naval Air Station Iwakuni back to the Japanese. Fifty years of keeping the peace in the western Pacific would come to a close. An uneasy future with a rapidly rearming Japan would begin.

A weak shaft of sunlight illuminated his window, then went dark as the sun rose into a dense cloudbank out over the Inland Sea. *Just about done,* he thought. The photographs, the awards, even his coveted Bear Trap citation, were now carefully stowed, ready for shipment back to Hawaii. One photograph was still hanging: the official portrait commemorating his taking the helm of VP-21. Patrol Squadron Twenty-one had been his for three glorious years. He unhooked the photo and held it under the lights.

The man receiving the squadron flag looked a great deal younger than Donovan felt today. The same solid chest filled out the Nomex flightsuit, the same insignia and patches adorned his leather G-1. He hadn't lost much more of the reddish blond hair that bristled from his scalp, thank God. But the face was not the same. The face in the photo had color, excitement. Donovan felt as gray today as the storm light coming through his window.

Donovan was leaving the front lines of maritime patrol flying. His new posting would be to a facility informally called Orion University, a training academy for Navy crews flying the big, four-engine P-3 Orion. With it would come his long-delayed rank of captain. All the same, Donovan knew his operational flying days were over. *It happens to us all.* He walked over to the last packing box and wrapped the photo with plastic blister sheeting. As he carefully packed the last photo, the powerful shout of a five-thousand-horsepower Allison engine made him turn and look outside.

He watched a P-3 of the Japanese Maritime Defense Force taxi off toward the runway. It had the rising-sun insignia on its wings. In a year, only Japanese planes would be flying from Iwakuni.

And then what? *Probably kick us off Oahu,* he thought. Donovan believed in a circular history. What goes around comes around. He knew the world was changing; what American military man didn't? Enemies were becoming friends and allies enemies, even if it was still considered impolite to say so. He stopped and listened as the Japanese P-3 roared off the runway and into the low clouds. The window rattled with distant thunder. *Crappy day to fly,* he thought. *I hope they enjoy it.*

Before it fell silent, the telephone rang. He picked up the old black handset. "Donovan."

"Good morning, professor. How's packing?"

"Just about done, Captain."

It was Capt. Henry Reynard, former Pensacola shipmate and Donovan's friend. He was also his CO. An abrasive, truth-telling officer, he'd run afoul of higher authority once too often. His latest brush had come after Desert Storm. All in all, it was a lousy war for the Navy. They'd run a distant last place to the Air Force and Army, media-wise. Reynard knew the real skinny; as commander, air group, aboard the carrier *John F. Kennedy*, he had launched the secret air strike against the Iraqi missile complex at Dahr Nema. The problem was geopolitical. Dahr Nema was in Libya, not Iraq; it was considered bad form by the Foggy Bottom boffins to call attention to Libya's dangerous hospitality. Reynard didn't like standing by, watching the wing wipers in blue slop up all the glory, and said as much to a reporter. His orders to Japan were waiting for him when *JFK* docked.

"What can I do for you, Henry?" asked Donovan. "You want me to send you back a case of something from Pearl?"

"Negative. I've got more urgent business with you. I've got a problem over at VQ-2," said Reynard. "In fact, it's sort of a revolt. I'd like you to take a shot at smoothing it out for me."

VQ-2 was the oddball squadron at NAS Iwakuni, flying an experimental version of the Orion, the EP-3. It was stuffed with gear to the overhead. All of it highly classified.

"Why me?" asked Donovan, puzzled. "Don't they work for you over there? Have they not felt the Hound Dog's nip?"

Reynard huffed. "I'd be happy to warm up their tailfeathers, but I can't. Not on this one. No way."

"Can't? Why not? The spooks have it wired?"

"Not exactly. I also thought you'd like a warm-up for

Orion U. Besides, I need this handled right. I also thought you might like a hop in this particular bird. It's the *Grape*."

"I see," said Donovan. The *Galloping Grape* was the secret squadron's technology test-bed aircraft. Unlike every other P-3 Orion in the fleet, the *Galloping Grape* was equipped to defend herself, not just snoop. She carried two AIM-9L Sidewinder dogfighting missiles under her long wings. She also came equipped with a device called the Sniffer. It stood for Scanning Neutron Interferometer. The proliferation of atomic weapons was finally setting off alarms in Washington. Simply put, the *Grape* had a nose for nukes. "Okay. What's the situation, Captain?" Donovan asked.

"Simple. I want you to give a check-ride."

Donovan scowled. "Hang on, Henry. I'm not checked out in an EP-3. Especially the *Grape*. And I'm probably not even cleared to step on board a VQ bird."

"You are now. Besides, what's the difference? It's got four engines. Two wings. A tube and a tail. Anyway, you won't be doing the flying. Just the watching."

"There's a big difference," Donovan replied. "That damned airplane is one solid computer. I can't even get the cash machines to work right at the exchange."

"Commander," said Reynard, his voice beginning to fill out with their difference in rank, "it would seem you aren't properly excited at the prospects of doing your generous CO a favor."

"And you haven't given me the particulars."

Reynard chuckled again. "Okay. I have a pilot who won't fly with his assigned copilot. Flat out refuses. He won't budge. It all came to a head about twenty minutes ago. The bird is out on the ramp and suddenly the pilot's out on strike."

"So? Fry him."

"Not so fast. I also have a very important mission on the boards for this particular aircraft and crew. And it has to be done yesterday. So frying is out of the question. I want this nipped in the bud before it gets loose and out of control, and I want the *Grape* ready and available to fly. It's that simple. I need the plane manned up and out of here. Quick."

"Why is it whenever someone tells me how simple a mission is, I get nervous?"

"Because you've become a suspicious old fart in your dotage. Look, you think I couldn't vaporize this kid's ass if it made sense to? Think a little deeper, Dickie. You're leaving in a couple of days. I have to stay here. So, if there's frying to be done, I'd rather you turn up the burner. I don't need any more enemies in Washington. Not these days."

"To think that I once believed you were the devious type. What does Washington have to do with it anyway?"

"You'll see. I told the pilot to walk over and talk with you. You know, a Dutch-uncle chitchat, paperwork to follow. Or even better, no papers at all. No need to write up a dash-one. You can keep your mouth shut. If you don't, some smart-assed lawyer would have a real . . . never mind. Will you do it?"

Donovan looked out the window. The deep belly of a thundershower was rolling closer. As he watched, a flash of lightning lit it from within. "It's not exactly good weather out there this morning."

"Damn, Dickie. What's a little rain to an old salt like you? So?"

Donovan shook his head and smiled. "I'm always at your service. But I still have never checked out in the bird."

"What's the deal? It'll be a piece of cake. Just look sage."

"Sage," Donovan repeated.

"I have the greatest confidence in you, Dickie. Even if you are a dried-up old fart heading for the boneyard."

"Stirring words, skipper."

"Call when you get back." With that, the phone line went dead.

Donovan stepped to the window. He caught sight of a flight-suited figure striding purposefully over from Ready Five, VQ-2's briefing hooch. Thunder rumbled from the squall line bearing down on the base from the Inland Sea. Across the bay, the lights of Hiroshima sprinkled on in the unnatural gloom. Donovan ran his hand through his close-cropped hair. *Check-ride?*

A few minutes later, three sharp raps came from his door. He sat down in his padded chair and folded his hands on the cleared desktop. He tried to look sage. Donovan cleared his throat. "Come!"

A young lieutenant came into Donovan's office, saluted crisply, and set a folder down on his cleared desk.

Donovan read the young man's nametag, squinting a bit to clear the gold blur on the lieutenant's chest. "Relax, Jameson. I don't bite. Captain Reynard says you have a problem with your copilot," Donovan said with a smile he hoped would put the young man at ease. "What's the situation?"

"The captain sends his regards, sir, and asked me to bring Lieutenant Harper's fit-rep for you to review." The young man nodded at the folder.

Harper? thought Donovan. Why was that name familiar? "I'll read it later," he said. "Why don't you fill me in on your side first."

"Yes, sir," said Jameson. "It all comes down to one thing: I won't fly with Lieutenant Harper."

Donovan raised his eyebrows together at such a bald

statement. "Why? Is there something wrong with the lieu-tenant's ability to fly?"

"No, sir," said Jameson with pursed lips. "Harper can fly just fine. But commanding a P-3 is more than stick and rudder. It's judgment and discipline. It's procedures, it's—"

"Okay, Jameson. I get the outline." Jameson was a sober sort. *Dry stick* was the name they had for them back at Pensacola. All wood and no sap. Donovan eyed the young pilot. *He'll probably make admiral.*

Donovan opened the folder and pulled out the fitness record of one Lt. J. P. Harper. He stopped right there.

The jacket bore a color photograph. Two piercing blue eyes stared back at Donovan from the face of what anyone might call a very beautiful young woman. *Harper!*

Now he remembered. She was one of the first women assigned to an operational P-3 squadron. *J. P. Harper,* he read silently. Her face bore the slightest hint of a cocky smile; her eyes seemed to challenge Donovan to find something, anything, amiss. He looked up at Jameson. "You know, son, I think the Navy has really changed. Time was half the wing would try to get her to fly right seat with them. Amend that. *The whole wing*."

"It's not a question of her being a woman," Jameson continued as he watched Donovan's surprise. "It's a matter of attitude. She feels the Navy gave her a raw deal by sending her out to VQ-2. She seems to think that flying the *Gr* . . . that our aircraft is a dead end. She's got this chip on her shoulder that gets in everybody's way. Like she has to prove herself every second she's flying. While she's pulling this macho number, she forgets she's there to command, not just fly. It's not just me—"

"Okay. Let me read," Donovan interrupted him. He slipped on his half-frame glasses and opened up the jacket of the report. He didn't have to go very far before coming to the first negative entry, this one made by her A Stage primary instructor back at Mainside, Pensacola.

The student's previous flight experience, although interesting (see attached) is not helpful in establishing proper procedures and methods.

P and M was what they called it, Donovan remembered. Entire classrooms chanting in unison the holy mantra of *one-ten, chop, drop and prop.* It was the prelanding checklist, reminding them of speed, power, landing gear, and propeller pitch for the T-34s they'd flown in training.

Donovan turned and saw a copy of a page extracted from Harper's civilian logbook. It contained nearly two thousand hours, a very considerable amount of flying time for anyone, much less a civilian. He looked more closely and was surprised to find a great many of those hours had been spent in crop-dusting biplanes. *Interesting is right,* he thought. Flying old Stearmans a foot off the ground didn't fit with Donovan's image of a typical teenage girl. He turned the page.

Day 5: Student is safe for Stage A solo, but is too confident too soon. Suggest we hold her back for the rest of her class. She likes aerobatics and unusual attitudes.

Donovan raised an eyebrow. Why had her instructor held such a gifted student back? He read on.

Day 12: Student performed low-level roll on her first authorized solo flight. Poor discipline and appreciation for course rules. Student has a natural ability but is very undisciplined. Likes to show up her shipmates in a demoralizing fashion. Harper is not a team player. Recommend a DOR.

Donovan stopped right there. This was the heavy artillery. DOR meant "drop on own request," a polite way for her primary instructor to suggest that she voluntarily get lost. Then the handwriting changed, and a new instructor's notes appeared.

A Stage completed satisfactorily. Formation work fine. Join ups are first class as is low-level nav. This student should be pipelined to Meridian.

NAS Meridian was a madhouse of runways with the permanent stink of kerosene baked into it by the hot Mississippi sun. It was also the Navy's primary fighter school, where every aspiring fighter-jock wished to go. Where women were not allowed. Donovan flipped the page. There, underlined, her instructor had written: *This gal was born for fighters.*

Donovan turned the page again and stopped, a chill rising up his spine. It was an accident board's final report.

The Board of Inquiry finds the cause of the accident of 2–22–86 to be improper diagnosing of a complete engine failure, incorrect manipulations of the controls, compounded by an apparent unwillingness to declare an emergency. Because the tower was not notified, equipment was not in place and the postcrash fire became intense, leading to total loss of the aircraft (T-34C) and one fatality.

Donovan breathed in deeply and let it out slow. The next page was a copy of her orders to NAS Kingsville, the Texas training ground for all multiengine naval aviators. Being pipelined into bigger, slower aircraft was the death of her dream to fly fighters. Like Donovan's orders back to

Orion U., it was a one-way trip. The Navy might change its policies regarding women in combat. But it would do so without Harper.

Donovan skipped through the entries, noted the number of requests for reassignment, each denied, that appeared as Harper made her way through a difficult career in naval aviation. He quickly turned to the last entry, the one made by the young officer standing uncomfortably before him. It was the most damning.

Harper is a danger to herself and to her crew. Her lack of organization and reliance on guesses and hunches won't hack it in the real world. She is an accident waiting to happen.

Donovan looked up as he closed the fit-rep. "Lieutenant Jameson?"

"Sir?"

"Are you sure you want it to read this way, son? She's dead with your eval reading the way it does. Not even the Air Force would touch her."

"I'm sorry for Harper, sir. She just doesn't want to fly Orions and it shows. That's what makes her dangerous."

"Don't be sorry to tell the truth. It only makes things worse in the end."

"Yes, sir. That's more or less what Captain Reynard said." Jameson shifted from one foot to the other. "You flew in Vietnam, didn't you, sir? With Captain Reynard?"

"Briefly." Donovan turned back to the problem at hand. "Okay. Ordinarily, with a jacket like this there would be no question about what to do. Harper would get the boot. But this, as I'm sure you know, is a little different."

"Because she's a woman? Sir, we can't afford to worry

about how it looks. I have the men in my crew to think about every time we fire up."

Thank you, Captain Reynard, thought Donovan. Reynard had said the problem with Harper would be good preparation for Orion U. Donovan looked back at Jameson. "What would you recommend?"

"Commander, I know what happened back at Pensacola. She nearly flunked Primary. She screwed up and killed her IP. She's been a thorn in everyone's side ever since. We can't take the chance of just shuffling her to some other squadron. If she screws the pooch, we'd still be responsible."

Donovan nodded. It was true. "I suppose the real question is, is she worth saving as far as the Navy goes?"

Jameson didn't hesitate. "Harper's got a single-seat mentality. She doesn't belong in an Orion. The rest is up to somebody else. As things stand, I don't think she's safe and I won't fly with her. Bottom line, send her back to dust cotton. If you don't believe me, you can make your own evaluation."

"If you won't fly with her, why should I?"

"Captain Reynard said you might like a chance to fly a P-3 Echo before you head back to the States." Jameson looked uneasy.

"Something else?"

"He also said you knew someone who got a raw deal once."

"I see." Donovan surely did: a young JG by the name of Richard Donovan. His own jacket contained the summary of an accident investigation board. And four men had died. Not just one. He looked up at the young pilot. "Captain Reynard is a devious old man. What's this hush-hush mission he alluded to?"

Jameson stared at his boots. "I'm afraid I can't ..."

"All right. Where were you headed this morning?"

Jameson looked relieved. "We were on the boards for a test run just offshore. There's a couple of Soviet . . . ah, I mean *Russian* cans inbound for a courtesy call and we were going to go rig them with the nose."

Rigging meant looking them over with a magnifying glass. But what was this nose? "I see." Donovan glanced outside. "This nose, what exactly . . . ?"

"The neutron scanner, sir. It sniffs out warheads."

"Oh. That nose." The storm clouds were darker, but they were to the east. The scheduled run would take them out west over the Sea of Japan. "Where is she? Harper, I mean."

"Preflighting the bird. We're due to crank in about twenty minutes." A brilliant flash strobed outside, followed by a long, rolling detonation.

Donovan looked around the office. There were still a few items to finish up. But when would he have the chance to fly a real operational mission again? He felt a decision click inside him. "Why not?" he said, pushing back from his desk. He stood up, his tan uniform immaculate. His barrel chest made him look shorter than his actual five eleven. "Where's the *Grape* parked?" Donovan asked as he grabbed his old G-1 leather flight jacket.

"South ramp, sir. You'll see it."

"I'm sure I will." The *Grape* was infamous at Iwakuni; the special nosecap needed to allow the Sniffer to work had weathered in the salt air to a lurid purple. Hence the name.

Donovan zipped up the jacket. The battered leather bore Patrol Squadron Twenty-one's insignia on the shoulder, a marlin spearing a Soviet sub, red blood leaking from the gash, with the words PATRON 21. "How's the aircraft, Lieutenant?"

"She looks chewed up by the techs, but she's a good

ship, Commander. And the crew's first rate and that's what they deserve out in front, too." The pilot watched as Donovan locked his desk. "Watch her, sir. Harper's quick. She can get you into trouble faster than anybody I've ever flown with."

Donovan looked up. "I will," he said as he handed the fitness report back. "And please give my regards to Captain Reynard. Tell him I'll find a way, somehow."

"A way, sir?"

"To get even."

4

SHE WHO IS TESTED

DONOVAN WALKED STRAIGHT TO THE SOUTH RAMP AND FOUND
tail number 003 without a moment's hesitation. With its
purple nose, the *Galloping Grape* was impossible to
mistake for any other P-3 at Iwakuni. *A neutron nose for
sniffing out nukes,* he thought. *Can we really do that?*

Rain began to spatter on the *Galloping Grape*'s aluminum
skin. Donovan ducked underneath, checking some of the obvious preflight items. Another flash of lightning made him
hurry. If they were going to fly at all, they'd better do it
soon. As he trotted for the boarding ladder, two muffled
booms came from a pair of F-14s as they started their engines. The storm cell was moving in fast, and everyone with
a destination was lighting the fires and heading for the hills.

He scrambled up the waist ladder as the rain came down
harder. Looking out to the east, he could see a solid black
curtain drawn down, blotting out the view across the bay. A
peal of thunder ended his sight-seeing. He ducked into the
cabin and looked around. Donovan whistled softly, glad
there were no crewmen around to see the shock on his face.
This, he thought as he examined the banks of humming
computers, *is going to be different.*

It looked too empty. All the usual workstations for sonar and magnetic-anomaly gear were gone. Even the sonobuoy racks had been pulled. Along the left cabin wall, a bank of glittering lights twinkled from racks of signal processors. Here and there, wires were strung from rack to rack, patching some of the more experimental boxes together. Most of all, there were no flight-suited figures rushing around completing last-minute jobs. Only the whir of computer fans. A normal P-3 required a crew of fifteen; the *Galloping Grape* demanded just four. Donovan secured the hatch, dogged it tight, and began to walk up the narrow corridor toward the cockpit. The odor of hot electronics was thick in the air. *Sage,* he thought, remembering Reynard's admonition.

As he walked forward to the flightdeck, he came at last to some occupied workstations: Lieutenant Carranza, the tactical coordinator (tacco), on the left, and Chief Svoboda, the nuclear detection/defensive systems operator, on the right. The two flight-suited men were sitting across the center aisle from each other just aft of the cockpit bulkhead. Each was head down and busy with preflight checklists. Donovan quietly moved by and pulled the curtain to the flightdeck wide.

Lt. J. P. Harper sat high in the Orion's cockpit, her face nearly against the windshield glass. She was looking out over its purple nose as the pair of F-14s thundered aloft in a formation departure. They went to afterburner with a concussion that shook the *Grape*'s windshield louder than thunder. Harper sighed as their nav lights became two bright dots against the storm clouds. The heavy plate glass of the *Grape*'s windshield seemed like the bars of a prison.

Chief Svoboda glanced up from his prestart checklist and saw the insignia of a full commander standing right behind Harper. He reached across the aisle and nudged Lieutenant Carranza.

"Oh, shit," whispered Carranza.

Donovan turned and held his finger to his lips for them to remain quiet.

"Well, Jameson," she said without turning to see who it was, "glad you decided to come along. I thought we'd have to leave without you." Her voice carried the clear accent of the Texas Gulf. "We're gonna run late as it is."

Donovan remained silent as he scanned the instrument panel, or at least what seemed to be the place where the instrument panel belonged. The *Grape*'s glass cockpit did away with virtually all the P-3's blizzard of switches and gauges, replacing the familiar crowd with just six CRT displays.

"Ready to crank?" Harper asked, still oblivious to the fact that it wasn't Jameson there behind her.

Donovan noticed her nails were polished and painted a bright pink. Harper was small and lightly built. Her short blond hair spilled over the collar of her Nomex flightsuit, thick and lustrous. Her flightsuit was baggy, at least a size too large, and Donovan could see the rudder pedals on her side had been cranked all the way up so that her legs could reach them. Her fitness report aside, Harper was just about the right size for the pointy end of an F-14. Donovan waited, one hand on the back of the copilot's seat. He finally cleared his throat and spoke.

"I'm ready, Lieutenant. If we're late, let's get a move on. You take left seat."

Harper froze, then spun in her seat. Her eyes went wide when she saw who was standing there. "Sir!" She stood up and hit her head on the overhead switch panel. "Commander!"

"Relax, Lieutenant. You know how to run this flying video game?" Donovan watched her initial shock turn to anger.

She knew what Jameson's absence, and Donovan's presence, meant. It was another rigged test. Another kangaroo court. She pursed her lips. "Yes, sir. I sure do." Her eyes glared back at Donovan. *Do you?* they challenged.

He listened and catalogued her accent. *Corpus,* he thought. Every multiengine-trained naval aviator knew what an angry woman from Corpus Christi sounded like. "You managed to scare off Mr. Jameson. Let's see if you can scare me." He pointed at the left seat and snapped his fingers. It was the place for the pilot in command. "Move."

Harper's blue eyes darkened, became clearer, hotter. "Yes, sir. It will be my pleasure to fly the commander anyplace he wants to go." She snatched the preflight checklist on the Orion's glareshield and stepped over the center console and slid into the pilot's chair. Donovan moved into the right-hand seat and cranked forward the rudder pedals Harper had adjusted for her short legs.

The cockpit was a study in grays; only the bright red seats, the black rectangles of the six CRTs, and the four blue power levers relieved it. The windshield was made up of five main segments, two to either side of a small, perfectly square panel in the center. Donovan looked around for something familiar. Only a few standby instruments fit the bill, their regular analog faces looking as out of place as Donovan felt.

He looked over as Harper reached up and hit the APU start button. She punched it hard. From below the cockpit, a whine built steadily into a low roar. A simple chime announced the successful start of the aux power unit, a small jet engine mounted right below the flightdeck.

"Tacco," she said to the tactical coordinator behind them, "get me the latest weather from the tower."

"Roger," said Carranza.

An instant later, all six CRTs suddenly flipped once and

then began running through their own diagnostic self-checks. The small turbine beneath the flightdeck was howling, putting out the electricity needed to start the *Grape*'s four big Allison engines. Harper looked over at Donovan as she cranked her rudder pedals full aft. "Sir, I hope this isn't a hanging party. If you'll just look with your own two eyes and forget the rumors, I don't think I'll frighten you too badly." When she smiled, her teeth were white and even, except for the one small gap up front. "Where do you want to go?"

"You've got a test flight scheduled," said Donovan as he slipped on the heavy, noise-canceling headset. "Let's fly it." A sidetone clicked on with a hum.

"Flight? Tacco here. If we're going, we better get a move on. Tower's painting cells all over the place out to the east. It's better to the north and west, but it could shut us down any minute."

Harper shot Donovan a questioning look. "If we don't go, what happens with my fit-rep?"

The blunt honesty of her question obliged him to return it in equal measure. "I'm scheduled to leave tomorrow morning for the States. Captain Reynard doesn't wish to stir up a hassle, so Jameson's eval will probably be left to stand."

"That's kind of what I thought. Okay, Commander, we're going flying." Harper's finger was poised above the start button for the first engine. "Crew, prepare for start," she called out over the intercom.

"Tacco's ready."

"Sniffer's up," said Chief Svoboda.

"Comm check complete. Starting two." She reached up, swung the selector switch to the number two position, and hit the start button. A faraway whine grew loud as the turbine began to turn the fat paddle-bladed prop, slowly at first, then faster, faster. The whine suddenly blossomed as the fires took hold. On Harper's master CRT, a simple green light announced the successful ignition. "Good start on two." The propeller blasted a cocoon of rain and wind back over the *Grape*'s long wing. In a moment there were four green lights, and all four Allison T-56s were spooled up hot and sweet.

Donovan watched and nodded. So far so good. The cockpit was all wrong, but one thing was still the same: the raw power vibrating through the Orion's body thrilled him. It also reminded him how long it had been since he had last flown. He ticked off the weeks on his hand and came to his ring finger. "What's our call sign?" he asked.

"Dragline Six, sir." Harper's CRT was scrolling through the pretaxi check. As Harper's fingers touched each of the killer items on the checklist, a soft chime sounded.

When she was through, Harper pressed the transmit button. "Iwakuni Ground, Dragline Six is up, Route Package Zulu, mission number niner three." The windshield wipers were slapping now, and the cabin lights were up bright.

The controller came right back at her. "Roger the route, *Grape*. We thought you were going to cancel on us today. Current weather is five hundred overcast, visibility three in rain and fog, dropping rapidly. Wind is out of the southeast, multiple echoes to the east, the south, and the north. We've got a thunderstorm in progress off the departure end, and more where that came from."

"Copy," she replied with a worried glance at Donovan that she hid behind a quick and determined smile. "Dragline Six is ready to go."

"Roger. Taxi to the runway, hold short for release."

"Dragline Six." Harper advanced the power levers for the two outboard engines and took her feet from the Orion's brakes, using the small wheel mounted on her left armrest to steer. She let the nosewheel wander first to the left of the yellow line, then back, then right.

Donovan wrote it up to nerves. After all, it wasn't every lieutenant who had a full commander for a copilot. He looked at the wholly foreign CRT panels. He hoped she knew her business.

Harper braked to a stop at the run-up area. "Okay, crew. Set Condition Five." Her small hands seemed to dance across the controls. "Servos are synced, fuel governors set, trim, flaps, and RPM set."

"Take your time," said Donovan. "It's not a race."

She turned up the speed on the wipers to keep even with the rain. "Power panel is green and oil doors are open." She looked over at Donovan. "Gonna be rough on climbout. Your harness locked, sir?"

Donovan leaned forward against his belts. "Locked."

She nodded and pressed the transmit button. "Tower, Dragline Six is ready to roll."

The Iwakuni controller's voice barked from their headsets. "Dragline Six is cleared for immediate takeoff. Turn left to zero one zero in the climb. That should put you through the lightest weather on my scope."

"Dragline is rolling." Harper ran the port throttles in, and the *Grape* powered itself around the arming pad and swung out onto the runway. The black asphalt ran straight and true, all the way to where it ended at a solid curtain of heavy rain. "Let's aviate," she said as she swept all four power levers full forward and took her toes from the brakes. The *Galloping Grape*, all one hundred thousand plus pounds of her, surged down the runway, the four Allison T-56s roaring with their twenty-thousand-horsepower voice.

"V-one," said Donovan. His eyes were glued to the tiny

backup mechanical airspeed indicator. He still hadn't puzzled out the CRT displays.

"Two-thousand-foot marker," said Harper as she quickly swiped a bead of sweat from her forehead. The rain came down as if a fire hose were pointed at the windshield. A brilliant fork of lightning struck an antenna off to the side of the runway. Harper didn't even hear the thunder. "Three-thousand-foot marker." She held down the wing of the big turboprop against the gusting crosswind, her boots dancing on the rudder pedals to keep them straight.

The airspeed needle rose steadily as they thundered down the runway. "Eighty knots," said Donovan. "Power check."

Harper glanced at the row of green lights that announced the health of her four engines. "Sweet."

"Rotate."

Harper pulled back on the Orion's big yoke. The nosewheel lifted free of the concrete, the purple nose pointing at the black sky.

"Positive rate," called out Donovan.

"Gear up." Harper pulled the handle out of its detent and rammed it up. "Flaps up." She swung the *Grape* north as they buried their nose into the low cloud. The turbulence increased exponentially, tossing the heavy turboprop like a sheet of paper.

The radio crackled. "Dragline Six, Iwakuni Tower. Contact Ocean One now on two five four point six. Good hunting, *Grape*, and we'd appreciate a ride report."

"Lousy!" Harper said as they bucked and shuddered away from the storm cell. A feathery tickle ran up her arm. She was about to turn her head to see what it was when a tremendous flash exploded right off the *Grape*'s nose followed by a titanic detonation. Almost immediately, all the instruments and cockpit lights blinked off. "Damn!"

"Primary bus failure!" Carranza shouted.

"Switch the load!"

Donovan had been blinded by the flash. As his eyesight returned, all he saw were six blank CRTs and a dead gray panel that merged with the guts of the storm cell out the windshield. He reached out at once to take command, but Harper batted his arm away.

"I've got it," she shouted above the rasp of rain on the windshield. "I've got it, Commander. You just watch and keep me honest."

Watch what? he wondered. What was she flying by?

The hum of the intercom suddenly came back along with the cockpit lights. Finally, the six CRT screens blinked once, rolled, and steadied.

"Flight, Tacco here. We're feeding off the secondary. The number one load bus is crisped."

"Roger, Tacco. Flight's got instruments and lights. Thanks." She reached up and swiped the sweat from her brow.

"Nice," said Donovan.

"No probs." She kept them climbing strongly to the north, then west. The rock and roll subsided. The clouds became thinner, the rain less of a torrent. Harper's hands went to her own communication subpanel to enter the new frequency, but then stopped. "Tacco, how about that freq?" she said instead.

"Flight, you've got Sasebo on button one. I don't know if the set took a hit, but it's showing okay."

"One way to find out," she said with a shrug.

Just then the *Grape* burst out into brilliant sunshine. Below them, a sea of clouds boiled, ramping up behind them into huge cauliflower thunderheads.

"Ocean One," Harper transmitted out over the burst radio, "Dragline Six is with you, climbing out of four thousand for flight level one eight zero in visual conditions. How do you hear?"

The big communications station at Sasebo boomed back immediately. "Contact, Dragline. Approved to enter Zulu Route Package Three as briefed. How was the climbout, *Grape*?"

"Be advised Dragline Six took a lightning strike. We're running power through the backup bus."

"A lightning strike?" Sasebo came back. "Do you require assistance?"

"Negative." She shot a glance at Donovan, then pressed the transmit button again. "Dragline is flying the mission as briefed."

5
—
STORM

THE *GALLOPING GRAPE* RACED BEYOND THE STORM'S OUTRIGgers and into clear air. Harper banked the patrol plane to the west. In the distance, across the mountainous spine of Honshu, a thin, cold blue line appeared. It was the Tsushima Strait, the Sea of Japan. Their destination.

Donovan looked over at the young woman. Her cheek was set with a tense line of muscle. He took hold of the yoke and wiggled it to gain her attention. She nearly jumped. "Mind?"

She shook her head. "Commander's airplane."

Donovan extended his feet to the rudder pedals and took hold of the yoke. God but it felt good to fly! He banked first one way, then the other, keeping the *Galloping Grape* in its steady climb. The mountains slipped below, then the western coast, and then the icy blue sea.

Harper gazed out the pilot's window. "Better check your power settings," she said almost absently.

"What?" Donovan scanned the engine CRT. *Where's the . . . ?* He hesitated, trying to make sense of the new displays. Where were the torque and temperature indicators?

With a quick sweep, Harper reached over and pulled the

turbines back to their cruise settings and with equal nonchalance, blipped the RPM toggles to match. She was still looking out the window, down at the sea.

Donovan finally found the four engine displays. They all were in perfect agreement. She had set the engines by ear. *How did she do that?* He leaned over to see what held Harper's attention.

Two gray darts flashed by several thousand feet below; the F-14s were part of *Eisenhower*'s airgroup en route to the carrier. "Ever try a fast mover?" he asked.

"No, sir. But I sure would like the chance someday."

"I guess the old *Grape* here is about as close as a P-3 gets to being a fighter," he said, looking out at the Sidewinders slung beneath the P-3's wing. The *Grape* was designed to go into harm's way. But where was that these days? Reynard had mentioned a special mission. But he hadn't elaborated.

Donovan rechecked each of the four turbine temperature gauges. They didn't differ by more than five degrees. *How did she do that?* he wondered again. It always took him a good minute or so to stabilize power at cruise. He cleared his throat. "Who knows? Maybe you'll get a shot at fighters someday. Your airplane, Lieutenant."

"My airplane." She shook her head. "No such luck, Commander." She turned to face him. "Not after what happened back at Pensacola. Not with all those guys getting RIFFed out of the fleet."

Donovan nodded. It was true. The Navy was shrinking with each and every turn of the budgetary screw. Fewer decks meant fewer squadrons. Fewer squadrons meant that a lot of hot fleet pilots were getting sent to the beach. "What exactly happened back at Primary?"

She looked at him quizzically. "Don't you know? I scared off my first instructor pilot. He didn't like gals in the cockpit. But the second one, he was good. Damned good." Her eyes seemed to flicker with doubt, but she covered it. "They say I killed him."

"Did you?"

Once again she seemed surprised. "We had an engine roll back on the approach into Saufley. I thought we could make it by gliding. At least, that's what I thought."

"What's a dead engine to a crop duster, is that what you mean?" he said, remembering her pre-Navy flying.

"Yes, sir. That's exactly right." She nodded as though she were grading Donovan on his homework. "Those old engines were always giving up the ghost. My father taught me to . . . well, never mind." She shook her head and buried the reference to her father. "I thought we could make it."

"Famous last words. Your father was a Navy pilot?"

Harper smiled and held up the old Navy Cosmograph for Donovan to see. "Fighting Six on the *Enterprise*, then the *Essex*," she said.

"Tacco here," Carranza broke in over the ship circuit. "We got Russians. Bed Check One is off the nose and twenty miles. She's supposed to be a Sovremennyy can, fourteen heads on board." The heads he referred to were the nuclear warheads mounted on the destroyer's SS-N-22 cruise missiles.

Harper squinted out through the big patrol plane's faceted windshield. They were still too far away to see something as small as a destroyer.

Donovan cleared his throat. "All right, Lieutenant, I'm supposed to observe your performance, and so far, I'd say you did just fine. Your ability to fly us out of that storm cell on partial panel was superb. Let's see a textbook ID run and you've got my up-check. Take us down and rig the bastard."

"Yes, sir." She pulled the throttles back and ran the

trimwheel forward. The patrol plane angled toward the sea. Neither of them spoke as the altimeter unwound.

Out ahead, Donovan caught sight of a bump on the horizon. "Tallyho," he said, nodding at the Russian ship.

"Flight," said Svoboda, the Sniffer man. "The nose has contact. No count yet."

Donovan watched as the bump grew to the shape of a Russian destroyer. She had a white bone of spray in her teeth as she plunged into the big swells. "By the way," he said, "who are we diving on?"

"A Sovremennyy tin can. Side number four three zero." Harper checked her list. "She's the *Bezuprechnyy*. Seven SS-N-22s plus seven reloads."

"I'm curious," said Donovan as they swept down on the Russian destroyer. "How'd you pick up your running name?"

She smiled and glanced back at the carefully painted red letters on her white flight helmet. It was hanging from the cockpit bulkhead. "Hot Dog? I guess you better ask Lieutenant Jameson."

Donovan smothered his chuckle. The *Bezuprechnyy* became a tiny toy of a ship, then a sleek greyhound slicing through the swells of the Sea of Japan. As Donovan watched, a light began blinking from its bridge. It had been a long time since he had tried reading light signals. But these were simple enough, even if they were also puzzling.

". . . *Grape* . . . hello . . . *Grape* . . . hello . . ."

"How'd he know who we were?" asked Donovan.

"The Russians are our pals now. Remember?" said Harper as she swung the Orion into a tight bank. The *Galloping Grape* pointed a long wing at the ship and circled as the Sniffer catalogued its dead cargo.

Donovan nodded. "I guess it's still a strange world for old-timers like me."

"Old?" She looked at Donovan. "You don't look broken to me." A sudden flash of worry crossed her face. Had she overstepped herself? "Sir," she hastily added.

Chief Svoboda broke the uncomfortable silence: "Flight, Sniffer's got the count." The clacking of a printer came over the intercom. "Confirm fourteen nukes, one-hundred-and-fifty-kiloton class. That's on the money. The nose is sweet."

Donovan watched as the light signals changed from the ship below. "What's he saying now?"

Harper glanced down the wing of the *Grape* at the spray-wreathed bridge of the *Bezuprechnyy*. She chuckled. "Have . . . a . . . nice . . . day."

They trained us to kill those bastards, thought Donovan. *Now we tell each other jokes.*

Suddenly, Carranza's deep voice came over their headsets. "Flight, Tacco here. You smell anything up in the cockpit?"

"Negative. What do you have?" asked Harper.

"I don't know, but it smells like hot insulation or something. I'm leaving station to check."

"Take a fire bottle with you," she said as she swung the nose of the *Grape* back to the east. There was a lot of cold ocean under the *Grape*'s long wings.

"Okay," said Carranza. "How do you hear me on the portable?"

"Five by," said Harper. "What do you see?"

"I don't know. It seems to be stronger back aft here. Wait. Okay. I'm opening up the door to the power distribution cubby." The small space was the electric heart of the patrol plane; it was so tightly packed with circuitry that a person wearing braces risked getting welded in place.

Donovan looked over at Harper. "Let's forget about rigging that other Russian can."

"Agreed," she said with a quick nod. She banked the *Grape* on a heading that would take them back to Iwakuni.

"Something's cooking but I can't see what it is," said Carranza. "It might be in a conduit under the floor. You want me to check?"

"Make a quick inspection and get back to your seat," she replied, then switched over to transmit. "Ocean One, Ocean One, Dragline Six is recovering to Iwakuni. We have possible smoke in the cabin. Say current Iwakuni weather."

"Roger, Dragline, stand by and I'll get it for you."

The intercom light winked back on. "I can't find the source of the smell," said Carranza. "It seems stronger nearer the deck."

"Okay, Tacco," said Harper. "We're headed back to the barn. Get strapped in."

Donovan crossed his arms over his chest, listening, weighing the options in his mind. *Harper can get you into trouble faster than anybody I've ever known,* he remembered. He caught a whiff of a sharp, cutting scent. Was it smoke or was it fear?

"Looks dark out ahead," said Harper as she nodded at the line of clouds over Honshu. They spilled over the high mountainous spine of the island in full flood, yet out here over the green water the air was calm and the sea sparkling.

Donovan took another snort of cabin air. There it was, definitely stronger than a moment before. Something, somewhere, was getting too damned hot. "You know, Lieutenant," he said, "it might not be a bad idea to give the fire crew a little thrill."

Harper nodded and pressed the transmit button on the *Grape*'s heavy yoke. "And Ocean One, Dragline Six is back with you. Go ahead and advise Iwakuni that we'll want the crash trucks rolling on arrival. What have they got for weather?"

"Roger the equipment, Six," said the calm voice in their headsets. "And Iwakuni is ceiling indefinite, sky obscured, one-sixteenth in heavy rain. There's a thunderstorm in progress. My screen shows most of the heavy stuff has already passed to the west of the station. You want vectors to divert or you want to pick your way through?"

"Stand by." She took a quick, tentative sniff. "Damn, now I can smell it." She shook her head as though now even the weather were conspiring to prove her incompetence. "Iwakuni's the closest place to recover. I think we better forget the divert and get this thing down on the ground."

"You're the pilot in command," Donovan replied, thankful that she had reached the same conclusion he had.

As they neared the Japanese coast, the dark line of the storm became a wall of boiling clouds, a slow-motion tsunami breaking across Honshu's mountainous spine. The *Grape* struggled east against a strengthening head wind, and in their headsets, both pilots could hear the crash and rattle of distant lightning strokes.

"Flight, Tacco. The smoke's really getting pretty strong back here. Definitely coming from under the deck."

"Okay, crew, go to oxygen masks and prepare to dump cabin pressure."

Donovan strapped on his oxygen mask and checked the flow as Harper opened up the *Grape* to the outside air. A breeze swept through the cabin as they depressurized. It would make the approach to Iwakuni a little less convenient, but it would deny a smoldering fire the air it needed. When the internal and external pressures equalized, she brought the cabin exhaust fan on. "Any better, Tacco?"

"I can't smell anything through my mask," he replied.

Harper swept her eyes over the storm front dead ahead. There was no way around the squall line; it extended north and south beyond the horizon. It was like a medieval castle's wall, guarded by high battlements of thunderheads surging twenty thousand feet above the mere rain. They could climb above the worst of it, but that wouldn't get them back down on the ground. They couldn't duck underneath, for that was where the mountains were; solid as the squall looked in the glass of their windscreen, granite was harder still. They would have to storm those walls, boring through the weakest point.

Harper pressed the intercom button. "Tacco, Flight. Optimize your radar display for precip and see if you can find us a way through."

"Stand by," Carranza replied.

"Looks pretty solid," said Donovan. He peered closely at a gap in the wall. It dipped lower to the north, but to either side of the saddle two monster cells cast long shadows across the sea. "Maybe a little lighter up by those two cells."

"Threading the needle," said Harper. As she watched, both cells lit up simultaneously with lightning. A slight bump shook the *Grape*, the first harbinger of the nearing storm. "Might be a sucker hole."

"Flight, Tacco here. It looks lighter to the north, but I might be seeing some attenuation from heavy rain. And it's getting hazy back here." The fire.

Just then, the radio center at Sasebo came back. "Dragline Six, Ocean One. Advise ready to copy a special weather observation from Iwakuni."

"Go," said Harper.

"Special Iwakuni weather, ceiling niner hundred broken, fifteen hundred overcast, three miles in moderate rain. Wind is now from the northwest at eighteen, gusts to three five knots."

She glanced over at Donovan. "Frontal passage," she

said. She hit the transmit button. "Dragline Six copies all. We're goin' home."

"Roger, Six, I show you about fifteen miles from the first precip. You should be seeing it pretty good."

"Yeah. We see it *real* good," said Harper. "It looks a tad better to the north, do you concur?"

"We had a MAC heavy go through that area and they reported hail and a pretty rough ride at angels three five."

"Thanks, Six out." Harper wiped a bead of sweat from where it threatened to trickle into her eye, then realized her eyes were tearing. "I think we'd better hurry this little procedure," she said to Donovan.

The sun dimmed as they neared the gray, woolly ramparts of the storm. The bright yellow disk turned bloodred as the thin veil of vapor thrown skyward by the thunderheads passed before its face. Harper banked north, aiming for the gap between the two monster cells. The light was definitely brighter straight ahead.

"Five miles to the front," said Carranza. "Can you run the exhaust any higher? It's starting to get bad back here."

"I'm running the fan on high," she said. "Okay, Tacco, take another fix on that gap and start shutting down. I'm shedding as much electrical load as I can. You, too, Chief."

"The nose is down and dark," said Svoboda.

Harper eyed the high towers of roiling cloud. It was going to be a rough one. "Tacco, go back quick and open up the sonochute door. Maybe that will suck some of the fumes out. And hurry back."

"You got it, Hot Dog."

"Chief, while he's back there, I want you to secure anything loose and strap in tight." She looked over her right shoulder at Donovan. "You, too, Commander. Lock your harness and lower your seat."

"My seat?" asked Donovan.

"Hail," she replied, tapping the cold glass of the windscreen. "If it busts through, you're going to want to duck." She reached overhead and ran the instruments up full bright as the sun was blotted from the sky. A cold breeze announced the opening of the rear sonochute door. The wall of clouds loomed high overhead, and the twin towers of the cells they were skirting disappeared into the stratosphere.

"I'm strapped down," said Carranza, out of breath.

"You'd better be." The color of the light straight off the nose deepened from yellow to a pale green. "Shoot." Harper knew at once what was there. She was from Texas, after all, and Texas thunderstorms were built to Texas scale. "We're gonna get a hosing," she said softly as she pulled back power to her four engines and trimmed up for a slower speed. Harper reached behind and took her white flight helmet off the bulkhead, HOT DOG, her running name, emblazoned across the crown.

"Let's go continuous on the ignition," said Donovan. "And fire up the anti-ice."

"Got it," she said as she put her pink fingernail over the touch-sensitive display screen.

"Dragline Six," the controller broke in, "Ocean One. Descent and deviation at your discretion. Contact Iwakuni Tower when you leave your assigned altitude. They should have vectors for the approach."

"Thanks for the help," said Harper as she strapped the helmet tight, then cranked her seat to the bottom of its travel. Short as she was, her eyes were level now with the top of the instrument panel. As she pulled off even more power, the *Grape* began to drop. A gust sent a long, ominous shiver through the aircraft. One wing bucked up, then dropped, then rose again. "Keep me honest," she told Donovan.

Why the hell am I up here? Donovan wondered as they

bored in between the two storm cells. *Harper can get you into* . . . He let out a long breath and cinched his harness even tighter.

"Smoke is getting worse," said Carranza.

"Shut your station down and hold on!" said Harper. The first dark wisps blasted by as they dropped toward the storm. The cells off each wing were like skyscrapers. The narrow slot that promised passage seemed terribly small. A flash of lightning lit the belly of the beast to their right, and the rumbling detonation of its thunder shook the *Grape*. Another flash came from the left. A high-voltage filigree snapped across the nose, branching into a fine electric web, the web of a titanic spider into which the *Galloping Grape* was steadfastly boring.

The air became dank and thick within the cockpit as one wing sliced deep into a bank of cloud and disappeared. Harper banked away from it back into the twisting corridor of clearer air. The sky ahead became threaded with gray streaks, a portcullis of ice and wind and rain dropping to bar their passage. There was no way around it now. Only through.

The light was tinted a dark, undersea green. "Here it comes," she said.

Before she could turn the wipers on full, the *Galloping Grape* smashed into a hurricane of wind and rain. It felt like granite. The windshield was fire-hosed with rain so hard the wipers themselves were invisible. The rush of the water drowned out the sound of the engines. Only the display screens indicated they were still functioning out on the wings. A fist drove up under the P-3's belly and blasted them skyward with a groan of tortured metal. Just as suddenly, they seemed to strike a solid ceiling. An instant later, they were falling straight down.

"Jesus!" Donovan grabbed for his control yoke as long-lost objects floated up from the floor. Coins, a broken pencil, a sharp, twisted strand of a safety wire, roamed like fish in an aquarium as the *Grape* fell.

"Flight!" Carranza yelled over the intercom.

"I've got it!" she yelled back over the roar of rain on the *Grape*'s skin. A brilliant flash of lightning exploded off the nose, coalescing into a white-hot sphere that came at them like a homing missile.

It arrowed straight for their right outboard engine and struck the prop, blasting through its composite-metal structure, vaporizing nearly a foot off each tip. Warning lights lit up in the cockpit at once, followed by the jangle of alarms. A thin wisp of acrid smoke drifted up from the glareshield air vents.

"I'll fly!" Harper yelled over to Donovan. "You get us shut down!" She was holding the yoke in a white-handed grip, fighting to average out the surges and drops of altitude.

Donovan reached up instinctively to where the emergency shutdown handle was in the P-3s he was used to. His fist struck blank metal.

"Damn it, Commander! Get it shut down!" The prop was beginning to run away, turning up faster and faster. It would tear itself, and the engine it was attached to, off the wing if left to its own much longer.

"I can't!" The whirling prop sent a distinct buzz through the airframe now, spinning faster and faster, the low growl becoming a high-speed whine.

"Take it!" She let go of her control wheel and the *Grape* suddenly lurched down toward the invisible ground. She punched the emergency shutdown button and kept her finger on it until she was sure. The engine spooled down, its fires quickly snuffed by the torrents of rain. But the propeller refused to turn edge on to the wind. "She won't feather!"

Donovan fought the controls as they bored through the murk, surging a thousand feet and dropping the same distance in a matter of seconds. A white stream of eye-stinging smoke now issued from the vents.

"I've got it!" Harper took the wheel back, slammed it full right and stomped left rudder. The *Grape* slewed into a skid.

"Harper!" Donovan knew this was the prelude to a spin. Beyond the *Grape*'s windscreen, there was no up, no down. A spin would be fatal. In the roiling heart of the storm, there would be no possible recovery.

But Harper knew better. She kept the crossed control inputs in. Flying almost sideways to the oncoming wind, the fuselage blanked out a portion of the right wing's airflow. The propeller began to wind down like a tired windmill; the high whine became a growl again, then a shudder.

A beam of white light strobed through the cockpit again, but this time it wasn't lightning. They blasted through a gap between towering cylinders of cloud into an alpine valley of clear air. They skimmed across the boiling tops of the undercast. Donovan winced when he looked out to his right wing.

The outboard prop was turning slowly, its damaged feathering system finally able to work against the air blast. All four tips of its fat paddle blades were crudely hacked away, and smoke was streaming back from the shut-down engine in a dark ribbon. He felt a lurch as Harper kicked them straight again.

"What do you see?" she asked, her breath coming hard and fast over the intercom.

"Looks like we took a real hit," said Donovan. "There's some smoke coming out of the nacelle."

"Hot hydraulics," she said. "Overspeed will do that." All the same, she reached up, pulled the oil-tank shutoff breaker, and hit the Halon release. "Bottles away."

Donovan saw the ribbon of smoke become a thread and finally snuff out.

She shut down all the aircraft's generators but one, pulling the boost levers to shutoff and killing nearly all electric power. The cockpit lights snapped off as did five of the six CRT displays. Only the one showing primary flight data—attitude, altitude, heading, and speed—remained.

"Can you fly us on that?" asked Donovan. His eyes remained glued to the tiny "peanut" artificial horizon.

She turned and smiled a weary smile as the air from the glareshield vents turned fresh and clear. "You tell me. Sir."

Donovan felt his heart subside as the air smoothed out and the clouds parted before them. "By God, Lieutenant, who the hell told you slipping her would shut that prop down?"

Harper scowled. She had just saved his hide and he was complaining? "It worked, didn't it?"

"No, I mean," he stammered, "how did you know?"

The *Grape* skimmed lower as the clouds thinned out below. There were patches of dark, rain-soaked ground showing through the breaks in the undercast. "Because," she said, "in spite of what you were told, I'm a damned good pilot."

The one radio still operating boomed to life. "Dragline Six, Dragline Six, Iwakuni Tower. How do you hear?"

"Five by, Iwakuni," said Harper with a swipe of sweat from her brow. "We made frontal passage and we're inbound for landing. We had some smoke in the cabin. It's electrical, but we got that straightened out."

"Roger, Six. The fire trucks will be rolling and we've got better weather for you. Ready to copy?"

"Stand by," she replied as laconically as she could. "Crew," she called out to the cabin, "rig for condition five."

"Nice going, Hot Dog," said Chief Svoboda with a long whoosh of breath.

"Hotel Sierra," said Carranza.

"Current Iwakuni weather is twelve hundred scattered, four thousand broken, visibility twenty. Winds are three ten at eighteen, gusts to thirty-two. Braking action is poor with puddles on the runway."

"Puddles, huh?" Harper looked over at Donovan and nearly giggled. "We'll be careful, Tower."

Donovan shook his head as the crisscrossed runways of NAS Iwakuni showed up ahead under a big break in the clouds. The sun streamed through the rain-washed air with supernatural clarity. "I never would have believed it," he said. "Slipping a P-3 to stop a runaway prop. I never would have had the balls to"—he stopped—"the guts to do that in the middle of a cell."

Harper looked over and smiled as innocently as she could. "Thanks, Commander," she said as she rammed the landing gear handle down and banked for her base leg to final. "Gear down and cross-check for three green."

"Dragline Six is cleared to land," said the tower.

Donovan remembered when he had opened Harper's flight records and seen her pretty face, her piercing blue eyes. She had surprised him then and she had surprised him now.

Harper flared the *Grape*, reaching for the runway. Their wheels kissed the soaked blacktop. "So do I pass, Commander?"

"Roll 'em again, Hot Dog," he said with a smile. "You haven't scared me off yet."

* * *

Donovan put the last words down on his evaluation of the day's flight and tossed the pen down on the bare table. *You pass indeed,* he thought. Harper's decision to fly in the first place was a bit sporty, but that wasn't all her doing. He had been an accomplice by hinting that as far as her flight career went, it was now or never. What would he have done?

Harper's flying was superb. She faced down an aviator's nightmare: smoke from an unknown source and weather that kept the ducks walking. And she had handled it all, quick as it came at her. Much quicker, in fact, than he would have. Or could have. Donovan sat back in his chair. She belonged in fighters. He could sense it and he could see it with his own eyes. She wanted them. She could handle them. It was a tragedy because the Navy would never give her one to fly.

Perhaps his reassignment tomorrow to the training command was coming just in time. Maybe Reynard knew him better than he knew himself. Maybe he was too old for frontline flying. Hadn't he frozen at the controls, in the heart of that storm cell?

He snapped off his desk lamp, sat back in his chair, put his boots up onto the desk, and closed his eyes, letting his mind go blank. Just as he began to drift into sleep, two sharp raps hammered the thin door. *Now what?* He took his boots off the bare desktop and sat up straight. "Come," he said, turning the desk lamp back on.

Donovan's commanding officer pushed his way into his office like a big bull released from a small pen. Capt. Henry Reynard was wearing a splotched raincoat. He carried a battered leather flightcase, the same one he had had back in Pensacola and in Da Nang.

"Well," said Donovan, "if it isn't Captain Iscariot himself. What now, Henry? You want to finish me off? Christ. After that flight today, what's left? Keelhauling?"

Reynard scrutinized him for an instant, then sat down on the one other chair in the nearly stripped room. "Evening, Dick. I heard you got a little wet up there. She do all right?"

"Better than that. She was outstanding. In fact, she saved my ass."

"She can join the club, then. Maintenance found the source of the smoke. A couple of wires burned through their jackets and got the padded insulation smoldering. Nothing bad. It's all put back together. They're hanging a new engine right now. She'll be ready to roll by morning."

"Really? That was fast. What's the rush?"

"I'll get to that," said Reynard as he unbuttoned his rain-coat. He reached into his breast pocket and tossed a thin envelope to Donovan. "You can read it later. You still keep your heart medicine in the drawer?"

"Aye, aye, Captain Iscariot. What kind of operation do you think I run?" Donovan reached into his bottom drawer and fished out a bottle of Jack Daniel's. "Henry," said Donovan as he poured two glasses, "I'm serious. This reassignment back to Oahu? It's the right thing. I'm getting too old to ride the pointy end. I was lost up there today. If it had been me and me alone, you'd be scraping my hide off the Eno Sammyaku."

"Now that would piss the locals off something fierce. Probably send us a bill." Reynard took a sip of whiskey. He held up the glass to the light. "Nice stuff." Reynard downed the rest in a gulp. "Now. Ready to listen?"

Donovan sipped at his drink warily. "Maybe."

"Dickie, you are one lucky son of a bitch. You were headed for the heap. Your flying days all over except for the shouting. I, your friend, your shipmate, and incidentally your commanding officer, have found a way to temporarily put off the inevitable decline by a couple of weeks."

"It better be something a little easier than the last one you came up with," said Donovan as he ran his hand across the nap of his hair.

Reynard reached down and pulled out a folder from the leather briefcase. It was prominently labeled SECRET-NOFORN. He passed it to Donovan. "Remember when I said we were planning to send the *Grape* out on a special mission?"

"Yes. So?"

"Well, this is the gem our good friends at the State Department sent via COMPACAIR. Read it later. You have all night before you need to blast out of here."

"Blast out?" Donovan put the file aside.

"Affirmative. Once upon a time, the Russians were the bad guys. Then they self-destructed. Now we're best friends with the sneaky bastards. They catch a cold in Moscow? They start sneezing in Washington. Nobody wants to rock the boat, just in case some wild-assed colonel gets it in his head to take over and straighten things out over there. Who lost Russia? That's a question nobody wants to ask. So, now that the world's so cozy, the Russians feel free to ask the State Department for little favors. Follow so far?"

Donovan sat up straight. "Like what kind of little favors?"

"It seems that they haven't managed to steal our neutron-detection gear yet. You know, the Sniffer? So instead, they'd just like to borrow an Orion with a good nose on board. Say, two weeks."

"Are they going to get one?"

"They are. And I want you on it."

"Me?" Donovan laughed. "You want me to help the Russians? Hell. I've spent my whole career hunting them down."

"That's why I want you, Commander, and not some dry stick lieutenant with his head up and locked. Tell me, did the *Grape*'s nose work okay? I mean, on that Russian ship?"

"You're asking me? I wasn't even 'officially' aware we had the capability. Yes, it worked. It picked up the warheads. The yields. The number on board. I was impressed. I wish we had one ten years ago. What do the Russians want a Sniffer for, anyway?"

"Remember Afghanistan? They lost twenty thousand troops trying to take the place over. In the end, they failed."

"What does Afghanistan have to do with a nose?"

"The short version is that our new buddies lost something a little while back. They'd like some help finding it."

Donovan felt the haze clear as he digested Reynard's words.

Reynard leaned over Donovan's desk and tapped the thin envelope. "This contains your orders, detaching you from your stateside command. I want you and the *Galloping Grape* ready in the morning. By then, the elves will have rendered today's excesses invisible. What's more, where she ... where you're headed, those Sidewinders on the wings may come in handy."

"Afghanistan." Donovan carefully poured his half-full glass of bourbon back into the bottle. "Who's my crew?"

"I should think you might have someone at the top of your short list."

"You mean Harper?"

"Hot Pants Harper. Dead on. You did say she could fly."

"But ..."

"Come to think of it, where you're going, Hot Pants might come in handy." He reached over and flipped open the secret op file to a marked-up map. "Your first hop is easy. You'll leave prior to local sunrise, overfly Kadena, and recover at Cubi. The locals will refuel you."

Kadena was in Okinawa, Cubi Point Naval Air Station was once the Navy's big base in the Philippines. Like Iwakuni, it, too, was in the process of closing down.

"And then?"

"Then it gets interesting." Reynard refolded the chart and pulled out another. The line that connected Iwakuni with Cubi Point abruptly changed direction, arrowing due west. "Da Nang. It used to be a crappy place, as we both know. I doubt it's improved."

Donovan whistled. "Christ. Vietnam?"

"I see your memory is still first rate. You'll pick up an aerial escort out by Dong Dao Island and proceed direct to Da Nang to refuel. Stuff it to the gills, Commander. The Russians are footing the gas bill. Besides, you'll need it. Your next leg is a doozy." Reynard steered his finger along the southern spine of the world's tallest mountain range. "From there you will head for lovely Kabul International, all expenses paid. The embassy has reopened there. It's all taken care of. A Russian company has done the advance work. MAYAK."

Afghanistan. Donovan silently mouthed the alien taste of the name.

"Still with me?" said Reynard. Donovan nodded, unsure. "Good. You have two weeks. As you may have read, a co-alition government took over from the old regime when Kabul fell. They had elections on tap. At least, before the heist."

"Heist? You haven't told me what we're looking for," said Donovan.

Reynard sat back in his chair. "Come on, Dick. Add it up. You know what the nose is supposed to find," he said.

6

—

THE NIGHT JOURNEY

THE SILENCE OF THE ABANDONED AFGHAN AIR BASE AT Bagram was broken by the whine of a starter motor. The first propeller began to spin, faster and faster. The whine disappeared beneath the cough and clatter of old pistons. A cocoon of oil smoke blasted back over a dark wing. The concrete ramp glowed under a dome of brilliant desert stars. The second engine caught a moment later.

The Lisunov Li-2 was thirty years older than Hessamuddin Badr, its pilot. A direct Russian copy of the venerable DC-3, the twin-engined plane could carry a tremendous payload into short, precarious airstrips. Badr had six passengers tonight: five heavily armed Uzbek mercenaries and one VIP. But the real cargo was stacked nearly to the roof of the plane's cabin: brand-new Kalashnikov 74s, fresh from manufacture; rocket-propelled grenades; Strela antiaircraft missiles. And a treasure trove of ammunition, from 5.45-mm RPK rounds to heavy 23-mm shells.

The Lisunov was a flying armory, and the cabin air was sharp with the distinctive tang of gun oil. At their destination, the smell would be replaced by the soft, seductive scent of poppy resin. Iron and steel for flowers, and flowers for hard cash. It was a transaction with a great deal of history behind it. Only the players and the currencies had changed over the years.

The pilot advanced both throttles. Dodging craters, he taxied to the end of the buckled runway. There he paused, thinking. Challenging the central highlands of Afghanistan at night was enough to make any pilot consider other careers. Badr patted the photograph of Michael Jackson he'd taped to the glareshield. It was his good-luck charm. He let out a long breath, gripped the throttles, and ran them full forward.

The Lisunov roared and rumbled, rolling like a truck with a stripped transmission. As the airspeed needle twitched to life, he hauled back on the heavy yoke and coaxed the laden ship into the night. The scattered cookfires of Charikar passed below. There, Badr turned west, heading for the mouth of the Bamian Valley. The old Li-2 shook as it struggled for altitude. Finally, Badr leveled off at thirteen thousand feet. He patted the good-luck photo as the last flat terrain swept underneath.

Ahead, dim in starlight, the Bamian Valley dissolved into a maze of canyons. He pulled back the throttles, set the props and mixtures. His scalp began to tingle as the valley narrowed. The opium run was very nearly a scheduled service, but he never got used to flying blind. Not in these mountains. Not at night. He banked first left, then right, threading a maze of unyielding stone.

Around a final bend, a sudden wall of rock stood squarely in his path. Beyond it lay a high, ice-carved bowl known as the Valley of the L'al. Three canyons slashed the granite wall; each was nothing more than a black slot, darker than the steep flanks to either side. Two were dead ends. One cut its way through to the valley above and beyond. Which one was right? He'd made this run twice before. Once at sunrise; once under a bright full moon. It looked very different tonight. Badr stroked the photograph, whispered a short prayer, and made for the southern chasm. The Li-2 was immediately swallowed. He could see nothing outside his cockpit.

Badr sensed rather than saw a sudden motion on the instrument panel. A needle was twitching. Above it, in Russian, was OIL PRESSURE 2. Badr tapped the glass face. The needle stopped moving for a moment. The engines droned on, steady. They'd better. There were no landing fields around. Not even a flat stretch of river bottom. And rescuers? None.

The oil-pressure needle began to vibrate again, swinging the full arc from red to green to red. Then, as he watched, the tiny needle, so small, so insignificant, took a steady, determined dive to zero.

He shot a look out the right window. The engine was invisible. He stared at the offending gauge, praying that the fault lay with the needle. Not the engine. He scanned the other instruments. Oil temperatures were good. RPMs steady. His airspeed had not decayed. But the number two pressure needle slept against its peg. Dead. Without pressure, the engine would seize. It might take seconds. It might last for a few minutes. Maybe longer. And if the engine seized at their weight, over such terrain, then . . .

The confining canyon suddenly opened up. He could see high white snowcaps all around him. The valley! He pulled back power to both engines and hunted the dark ground. He wanted a runway. Now. The right engine began to vibrate. Or was it his imagination? He held his breath, feeling the old machine through his fingertips. No. It was real. Faint. Then stronger. More insistent. Something was wrong out there.

Suddenly, out of the blackness dead ahead, two bright lines of white fire erupted. Badr dove for the outlined runway. Both engines backfired, strobing the rapidly nearing ground with blue flashes. He pulled out the massive gear handle and rammed it down. The slipstream roared against the Li-2's wheels. The gear lights showed green. He stroked his sacred photo again. Who knew what worked and what did not?

Badr lined up on short final and dropped full flaps. The plane struck an instant later. The ride was rough. The tail fell with a loud thump and a bang. The runway lights went out, leaving him utterly blind. He gingerly brought the plane to a stop, then pulled back the red mixture controls. Both engines died with a shudder. They were down. Alive.

The curtain behind the cockpit swept open. The broad, flat face of the VIP appeared, his pale skin glowing like a moon in the night. "Good work."

Badr let out a long breath and nodded. "We have a problem with the number two engine."

"Can it be fixed?"

"Sure. In Kabul."

The foreigner snorted. "See what you can do." The curtain fell closed.

"Exactly so," said the pilot, mocking the mandatory response of a Soviet Red Army soldier. He knew one thing: they weren't flying anywhere else tonight.

The foreigner walked downhill toward the hatch, through the narrow aisle between stacked ammunition crates, beyond the five Uzbek mercenaries. He was dressed in jeans and black leather jacket. He unlocked the hatch and threw it open.

He could smell the dust blow in as the boarding ladder dropped to the ground. The instant he stepped out, a hot beam of blinding light pinned him in its glare. It seemed to burn through his eyelids, through his skull. He held up his hand against it.

"Come down!"

Halfway to the ground, the spotlight snapped off. He squinted, trying to make sense of what seemed a mass of shifting, irregular shapes below. One shape, dark and hooded, broke away from the mass and approached.

A strange vision confronted the foreigner as he stepped down to the dust of the Valley of the L'al: the glittering black eyes of an insect peered out from beneath a mullah's robe. As the nightmare drew near, he saw the insect's eyes become the lenses of a pair of Red Army–issue PNV-57 low-light goggles. A wire came from them and buried itself under the dark, flowing mullah's robe. "You're late," said the Baluchi as the Uzbeks began to unload the weapons. A pile of poppy-resin bricks stood nearby.

"I'm here. There's fighting in Kabul."

"Thanks to Allah, not for much longer."

"Thanks to Allah," replied the foreigner, "and MAYAK."

7

PILGRIMAGE

LT. J. P. HARPER TURNED UP THE BRIGHTNESS OF HER CRT display to match the glare of the morning sun. Everything was running sweet and right with the *Grape*. It was a testimony to the work of the maintenance crews as well as to the importance of the mission. *Somebody busted their asses getting this beast ready to fly again,* she thought. It had taken them all night to rewire the burned circuits and hang a new engine and prop on the *Galloping Grape*'s wing. She glanced out at the new turbine. *So far, so good.*

The sunrise painted the South China Sea the color of mercury. They were westbound, one and a half hours out of Cubi Point, nearly six from home at Iwakuni. Donovan still hadn't briefed them on the mission. What were they doing headed straight for Vietnam? If they didn't turn soon, they'd be feet dry over a place naval aviators still called Indian Country.

"Commander?" she said as she unbuckled her shoulder harness. "My legs need a stretch. Can I bring you something up from the galley?"

Donovan looked over. "Coffee sounds pretty good." Harper's face was softly lit by the glow of her instruments.

Damn it, he thought, *lieutenants aren't supposed to be pretty.*

"I'll be right back." Harper pushed aside the blackout curtains and stepped into the *Galloping Grape*'s cabin. To the left, Chief Svoboda, the Sniffer man, was asleep with his head against the padded cabin wall. He still wore his heavy green headset.

To the right, Lieutenant Carranza was head down over his circular radar display. The green glow coming from the sweeping radar plot gave his hawklike features a ghoulish tint. She watched as he adjusted the sweep of the radar, optimizing the presentation until a ragged line of coastline showed in the upper corner.

"Hey, Hot Dog," said Carranza. "What gives?"

"Morning, Tacco. Want anything from the galley?"

"You bet," said Carranza as he pushed one earphone away from his head. "I'd like to know where the hell we're headed." Even now his flightsuit was pressed and immaculate, his logs meticulously kept. His compact frame, dark hair, and carefully trimmed mustache all evinced a certain precision that matched his approach to his job. He jabbed the wavy line on his screen. "You know what's out ahead, don't you?"

"Yes. Where are we?"

"We just passed the Dong Dao beacon." Carranza pointed to a jagged white line that slashed across the upper edge of the circular screen. "I'm picking up the Vietnamese coast plus a whole lot of radiation from defense radars. They sure as hell know we're out here. I hope they're expecting us."

"Me, too." Harper glanced across the aisle to where Svoboda slept. "Better get the chief up. We'll be landing at Da Nang."

"Say again?"

"Da Nang." With that, Harper walked aft.

The name seemed to ring a loud alarm in Svoboda's ear. Unlike Carranza, he was old enough to have been there before. He suddenly sat up, his face red from where he had leaned against the cabin wall. "Da Nang?" he said. "Did I hear that right?" Svoboda was as fair and beefy as Carranza was dark and compact. His hair had once been blond, but too much exposure to officers had tarnished it gray. "What's going down?"

"Not us, I hope." Carranza shook his head and glanced across the aisle at the Sniffer operator. He tapped his radar screen. "I figure feet dry over Vietnam in forty minutes."

"Sheeit. And the gooks know we're inbound?"

"Hot Dog says so," replied Carranza with one dark eyebrow arched.

"Sheeit," Svoboda said again as he punched up the armament panel. Two AIM-9Ls weren't much in the way of self-protection. But it made him feel better all the same. You never knew.

Harper walked back through the *Grape*'s midsection, racks of electronics with twinkling, multicolored lights to either side. She could feel the heat of the equipment on her face.

She stopped at the galley and peered out the small porthole. Harper could feel the Plexiglas tremble. Vietnam was out there, drawing closer at the rate of five nautical miles a minute. She leaned over. The P-3's starboard wing looked black against a steely blue sky. She could just make out the silhouette of a single Sidewinder slung under the wing.

She turned away from the porthole and walked back to the cramped galley. The hot can still contained fresh coffee taken on at Cubi. She poured a cup, adding a bit of salt, just as her daddy had shown her back at Corpus.

When she returned to the cockpit, Harper discovered that

Donovan had moved over to the left seat. He was just reaching up to the overhead switch panel to flick off the nav lights when she swept the blackout curtain aside and stepped into the cockpit. "Navy black," she said, handing him both cups.

"Thanks." Donovan took a sip and smiled. "Just right. By the way. I was wondering"—he stared out at the flat gray plain of the South China Sea—"what exactly did you do to put the bee in Jameson's bonnet?"

She looked away. "Lieutenant Jameson can be touchy sometimes. I sort of surprised him. That's all." She suddenly found something to adjust on her attitude display. She hoped Donovan would drop it.

"Exactly how did you surprise him?"

She looked up. "Well, I was saying that as far as Carranza knew, he was on a submarine. Svoboda, too. I mean, those guys back in the tube don't even look out the window."

"Uh-huh. What happened then?"

She flicked a dust mote from the shoulder of her flightsuit. "Jameson said the guys in back had a better picture of what was happening than we did up here. You know, radar, the Sniffer, ECM, all the sensors they stuffed us with. I said anybody'd believe that ought to drive a pencil, not an airplane."

"I see." Donovan smiled. He might have said the same thing. Still, he was a commander. He could get away with it. He scrutinized the young lieutenant. "Was there something else?"

"We sort of got into a discussion. I told Jameson I could prove it." She looked pained. "I said that Carranza and Svoboda wouldn't even know if we were upside down."

"That's crazy. Of course they'd know if you rolled inverted."

Harper's blue eyes flashed in the silver light of dawn. "Not if you kept one g positive," she said earnestly. "Sir."

Donovan examined her face to see if she might be pulling his leg. Harper swallowed under his stare. He glanced at her flight helmet hanging from the bulkhead, saw her running name emblazoned on it, HOT DOG, and looked back at her. "You mean to tell me," he said at last, "you *rolled* a P-3? You didn't, did you?"

Suddenly, the intercom came to life. "Flight, Tacco here. We've got company. One bogey at eleven for ten o'clock, twenty miles, big and slow moving. Looks like a sortie out of Da Nang."

"Roger. Not to worry," Donovan said. "That bogey's our escort." He paused and looked at Harper. She was sitting very still, wondering whether it had been right to speak the truth to a commander. "By the way," he said to her. "How'd she roll?"

Harper broke out into a bright grin.

"I see," said Donovan. *Harper can get you into trouble faster than anyone I ever knew. . . .*

"Flight," said Carranza, "that bogey's on an intercept. He's moving to our ten-thirty, range ten. He's probably getting blind vectors from coastal radars."

Donovan saw a glint of sun off the wing. Then a shape that was at once familiar and alien. "Tally the bogey," he said. "It's a May." The Ilyushin-38, known to NATO as the May, was a four-engine antisubmarine plane that was a virtual double for the P-3. It still sported the bright red Soviet star on its fin, even though there was no Soviet Union anymore.

Harper looked over at Donovan. "Our reception committee?"

Donovan nodded.

"Sir? I was wondering, the crew's wondering, too, about, I mean, where this mission is headed."

"Fair enough. It's about time, anyway. I wanted to wait until after we put Cubi behind us." He watched as the Russian plane took station off their left wing. "Here's the deal. We'll follow the May into Da Nang, refuel, and take up a course for the Bay of Bengal."

"Is there a fleet-ex?"

"Not exactly. We'll fly on to Kabul. As in Afghanistan."

Harper whistled softly. "That's a long way from the ocean."

"That's what I said to Reynard . . . ah, Captain Reynard. But our friends at the State Department have the route all approved. All we have to do is fly it."

The intercom interrupted him. "Flight, Tacco here. The May is at nine o'clock and two miles. Is there a freq I can hail him on?"

Donovan flipped open a pad of paper on his kneeboard. "Try two six two point five."

"Sir?" asked Harper. "What's happening in Afghanistan that needs an EP-3?"

"Not just any Orion," Donovan corrected. "But one with a nose."

"Flight, Tacco has the May on two six two point five."

"You fly the airplane, Hot Dog," said Donovan. "I'll talk with the Russians. When we're all set up, I'll fill you in on what I know." Donovan checked the kneeboard scratch pad once again and pressed the transmit switch. "Black Eagle Nine, Grape Six is with you. How do you hear?"

The answer from the Russian patrol plane was immediate. "Black Eagle copies your transmission, Grape Six." The Russian pilot's English was excellent. It made Donovan suspicious. "We have you in sight. Follow us and do not transmit to the tower. Acknowledge."

"Pushy son of a gun," said Harper. She fought back the

urge to needle the Russian somehow. All her life, whenever someone had pushed, she had learned to push back harder.

The May glinted in the brilliant morning sun. "Remain on our wing, Grape Six. Black Eagle out."

Harper looked beyond Donovan at their escort. "Nice copy," she said. It looked almost exactly like an Orion.

Donovan looked over at the May. The IL-38's tail even had the long stinger of a magnetic-anomaly detector (MAD) device. Like the Orion, the May was a hunter. The enemy. There was the bold red star on its steeply raked rudder to prove it. Just what the hell were the Russians these days? Enemies? Friends? Just what?

"All right, Lieutenant," said Donovan. "Here's the outline. It's really pretty simple. The Russians lost a nuke. We're going to help them find it."

"A nuke boat? In Afghanistan? I mean, how can you . . ."

"Not a nuke boat. A *nuke*. As in a bomb. Our friend over there"—he nodded at the May—"doesn't have a Sniffer. We do. A loose nuke makes Washington a bit uneasy. I guess it makes us all a little uneasy."

Harper took this in silently. How did you just lose a nuke? She kept a wary eye on the Russian aircraft ahead and to their left. "So the Navy volunteered us?"

Donovan shook his head, thinking of Reynard. "I doubt it. But you know how tough things are right now. The fleet's getting smaller with every budget. Lots of good sticks are getting RIFFed out. I guess someone back in Washington decided it was a way to do well by doing good. Anyway, we'll run this little op for about a week, maybe two, and then return just like we came. After that, I'm off to Oahu. And you, if you're good and lucky, will—"

"Grape Six, Black Eagle," said the Russian pilot. "Begin your descent now. Da Nang weather is clear, winds light and variable. We will take you down to Runway Thirty-five Right and break off the approach. You will have three thousand meters available. Acknowledge."

"Grape Six acknowledges." Donovan was glad that the approach would be entirely visual. Very glad. He looked at Harper. "I've got the airplane." He took the yoke and pulled the power levers back a touch, keeping precise station with the Russian May off to their left as they started their descent.

"I've got terrain off the nose, Commander," she said as she peered out ahead. "Looks like a big hill."

"Monkey Mountain," said Donovan without so much as a glance. "It's bigger than you think. I know. I'm the guy who established its true elevation."

"How?"

"The hard way." Donovan didn't seem to wish to delve any further into it.

Harper rustled open a chart of Da Nang. The date at the bottom made it a relic of the 1960s. "Monkey Mountain it is," she said. "Fourteen hundred meters and change. It's not so big."

"God damn." Donovan looked down at her opened chart. "Does it really still say that? Fourteen hundred?"

"Yes, sir. Why?"

"Because it's three hundred and twenty-two meters higher," said Donovan quietly. "That's why."

"You'd think somebody would have caught it."

"Somebody did." Three hundred meters was a very big difference when you were solid in the clag, with nothing beyond your windshield but gray milk. It was all the difference in the world. Donovan watched as the rocky hump grew larger on the horizon. The white fringe of distant beach showed at its base. How many times had he seen that beautiful green bay sweep beneath his wing? Vietnam seemed a geologic age ago.

"He's slowing up, sir," said Harper, nodding at the Russian May.

Donovan blinked, forcing himself to see the here and now. To *be* in the here and now. He pressed the intercom button. "Crew, Flight here. Set condition five and perform your prelanding checklists and prepare to depressurize."

Harper reached over to the Sidewinder panel. "Master Arm is off, circuit breakers set, wheel warning breaker is on." She spun the pressurization controller to the dump position. "Cabin pressure is bleeding. ESM to safety, chaff and flares are disarmed. Weights and speeds are on your display, Commander."

"Let's head on down." Donovan nosed over and began the long glide to a land that had once been utterly familiar and now was utterly alien. *Maybe,* he thought, *it always was.*

The coast of Vietnam appeared as a range of green hills with a fringe of white surf at their base. Monkey Mountain stood head and shoulders above all the others. Donovan banked away from it. Da Nang Bay became visible as a cobalt blue jewel gripped by bony, mountainous fingers of land. The red metal roofs of town clustered tightly to the south shore like an encrustation of barnacles.

To the north, the hills ramped up into serious mountains. The old air base occupied the coastal plain just beyond the beach but before the hills climbed up in earnest, the two parallel white strips of concrete in sharp contrast to the dark green of the surrounding jungle.

The Russian subhunter took them down on a wide base leg, turned north over town, and dropped its gear. Turning a high final, Donovan brought his engines back to flight idle and retrimmed the *Grape* for final approach speed.

"Gear down," he called, and Harper pulled the handle from its detent and rammed it down. "Flaps set to approach."

"Flaps to approach," she called back. The whine of electric motors filled the cockpit, along with the thunder of air spilling by the gear doors and the wheels themselves. Ahead, the May wagged its wings as the tire-streaked white concrete swept closer. "Three green," said Harper, checking the gear indicator lights. "Brake pressure is up. Taxi lights are on, landing lights are on. Harness is locked."

"Landing flaps."

"Coming down," she said with a nod. "Nice setup, sir."

"I did it a few times before." Donovan retrimmed as the *Grape* slowed down even more, the airspeed dropping through 140 knots. The May suddenly banked up on a wing and thundered away, four tongues of orange flame visible from its engines, its wheels folding back into their wells.

As the concrete blurred under the *Grape*'s purple nose, Donovan pulled off the remaining power to his engines and flared. The P-3 settled in with a double chirp and two clouds of blue tire smoke. They were down, rolling out along a runway built by the French, expanded by the Americans, blown up by the North Vietnamese, and now rebuilt a third time by the Russians. It hadn't brought anybody much luck.

"IFF is off, flaps are coming up, and the boost pumps are off," Harper called off as she ran down the postlanding items on her list. She glanced out toward a deserted-looking terminal. "I see the taxi guide." Harper nodded at a jeep that scuttled across their path with double checked flags flapping. "I don't know the taxiway layout here, but it looks like you could—"

"I do," Donovan replied.

They taxied by a line of ruined hard shelters, their arched roofs caved in, then by an airplane cemetery. All these shiny clever machines brought halfway around the world now sat sinking into the tarmac, rotting, picked over.

"Wow," said Harper as they taxied by the chaotic jumble of wings, engines, broken fins, and hydraulic lines. "It looks like a junkyard. Hey! Look!" She picked up a familiar shape in the incredible mess. "That's an A-4 sitting out there!"

"Don't get your hopes up, Hot Dog," Donovan said with a weary smile. "Unless you're prepared to buy it."

The Russians had built a brand-new hangar for their own use across the runways from the passenger terminal, but that was not where the *Grape* was being led. Four IL-38 Mays sat in a row in front of the older building. The jeep slewed to a stop and a man jumped out. His blond hair was plastered to his head. A Russian. He signaled them to slow, slow, and stop. A slashing motion of his hand demanded engine shutdown, and Donovan complied. From medium distance, the *Grape* could be the fifth May except for its Stars and Bars, its purple nose, and the words US NAVY on its side.

"Welcome to Vietnam," said Donovan as he shut down the last engine. A refueling truck was already hurrying across the runways from the big new Russian hangar. "You supervise the refueling. Have them top off everything. The mains, the pods, and the auxiliaries. Everything. We'll need the gas. And keep the locals away from the Sidewinders." Donovan looked out the window at the approaching Russian truck. "In fact, keep them away from everything except the fuel points."

"Will do," Harper replied as she unlocked her harness, released the shoulder webs, and stood up. "Are you coming out, sir?"

"No. I've been here before."

Donovan watched as Harper went aft. He heard the main

crew door crack open, heard the voices of his crew, excited, encouraging the refuelers to hurry up with the boarding ladder so that they might feel this fabled alien earth beneath their boots. A moment later, he smelled it.

It was a dank, lush odor of too much rot and too much life all at once; sweet and rancid; dense enough to slice. A strange, yet horribly familiar stink that the rich kerosene fumes rising from the Russian refueling truck could not mask. Sweat popped out on his brow as he listened to the voices below and smelled the nearby jungle. Donovan felt the world tilt and collapse in upon itself, until the years were condensed to the thickness of his logbook. With the smell of the jungle, the voices were not far behind. He picked up Harper's chart and saw the fatal error repeated on the elevation tag for Monkey Mountain. He closed his eyes. The memory came at him like a runaway freight train.

Whiskey Niner Five is cleared for the Da Nang GCA. No need for further acknowledgments. Da Nang weather is ceiling two hundred, one-half mile in fog and rain.

Too bad. It's nice and sunny up here.

Yeah. It's wet and ugly down there. Here we go.

Donovan's old SNB Twin Beech skimmed through the tops of the clouds, pinned in the glare of hot sunlight, then burrowed into a humid, gray world. All was as it should be. The altimeter unwound but not too fast; the course was perfect. The approach was supposed to keep them well clear of the terrain.

But it didn't. Suddenly, the gray clouds turned dark with rocks. A thump came from the SNB's belly as it slewed violently to the left. Both wings snapped off and the fuselage plunged through the jungle canopy, burying its crumpled nose in red earth. Then came the silence.

The Board of Inquiry finds that the cause of the accident

of three November, nineteen sixty-seven, to be a premature descent from safe altitude . . .

"Sir?" asked Harper. She had to shake Donovan. "Sir? We're finished refueling."

"What?" How could that be? He had just seen her walk aft. He looked outside. The Russian truck was nowhere to be seen.

Harper dropped into the copilot's seat. Her blond hair was plastered to her forehead by the dank heat. "Damn but it's Texas humid out there. We're ready for the start, sir." Harper narrowed her eyes. "Are you feeling all right?"

"Fine. Just fine. Tell you what," Donovan said as he took his hands from the *Grape*'s controls. "You make the take-off."

The smell of the jungle permeated the cockpit, brought in on her sweat-stained flightsuit. Ten minutes later, he could smell it even as the *Grape* climbed out, leaving Da Nang behind in the orange glare of the rising sun.

8

—

THE WINDS

BELENKO WAS RIGHT: MONEY TALKED. EVEN WITH ALL AIR SERvice canceled into war-torn Kabul, the International MAYAK Corporation, Ltd., had found a way to fly him in. The chartered twin-engine Antonov AN-26 still carried Aeroflot markings on the tail, down to the red banner with its hammer and sickle. The fuselage had been stripped to an anonymous white. He imagined what it would look like to a *mujahed* with a missile, buzzing across the cloudless blue sky. It was not a comforting thought.

The Antonov struck the runway hard, drawing shrieks of protest from the tires. There was no time for finesse. The pilot was in a hurry. The airport had always caught more than its fair share of rebel rounds. The AN-26 swerved off the runway and fast-taxied to the last undamaged terminal building. The burned remains of aircraft caught too long on the ground were scattered across the parking areas. They looked like rotted corpses baked black by the merciless Afghan sun.

The pilot cut one engine, leaving the other one howling, ready for a quick turnaround. The curtains separating the cockpit and the cabin opened. "I'm taking off again in three minutes," the pilot said to Belenko. "Welcome to hell."

* * *

Pavel Markelov sat waiting in a room chance had saved
from the rain of shells and rockets. A bush jacket, fes-
tooned with straps and pockets, had replaced his blazer. The
room was painted in the blue and white colors of Afghan
Ariana, the old prewar airline. On the walls were travel
posters and photographs of tourist sites even a tank regi-
ment could not safely visit. He looked out through the
cracked window glass. One man, and only one man, came
down a ladder someone had hastily pushed against the
transport. Markelov put on his sunglasses. Belenko.

The heat was a white glare off the ruined concrete.
Smoke-ringed craters had turned the taxiways into an obsta-
cle course. Concrete rubble had been blown outward in perfect patterns of circular ejecta. Like the moon. Kabul.

Before Belenko made it under the tattered shelter of a
canvas awning, the AN-26 spun up its second engine and
taxied away. *Welcome back, Aleks,* he thought as he
watched Belenko trot toward the terminal. He heard
Belenko's footsteps scuff up the concrete stairs. "So you
made it."

Belenko brushed his sweaty hair from his eyes and took
off his overcoat. There was no need for it in this heat. "I
made it, thanks to the MAYAK air force."

"Money talks and nobody walks," Markelov said in English, then chuckled at his own joke. But then his face registered a look of serious concern. "So tell me, Sasha, what
did you learn up at Khorog?"

"Some things." Belenko glanced around the waiting
room, remembering when this place was new. The Americans had built it when Kabul International was going to be
a busy refueling hub for trans-Asia flights. It had been a big
indoor bazaar back then, bustling with vendors of bus tours,

newly antiqued rugs. Opium, too. Once again, Belenko's face registered the presence of ghosts.

"Things?" Markelov's eyes were invisible behind the deeply tinted glasses. Somehow his face looked frozen, not flushed by the morning heat.

"For one, you are right. Hekmatyar's men did it. I saw them there."

"Alive?"

"Very dead. And another thing. The weapon went armed."

"Mother of God," Markelov whispered. "The worst-case scenario."

Belenko nodded. "I suppose so." He glanced beyond Markelov. The door was guarded by two soldiers, their AK-47s loaded and their expressions professional. Neither one wore Red Army–issue uniforms. Both were tall, menacing Slavs. "MAYAK has a militia, too?"

"Kabul is a dangerous place. Especially for us. For them"—he nodded derisively—"it's a job. Better than Moscow."

"Too bad MAYAK didn't run the war. We might have won."

"Exactly so. Still, I shake my head when I think how naive we were once to deal with that devil. We should have known," Markelov continued. "I never trusted Hekmatyar. You knew him, didn't you?"

"At the university. He was in my Russian-language class. He cheated."

"So nothing has changed."

"Everything has changed." Belenko looked beyond the soldiers, through the half-open door, to the empty corridor outside the reception room. "Tell me, Pavel Ivanovich. Why was that missile battery in Tajikistan?"

"You asked me that in Moscow. I still have no idea."

"It makes no sense. I asked around. They were ordered out of Kazakhstan and told to meet a train in Dushanbe. A strategic withdrawal, they said. To keep the bombs out of the woodchips' grasp. The old weapons would be decommissioned. The new ones recycled into Russian stocks. Makes sense?"

"Indeed." Markelov's face was utterly blank as he listened.

"But why Dushanbe? They could have gone home from Alma-Ata. Khorog is not on the direct route anywhere. If they wanted security for that missile battery, sending them a stone's throw from the Afghan border hardly seems wise."

"In retrospect, no. You have some private conclusions?"

"Suspicions." Belenko looked back at Markelov. "Consider this: who knows where a missile battery is from day to day?"

"The Army. The Strategic Command. STAVKA."

"The local commander? His adjutant? The mess sergeant?"

"Sasha! Surely you don't believe . . ."

"Why not? Perhaps the International MAYAK Corporation is not alone in joining the world of private enterprise. The Red Army stripped to its underwear to sell their gear to the Germans. How much do you suppose a nuclear warhead might sell for? A small one, as you said. But all things are relative. How much? A million? Two? And not rubles. We speak of dollars now. Or would it be francs?"

Markelov's voice dropped to a whisper. "You think *Russians* were involved?"

"Twenty percent of Missile Battery Alfa was non-Russian. Mainly Tajiks. Including some of its officers. I checked that, too."

"Your mind is sharp, Sasha. Like a razor. But still, such

a notion boggles the mind." Markelov checked his watch. "To think that some filthy Tajik officer might sell a . . ." He stopped and scowled. "I *knew* we were right to bring you in on this. We'll make the necessary inquiries back at the embassy. Let's get your things into the car." They began to walk down the ruined corridor, an armed soldier to either side. A radio strapped to one soldier's belt suddenly buzzed.

"They have crossed into Afghanistan," the mercenary told Markelov.

"They?" asked Belenko.

"Oh. Yes," said Markelov. "Didn't I mention it to you? We are getting some help from the Americans on the recovery effort. They're due in today as well. I thought later, but sooner is even better."

"The *Americans*?" Belenko was shocked. He'd lost many friends to weapons smuggled into Afghanistan by the CIA, and its local toadies in the Pakistani ISI.

"Something the matter, Aleks?" asked Markelov.

"No, of course not. The Americans have always been so helpful. Guns, ammunition. Heroin for our troops. Stinger missiles for the *mujahedin*. What kind of help are they offering now? A knife to slit our throats with?"

"Old thinking." Markelov waved away Belenko's words as though they were a poorly told joke. "You'll see."

Belenko remained silent. He switched subjects as they came to a relatively undamaged lobby. "Where is Nazipha Popol?"

"She's still at the hospital."

"Which hospital?"

"The only one left. Wazir Akbar Khan. Frostbite here and there. Nothing immediately serious. In a few days she might become useful."

"She's useful right now," Belenko said, his voice carefully flattened, all emotion drained. "I'd like to go there straight from here. How is the care?"

"Better than in the hills."

"I want her moved to the embassy."

"In due time, Aleks. Relax. We'll wait for the American plane to arrive. It won't be long. I'll introduce you."

"Wonderful." Belenko examined the little emblem on Markelov's jacket. "No more Polo?"

"Banana Republic. One hundred percent."

Harper read the note Carranza passed forward. "I'll be glad to get out of this thing and walk around. It feels like we've been airborne for a month. At least the weather's supposed to be good at Kabul. Ever been there, sir?"

"Never have, never thought I would," said Donovan, but the long flight had emptied him, too. This was where it could get dangerous. Sloppy. He checked the altimeters, saw they both agreed at twelve thousand feet. He scanned the fuel totalizer, his eyes lingering on the CRT, trying to make sense of what would normally be a very simple display. He saw the numerals showing the available fuel were displayed in cautionary amber. Hadn't they been green before?

"Running a little tight," said Harper. "I hope they have fuel at Kabul."

Donovan nodded. "I remember being told the only time you have too much fuel is when you're on fire." The long journey across Asia on a single tankup had left them with little in the way of reserves. Donovan looked out off the left wing.

The afternoon sun was hot and penetrating, the sky a dark blue stitched to the earth at the horizon by a line of undulating mountains. Down below, the greens and lush browns of Pakistan had disappeared, drained to a sere tan amid the shattered rocks of Afghanistan. The bombed-out city of Jalalabad passed under the *Grape*'s purple nose. It was lifeless and still, baking in the afternoon heat.

"Flight? Tacco here. Kabul International's at twelve o'clock, fifty miles."

"Might as well start down," said Harper. "Save some fuel that way."

Donovan shook his head. "No. Not yet."

"Why?" She pointed to the amber lights illuminated on the fuel panel.

"We'll stay high until we're right over the field, Lieutenant," Donovan snapped. He shook his head. "Sorry, Harper, I'm tired. I think it's safer to stay high until we scope the place out." The Orion's engines hummed a dangerous lullaby as the broken landscape scrolled underneath them.

Finally, Harper spoke. "You think they're still shooting down there, sir?"

"Let's do our prelanding drill."

She pressed her intercom button. "Okay, crew, set condition five and perform your prelanding checks."

"Flight? Kabul elevation is fifty-eight hundred feet," Carranza prompted. Why the hell were they still at twelve thousand? "We can start our descent any . . . stand by." In a moment, Carranza spoke again. "Flight, Tacco here. Bad news. Kabul tower says the airport is under rocket attack. They want us to hold west until they give the all clear."

Harper looked over at Donovan. "Now what?"

"We wait." Donovan banked the big patrol plane away from the airport. From thirty miles out, the black pillars of smoke rising from the field seemed insignificant. Donovan knew they were anything but. The Viet Cong had used similar weapons against him at Da Nang. Elephant Feet they called them, for the thumping crash they made as rounds were walked across the tarmac. He had no wish to hear that sound again. But without fuel to reach an alternate, he had no choice but to find a way to land. Somehow.

"What do I tell Kabul, sir?" asked Carranza.

Donovan hesitated, his jaw working. Was it a nuisance attack or the start of something bigger? Were they gunning for the *Grape*? Or was it just coincidence?

"Can't stay out here too much longer," said Harper. Her pink fingernail tapped the CRT screen. The fuel display had turned from amber to red.

Donovan looked toward Kabul. As he did, he saw another fountain of dirty smoke begin to rise. He pressed the intercom button. "Tell them we'll circle for five minutes, then we're on our way in." Donovan glanced to his right. "Take it for a second, will you?"

As Harper took hold of the yoke, he pulled off his headset and rubbed his face. How many hours had they been traveling this day? The sky was cloudless, but his brain was fogbound. The steady, unmuffled din from the *Grape*'s four T-56 turbines was reassuring to him, the sound of safety, security. But they needed fuel, and there was no way he could get it up here. He slipped the headset back on.

"Flight? Tacco here. Kabul says come on down. The attack's over."

Donovan smiled. "Thanks, Tacco." He swung back to the field. Black smoke clouds were slowly drifting away. "Flaps to approach. Set condition five."

"Coming out. Prelanding checks complete. We're real high, sir."

"Not for long." Donovan swung the yoke right and stomped full left rudder. Skidding sideways, the *Grape* plummeted with all the aerodynamic finesse of a dropped safe.

"Not in the book," Harper said with a nod. "But nice."

"I saw a young lieutenant do it. I figured if she could

hack it, I could, too," Donovan replied dryly. The east-west runway at Kabul International appeared straight off the nose. To the left, the low mud-colored capital baked like pottery under the searing sun. Half a dozen fires were burning, sending plumes of smoke against a brassy hot sky. Farther south, a brisk firefight was under way, the muzzle flashes visible even from the *Grape*'s distant vantage.

"Gear down."

The rumble of the slipstream blasting by the *Grape*'s wheels vibrated through the fuselage.

"One thousand feet, three green, landing checks complete."

"Full flaps." Donovan released his crossed controls and the P-3 straightened out with the runway rising up fast to meet them.

"Flaps all the way," Harper answered.

The *Galloping Grape* glided toward the runway. Donovan felt a gust push at the *Grape* and lowered a wing into it. The P-3 shouldered its way through. He pulled back power and started to flare.

"Thirty feet."

The airspeed bled down as two distant thumps sounded from the main wheels. He pulled the engines back to flight idle. A crater the size of an automobile whizzed by. Suppose they'd struck it? *Time to get this puppy stopped.* Donovan brought the propeller controls into full reverse and fed power to all four engines. It threw them both forward against their restraint harnesses.

Harper watched as they rolled by the carcasses of burned aircraft. "These bastards are serious."

"Bet on it, Hot Dog." Donovan brought them to a stop square in the middle of the runway. He pressed the intercom. "Carranza, tell Kabul tower we've arrived."

* * *

The last *crump* had barely subsided when the telephone rang.

"Chinese one twenty-twos," said Belenko as he stared out the cracked plate-glass window. "Fired from the hills to the west."

"Such a connoisseur," said Markelov from underneath the desk. The phone jangled. "What would have happened to you if one of them landed on us?"

"The same thing that would happen to you underneath that desk." The phone buzzed again. "Aren't you going to answer it?"

The telephone hanging from the Ariana bulletin board trilled again.

"Yes, yes," said Markelov as he eased out from beneath the desk. "Please, Sasha. Stand away from the window? Just a few feet?" He walked up to the jangling phone, noting that the airline schedule still listed flights to cities that had been leveled into dust two years ago. Markelov spoke a few words of serviceable Dari, nodded his head, and hung up. "The Americans have just arrived. Please try to live long enough to meet them. All right?"

Belenko walked over to the broken part of the window and sniffed. The smell of cordite from the rocket warheads cut the air. "It would seem that you were not the only ones who knew of their arrival time." Then, accompanied by the scream of four howling turbines, a great purple nose appeared, glinting hotly in the sun. The wings cast a deep black shadow on the white concrete ramp.

It was ten minutes before the hatch on the Orion was cracked open. Belenko watched as two figures descended the stairway that unfolded from the plane. "Only two for such a big airplane?" he said as they made their way toward the ruined terminal.

"American technology."

Two knocks on the door announced the Americans' arrival. Comdr. Richard Donovan, drenched in cold sweat, entered with Lieutenant Harper right behind.

"Welcome to Kabul," said Markelov as he strode over, his arm outstretched American style. His English, Belenko noted, was quite a bit better than his Persian. "I am Pavel Markelov." He produced another card from his seemingly inexhaustible supply. "I'm from MAYAK. This is my assistant."

Belenko's eyebrow, the white one, raised. "Aleksandr Belenko," he said.

"Commander Richard Donovan, United States Navy." Donovan slipped the card into his flightsuit pocket. "I was briefed your company would help smooth things out for us while we're here. Did the fuel arrive?"

"Absolutely." Markelov turned to Harper. "I see you have brought your assistant, too." His sunglasses lingered on Harper. A muscle in his face twitched. "She is much prettier than mine."

Harper bristled and was about to speak when Donovan took her by the shoulder and squeezed. "This is Lieutenant Harper. I assure you, she's nobody's assistant. She's the pilot of that plane outside. I'm leaving two other crewmen here for security."

"Of course," said Markelov. "You both have my apologies then." He kept staring at Harper, a strange smile on his face. "But such a world we must endure when it becomes impossible to compliment a woman."

Donovan squeezed her shoulder again. "Apologies accepted," he said. "Will my aircraft be secure out in the open?"

"Secure? There's no place in Kabul that's safe," said Markelov. "That's why we must move smartly along. The sooner we find what we are looking for, the better, yes?"

"That's why we're here," Donovan answered. "We can begin flying sector searches in the morning."

"It's too late now, I suppose," said Markelov.

"We've flown fourteen hours getting here and I'm bushed."

"Amen," said Harper.

"Of course, of course," Markelov said. "Your men and your airplane should be safe enough tonight. The woodchips are all to the south."

"Woodchips?" Donovan looked at Harper, then back at Markelov.

"He means Afghans," Belenko corrected. "But some are not far away at all."

"We saw the rockets," said Donovan. "Where will we be staying?"

"The MAYAK office is very sparse. It will get better, but for now, you will be happier at your own embassy," said Markelov. "Someone should be here within the half hour."

Donovan eyed Belenko. "I understand Hekmatyar's headquarters complex is known?"

"Ah," said Markelov. "Yes. Khadir. It will make a splendid place to begin. Very sharp, Commander. Very sharp."

"I doubt it," said Belenko. "Hekmatyar is much smarter than that."

Donovan glanced at the tall, silent man standing behind Markelov. He seemed older and his silence made him seem wiser. How was it that he was the assistant? "You have some idea where we should begin, Mr. Belenko?"

"Perhaps. But remember. Afghanistan is a big country. It was big enough to swallow the Red Army. It is big enough to swallow one airplane."

"Thanks for the warning," Donovan said to Belenko. "I'll keep it in mind."

The two MAYAK mercenaries flanked the two Americans as they walked toward the main entrance of the ruined terminal. Markelov and Belenko trailed behind. The soldiers' assault rifles were held at the ready, safeties off. They weren't along for ceremony.

The old main lobby was scarred with burn marks and holes blasted by rebel-fired rockets. No window held a fragment of glass. The entrance lay buried under chunks of fallen concrete. A sign pointed off in the direction of Customs, but there was nothing there but a great hole in the concrete wall and a tangle of steel reinforcement bars. Through the hole, a black Jeep Wagoneer could be seen.

"Commander Donovan?" said Markelov, nodding at the hole. "Your people have arrived."

There, picking daintily through the hole, came a short, black-haired man. He was dressed head to foot in khaki, with a sleeveless vest over a short-sleeved shirt. Donovan assumed he could only be a journalist, but in this he was mistaken. Afghanistan had been an American victory, and in victory even the spies were permitted to dress for the occasion.

The short man stepped forward, holding a slim vinyl case to his chest. He wore impenetrable sunglasses. The dark lenses hovering above a luxuriant black mustache gave him the look of a wily bandit. "Commander Donovan?" the man with the case said. His lenses lingered on Harper for a moment. His mouth turned down and he shook his head. He held out a hand to Donovan. "Floyd Brown. I'm from the embassy."

"What?" The name was like a jolt of electricity to Belenko. He squinted as though his eyes had failed him. "Brown! You?"

Brown turned and smiled. His teeth were very white. "Talk about a small world. I heard from Pavel you might be paying us a visit. You'll liaise with the locals, right?"

"What brings you back to Kabul?" said Belenko. "Business?"

Floyd Brown, the CIA's station chief in Islamabad, had been the very man to bring the first shipment of Stingers across from Pakistan.

"I'm here to help the Coalition get on its feet. You know. Elections. Straightening out currency markets. Can you believe it? The joker the *muj* have running the Central Bank can't add or subtract. How's he gonna do his work if he can't add or subtract?"

"Good thing you're here to help," said Belenko. "You used to specialize in small arms. A Stinger now and then. I'm surprised you've moved up to helicopters."

"Huh?" Brown smiled and looked at Markelov. "What's he talking about, Pavel? He isn't tracking."

"I have no idea," said Markelov with an icy glare pointed square at Belenko. "Nor does Aleks. He's had a long flight today."

"Very long," Belenko agreed. "In any event," he said to Brown, "I'm back, thanks to your bandit friends. I told you a long time ago you'd regret climbing on the tiger's back."

Brown's smile faded slightly. "That's the trouble with you, Aleks. You always sounded like you knew more than you did."

Belenko fought the impulse to strangle the cocky American intelligence officer. Why had history handed victory to men such as these?

Brown turned to Harper. "Whose idea was this?" he said to Donovan.

"This is Lieutenant Harper," said Donovan. "She'll be flying the search for us. I'm just along for the ride."

"Oh?" said Brown. "That's something of a surprise."

"Why is that, Mr. Brown?" asked Harper, a combative edge in her voice.

Brown ignored her and spoke to Donovan. "We'll get into this later. At the embassy."

"What about airport security?" asked Donovan. "I've left two men at the airplane."

"I wouldn't worry too much. They aren't shooting small caliber at the airport anymore."

"Just rockets," Belenko observed.

"No more than get lobbed into town," said Brown with a shrug. "Take your choice."

"When do we fly the first sector?" asked Harper.

Brown didn't seem to hear her. He turned to Markelov. "Let's plan to meet here for our morning brief. Oh six hundred soon enough?"

"That will be fine," said Markelov. "We shall be here."

"Okay, Commander," said Brown as the two aviators wearily piled into an armored Jeep Wagoneer. Both U.N. and American flags fluttered from the front fenders. "I've got some updated information for you." He carefully rolled up his window, looked around and checked to be sure that all the other windows were up, and started off toward town. "First, how much have you been briefed on here?"

Donovan cleared his throat. "I'm not sure I'm free to speak about a mission brief, Mr. Brown."

"Floyd. Fine. Good answer. Then listen. There's been some new developments." Brown took off his sunglasses. His eyes were dark, almost black. Olive skinned, with only a touch of silver to streak his jet hair, he looked more than a little like a local. His face wrinkled in amusement. "Here's the straight poop. The Russians have gotten their tail in a deep dark crack. You know how they hate to throw anything away, right? I mean, they have artillery pieces from the siege of Stalingrad sitting in warehouses."

"So?" asked Donovan.

"Well, they had these medium-range nukes that were supposed to get cut up according to a treaty we signed with them a while ago. An embarrassingly long while ago. We're talking *Nixon*. Instead of melting them down, they retargeted them against the Chinese. Why not? Who'll notice? Well, somebody noticed real good. They meandered a little too close to the Afghan border, and the *muj* cleaned their clock. That's why it's important you find the damned thing ASAP. The Russians are riding a rocky boat, folks. Riots. Breadlines. They're on the IMF hit parade. We don't want to start jumping around. They could sink. Then what?"

"I thought we needed to find it because of the elections," said Donovan.

Brown turned and looked at Donovan as though he'd just spoken Esperanto. "Sure."

"Where do we start looking?" asked Harper.

"Hekmatyar's HQ." Brown swung wide around the wreck of a big Russian truck. "Khadir's in south-central Afghanistan. Right in the heart of Herati country. The most fundamental bunch of ragheads around. Hekmatyar's a fish in the sea down there. No way in on the ground."

They were passing through the suburbs of Kabul. Not a single building was standing undamaged. The light tan stone that had been used in nearly all the construction lay heaped like archaeological ruins.

"You were saying something about the weapon being in Khadir," said Donovan.

"Best guess," said Brown. "Markelov is a real help to us. He used to be with the opposition. You know. The Committee."

"Which committee would that be?" asked Donovan.

"The KGB. Now he's the local MAYAK rep. Recycled, you might say. But still in the information business."

"MAYAK?" asked Harper. "Is that some kind of company, or is it government?"

"Some and some. In any event, Pavel showed me a preliminary report from the site of the raid. It confirmed that our old friend Gulbuddin Hekmatyar had his fingers in the pudding. So first thing, you guys are going to Khadir. It will be well defended." He turned to Harper. "Women aren't supposed to be on combat missions."

"Good thing nobody noticed back at Iwakuni," said Harper.

"Why would he do it?" asked Donovan. "This Hekmatyar."

"He's been frozen out of a deal he figured he had wired. That's my guess. You know what happened in Kabul. Well, when the city fell to the *muj*, there was a real scramble. Seven different rebel groups. Six of them banded together. The Coalition. One got left holding their . . . got left out. Hekmatyar is not a man to be left out. Not for long."

"So he swipes a nuke?" asked Harper.

"Correct. Now he's got a pile of chips to dicker with. He's put Washington on notice that unless we suspend our aid to the new Kabul government, that little item he stole might find its way someplace. Someplace we might not like. Result? No aid. No aid? No election. And no way we make an issue of the nuke. I mean, if it comes out the Sov's blew us off on a treaty once, they might do it again. Huff and puff back on the Hill, guaranteed. The stakes? Mucho dinero. Farm-aid packages. Consultants out the yin-yang. MAYAK would scream bloody murder. Negative."

Harper and Donovan exchanged looks. What?

"So that's why you're here." Brown turned to face Donovan. "You really can find it, can't you?"

"Like Markelov's assistant said," Donovan replied. "It's

a pretty big country out there. But even if we find it, someone has to go retrieve it."

"Not exactly. Anyway, like I said, Markelóv's been
tremendously helpful. MAYAK's made the technical ar-
rangements. You find it, we'll take care of the rest."

Brown slowed down as they came to a bridge. White
banners fluttered from the parapets, held aloft on slim
wooden poles.

"What's the celebration?" asked Harper. There were hundreds of them.

"Celebration?" Brown shook his head. "Those are for the
shaheen. They're death markers, one to a corpse." The Kabul River was a snaking trickle in its wide, parched bed.
The Wagoneer thumped over and crossed to the embassy
district of the Carte Seh.

Donovan stared out at the incredible jumble of stone,
concrete, and reinforcing bars that had once been homes
and apartments.

"What a shit hole," Brown muttered. As though to punc-
tuate his words, something struck the Jeep's Kevlar-plated
roof and spanged away. "Small caliber. Don't worry. They
see uniforms around here and they think *shouravi*. That's
the Russians. We're *all* Russians to the locals."

Another sharp tick made Harper duck. She looked
around at the empty, black eye sockets of windows in the
heaped ruins. There was nobody.

"Anyway, about Hekmatyar's AO," Brown continued.
"Khadir is an old Silk Route way station. A fort. Now it's
mostly ruins. The Russians flattened the place. It just drove
them underground."

"Like Vietnam."

"Worse. Imagine Charlie with heat-seeking missiles,
radar-guided guns, and an unlimited bank account. This
area? Herati? It's number two on the opium hit parade after

the Golden Triangle." Brown nodded at the case on the seat beside him. "You'll find maps, a breakout of our intel on the various groups, their operational areas, our . . ." There was a sudden movement on the street ahead. Three men in brown *patous* darted across the street and disappeared into a building. A wall had given way ahead, partially blocking the road with rubble.

"Damn," said Brown. "Hang on." He floored the Jeep, but with the weight of its armor the acceleration was less than breathtaking. "You two best get down." As Brown yanked the wheel to steer around the pile of stone, a rock storm descended on the Jeep, hammering the roof and thumping off the sides.

"Rag-headed assholes," Brown muttered.

Harper sat back up as they slowed, out of rock range. "Nice place you got here, Mr. Brown," she said. "Kind of reminds me of Brownsville on a hot night."

"Miss," Brown said, "when they give the world an enema, this is where they'll stick the tube." He turned to Donovan. "Anyway, MAYAK's taken the lead in Russia, and in this pest hole, when it comes to nuclear-security issues. They've got the experience, after all."

Donovan eyed the deserted buildings as if each one held a rifleman. "So?"

"So MAYAK hired a bunch of otherwise unemployed Russian bomb designers. We're talking technical means. Remote. You find it, and the bastards that stole it are gonna be one sorry bunch of *muj*. The last thing they'll see this side of paradise is a United States Navy airplane."

"I don't get it," said Harper. "We might be able to find the warhead, but it won't put an air strike on them. And we sure can't land to retrieve it."

"Retrieve?" Brown shook his head. "Who said anything about retrieving it?" He pulled up to a massive concrete bunker of a building. He hit a dash-mounted button and the steel garage doors opened. He quickly gunned the Jeep inside, hitting the door switch before they had even stopped. "You find it," he said to Donovan, "and they'll make sure it gets taken out."

"Taken out?"

"Absolutely. Right where it sits."

9

—

THE CITY

"So you've met Brown," said Markelov as they walked behind the two MAYAK guards to the Russian embassy car. It was another American Wagoneer, engine running.

"I know Brown," said Belenko in a hostile voice. "I wouldn't be at all surprised to discover he had something to do with the raid. The theft. Getting their hands on a Russian weapon must still count as a prize for the CIA."

Markelov snorted. "Don't be cynical."

"I'll try my best."

Markelov took him by the shoulder. "You can try what you will, but the truth of the matter is that we are on the same side. Besides, the Americans don't need to steal a Russian warhead, Sasha. We could arrange to sell them one, if it came to that. In fact, it is in the works already. I have seen the documents. For peaceful uses only, of course. Nothing eliminates toxic waste like a hydrogen bomb."

"Be serious."

"I am."

Belenko stared. "Tell me, Pavel, if you'd sell the CIA a bomb, who *wouldn't* you sell one to?"

"I worry about your attitude. You've been down in your

little basement room for too long. The world changes, Aleks, and you must learn to change with it. Those are the facts."

"Facts," Belenko repeated with a curl to his lip. "The facts are that your good friend Brown brought the first load of Stingers in from Pakistan. He has Soviet blood on his hands. Good men died because of him."

"Please. Where are these Soviets? You speak of the ice ages." Markelov waved away Belenko's words. "All of that is done with. Ancient history. These Soviets? They lost their war. Now it is our time." Markelov opened the door of the armored Jeep wagon.

"Where else but Russia can history be so unpredictable?"

Inside, Markelov went through his own careful check of each of the car's bulletproof panes. When he was satisfied, he rapped on the glass separating the front and back seats. "Let's go," he told the driver, who in any event needed little encouragement. The armored Jeep lumbered away from the terminal and out onto the road connecting it with the capital.

"So," Markelov said as he sat back in the car's plush seat, "let's start with how we will best use your time. Tomorrow the Americans can begin to scour the mountains with their airplane. I believe they should begin at Khadir. But as you said, the country is big. There are many places to hide. We will need to determine where they should look if Khadir comes up empty. Tell me, what did you think of the blonde?"

"What blonde?"

"The pilot. Harper."

"I think she would hand you your head."

"A spitfire." Markelov nodded eagerly. "Who knows what might happen? I keep wondering what she might be hiding underneath that flightsuit. Where should I begin?"

"That's your concern. I'd like to begin with Nazipha Popol. Has anyone spoken with her?"

Markelov shook his head. "No. She's not in good shape. Her thinking is still unclear. Perhaps tomorrow we could—"

"I want to see her this afternoon."

"In good time, Sasha. In good time. What else is that devious mind of yours working on?"

Belenko eyed the first pile of rubble to appear beside the road. It had once been a block of apartment houses. He watched the ruins drift by the quiet American car. "I still think the Red Army angle should be investigated."

"Theories. We should concentrate on facts."

"Very well." Belenko sat up straight. "Take me to Nazipha. She is the only one who might have some."

"Tomorrow."

"I want to see her. Not tomorrow. Now."

"She'll be there, don't worry," Markelov said as the Jeep picked its way through rubble barriers. "But first things must come first. We have to get you checked in at the embassy, get your briefing under way, outfit you with—"

"No. All that can wait. I want to talk with her."

"Soon enough, Aleks. There's a special aspect to this hunt that must be discussed. A technical solution MAYAK has devised for us."

"A what?"

"A technical approach. You'll see," Markelov said patronizingly. "Things really have changed since you went down to your basement. You'll see."

The road followed the course of the Kabul River in toward the capital, with mounded hills to either side. Two- and three-story apartment flats clung to their slopes, all executed in identical dun sandstone. Their dark, glassless windows were like eye sockets on a bleached skull. The

Jeep weaved along the once-grand boulevard. Rockets had blasted respectable craters in the roadbed.

Belenko watched as the car nosed deeper and deeper into what had once been a prosperous commercial suburb of Kabul. Gone were the *serais*, gone were the corner bazaars, gone were the high-walled houses of the rich merchants. Only the grid of streets remained to separate piles of dusty stones. *A graveyard.* He sat back in the seat and folded his arms. *I should never have come back.*

"Now, I want to go over the ground rules before you start spinning any new webs." Markelov opened a leather attaché. "I think you'll be impressed with the work we've done. MAYAK has been given full cooperation at the embassy."

"How much did that cost?" Belenko asked.

"Nothing. We used rubles." Markelov shuffled through a thick pile of briefing papers. "Geneva has prepared the necessary documents for you. We have a breakout of friendly, neutral, and hostile villages for the entire country." He smiled, obviously pleased with himself. "It's automatic. Ethnic makeup. Language. Religion. All done by computer. We have to do things efficiently now. It's all according to the bottom line. You can see your old friend after we lock you into the program and bring you up to speed."

Belenko turned in his seat and looked at Markelov. "Lock me *where*?"

"It's just an expression."

"Spare me. There will be time for all of that later. For now, I wish to see Nazipha Popol."

Markelov shook his head. "I'm sorry, Aleks. But it's already planned. Brown and I have already discussed how you will proceed. We can't have you running around uncontrolled. Not with a bomb loose. Not with elections coming so soon. What would happen if you were killed? You think you can still pass for a local?"

"Yes."

"No. We'll plan this out at the embassy, see what fits, and then set you sniffing like the bloodhound you once were."

"I see. You and Brown have worked this all out."

Markelov smiled. "Geneva, too."

Suddenly, it was too much. Belenko reached forward and tapped the glass partition. The driver glanced back, touched a button, and the panel slid down. "Stop," said Belenko.

"What?" said Markelov. "Here? Why do—"

"I said *stop*!" Belenko issued the command with an old voice, a voice that belonged to a man used to getting his way. Surprisingly enough, it still worked.

The driver turned off the road and braked to a halt. He looked at Markelov.

"Aleks," said Markelov, "I think we had better establish something here. I take orders from MAYAK. You work for me. You can't just issue—"

"No. I'm not interested. This is a mistake. I should have known. Take me back."

"You can't back out now."

"Oh?" Belenko opened the door and got out.

"Aleks!"

"Tell Geneva you made a mistake. The bottom line is in revolt. You don't need an OSNAZ man here. Just technical alternatives and computers and reports to lock people into. No thanks, Pavel, but it's not the same world. I don't belong here. Good luck."

"Wait." Markelov shook his head and sighed. "I told Geneva you would be trouble."

"Geneva should have listened."

"Will you *please* get in so we can talk?"

"Take me to see Nazipha Popol," said Belenko firmly. "Then we can talk. Otherwise, I will walk there if I have to. That's my last word."

Markelov stared out the window at the bleak, ruined town. "OSNAZ," Markelov said with a shake of his head. "All right. Get in, cowboy."

"We were never cowboys, Pavel. We were the Indians."

Wazir Akbar Khan Hospital was the biggest building left standing on its block, seemingly untouched by rebel rockets. It was a testimony to its stout construction and not the merciful intent of the rebel missileers; the accuracy of the guidance circuits mounted on the big 122-mm warheads fired from the surrounding hills was notoriously bad under the best of conditions.

As the embassy car neared, Belenko saw that the hospital was not entirely undamaged. While its thick walls had protected it, most of the glass on the lower three floors had been blown out, and ragged curtains swung in and out with the wind.

Sandbagged sentry posts, each with a ragged Afghan soldier holding a Kalashnikov, guarded the door. They wore composite uniforms, part old Army, part *mujahedin*. They were the only obvious signs of human life Belenko had seen since leaving the airport.

"Don't be long, Aleks," warned Markelov. "I'll send the car back for you in half an hour. You don't want to be out after dark. It's not safe. Not even for Indians."

"Fine." Belenko got out and slammed the door shut. He watched as the Jeep hurried away.

Kabul. Belenko turned, all his antennae out, listening, feeling the old city. When had Kabul seemed so empty? Even where the buildings were intact, all the windows were tightly shuttered. No smoke rose from cookfires, no swarms of children flashed down the streets like flocks of wild pigeons. No sad music drifted up from crowded alleys. Nothing. Kabul looked dead to Belenko, and Wazir Akbar Khan looked more like a headstone than a refuge for the sick.

He drew in a lungful of air. *Not quite dead,* he thought as he smelled the distinct odor of a charcoal brazier's fire. He scanned the deserted street. Somewhere nearby a samovar brewed. It was a sign of life and buoyed his spirits tremendously, not only because it was a sliver of the present that matched his memories, but for more practical reasons: with the bazaars all shut down, a samovar was just the sort of place where information might still be for sale. The smoke made him oddly hungry. He patted his breast pocket for a Prima, but the sound of a racing engine drawing near made him stop and turn.

A battered ambulance skidded up beside the main door. It flew U.N. flags from its front fenders, but the back was painted with the markings of *Médecins sans Frontières,* the French relief agency. Belenko waited, watching as its driver and a young boy pulled a rough wooden stretcher from the back and hoisted it to their shoulders. It was little more than planks of wood lashed together at each end. A man was tied to it by the expedient of having a sheet wound around him and the planks, mummy-fashion.

Only his face showed. His head was wrapped, Nuristani style, in a filthy turban. The sheet was covered in dark brown splotches of dried blood. It was impossible to tell where or how he had been wounded. The man's dark brown eyes stared back at Belenko as he was carried inside. Belenko followed.

The Coalition guards flanking the hospital entrance didn't even look up as Belenko walked in behind them. He followed them inside, to the stairway, their footsteps echoing on cold stone. A grim gray light filtered in through the shattered windows. The main desk was unoccupied. Jumbles of wires spilled from the switchboard like entrails. He began to climb, his shoes scraping grit as he ascended the stairs.

He stopped when he came to a landing, listening, as the two bearers carried their cargo upstairs. A low, constant wailing punctuated by the sharp spikes of screams came from above.

Then a man dressed in stained hospital whites appeared on the stairway, his head down, his thin hair plastered by sweat to his skull. The emblem of *Médecins sans Frontières* showed through the bloodied operating smock. The man came to Belenko's landing and nearly collided with him. "What do you want?" His gaunt face bore the marks of pure and unmistakable exhaustion, his eyes red and his skin the gray of a man in pain himself. He looked as though he hadn't slept in a month. *"Journaliste?"*

"Mais non," Belenko replied.

"Then what do you want here? You are a Russian, aren't you. I can smell the smoke on you."

"I am looking for a patient."

"There is no shortage." The doctor's voice had a wild edge to it. "We have plenty. Thanks to you. There's no medicine, no antibiotics. No surgical equipment. But patients? We have no shortage of those." He took Belenko by the shoulder. His fingers pinched him hard. "Listen. *Those* are your patients." He stepped closer, pressing his face near to Belenko's. "You're worse than the Nazis. At least they killed their victims. You only maim them."

Belenko remained silent.

"A land of butterflies. That is what this country has become," he said, referring to the most common Soviet antipersonnel weapon. Seeded by aircraft, their plastic wings spun them down to the rocky soil. Children were especially drawn to the colorful plastic devices.

The doctor whispered, "Bastard." His breath smelled acrid as he spoke. "You made them small. Just right for a hand, a foot. Maybe a leg, yes?" His dark eyes glittered. "They come in here looking like meat. And what do we have to give them? A knife and maybe one aspirin. No anesthetics. Tell me. Do you know what happens when the knife first strikes bone? Do they teach you that in Russia?"

Belenko looked down. "I have been away."

"Then you should have stayed away." The doctor let go and made to leave, but Belenko stepped into his path and blocked him.

"I am looking for a woman. She was brought in with frostbite. Nazipha Popol."

The doctor's eyes narrowed. He nodded up the stairs. "She would have been better off in the mountains. The snow is a clean way to die. Fifth floor." He turned away and walked downstairs, leaving Belenko on the landing with the voices from above. Once more, Belenko began to climb.

The sounds became more distinct. So did the smell. The gagging stench of death and decay assaulted him until he had to breathe through his mouth. Still he climbed, third, fourth, and finally the fifth floor. What seemed like a band of refugees from a Stone Age tribal war sat camped in what had been the fifth-floor nurses' station. They did not move as Belenko carefully stepped around them, but they followed him with their eyes. Finally, one spoke. *"Duktur,"* a young man with a stump of an arm whispered. *"Duktur."* The low moaning stopped and the word was taken up as a chant by the broken men and women. *"Duktur. Duktur."*

He looked beyond the suffering to find a real doctor, a

nurse, anyone in charge. On one wall, a passage from the *Qur'an* was executed in graceful script.

Each other's limbs are Adam's Sons,
Who of one substance were created.
Should fortune topple one of them,
The others cannot keep their balance.
Impassive at your brother's fate?
You cannot call yourself a human being.

"Duktur!" The voices became more frantic as he began to walk away. *"Duktur!"*

Down the hall he went, running a gauntlet between a double row of wounded waiting for salvation or death. It was clear from their expressions that either one would do. *"Duktur. Duktur!"* Hands clutched at him as he walked by.

He peered into each room as he went. Beds were arrayed haphazardly in each, three, sometimes four to each dank chamber. Where was Nazipha?

Then he found her. There were three beds inside, one along each wall and one against the back. The two patients to either side were silent, motionless. The one in the center was not.

Belenko could scarcely recognize the young woman he had recruited, loved, and then sent out of the country for her own protection. "Nazipha." Belenko stepped closer. Her small face was on fire with fever. Her skin was stretched tight over her face, her long dark hair spilling over and off the bed. She rocked her head back and forth, her eyes tightly shut. "Nazipha," he said again. As he reached out to touch her skin, her eyes blinked once and opened. It was the green of them, the green of new spring growth, the green of hope and courage that defied the desert, the mountains. Defied even time itself. It was the green that summoned Capt. Aleksandr Belenko back to life.

"Sssshhh . . ." Her voice gathered strength like a steam pocket ready to blow. *"Sasha?"*

"Nazipha!" Belenko reached over and took her by her shoulders, pressing her to him. All the time and distance fell away to a pinpoint and he was there again, young, a warrior in a land he had been trained to undermine but that had, instead, infiltrated him. Her bones felt ready to crumble under his hand. "Nazipha!" Her fever glowed through the thin sheet.

"Sasha," she repeated. "Am I . . . dead?" A violent cough made her stop. A cold shiver wracked her small body, and a flash of clarity passed over her face. She licked her lips.

"No!" He held her close. "No. What happened? Where did this happen?"

She shook her head. "You," she said. "I failed . . . my brother. My brother. Gone. You, too."

"No!" Belenko stopped her. "I tried to find you! I looked everywhere. I came to your home and—"

"Gone. All dead." She swallowed hard. "My brother. Failed . . ."

"Where is Hekmatyar?"

Her eyes widened once again, a flush of heat rising up her neck. "The Cave. At the Cave . . ." She drew in a long breath. "You should never . . . have come here. I should never have . . . left."

Belenko kept his eyes on Nazipha. "Who helped Hekmatyar?"

She shook her head so violently the filthy sheet that covered her half fell from the bed. Her body was covered with scratches. She swallowed again, fighting to keep her mind focused, her lips under control, each breath a rasping, grating wheeze within her chest. "I did."

Belenko felt his face burn. Markelov had been right.

"The Cave. Must . . . go to the Cave."

"At Khadir?"

"The Cave."

What cave? thought Belenko. Belenko leaned over Nazipha's burning face.

"Aleks. Aleks." She forced the fever from her mind, her green eyes blazing with it just beneath the surface. "My brother . . . my brother is dead. Killed. You . . . must tell . . . my parents."

Belenko felt his fist ball. He'd seen the rubble of her house. "I will," he said at last.

"All . . . the killing . . ." She closed her eyes. "Hekmatyar said . . . promised. An end."

Belenko stood. *Hekmatyar. A cave.* He watched her chest rise and fall as she took quick, shallow breaths.

"The sky," she said, her eyes still closed. "I fell. Fell. All . . . dead." Her words fell away to silence as she dropped back to sleep.

He glanced down at Nazipha Popol. A fine sheen of sweat glistened from her forehead in the dim light. He could see the fever rise within her skin like a lamp glowing from below parchment. She had not given him much more than a place to begin. Gulbuddin Hekmatyar. A cave. As he started to leave, she spoke again.

"Wait, Aleks. Just a little."

He stopped. "Nazipha," he said as he returned to her bed. He sat on the edge and stroked her hot brow. "Nazipha."

"Stop them." She closed her eyes and sagged back, receding into a troubled sleep, exhausted.

"I promise," he said to her sleeping face. "I promise." Grabbing a doctor's white coat on his way out, Belenko took the stairs down two at a time. He wrapped the blood-stained jacket around him and stepped out onto the sidewalk. A desert sunset washed the gray masonry with purples and reds.

The embassy car was back. The driver sat up straight as Belenko pounded on his window.

"Who is the mission doctor?" he demanded.

The driver had seen Markelov humbled before his own eyes. This Belenko was supposed to be nobody, but he clearly was far more than that. "Abrosimov," he said quickly. "Dr. Sergei Abrosimov."

"Go fetch Comrade Abrosimov." Then Belenko remembered the soft moaning of the broken men and women, the innocent armies of the maimed. "Tell him to bring all the medicines he has from his stocks. Anesthetics. Antibiotics. Everything he can. We can get more." He glanced up at the grim gray stones.

"He is not permitted—"

"He *can* and he *will*. Tell him he has a patient. Nazipha Popol, on the fifth floor. I want her taken back to the embassy infirmary. *Go!*" Belenko roared. The driver nodded, rolled up his window, and drove off with a screech of tires.

Belenko watched as the Wagoneer disappeared toward the embassy district. The Carte Seh was a good twenty-minute drive away. That left Belenko with just enough time.

The smell of charcoal smoke drifted by again. He turned one way, then the other, his nose directing him.

Hekmatyar, he thought as he walked the deserted street. He saw a puff of smoke rise from the stub of a chimney ahead and found his way to its source. *The cave.* Was it an underground bunker at Khadir?

The door to the *tai chanha* was made from wooden planks scavenged from a looted depot. They still bore Cyrillic markings. Belenko closed the white coat around him and pushed. The sound of voices spilled through the crack, but they came to an instant hush as he opened the door and stepped inside. He looked around at the faces of the dozen men seated around a raised platform. One place was free at the low platform. The seated men looked up at him with frank and hostile appraisal. If their eyes had been X rays, Belenko would have been killed on the spot from overexposure. *"Salaam,"* he said to them. "Are your souls in harmony?"

Harper stifled a yawn. She glanced at Donovan with a questioning look on her scrubbed face. Despite the shower and the ample dinner, or perhaps because of it, she was ready to collapse into sleep. Fourteen hours in her flight log made it a long day. Donovan nodded as Floyd Brown fiddled with an attaché case at his feet. "Well, gentlemen," she said as she stood up, "I'm bushed." She was wearing her spare flightsuit. It felt cool and crisp after the sodden mess the long day had made of her other one.

The hydro site at Sorubi had been dynamited again, leaving the American embassy on its own generator. The room was lit by a single yellow lamp. It cast long, hypnotic shadows. The deep carpet on the floor and the utter quiet afforded by its foot-thick walls was an effective sleeping powder.

Brown looked up. "You have everything you need?"

"I'll be just fine, Mr. Brown," said Harper.

"Good gal. Hot water comes on . . ." He stopped when a distant thud shook the heavy concrete floor.

"What's that?" asked Donovan. A second detonation rumbled through the rocketproof embassy annex, then a third, then a fourth.

"The *muj* are saying good night."

"My men at the airport . . ."

"Don't worry. It's coming from the south. Your guys are safe." Brown turned to Harper. "Hot water comes on at six. Knock on my door if you get scared." He winked.

"I don't think I get that scared, Mr. Brown."

Donovan listened as the distant thuds fell silent. "All right, Lieutenant. Let's plan oh four-thirty for a five-o'clock brief." Donovan's eyes felt as though they were ready to drop from his head and roll across the floor. "Wake me up if I don't get up first."

"Aye, aye. Good night, sir."

Brown watched Harper as she left the embassy reading room and disappeared down the hall. When he was sure she was out of earshot, he turned to Donovan. "Tough little broad. At least she seems to think so."

"She's had to be," said Donovan. "Any problem driving us out to the field that early?"

"None compared to what happens once you get there."

"Why?"

"I don't like the fact that some asshole saw fit to send a woman out here," Brown said, jerking his thumb at the now empty hallway. "It's just stupid. This isn't the place for making statements, you follow? If they've got to prove they've got the balls to do a job, let them do it where it doesn't count. Afghanistan's the real thing."

"So is Lieutenant Harper." Donovan stood up and cast a longing look toward the hall leading to the embassy's dormitory wing. "We're here to fly. She's a pilot. A damn good one, too. That's all there is to it."

"I don't think you get it, Commander. Listen, this is a fucking dangerous place. It's one thing for a man, but it's a whole different game for a woman. Do *you* have any idea what I'm talking about? I mean"—he shook his head—"what if you get nailed and have to walk out?"

"Nailed? Why would anybody shoot at us? We're the good guys."

"Jesus." Brown looked at Donovan as though he were an idiot. "Where have you been sleeping these last couple of years? The only airplanes the *muj* know about are the ones that drop nasty things on their heads. You know? Gas. Napalm. Mines. Millions and millions of mines. Remember something, Donovan. This was the place where the Sovs were going to learn from our fuckup in Vietnam. They were going to do it right. No holds barred. We blasted a jungle or two, but the Sovs bombed the whole fucking country. Something moves on the ground, they hit it. So it's not exactly a shocker that the *muj* see something flying, it's the enemy. Now do you get it?"

Donovan felt a chill run down his body as he nodded. "Go on."

"It's simple. Your typical Afghan lives for revenge. You go down in the boonies, you'd be the lucky one. You're dead, but so what. But her? A woman? An *unbeliever*?" Brown shook his head. "They wouldn't let her go to waste. Follow?"

10

—

COUNSEL

No one answered Belenko's formal greeting. A dozen pair of dark eyes followed him as he approached the one open space left at the low wooden platform. It was all so familiar. The dirt floor was covered with piles of carpets, their brilliant hues muted by dust, age, and the dark. The wool smelled musty, but the scent of smoke, tea, hot bread, and rice made him feel more at home than he had in years. A powerful wave of perfume washed over him. He turned to find its source.

A portly merchant swiftly turned away and took up his haggling with a leaner, rougher-looking customer, a *mujahed* dressed in the distinctive outfit of the Panshair Valley. A small pile of purest lapis lazuli sat on the table between them. The merchant was an Afridi, a pirate-trader from the lawless Pakistani borderlands. The *mujahed* was probably a Massoud man, and that made him interesting indeed. Belenko recalled the pile of bodies at Missile Battery Alfa. They were all Hekmatyar's men; and Hekmatyar was Massoud's sworn enemy. *Perhaps.*

Belenko wrinkled his nose as another tide of aftershave rolled over him. The merchant's *shalwar kameez* was rolled up at the sleeve to expose a cheap digital watch on each wrist. Each gesticulation sent more perfume his way. The Afridi looked up and caught Belenko's gaze.

"*Salaam,*" said Belenko, but the man sneered a silent reply.

To Belenko's right, an old man sat sipping tea. As Belenko was about to greet him in Dari, the man let fly a wad of tea leaves right onto Belenko's shoe. The ancient face screwed up into a toothless grin, the folded eyes unblinking as a lizard's.

"*Salaam,*" Belenko forced himself to say, but the old creature didn't respond with the customary *salaam alekum.* Belenko sighed. The Afghanistan he remembered had been a desperately poor place, a dangerous place as well; but one in which the small courtesies could be relied upon. No more. Belenko shifted his gaze and tried to catch the proprietor's eye.

Behind a second wooden platform, a young boy dipped a plate into a bowl of sudsy water twice, then handed it to the *samovarchi.* The proprietor of the teahouse dried it with a rag and tossed it onto a stack of battered crockery. He looked up at Belenko. "*Eh bien?*" he asked in guttural French. "What do you want?"

"He is a foreigner," the old man to his right whined to the *samovarchi.* His face looked like a topo map of the Hindu Kush, a crosshatch of wrinkles overlying wrinkles from the fringe of his scraggly white beard to the worn *kola* cap. His legs were exposed by an opening in his robe. They were two matchsticks, the minimum covering of skin necessary to go from knee to ankle. The old man pointed a bony finger at Belenko. "Why is he allowed? Why must we sit and eat with such devils?"

"He is a *duktur,*" the proprietor said with a nod toward

Belenko's stolen hospital coat. "He does not have to be here."

The Afridi chuckled. "Then he is a foreigner *and* a fool."

"Better than a thieving Afridi," said the *samovarchi*. It was a long tradition for the owners of teahouses to keep the peace as well as serve the food. He turned to Belenko and spoke once more in battered French. "What will you eat, *duktur*?"

Belenko held up both hands. "Is it not the custom," he said in perfect Dari, "to wash before eating?"

"Ack! He speaks!" the old one said in openmouthed astonishment. A foul stench came from his rotted gums. He had exactly three teeth remaining in his jaw, none of them straight. He moved away from Belenko warily as though this *duktur* might be a dangerous jinn.

"Is he a Moslem?" the Afridi merchant asked, equally surprised. His fat jowls puffed in a way that reminded Belenko of an offended frog.

"He is an unbeliever!" the old one insisted.

Belenko spun on the old heckler. "Who are you to judge, *baba*? It is for God to judge men, not you." Belenko was on safe ground. It came straight from the *Qur'an*. The room hushed as the denizens watched and listened to the evening's entertainment.

"Aye. What he says is true," said the owner of the teahouse. He shoved the washboy toward the copper bowl of water. The urchin dipped an ewer into it and came to Belenko's table, holding it beneath Belenko's hands, splashing the soapy water over them in the proper fashion. The boy then took a rag from over his shoulder and dried Belenko's fingers, one by one.

"Thank you," said Belenko to the sullen child. He turned to the *samovarchi*. "Tea, and *kabli*." How long had it been since Belenko had tasted that delicious concoction of nuts, raisins, rice, and carrots?

"But *duktur*, we have only a poor pilau," the owner apologized. "It is all we can get these days."

"A feast," Belenko replied in formal Dari.

The *samovarchi* smiled approvingly and began preparing Belenko's dinner.

The merchant went back to his negotiations with the young warrior, but the old one stared at Belenko with unmistakable antipathy.

"I have heard," he said in a high, singsong voice, "that the *Amrikans* have visited the moon. That they have conquered death itself. Is that why you are here, *duktur*? Is there no death for you at home anymore?" As he waited for Belenko to reply, a series of distant explosions made the air tremble. "What do we have here but death?" The ancient one grabbed a fistful of Belenko's stolen hospital coat. His fingers gripped like talons. "You speak our tongue. Answer that one, unbeliever. What else does this poor nation have in such abundance?"

Belenko watched as the rest of the patrons watched him. The Afridi smiled his sly smile. The *mujahed* stared at him intently. The pale blue lapis shimmered like crystallized mountain air. All conversation came to a stop, as though his very life might hang upon his next word. Who could say that it didn't?

"Well?" the old one said in triumph.

"The Arabs have oil, the *Amrikans* have gold," said Belenko. "But the Afghans have two things in vast supply. More than anyone."

"Oh?" said the Afridi. "And what are they?"

"Honor and courage."

The silence hung heavy across the smoky room for a long second, then broke.

"*Bi-khuda,* he is almost right," the young *mujahed* nodded with new appreciation for Belenko. "But there are two other gifts that God has given us: mountains and *badal.*" It was the Pathan word for vengeance.

"And poppies," someone else added with a chuckle. "Enough to cover mountains and vengeance."

The Massoud man spun on the man, a solitary figure in the far corner. Despite the dark, the man wore sunglasses as he sipped his hot tea. He had the *kaffiyeh* bandanna of the *Hezb Islami* around his neck. One of Hekmatyar's men.

"Poison is your lot in life," the warrior shot, "but it is not mine."

"Of course," the other replied, his dark sunglasses unable to hide a snide smile. "Your guns are bought with almonds and dates and little pieces of blue stone. We all know."

The young *mujahed* was on his feet like a striking snake. He had his sinewy hands around the man's neck a moment later. The bandanna fell. A knife blade flashed in yellow candlelight. The sunglasses flew off the man's head, clattering in the corner as the *samovarchi* ran to break up the fight.

"Enough!" the proprietor cried. "This is no place to fight! Stop it!"

"You see?" the old man rasped, pointing a bony finger at Belenko. "You see what happens when they are allowed to eat with human beings?"

The *samovarchi*'s hands were bloodied. The Massoud man stood with his arms on his hips as the other hastily put his dark glasses back on and rubbed his neck. A stream of red trickled down a shallow cut that extended from ear to ear. The cut was meant more to humiliate than kill. The *Hezb* fighter glared back pure hatred as he snatched up the bandanna and wrapped it over the wound. "I will not forget." He gathered his things, stood up, and left.

"Bah!" the old man said with a spit of tea onto the dirt floor. "You see what good comes of having them around? All of you are witched by him. But not me. Not me."

"I am sorry, *duktur*," the proprietor said with a deep bow to Belenko as he placed the rice dish before him. "But sometimes . . ." He shrugged and turned back to his dishes.

Belenko picked at his food as the room began to buzz with low, conspiratorial voices. He checked his watch. The embassy driver would return soon with his load of drugs for the hospital. *Poppies. Drugs,* he thought. He knew all the guerrilla groups dabbled in it, although Massoud really did have a mountain of pure lapis to exchange for guns and ammunition. Was the *Hezb* now running the drug trade in Afghanistan? Was Gulbuddin Hekmatyar, the Islamic fundamentalist, selling poison? It was ironic, but . . .

Suddenly, the young washboy darted back into the teahouse. Belenko hadn't seen him leave. He hissed one word that froze all conversation at once. *"Hezb!"* The affronted *mujahed*, a member of Hekmatyar's Party of Islam, had found some friends.

In a clatter of overturned chairs and crashing plates, the teahouse emptied out the back door. The Afridi merchant was already gone, but the young *mujahed* stood firm. A Kalashnikov suddenly materialized in his arms. A shout came from outside the door of the teahouse. Suddenly, four shots sounded in quick succession. A fifth shot brought forth a scream.

"Get out!" the *samovarchi* yelled to Belenko as he himself ran out the back.

"Or die," the young *mujahed* said. His face held a frozen grin made up of equal parts of eagerness and fear.

Belenko ran toward the main door. He threw a heavy iron bar across it just as someone tried to push it open. The wooden planks strained but held. *Good Russian timber,* he thought. The rival *mujahedin* began hammering on it with the butts of their rifles as Belenko ran back.

The young man snapped the AK's safety lever off and pointed it right at Belenko's chest. His eyes swung from the door to Belenko and back. "You should have run," he growled. "You wear the coat of a *duktur*, but I know better. I saw you get out of the *shouravi*'s car. You look like a *rus* and you talk like a Moslem. That makes you a spy."

"Listen to me . . ."

The *mujahed* thumbed the Kalashnikov onto single fire. "One bullet is all that you are worth," he said, a glazed, murderous look across his eyes. "And one is all that it will take."

The rifle was crude and evil looking, not even a good Peshawar copy of the Soviet weapon. But Belenko knew the *mujahed* was right. One bullet was all that it would take. Belenko braced his belly against the round he knew was just about to leave the black circle of the rifle's muzzle.

The door thumped loud, this time splintering the wood behind one of the iron hinges. A shot was fired through the planks. As though guided to the very heart of this place, it found the samovar. A gusher of hot tea arced across the low tables. Steam whistled out the puncture, filling the room like a sauna. The jet caused the vessel to tilt and fall, overturning its platform as it crashed to the carpeted floor.

The *mujahed* grabbed Belenko by the shoulder and threw him to one side. He then lifted the muzzle of the assault rifle and pumped three shots in return. Yellow flame arced halfway across the room. The heavy slugs tore through the weakened wood, and another scream split the steamy air. The men outside retreated for only a few seconds, and then the pounding began afresh. The wood screeched like a tortured animal. Then, with a dry crack, it tore free from its hinges.

A *mujahed* jumped through dressed in dark battle fatigues, his face covered by the *Hezb* bandanna. His assault rifle swung in a hungry arc, settling at once on the Massoud man.

Belenko felt a strange, exhilarating power course through him. Time slowed as his muscles moved faster, faster. Without a thought to which side was which, he grabbed a plank of wood from the overturned samovar platform. "Hey!" he shouted. "You!"

The *Hezb* man turned in time to meet the rough-sawn wood face on. With a wet thump, the guerrilla went down to the carpeted floor.

Another voice came from beyond the front door. There were more of them out there. *What am I doing?* Belenko wondered. *What side am I fighting for?* The brains of a scholar, the arms of a soldier. That was the old OSNAZ motto. His brains were still considering the situation. His arms had already chosen.

The *mujahed*'s dark eyes seemed to pierce Belenko as he prodded the unconscious man with his boot. "You did well. What was it you said to the old one? Courage and honor?" He placed the muzzle against the *Hezb* bandanna and fired one shot. The man's head exploded.

Belenko was rooted in shock. His shoes were covered with brains. Blood. He watched as the Massoud man stripped the guerrilla of his valuables.

The *mujahed* stood up. Voices called from beyond the door. "You'd better get out of here." A shout came from outside. Belenko turned in time to see a grenade sail in a lazy arc through the shattered door. Its fuse sputtered like a party sparkler. The *mujahed* ran to it and tossed it back outside. A flash white as lightning strobed through the wrecked teahouse, followed by the concussion. The silence that followed was heavy as syrup.

A smile crossed the *mujahed*'s hawklike face. "Spy, I owe you my life," he said as he walked up to Belenko. "I will help you escape." The young warrior took the wooden stock of his Kalashnikov and swung it up against Belenko's skull. The man who found himself caught between two equally dangerous worlds dropped like a sack of flour, right beside the dead *mujahed*.

11

REVELATIONS
WELL EXPOUNDED

HARPER ROUNDED THE CORRIDOR AND SAW THE LOW MORNING sun stream through the open door to the conference room. It beamed into the embassy annex with laser brilliance, a combination of Kabul's altitude and the building heat of the summer's day. Two voices also came from within the room; one was Donovan's, the other was Brown's.

". . . sorry, Mr. Brown," said Donovan. "It's a technical limit that I can't do much about. Frankly, I don't *know* much about it, either."

"Figures. Listen, Commander. All I need from you is to get near. I don't want the damn thing in my lap. This Russian box is designed to work from a distance."

"How much of a distance?"

"Markelov will brief you on it. A couple of miles is . . ." He stopped when he saw Harper.

She waited for a moment at the door, checking her father's old Cosmograph. It was five-ten in the morning, Kabul time. She rapped three times on the doorframe and stepped inside.

Donovan looked up from the unfolded navigation chart.

"Good morning, Lieutenant." He put his coffee mug aside. "Sleep all right?"

"Yes, sir. After all that flying yesterday, I was dead to the world."

"Come over and join the briefing," said Donovan. "We're just getting into it."

Floyd Brown looked up from the large-scale topo. "Yeah, your commander was telling me what you couldn't do. Maybe you can start out with what you can."

"What's the problem?" Harper walked up to Brown and peered at his chart.

"The problem is we've got a bunch of ground to cover and not much time," he said. "If the weapon isn't in Khadir, then we have to go house to house. There's a lot of nooks and crannies in this country."

"What's the source of the deadline, sir?" Harper asked.

"Elections," said Brown with a sour look on his face. As though to say, don't blame *him* for something so ridiculous. As she stood next to him, he smelled a clean, fresh-scrubbed scent cascade from her skin. It was amazing that he could find a standoffish blonde in a green Nomex flightsuit enticing. But in Afghanistan, clean had an appeal all its own. Brown unfastened the topmost button of his khaki shirt. A tuft of black hair coiled into view. "The nice people at the State Department are on my ass. You know the threat they received? If the Coalition goes ahead with the elections, then something unpleasant happens with the stolen nuke. So if we don't find the device and deal with it, the elections won't happen. Stone simple. If they don't happen now, they never will. The Coalition fails. Hekmatyar walks in and takes over. You know. Today Kabul, tomorrow all of central Asia. Next week, who knows? Maybe the whole damned continent turns into one big Yugoslavia.

Everyone at each other's throat. Very unstable. Very dangerous."

"I see," said Harper. Before them was a large-scale map of Afghanistan. It was broken into a grid of squares, each a hundred miles on a side. There were twelve sectors running east to west, and six stacked north to south. "Okay. Let's get oriented." Harper unzipped her breast pocket and pulled out a smaller version of the map spread before them. She turned it to match the larger one.

Donovan nodded his approval. "I've been briefing Mr. Brown on the limitations of our equipment. But I don't know as much about it as you. I think we have a whole bunch of territory to cover, and I can't seem to fit it into the three-week timeline. Not with the limitations I'm aware of on the nose."

"Well, sir," Harper said, "the Sniffer can spot a warhead and spit out its name, rank, and serial number in a few seconds. You know that. But it has to be in range."

"That's the problem." Donovan nodded. "If we fly low, we stay in possible range of the warhead. And we're also in range of anyone with a half-decent antiaircraft weapon, too. But if we're down in the weeds, we don't cover much terrain. High and safe, we might miss the warhead altogether."

"So we're screwed?" asked Brown.

"Maybe not." Harper examined the chart. It was ONC-6, covering nearly all of Afghanistan plus some healthy chunks of Pakistan, Iran, and the former southern republics of the old Soviet Union. "The Sniffer is made to find and catalogue nuclear warheads. But we're here to *find* a warhead. Not catalogue it."

"What's the difference?" Brown's eyes had come to rest on a triangle of bare skin exposed at the top of her flightsuit

Harper saw his glance and decided to ignore it. "Big difference, Mr. Brown. All the resolution that's built into the nose is designed to distinguish one nuke from another. But getting a hit on the nose is a lot easier job than figuring out what kind of hit it might be. If there's just one fish in the lake, and we get a nibble on the line, we don't need to wonder who it is. It's probably our fish. You see?"

"I'm beginning to," said Brown with a wolfish grin. "I like."

"How do we make field changes in the nose, Lieutenant?" asked Donovan. "We're not equipped to monkey with the gizmos."

"It's not a hardware problem, sir. We can reprogram the ID software, take away the automatic gain filters. That way we'll stand a better chance of picking up the weapon. And we do it from a higher altitude. Fly high, we stay out of triple-A range and cover the search sectors more efficiently. Win-win. We should be able to handle one morning patrol, recover to Kabul to refuel, and go out again in the afternoon. I'd rather not fly at night."

Brown nodded. "Go on, Miss Harper."

"I'm a lieutenant, sir. Now, instead of one or maybe two sectors a day, we could sweep eight. Four in the morning. Four in the afternoon. By my calculation, we run out of places to look in about nine days if everything keeps working and if the target doesn't move on us. That's a big if."

"Good brief, Lieutenant." Harper had done her homework. Donovan glanced at the map with its myriad search areas, then at Brown. "You have some of these squares colored in. Is that some kind of a hit list? Can any sectors be ruled out?"

"Very iffy intel," said Brown. "We know where this bird

hangs his hat. But he's crafty. He knows we know about Khadir. Hell, even *I've* been there. So chances are, he's holed up someplace else. Our friends over at the Russian embassy were supposed to brief us on where we should start."

Donovan checked his watch. "It's five-twenty local. Your friends were supposed to be here by now." He looked up at Brown. "If we have to wait much longer, we'll miss the whole morning's search. What about the equipment they're supposed to be bringing? The destruct device?"

"I'll have to check," said Brown. "Markelov is usually pretty punctual. I wonder what's keeping him?"

It was the fever that woke him.

"Aleks?"

There was something familiar about the voice. Belenko moved his head and sweat dripped off. Gallons. It felt as though his skull had been filled with lead shot, heavy but loose. The very act of thinking was giving him the most astounding headache. He tried to open an eye, but found it glued shut.

"He's coming around," said another voice.

"It took long enough. Give him some more."

"It's dangerous."

"Sodium aminate? Mother's milk."

"Maybe to the KGB."

Silence. "Do I have to ask again?"

Belenko felt his arm rise, a pressure clamped around his wrist. A sharp jab. "There could be a reaction."

"Don't talk to me of reactions, Abrosimov. You have no fucking idea. Aleks?" said the first voice again. "Aleks? Can you hear me?"

Belenko managed to force both eyes open. A two-headed

version of Pavel Markelov confronted him. His vision was clearest in the middle, gray at the edges like an old photograph. And he was hot. Feverish. How the hell had he come down with ... *Ah. Sodium aminate.* Not fever. He was being interrogated. Belenko watched as the images slowly merged. Markelov was dressed in a dark blue jacket and a red tie. What was the occasion?

"Welcome back to the land of the living," said Markelov. "You OSNAZ men always had hard heads. Good thing."

Belenko licked his lips, loosening them. "Pavel ..."

"Very good. Now," said Markelov, "perhaps you will tell me what happened last night? Do you know how close you came to getting killed? You think we need that kind of complication right now? I didn't bring you out of your hole to cause a problem. Geneva will have my ass. You had brains on you, Aleks. Fuck your mother. Brains. At least they weren't yours."

"It's still too soon," said the other man. "The drug is only—"

"Quiet," Markelov snapped. "Go place the call to the Americans. See if they've already left for the airport."

"Very well." With one last glance at Belenko, Abrosimov turned and left.

"My head," Belenko said. "It's hot."

"Kabul in summer. What did you expect? Snow? What were you doing in that place?"

What place? A smell came back to Belenko, drifting through the rigid fibers of his brain like a sea fog. He looked across at the shuttered window. The room was a hundred miles wide. The ceiling was on Mars. He was a dust speck. A mote in the middle. Useless. *Money talks, nobody walks.*

"Aleks?"

Tea. "Teahouse," said Belenko. "I was eating . . ."

"Eating?" Markelov laughed. "It must have been some party. Four dead men outside on the street. One next to you on the floor. Blood everywhere. The militia wanted to question you. Very inconvenient. Not on the schedule, Sasha. Not at all. I warned you about independent acts. Now do you believe me?"

"My head," Belenko said again.

"Take care. Someone may wish to keep it for a souvenir next time. Now. What were you up to in there?"

"What?"

Markelov reached over and shook Belenko by the shoulder. "Come on. If you have anything, give it to me." He shook him again. "We know you spoke with her. I'm meeting the Americans, and if you know something, then I want to know it, too. You were with the woman. You had her brought here."

"Where . . . ?" Belenko swung his head to one side, and the dull ache flared like a breathed-on coal.

"She won't talk to me, Aleks. Perhaps you will let me know what was said?" Markelov checked his watch. "Don't make me fish for it. We're on the same side, aren't we? What did she tell you?"

Belenko eyed Markelov. He hovered like a thunderstorm way up in the heavens. Sparking. Angry. "It was Hekmatyar," Belenko said at last. "A cave. Drugs. Pavel, open the fucking window."

"I see. All we have to do is look inside a cave. Too bad there are half a billion of them in Afghanistan. Shall we start in one corner and work our way to the other? Fuck your mother. You couldn't find your prick if it was nailed on. A cave. Wonderful." Markelov cocked his head. "Or was there a particular one?"

Belenko looked at the window. He felt like crying. It was so far. So cool outside. But so far.

"Just a cave, then? Nothing more helpful than that?"

Belenko blinked again, trying to clear his eyes. The details of the night were slowly coming back. He recalled the fight. "No. Nothing."

"Think."

Just then, Abrosimov the doctor came back into the infirmary. "They left for the airport fifteen minutes ago," he said to Markelov. He glanced down at Belenko. "I told you to be careful with him. The drug is un—"

"Watch your patient," Markelov ordered. "We will perform a full interrogation of the woman when I get back. I want her ready and alert. Do what you must."

"She's too weak," Abrosimov objected. "She could have a systemic reaction."

"She needs to be awake for the interrogation," Markelov explained patiently. "The rest is of no consequence." Markelov looked down at Belenko. "I think your memory might need some help. You visited the hospital, spoke with your little woman, and then found yourself in the middle of a firefight. I will give you a few hours to collect your thoughts. Perhaps by the time I come back you will remember more. A cave. Idiot." With that, he spun on his heel and left.

"Ready to visit Khadir?" asked Donovan.

Harper nodded as she carefully placed her headphones on. She winced as they clamped down tight. Her ears were still sore from wearing the headset all the previous day. She toggled the auxiliary power unit to life. The whine of the APU turbine grew to a howl beneath the flightdeck. When the annunciator flashed its readiness, she powered up the main instrument bus, causing all six CRTs to flip and then steady. She checked her instruments and pressed the intercom button. "Okay, crew. Comm check time."

"Tacco is up," Lieutenant Carranza called in. "Let's fly."

"Sniffer's a go," said Chief Svoboda. "The nose is running at full gain, so we're gonna pick up a lot of false hits, but we'll sure as hell know it if it's out there."

"Thank you, gentlemen." Harper leaned forward, putting her nose nearly to the windscreen glass. She could see the high mountains north of the airport with crystal clarity. She glanced at her chart, matching its features with the view outside.

Running from its northeast corner down to the southwest, the Hindu Kush mountains gripped Afghanistan like a gnarled tree root branching out from the trunk of the high Himalayas. Rising to twenty thousand feet in some places, they divided the country both geographically and culturally. Tajiks and Uzbeks occupied the upper zone; nomad Pathans roamed the south. In between, the central highlands were held by orthodox Hazara Shiites. There, protected by walls of granite, the Hazaras practiced their ancient, unadulterated version of Islam. There lay the lair of Gulbuddin Hekmatyar: Khadir.

"Ready?" Harper asked Donovan.

"Let's get them turning," said Donovan as he refolded a chart to expose their first search sector.

She turned the engine start select switch on the overhead panel to the number two position and pulled the autostart. "Starting two." The exhaust-temperature display shot up through seven hundred degrees, stabilized, and then fell back into the normal range. "Good start on two." She swung the selector switch around and a second engine began to spool up. In a moment, all four Allisons were up and running, the big paddle-bladed props biting the dusty air.

Harper placed her hand on the four throttles and inched them forward, taxiing cautiously toward the single long runway of Kabul International. It pointed nearly due west, right at a second range of mountains arcing off the main spine of the Hindu Kush. She snubbed the *Grape* to a halt, then ran her polished pink nail down the CRT's checklist. "Fuel governors, flaps, and RPM."

"Ready."

"Trim tabs and flaps."

"Takeoff," Donovan answered.

"Harness."

Donovan pushed forward against his straps. "Locked."

"Killer list is complete." Harper pressed the transmit switch on her wheel. "Kabul Tower, Grape Six is ready to roll." The tower came back with a strange mixture of English and Russian that Harper took for clearance. She knew where they were headed, and that was all that counted. "Here we go," she said, advancing all four throttles while still holding on to the *Grape*'s small brakes. The engines rose to a twenty-thousand-horsepower shout. Harper released the binders and the P-3 surged down the runway.

"Eighty knots," Donovan called.

Harper rotated the nose and the *Grape* immediately ramped up into the air. "Positive rate," Harper called out as they lifted off toward the mountains dead ahead. "Gear, please."

Donovan pulled the gear selector handle out and rammed it up. "Coming up."

They leveled off at eighteen thousand feet, following the southern flanks of the imposing Hindu Kush. The bare, shattered mountains of central Afghanistan lay directly to their right, range after range, like enormous storm waves marching to the horizon. To the left, the open *dasht* baked under the merciless sun.

Harper checked their course against the line marked on her chart. The route took them directly west, up and over the spine of the high Selseleh Koh. "Sir?" she said to Donovan. "What do we know about activity down in this sector?"

"Khadir's well defended. But other than that, I don't have a clue. That's what the Russians were supposed to give us." Donovan looked down off the *Grape*'s purple nose. "Why?"

"Well, sir, we're safe at this altitude from any hostiles in the valley. But we're going to make a fat target if there are any shooters in the hills."

Donovan remembered his little chat with Brown the night before. The guys on the ground saw an airplane and thought *enemy*. They didn't wait to see which country had its name painted on the wing. "Okay. Tell the chief to warm up the ESM," he said, a furrow of worry on his brow.

"Roger," said Harper.

The ESM computer managed the defense of the *Galloping Grape* by automatically sensing and cataloguing threats and defeating them with radar and infrared jammers. Heat prisms on each wing were controlled by the ESM to lure infrared missiles off track. Flares and chaff completed the passive defenses. Two AIM-9L Sidewinder missiles were there to deal with air-to-air threats. They were known more casually as Snakes.

The ESM electronics suite had proven remarkably effective against Soviet equipment, but the locals were equipped with a smorgasbord of deadly weapons from a dozen nations.

Harper shifted in her seat as she told Svoboda to run the self-test routine on the defensive electronics.

"ESM is sweet," said Svoboda at last. "Chaff dispenser

is armed. Prisms and jammers are up and running. The Snakes are in chill mode."

"Hope we don't need them." Harper looked over at Donovan.

"Me, too, Chief," Donovan replied as the sere moonscape below began to rise toward them.

The battered Toyota pickup slowly ground its way up the west side of the Bamian Valley. The white concrete of the old highway was now four thousand feet below them. They had another mile to climb on their way to the mountain village of Sange Sanda.

The small truck's springs were completely flat under the load of men, weapons, and ammunition in the back. Five guerrillas were crammed in the front seat, their rifles poking out through where windshield and side windows had once been.

Ornate tapestry dangled from the empty window frame, the tassels getting in the way of the black snouts of their AKs. In the back were another fourteen fighters, wedged in by boxes of ammunition, mortars, rockets, and most prized of all, four new tubes of Stinger missiles, fresh from the Peshawar bazaar.

"It is good to leave the city, Wakhil," an older fighter said to the hawk-faced man standing next to him. The old one was perhaps thirty. He looked sixty. He wore a dark green Nuristani-style turban. The others wore flat-rolled *kola* caps. "Kabul is a dangerous place. There is too much air." They swayed as they took an unbanked curve. They were packed too tightly to risk falling out.

"Too many women, too," said someone else.

The older man spat a gob of *naswah* over the side. "The city is for women. The mountains are for Pathans."

"And goats."

A gust of hot wind plucked at their thin cotton shirts. It caught the old man's green turban. It sailed up and over the side.

"Son of a whore!" the man bellowed, his scraggly dark hair flying in the wind. He pounded on the top of the cab. "Stop! Stop!" The Toyota swerved to the side of the gravel road and came to a stop as much by gravity as by its brakes.

"Now what is it?" the driver demanded. To drive the exposed road up from the valley floor was a risky proposition at best. Rival bands of *mujahedin* roamed these hills. A truck was a prize worth killing for, not to mention the Stingers.

"My hat!" The old *mujahed* fought his way from the grip of bodies and weapons and jumped down. The others, seeing in this an opportunity not likely to be repeated soon, hopped down to the gravel and stretched their limbs and relieved their bladders. The Toyota, like a horse with more spirit than muscle, slowly staggered level as the last of them tumbled out.

"Hurry up!" the driver shouted to them. With turban recovered and tightly tied once more, the old *mujahed* was the first back on board. Others soon followed. In under a minute, with hat retrieved and bodies relieved, the Toyota's engine coughed to life. Wakhil put his hand on the battered metal skin to lift himself up when he heard an odd sound.

At first he thought it was the engine. But it didn't sound right. The Toyota sputtered. This was a deep growl. He glanced up into the cloudless blue sky. It wasn't the truck. He looked down into the valley. There was nothing on the road. He looked up again.

"Aircraft!"

He spun to face the mouth of the valley, to the south, and saw the flash of sun on metal.

"Aircraft!"

The guerrillas exploded from the back of the truck in all directions, leaping to the ground to either side of the gravel road. Some covered themselves with their dun-colored *patou* blankets. Some squinted up to find the intruder, their rifles at the ready. The sun's glare was intense off the light-colored rock. Not one man wore sunglasses.

"Forget your popguns!" a man bellowed.

Wakhil turned and saw that it was the old one. He was breaking out the long green tube of a Stinger surface-to-air missile. The *mujahed* ripped the green plastic that protected the weapon's circuitry from the harsh elements and threw the casing aside. With the easy movements born of experience, he elevated the tube, clicking off the safety with his thumb as he nestled the launcher against his cheek. "Now see how a man fights," he told Wakhil as he tracked the approaching aircraft.

Wakhil could hear the growling warble of the Stinger's activation circuits. The missileer moved it slightly higher, lining up the forward and rear sights. His thumb uncaged the rocket's own seeker head. The tone changed at once as the single-minded guidance system began tracking a live target.

The sound of flying engines grew louder as the aircraft approached from the south.

"Allahu akbar!" shouted the old fighter. He pressed the firing button, and in a cloud of ocher dust and burned propellant, the Stinger blasted into the blue Afghan sky.

"Fifty miles out of Khadir," said Tacco. "We going in dumb?"

"We'll start a climb soon to stay out of triple-A range, Tacco." Harper watched the terrain roll below their wing.

"Maybe we should start a climb now," said Donovan.

"Good idea." Harper placed her hands on the throttles.

"Missile!" It was Chief Svoboda. His threat board was blinking urgently red. The vector arrow on his display showed that it had been fired from the mountains below. The computer flashed *IR*. "Heat seeker at three o'clock!"

Harper swung in her seat, hunting below the *Galloping Grape*'s right wing for a smoke trail. "I don't have it!" she yelled. "Chief! Keep talking!"

She rammed the throttles full forward and stood the P-3 on its wing and banked into the threat. There was nothing. She looked out at the IR jamming pods on the wing; one jammer pointed aft from the nacelle of each engine. They contained heating elements and focusing optics designed to give an infrared missile too much to think about. "Come on, Chief! Where is it?"

"Missile is now at one to one-thirty! It's closing!" Svoboda shouted. The range tone was getting higher and higher as the distance between the *Grape* and the Mach 3 missile shortened. "Steer two niner zero!"

Harper reversed her turn. "Two niner zero."

"Steer three one zero!" Svoboda called.

"Back to three ten." Harper threw the *Grape* into a savage bank to the north. Two distant thumps could be heard above the snarling engines. Harper briefly shut her eyes.

"Chaff's away! Flare's away!"

"What's the range?" Donovan demanded.

"Hold it, hold it," said Svoboda. The tone wavered, then held constant. An indicator marked OBL glowed on the threat board. "Flight! We broke lock on him. Distance is opening."

"Confirm it!" Donovan shouted.

"That's it. It's going unguided, sir. Clear board."

Harper leveled the wings and looked over at Donovan.

"Khadir is twelve o'clock and thirty," said Carranza with a slight waver in his otherwise unflappable tone.

"You know what?" she said. "I think three weeks around this place is starting to look like a mighty long time."

12

—

WORLDLY GAIN

SHE NEEDS TO BE AWAKE FOR THE INTERROGATION. MARKELOV'S words swam back to Belenko out of the darkness. *Nothing else is of any consequence.* He opened his eyes. The room was stuffy and airless, and nearly as black as it had been with his eyes shut. But his fever was gone. So was the sodium aminate in his blood. How long had he been out?

He willed his arm to move out from beneath the blanket. The tiny green phosphor stars on his watch were an unreadable nebula. *What time is it?* Belenko wondered. He tried to focus but his eyes refused to obey. How much drug had they given him? Why couldn't he think straight?

He saw a thin gold edging of light from around the blackout curtains. *Daytime,* he thought. *But what day?* Had Markelov already . . . No! He refused to allow that thought to gain a foothold. Why drug Belenko to interrogate him? It was the act of a fearful man. But what did Markelov have to fear? Then, out of the soft, insulating quiet and dark, Belenko heard the muffled thump of footsteps outside his room. He shut his eyes as the doorknob clicked.

Doctor Abrosimov walked in, a hypodermic needle in his hand. The embassy doctor didn't like the idea of using so much mother's milk. Not on an unconscious patient. He approached Belenko and snapped on the lamp beside the bed, checking for any sign of wakefulness. He pulled the rubber cover off the syringe, squeezed out an amber drop, and placed it on the bedside table while he took Belenko's pulse and listened to the sleeping man's slow, deep breathing. *Markelov be damned. There's no need,* he concluded, placing the cover back over the needle. Abrosimov snapped off the lamp, turned, and left.

Belenko opened his eyes as soon as the door shut. Careful not to make a sound, he peeled back the blanket and sheet and sat up in bed. Almost at once, the pounding headache flooded back. The pain sharpened his thinking. *Nazipha.* He had brought Nazipha back to the embassy, and to Markelov. What game was he really playing? Something smelled. Why had he insisted on bringing him here to Kabul? Why the sodium aminate? Was the theft of the hydrogen warhead an arrangement MAYAK had made, a sale, even, but one that had somehow gone sour? He thought of men, Russians, handing over a nuclear weapon to the Islamic fanatics. *No. Impossible.* No amount of gold was worth so great a risk. Not even to MAYAK.

Or was it?

His eyes slowly adjusted to the dark. In the soft glow penetrating the thick window curtains, he saw new clothes neatly folded on a chair by the door. Would there be a guard outside? He blinked, trying to regain the tight focus, the nerve, to do what he now knew must be done. His head as heavy as lead, he stood, staggering slightly as he sought his balance, and made his way to the window.

The brilliant morning sun scalded him when he pulled the drapes open an inch. A narrow sleeping porch extended just outside his window, ending in a delicate wooden screen through which he could see the ugly, squat mass of the new embassy building. Blind as a turtle's shell, it was a humped, rocketproof mass of concrete and reinforcing steel. *Good,* he thought. He was in the old annex, the original embassy structure built in the twenties, used as a dormitory for those not sufficiently high-ranking to deserve bombproof accommodations.

Below, the courtyard at the heart of the embassy compound was deserted except for two guards at the gated entry. A desert-tan UAZ-469 jeep was parked beside them. At the other side of the gate, a hulking BMD armored personnel carrier sat parked, its dark green hide baking in the hot sun, its 73-mm cannon leveled at the gate.

Belenko let the drapes close. He found clean clothes and dressed quickly and silently in light pants and gauzy Afghan shirt, billowing loose and tied with a cotton belt. Neither one bore the labels Markelov so appreciated.

How long has Markelov been gone? he wondered. His senses were completely askew. One thing he knew beyond question, though, was that he had brought Nazipha back into danger. That sure knowledge coursed through him like a powerful antidote to Abrosimov's drug.

He put his hand on the doorknob and slowly turned it. The clack of its retracting tongue was impossibly loud. *No guard,* he thought with a sigh of relief as the door swung open. What would he have done if there had been a sentry? Killed him? *Which side are you on, Aleks?* He edged into the hallway.

Bright morning light came in from a window at one end of the hall. To either side were rows of identical doors.

He turned right, put his ear to the wood of the first door, and listened. When he was certain there was no sound, he quickly opened it and saw an empty bed. He softly shut it and checked the next. Deserted. *Could they have her in some other part of the compound?* But where? He came to the last door. Belenko twisted the knob. This one was locked.

He listened. There were no sounds beyond. That could mean anything. Was Nazipha in there? *Now what?* He crouched and pressed his lips to the keyhole. "Nazipha!" he whispered. "Nazipha!"

"Hey!"

Belenko spun just in time to see one of the MAYAK guards, his battle jacket unadorned by rank or unit blazes. He was thickly built, and his face held the permanently angry look of a noncommissioned officer. If his expression was informative, the heavy Makarov in his hand was even more so. "You!" the man shouted. "What are you doing!" He leveled the 9-mm in a two-handed grip and advanced. "Get away from the fucking door!"

Belenko stood up, his palms open to show he was unarmed. He smiled. "I was hoping someone would come by," he said as the guard drew near. *Come on,* he urged. "I must have made a wrong turn back at the annex." *Just a bit closer.*

The mercenary kept coming, the black automatic leading the way. "Stand away from that door! Who the fuck are you, anyway?"

Closer! "The new cultural attaché. You haven't heard?"

"Who?"

Belenko glanced at the Makarov. The weapon was safed! *Some soldier.* Belenko would have thrown him out of OSNAZ in a day. *Almost. A little closer, comrade.* "I was wandering here for ages. I thought I would never see a—" *Now!* Suddenly, with a smile still on his face, Belenko shot a side kick directly into the guard's groin. The sergeant's breath exploded from him as he went down, his finger drawing tight on the trigger in reflex.

Two shots blasted into the plaster ceiling.

Belenko's ears rang. He shook off his surprise and snatched up the smoking automatic and pointed it at the soldier. He observed the safety lever, then the two craters in the ceiling. *Another black mark against Soviet quality control.* He motioned for the man to get up. "Open the door," he ordered as the agony boiling in the soldier's testicles began to subside. "Come on!"

"Aysssh ... bastard," the man said between wheezes. "You fucking sneaky—"

"Don't speak harshly of the cultural attaché," said Belenko. "On your feet." He pointed the pistol at the guard's head. The man's eyes nearly went double as they peered back up the smoking barrel of the weapon. Slowly, painfully, he got to his feet. Belenko kept a circumspect distance. "Unlock the door."

"I ... I can't. I don't have the key. What do I look like?"

"A very lucky ex-sergeant." Belenko eyed him closely. He didn't have time for persuasion. "Nazipha! Stand away from the door!" Quickly, before the MAYAK mercenary could react, he swung the muzzle of the Makarov and loosed three quick shots into the door's lock. A cloud of dry wood splinters blasted into the corridor.

"Fuck your mother!"

"Quiet!" Belenko ordered. "Open it!"

"You're crazy!"

"Absolutely. Remember that. Now open it."

The man pushed at the broken door. It swung open easily.

"Inside!"

Belenko followed him in. The room was unlike the one he had left. It was dark inside, but the door let in enough light to see by. There was no bed; no window here, just piles of cardboard boxes stacked almost to the ceiling. There was a strange, sickly sweet scent as well. *Food?*

Why would they store emergency rations in the part of the embassy susceptible to rocket attack? He sniffed again.

"Look," the guard said, his eyes pleading. "Let's just forget that—"

"Open one." Belenko motioned at a box.

The mercenary was beginning to panic. "What for? They're just—"

"You're beginning to upset me." The muzzle swayed in the direction of the guard's gut.

"Watch where you point that thing!"

"I am. Now. Think, Sergeant. What is worth dying for here? Tell me. MAYAK? How will your tragic death advance the cause of bringing capital and technology together? Think."

"Fuck." The guard pulled a box from the top of the nearest pile. He got his fingers under the sealed flap and pulled it open. "All right?"

Belenko advanced and looked inside. The box contained hundreds of clear plastic pouches, each filled with a light-brown, gummy substance the consistency of spoiled, crystallized molasses. Belenko knew exactly what they were. *You shit,* he thought of Markelov. *You filthy little shit.*

The stacks of cardboard boxes held enough opium resin to make their owner a very rich man. Even in rubles. *You little shit.* He remembered Markelov's boast of MAYAK's vast resources. *Money talks. Nobody* . . .

"What difference does it make?" the guard said, his voice more resolute.

"Shut your mouth!" Belenko felt his blood pound. The opium wasn't all headed to America. The poison had raged through the Red Army during the war; it had killed his friends. Belenko's finger tightened on the pistol's trigger. Killing was something Belenko had almost forgotten. Almost.

The guard saw it in his eyes. "Don't!" He scrambled back and away from Belenko. The 9-mm was a black accusing finger pointed at his chest. "Don't!" The guard fell backward over a box of resin, toppling with them into a heap. Belenko walked over to him.

"No!"

Belenko flipped the automatic, grabbed the barrel, and swung the checkered grip down onto the guard's skull. Belenko had seen a flicker of relief the instant before steel struck bone, but then the man's face went blank. *Capital and technology. And opium, too,* he thought of Markelov. MAYAK wasn't a company. It was a Russian Mafia where ex-KGB men turned in their cloaks and daggers for Savile Row and calculators. Where everything was sold, everyone had his price. Money talked. Nobody walked. The future.

"Fuck."

Out in the hallway again, Belenko turned left, passed his own room, and came to the next door beyond. He turned the knob and pushed. The hinges squealed as the door swung inward.

Leaving the door open to admit enough light to see by, he walked softly but swiftly to the bed. *Nazipha.* Belenko watched as her chest rose and fell. The sweat, the fever, seemed to be gone from her. In the dim light, she looked very much like the woman he had known so long ago. Had the world really changed so much? He reached out to touch her brow. It was cold now, the fever gone under Abrosimov's antibiotics. What would have happened if he hadn't brought her out of that hellhole of a hospital? She would surely have—

Suddenly, fast as a striking cobra, her arm shot out from beneath the covers, and before he knew what had happened, her hand had closed around his throat. She kicked the blanket off and pulled him down to the bed. Caught off balance,

Belenko fell with a loud thump that shoved the bed across the bare floor with a shriek.

In a flash, with one sharp knee buried in Belenko's groin, she was on top of him, squeezing the air from his throat, a hard, glittering light in her eyes. Naked except for her hospital gown, her muscles tensed like steel cables under her skin. A bandage was wound tight below one knee. The skin was swollen above and below it. "Pig," she cursed, her other hand a claw poised to strike at his eyes.

"Stop!" Belenko tried to fend her off, but her grip was unyielding. ". . . me!" he croaked out from his constricted windpipe. "Me!"

Her grip loosened a fraction as she peered at him. "Sasha?" she whispered. "Sasha?"

"Let go," he whispered back, half listening for sounds in the hallway. "Nazipha! Stop it!"

She loosened her grip another increment and peered at Belenko. "Sasha! What are you . . . ?"

"Finally," he said, squirming out from under her. He took her hand away from his throat. "I thought you were asleep."

"I thought . . . ," she stammered, "I thought it was that pig. . . . I heard him shoot you and—"

"Markelov is gone. For now." Belenko took Nazipha by the shoulders. "There's not much time. We have to leave this place." She stared at him without a hint she had heard.

"Sasha." She wrapped her arms around him and pulled him close. "I never believed . . . I thought it was a dream."

"At the hospital?"

"But then I woke up here with . . . with him standing over me."

"Nazichka," he said softly, "I promised, didn't I?" He stroked her dark hair, feeling the thick coarseness he had found so shocking and so appealing when he had first touched it. It felt like a wild horse's mane, blowing free in the wind. "I'll get you out. Someplace safe. Don't I always do my duty?"

She stiffened in his arms and sat away from Belenko. "I heard him order that doctor to stick you with . . ." She stopped. "Sasha, don't do this. Go away. You don't belong."

"After ten years you tell me to leave?"

"If you're smart."

"Too late," he said, wondering how long the guard would remain unconscious. "Trust an old OSNAZ. I'll get you out of Kabul."

"Kabul is barely a beginning." She touched the hot skin below her bandaged leg. "And where can I go?"

"What about the cave?"

She stared at him. "What do you think you know?"

"You babbled at the hospital. Hekmatyar. I know the bomb is there. You tell me the rest. What cave? Where is it?"

"In the *Qur'an*."

"What?"

"The mullah. The Baluchi. He said they were going to the Cave of the Sleepers. There's your cave. Go to the mosque. You'll find it in a book. It was a fever, Sasha. A dream."

"You mean it's not a real place? Just a story?"

She shook her head. "Sasha. I'm sorry."

Belenko sat back on the bed. This changed things substantially. He couldn't go charging off into the pages of a book to find a hydrogen bomb. Something pricked his memory. Another book. "I remember something. I once heard a story about a shrine. A real cave. With real sleepers. A British text."

"Stories. Even if it were real, what does it matter? We can't get there. And if we did . . ."

"We might find a way. Suppose."

"If we did, I would kill him. I promise you. I would kill him." But then her anger melted. "It's my fault, Sasha. I gave it to them. I wanted to save Ghulam."

"Your brother."

"I didn't care what happened. Not to anyone else. It's my fault. Now there's no way."

"Nazichka, I promise. We will find this cave." He turned and saw a *chador* tossed onto the floor. He leaned over and gave it to her. She put the *chador* over her head and threw back the hood. Belenko's eyes saw the hardened face of a survivor, but his mind saw only the picture he had carried around in the sweatband of his black beret. He stroked her hair again. "We'll get out of—" A sudden sound outside made him stop.

"Who is it?"

"Quiet." He stepped to the window and opened the curtain enough to see. Through the carved wooden screen, Belenko could see the two sentries by the gate move to attention. One saluted, then manipulated the controls to swing the iron gate open. Outside, a dark Jeep Wagoneer sat gunning its engine impatiently. Someone in the BMD minitank had trained its rapid-fire autocannon on the embassy car. "Markelov." Belenko let the curtain fall shut. He pulled Nazipha to her feet as the Wagoneer's engine roared outside the window and then, ominously, shut down. "Can you walk?"

"With you."

"Then come."

The Bamian Valley of central Afghanistan grew tighter and its walls steeper as the *Galloping Grape* droned west.

Off the right wing, the high peaks of the Hindu Kush left
scars of blowing white snow scratched across the blue sky.
To either side, the walls were drawing in closer and closer,
their flanks covered with shattered rock and their side valleys deep and shadowed despite the hot, clear sun.

"Flight, Nose here," said Chief Svoboda. "Khadir's
clean. Could you give me a turn to zero one zero?"

"Coming north." Harper banked the patrol plane around.
Khadir was nothing more than an elevated pile of rubble
nestled in an abandoned valley. If Hekmatyar was there, he
was hiding under the rocks. Nothing.

"Stop turn," said Svoboda. "Okay. Hold it. I'm clearing . . . Okay. I may have something. It's a nibble at max
range." He adjusted the sensitivity setting on the nuclear
detection gear. "Can't really say for sure. Might be an
anomaly or we might be picking up something over the
tops of the hills far off. Fly zero one five and give me a
climb."

"Zero one five." Harper banked the big turboprop northeast. She advanced the throttles and put the patrol plane
into a climb. "If it's out in those mountains—"

"Damn. It just went dark. False alarm. Sorry. I thought
we had something."

Harper quickly banked away from the wall of rock.
"Sir?" she asked Donovan. "That about covers this entire
valley. Khadir was supposed to be our best shot. It's cold.
Either it ain't down there, or else we aren't picking it up.
I say we recover and talk to the Russians. See if they know
someplace else to hunt."

Donovan gazed out at rank upon rank of mountain and
valley. "I think you're right. Let's head back to the barn
and see if we can narrow this operation some."

"Coming around." Harper kept the bank in until they
were once more pointed at the wide mouth of the valley.

* * *

They were nearly to the end of the bedroom wing's corridor when Belenko heard the pounding of feet on the stairs.

"Sasha!"

"In here." He shoved open the door to the last bedroom, the opium storeroom, and started in, but then he stopped. That room had no window. The footsteps were loud and close now. He had seconds. He chose the next room, pulled Nazipha inside, and shut the door.

"Come on." He made his way to the window. He pulled the curtain aside as several men walked outside their room. A voice was raised, then the steps came faster.

The open-air sleeping ledge was covered with pigeon droppings, and the wooden screen was broken where a large pistachio tree had grown against it. Below, the two sentries were resting in the shade by the gate. The dark green BMD had its 73-mm cannon pointed skyward. Markelov's American car was right below them, parked under the spreading pistachio.

She looked beyond him. "I can't jump."

"You want to find the mullah? The Baluchi?"

Her eyes clarified. "You know."

"Then you jump. Take this." He handed her the guard's pistol.

She gripped the Makarov with sure, certain hands, even checking to be sure the safety was now off. Belenko eyed her briefly, wondering how many other ways the Nazipha of today was different from the one he had known and . . . no. He couldn't say that. Not even to himself. "When I signal, you follow me. Clear?"

She nodded.

Belenko eased out onto the old sleeping deck and made his way to the tree. Its branches, reaching well above

Belenko's second-floor vantage, were covered with millions of green, unripe nuts. "Nazipha," he whispered, "wait until I signal."

The sleeping deck was a narrow affair, barely four feet wide, built as a convenience long before the advent of air-conditioning and now long unused. The carved wooden screen had once been a triumph of the carpenter's art, a three-dimensional tapestry of geometric forms, stars, and moons. But the wood was rotten, crumbling in Belenko's hand as he broke an opening large enough to squeeze through.

The pistachio was in full leaf, its dense green heart nearly black in the hot sun. He leaned out through the break in the screen and grabbed hold of a branch stout enough to bear his weight. He eased his way through and let the tree pull him from the ledge.

For an instant Belenko was airborne, supported by neither the building nor the branch, swinging, falling. The pistachio branch began to crackle as it bent, its flexible wood strained to the point of failure. A rain of hard nuts fell to the ground, pelting the roof of the parked car directly below. Then Belenko's foot caught a firmer hold. He swung to a stop. The sentries, assuming all danger came from outside the embassy compound, were still facing the empty street. He let out the breath he had been holding and looked back to the ledge.

Nazipha was there, her face framed in the broken gap of the decrepit wooden screen. Suddenly, she turned away, looking back into the room, then back out again. Her expression shouted what she could not. *Hurry!*

Belenko twisted in his perch, feeling some of the old reflexes flow back into his muscles and sinew. He watched the drowsy guards at the gate, measuring their motions and their reactions. They were Russians, just as he was; they weren't even MAYAK slugs. Just draftees standing in a hot, foreign sun because someone had told them to. They were soldiers, just as he had once been. They surely wouldn't volunteer to open the gate. How far was Belenko willing to go? Shoot over their heads? Shoot them down where they stood? How far? Mercenaries were one thing. But these men?

He turned once again and saw a flicker of panic pass over Nazipha as she edged her body out through the screen. It was the look of a person standing in the window of a burning building.

The buzzer rang at the gate guardbooth, and the nasty, cutting sound cleared Belenko's mind and energized his body. Dropping silently from branch to branch, letting his OSNAZ training flow into his arms and legs, Belenko made his way through the thicket of pistachio branches to the ground. He put the thick trunk between him and the two guards. *How many are there?* He could see only two, but someone was operating the gun turret inside the BMD. Belenko could well imagine the man sitting at the breech of the autocannon; sweat would be running down his face as he baked inside the turret. Even with its two rear doors open and the top hatch flung wide, the squat armored personnel carrier shimmered with heat waves.

The gate buzzer rang again and stopped when one of the conscripts picked up the telephone. Belenko sucked in deep breaths of the hot, thin air, charging his body and clearing his mind. He bunched his thigh muscles like a sprinter waiting at the block, tightening them.

A shot sounded from behind and above. He looked up and heard shouts. *Now!* Belenko exploded like a spring and ran for the BMD.

Fifteen meters. His legs pounded like pistons. The two guards were still occupied. *Ten.* One of them began to turn in his direction. The sun was hot on Belenko's dark hair. He was utterly exposed by the cloudless Kabul sky, as though a spotlight followed him as he ran across the cobbled court. *Which side are you on, Aleks?* The stacks of boxes loaded with their poisonous freight came to him, making his legs strong. He saw the soldier at the telephone reach for a sidearm. *Five.* The clamshell doors were open, the black cargo deck of the BMD right in front of him. How many were inside? It was too late to wonder.

With a final leap Belenko jumped into the maw of the armored vehicle. The thick steel hide masked the sound from the two guards, but not from the gunner.

Belenko saw a white sweatband swing his way in surprise.

"Hey!" the soldier shouted. "Who—"

Belenko dived onto the steel decking, rolled, and came upright just beneath the elevated dais that held the gunner's seat. He realized with a flash of terrible understanding that it would be far easier to kill than to incapacitate. But the man was a Russian! His indecision vanished as the gunner reached for a rifle. The soldier's eyes glowed as white as his sweatband in the dim interior of the turret.

Belenko didn't wait. He jumped over the gunner's seat and rammed his fist square into the young boy's face. The sweatband flew off as his head snapped back and struck the turret wall. The rifle clattered to the steel deck. The gunner started to rise. Belenko struck again. Harder. Enough.

Belenko's nostrils flared as his muscles began to shake. He stuck his head up through the turret hatch. Another single round cracked from the second-floor annex, but this time the fast *pop pop pop pop* of an AK on full automatic answered. *No!* Nazipha suddenly appeared through the screen, clinging to its rotten boards, but not yet in the arms of the tree. He whistled, but she was frozen like a deer in the glare of a poacher's headlight, looking down between her feet at the fall, shaking her head and mouthing *No!*

More shouts came from behind her. With the hopeless look of a suicide, she let go of the broken screen and fell into the branches of the pistachio. Her dark *chador* was almost perfect camouflage.

Belenko turned the other way and saw the first guard level his Kalashnikov. An alarm bell began to ring. The BMD's radio suddenly squawked to life. He eased into the forward compartment. *I hope,* he thought as he dropped into the driver's seat, *they haven't changed this, too.*

He ground his heel where he remembered the starter pedal to be. The V-6 diesel immediately roared to life behind him. *A plus for Soviet quality control.* He scrambled back into the gunner's chair and grabbed the twin handles of the autocannon traverse, swiveling the turret back, away from the gate and toward the embassy.

Belenko stuck his head up through the open hatch for an instant. Long enough to draw a series of shots. The heavy slugs spanged off the armored hull in a shower of sparks. He saw Nazipha on the ground now. She'd fallen! He dropped back down and put his eye to the viewing prism, elevating the autocannon, slewing it sideways, then back, centering the cross hairs on the blank portion of the annex's second-floor wall. The room without a window. Another burst of small-arms fire raked the BMD. His hand convulsed on both firing triggers. The autocannon roared as he walked a dozen 73-mm shells across the face of the embassy annex, sending stone, wood, and opium blasting into the arid sky.

The BMD's fire sent the gate guards running. Belenko used the moment. There wouldn't be many more. He dropped out of the turret and into the driver's seat. With a yank on the steel levers, he engaged both tracks, clutched the hulking beast into ultralow. Like a blind turtle, the BMD lurched forward in a cloud of black diesel exhaust.

Belenko slewed the tank right, watching through the driver's prisms as the iron gate swung into view directly ahead. When he was satisfied, he locked both track levers, stood up, and ran back aft toward the tank's clamshell doors. The BMD gathered speed as it rumbled straight at the gate. He collided with Nazipha coming the other way.

"What are you thinking—" she began, but Belenko grabbed her and slammed her flat to the armored side of the tank. The first shot sparked off the armored hide of the tank a microsecond later.

Belenko looked back and saw men spill out of the main embassy building like ants from a kicked-over mound. The annex was burning vigorously. But then, running out from the burning building, he saw Markelov. He was still in his dark fancy jacket and tie. He pointed straight at the BMD. A whine ended in a series of ricochets that caromed through the BMD's hull. The crack of the pistol followed in the bullet's wake.

Any second. Belenko braced against the tank's metal frame. "Hold on," he told Nazipha.

The heavy BMD struck the iron gate with a scream of metal upon metal. The tank shuddered, its tracks digging up the cobbles and flinging them backward as it regained its footing and blindly pushed its way ahead. With a crash, the gate smashed flat to the stones. The tank surged forward.

"Stop them!" came the voice from far behind. But the gate guards had seen the autocannon at work. They were flat on the cobblestones, sheltering behind a jeep. Markelov was in a combat crouch, his pistol pointed straight at them again. A cloud of blue cordite erupted. *Crack!* The report echoed across the courtyard. The bullet struck the lip of the tank and disappeared.

Belenko waited until the tracks clattered over the broken gate, then jumped down off the decking, pulling Nazipha with him. He ran straight for the UAZ jeep.

"Hey!" said one of the guards as he looked up.

"Go home!" Belenko leaped into the seat, hit the starter button, and threw the little jeep into first. He shoved Nazipha into the space in front of the passenger's seat. Another shot shattered the windshield. He gunned the throttle, and with a chirp from its wheels, the jeep leaped over the flattened iron gate and out onto the street. He swung the wheel right, putting the lumbering, driverless hulk of the BMD behind him, and dove into the maze of streets of the Carte Seh district.

"Where are we going?" asked Nazipha, still crouched into the passenger's footwell. Her face was bleeding from slivers of glass.

"A mosque."

"A *what*?"

Belenko turned into a narrow street that led down to the river. He had no hope of breaking out of Kabul by main force; he planned to do just the opposite. In true OSNAZ fashion, he would escape by driving deeper and deeper into the heart of the ancient city.

He turned onto a ramp. It led to a narrow stone bridge spanning the bed of the Kabul River. Belenko gunned the jeep out onto the bridge and across. A deserted bazaar appeared on the other side. They were through.

The road he was on was like a river. Belenko drove the jeep upstream to its source. The river became a stream, the stream a creek, and the creek a dry rivulet. An alley, shadowy and cool. Ahead was an abandoned *serai*, a place where poor merchants had once come and stayed on their marketing trips to the capital. The ground level was taken up by a row of boarded-up stables. The minaret of a poor mosque was crudely hacked off two-thirds of the way to the top, its roof tiles scattered like bones across the street. Belenko slowed to a stop, listening for signs of pursuit.

Broken telephone lines dangled from overhead. The windows were as empty as the gaze of a dead man. The smell of dust cascaded down from the plastered walls.

At the end of the row of empty stables, one door was incompletely boarded over. The black interior beyond was visible, dark and inviting.

"What are you thinking of?"

"Here." Belenko drove up to it. He jumped out and pulled apart the broken boards that barred the entry.

"Sasha, what have you done?"

"Almost there." Belenko eased the UAZ into the old stable.

He shut down the engine and pulled the ramshackle doorway closed behind them. Light streamed through its cracks, covering them both in stripes of light and shadow.

"Almost there," she repeated. "But where?"

It had been luck, not skill, that had brought them this far, and Belenko was wise enough to know the difference. "I'm not sure. Markelov is . . ." He stopped. It was so hard to believe! "Markelov is involved with shipping opium. Maybe on the side, without Geneva knowing. That bastard. I wouldn't put it by him to have his hands dirty with that bomb, either."

"Theories."

"And stories. What if the Cave of the Sleepers is real?"

"Then I'm in trouble. Maybe I should have stayed a believer." She nestled against him and closed her eyes. "What do you know, anyway?"

Belenko didn't have an answer. He looked away at the light streaming through the broken boards. The shadows were like the bars of a cell. They striped across the stolen jeep. Suppose the Cave was real? Suppose. Theories and stories. He didn't have time to hunt down an ancient riddle. *Cave of the Sleepers!* He looked around the stable. He had more than enough riddles right here. In his arms.

"Okay, crew," said Harper, "set condition five and perform your prelanding checks." She pulled back the throttles and the purple-nosed patrol plane angled down toward Kabul International. The ring of snowcapped mountains that surrounded them rose higher and higher as they descended.

"ESM is secured," said Chief Svoboda. "Flares and chaff dispensers are disarmed. Glad we had 'em."

"A-firm," said Harper.

"Hope nobody takes another pop at us," said Donovan. The ESM defense system had saved them at the mouth of the Bamian Valley by decoying the infrared-homing missile someone had fired. Now all the rocks below looked dangerous.

Harper rolled out of the descending spiral with the nose of the *Galloping Grape* pointed at the long runway.

Suddenly, a flash erupted at the far end of the Kabul runway. A filthy black pall billowed up from the rocket strike, orange fire pulsing at its heart, sending chunks of concrete flying. A second strike blew a ragged hole a hundred feet closer.

"Abort!" Donovan shouted, but Harper's hand was already on the throttles. The *Grape* surged back into the relative safety of the sky as another rocket burst to the left of the main runway. With gear tucked in and props biting the thin air in high pitch, they circled warily to the east as Kabul International was pounded by the big 122-mm rockets.

"Someone's too goddamned good with those things," Harper said. The rockets had been walked down half the length of Kabul's one and only runway.

One last spout of fire and smoke brewed up from a parched field outside Kabul's perimeter fence. A yellow haze of detonated explosive wafted off on the breeze. "I think that's it," she said. "I'm damned glad we were watching the show from up here."

"Roger that," said Donovan. The *Grape* felt so solid and secure in the air, but down on the ground, against a fifty-kilo warhead? He might as well be wrapped in aluminum foil.

Harper pulled back the power again and set up for another approach. She watched the cordite smoke dissipate. "I think they left us with just enough room. Maybe they aren't such good shooters after all."

"Maybe they were just reminding us that there's a war on."

She nodded.

Donovan cocked an eyebrow as they ramped down toward the runway. "Take it easy, Hot Dog. This is a big airplane. Big airplanes use lots of runway."

"What, this old bird?" she said with a tired smile. "It's just an overgrown cub." She sized up their sink rate and rotated the nose until the *Grape*'s wings were nibbling at the stall. "Flaps to full," she called out.

"Full?"

"Full."

Donovan hit the flap lever and the *Galloping Grape* seemed to come to a stop in midair. He eyed the airspeed display on his flight-data CRT. They were very slow.

"We're gonna make this one short and sweet," she said. "I don't want to motor along that runway any longer than I have to." She jockeyed the throttles as they dropped to the runway. The deck angle was way too high; she was using the prop blast to keep them in lift. They were hanging on their engines.

Donovan watched the rocket-pocked runway rise up fast. "Easy! Take it easy!" He reached for the yoke and throttles, but forced himself to let Harper have the landing. He braced in his seat as the *Grape*'s long wings came level.

She pulled off power and they settled in. "Hang on," she told him as they slammed down onto the concrete. Two clouds of blue tire smoke billowed from the main gear. She pulled back the prop levers into reverse and shoved the throttles full forward. The Allisons yowled in protest as they were flung hard against their harnesses. In under six hundred feet, Harper swung off the runway. The tower was still silent. "Probably in the bomb shelter," she quipped as they nosed along the shell-pocked taxiway toward the place they had met the Russians the day before.

Donovan unbraced himself. "You know, I think you could get your carrier qualification chit real fast."

She looked over at him and smiled. "When we get back to the world, I assume the commander will put that in writing?"

"You really want to fly fighters, Hot Dog?"

"More than anything, sir. More than anything."

"We'll see," he said as they nosed up to the deserted terminal and snubbed to a stop.

"How long have I been asleep?"

"You needed it." Belenko stroked her hair. A series of heavy crumps shook the air, sending a shower of dust raining down on them from the dark rafters of the stable. "Better now?"

"What's that?" Nazipha pulled away from him. The slant of light coming through the door was lower now, skimming through the slats and illuminating the far corner of the empty stable. "Sasha, do you hear . . ."

"Rockets," said Belenko, his eyes still closed. "They sound like Grads. Far away."

She moved away from him. "I don't know how to find the bomb, Sasha. Or how we'll get there."

"I do. Come." He held out his arm for her. "Sleep. Just until dark. Then we leave."

"How?"

"Like Markelov says. Money talks. Nobody walks."

"Until dark," she said as she nestled back against him.

13

—

THE DECLINING DAY

"HELL OF A DAY," SAID DONOVAN AS HE STRETCHED HIS ARMS out above his head. His fingers brushed the padded overhead of the *Galloping Grape*'s cabin.

"And it's only half over," said Harper. "We've got company." She nodded out the single porthole installed beside the nuclear detection console. The black Russian embassy car had pulled up outside. Chief Svoboda, the Sniffer operator, was rewinding the flight tapes from their morning mission over the Bamian Valley to Khadir.

"It's Markelov," said Donovan.

"I don't know how he can stand to wear a leather jacket in this heat," Harper said. Markelov's red hair was plastered to his skull with sweat. But he still wore the waist-length jacket, black and shiny as though the cowhide were sweating, too.

"I hope he has some intel for us," said Donovan. "Go greet our guests, Lieutenant, and make sure Carranza has the fueling under control."

"Yes, sir," said Harper as she walked back toward the *Galloping Grape*'s hatch.

Donovan tapped Chief Svoboda's shoulder as he stood behind him. "Roll 'em."

Svoboda hit the replay switch, and all the signals picked up by the Sniffer began to scroll across the chief's central CRT. "See, this is where I ran the calibration right after we took off this morning." The CRT flashed with a waterfall of signals and messages, but the letters *BIT* glowed red at the upper right. "The box checked out and started scanning," Svoboda explained as the CRT settled down into a series of horizontal lines. Each line represented a detection range, and all were depressingly flat. "It stays like this for a long while, sir." Svoboda fast-forwarded. "Now watch."

"Commander?" came a voice from the aft fuselage. Donovan looked up and saw Pavel Markelov walking briskly up the aisle toward him with Harper in tow. He was struggling with a large, polished aluminum case, carrying it with both arms.

"Sir?" Svoboda nudged Donovan. "Here's the part where we were fired on."

The CRT blinked and shifted as the tape replayed the desperate maneuvers Harper had used to evade the heat-homing missile. The digital heading display at the top of Svoboda's CRT flashed through north, then west, then north, then west again faster than Donovan's eyes could make out the individual numbers. *Good flying, Hot Dog,* he thought. *She really does belong in fighters.*

"Commander?" Markelov said as he joined them at the Sniffer station. His face was flushed red and his breathing came in noisy, sucking gasps. He placed the heavy box carefully on the deck.

"Good afternoon, Mr. Markelov." Donovan nodded at the Russian's black leather jacket. "Kind of hot, isn't it?"

"Always. There was a problem with the embassy laundry," said Markelov, not mentioning that it had been blown up by tankfire. By Belenko.

"Here it comes," said Svoboda. As the *Grape* climbed away from the missileer, the bottom line of the Sniffer display, the one that represented maximum range detection, suddenly twitched. Svoboda stabbed the freeze button. "There! It's not much more than noise. Not enough to run through the processor." He looked up at Donovan. "Just when we cleared the wall of the valley. It ain't much, sir. Just a nibble."

"Commander Donovan," said Markelov, his breath back. "I am sorry I missed you this morning. I arrived a little after you departed. I trust the bandits didn't disturb your landing?"

"No," said Donovan. "I got the feeling that if they wanted to, they could have been a whole lot more disturbing."

"Yes, well, in any event, we had a few matters of unexpected urgency at the embassy."

"We had a little excitement ourselves," said Harper as she walked up behind the Russian. "We were fired on over the Bamian Valley. A heat-seeker."

"Probably one of your Stingers. What happened at Khadir?"

"Dead as a doornail," said Harper.

"Do you have any better intel for us?" asked Donovan.

"Perhaps." Markelov narrowed his eyes and nodded at the CRT. "Have you come up with something?"

"Probably not," said Donovan. "Maybe a place to look. A nibble, as Chief Svoboda puts it. We were hoping you might be able to help us zero in some."

"I may. Tell me about this nibble."

"Could be nothing at all," said Donovan.

"You were in the Bamian Valley?"

"Yes. This hit looks like it's from the next valley north." Donovan refolded the chart. "The L'al."

"Then I can assure you. There is nothing out there," said Markelov. "It's totally uninhabited. Glaciers. Rocks. Nothing more. Our next best chance is here." He pointed to the open desert well south of the Bamian.

"Still, it might be worth a second look." Donovan glanced at the aluminum case. "Is that the MAYAK equipment we were told to expect?"

Markelov picked up the heavy case with a grunt and set it down on Svoboda's console.

"Careful," the chief said, pushing the case away from his keypad. Didn't this guy know anything about electronics?

Markelov took out an odd, tubular key from his pocket and unlocked the case. The hasps snapped open to reveal a row of batteries, a coil of coaxial wire, a small whip antenna, and a switch-studded electronics box.

"Wow," said Svoboda. He looked at the assembly and wrinkled his nose. "Where'd you find this? Radio Shack?"

Markelov looked at him with a sour expression. "The best brains of the Ministry for Atomic Power and Industry assembled it."

"No wonder you guys had Chernobyl," said Svoboda.

Donovan looked down at the box, then up at Markelov. "Brown didn't know the operating range."

"Frankly speaking, the closer the better. We must have a clear view to the warhead's built-in receiving antenna. Line of sight. No farther than ten kilometers."

"Ten klicks," Donovan repeated. "What will the weapon effects be at ten kilometers? I wonder."

"Maybe we can patch it into one of the *Grape*'s whiskers," said Svoboda. "We should be able to keep a safe distance that way."

"Whiskers?"

"Antenna," Harper explained. She checked her watch. "The one thing I know is that it's getting late for another launch. If we want to check out that nibble, we better get a move on."

"Knowing the terrain as I do, it would be a waste of time to go up into that valley. Hekmatyar's family is from here." Again, the finger pointed south.

Donovan glanced at Harper. Why did it seem as though Markelov was steering them away from the one nibble they'd managed to get? "You feel like flying another run today?"

"So long as we get back before dark. I don't want to risk landing on a damned rocket crater."

"I agree." Donovan looked at the aluminum case, then at Markelov. "Very well. I assume you'll want to accompany us, Mr. Markelov?"

"Absolutely."

"Fueling is complete," said Carranza as a truck pulled away out on the ramp.

"Right. Don't touch that button unless I order it," Donovan warned the Russian. He turned to Harper. "Okay, Hot Dog. Let's fly."

Nazipha moved against him and Belenko sat up. What time was it? He brushed the dry hay from his chest. The air was still and hot; a fine, choking grit floated through the beam of golden light coming from the broken slats of the stable door. It was still too light outside. In one corner, heaped with dead, dry grass, an ancient tonga cart sat abandoned. *No one's been here for years,* he thought.

Time to get oriented. He stood up and walked silently over to the stolen jeep. He didn't know what he was looking for. An answer. Something. He hunted through its var-

ious nooks, but found no maps. Nothing but a cheap
Japanese transistor radio, its two halves taped together.

A rustle of hay. "Sasha?"

"I'm here."

"Is it time?"

"No. Not yet. Soon." It was strange how natural it felt to
speak Dari with her. How distant, how strange, Russian
tasted in his mouth. "It will be safer after sunset. Then we
can go." He joined her in the sweet-smelling pile of hay.

"Where?"

"Rest." Belenko knew the name and nothing else. The
Cave of the Sleepers. A story in the *Qur'an*. A myth. How
long would it take to drive all the way to a legend? He
stroked her hair. "Nazichka, the helicopter. The one . . ."

"I know." She still saw the world spinning, flashing dry
snow crystals as she fell, thrown from the Baluchi's helicopter. Given up for dead. The silence. Snow packed tight
into her ears. The cold that never let up, the ice that melted
only under her fury.

"Did you see, did they say anything else about where
they were going? A direction?"

"It was going up. I was falling. It's a matter of relative
motion, as they would say at the Polytechnic."

"Nothing more?"

"The mullah did the talking. The Cave of the Sleepers is
all he said." She sat up. "Sasha. It's not a real place. We'll
never find it. Not on earth, anyway. We can't lose ourselves
in the pages of a book. We need a more practical plan. You
of all people should know."

"Just now, finding a place that exists only in a book
seems very practical."

"Given the alternatives."

"Yes." He tried to remember his OSNAZ training course
on the holy *Qur'an*. He'd once memorized most of the

thirty sura, or chapters. Not in detail. But in substance. The story of the Cave was written in the eighteenth sura, called *Al Khaf*. It grew, the instructor had said, from an even older story, one that Gibbon related in his *Decline and Fall of the Roman Empire*.

Seven Christian men, hounded by persecuting Romans, hid themselves in a mountain cave above Ephesus. They fell asleep, entranced, sealed within the rocks of centuries, only to awake very hungry. They made their way back to town and discovered that Christianity had triumphed in their absence. The Romans were gone. Their hideout, the cave, became a holy shrine. The Islamic version tracked the Roman original. *Or was it the other way around?* Belenko wondered.

The Cave of the Sleepers. The Cave of Ephesus. Ephesus was near Smyrna, now called Izmir. Surely the bomb was not hidden on the Aegean coast of Turkey. Forget politics. A Russian Mi-8 couldn't fly there from Afghanistan. That was practical.

"What are you thinking?"

"Rest," he said. He closed his eyes, bringing back the memory of the opening lines of the strange tale:

In the name of God, Most Gracious, Most Merciful, praise to Him ...

"What did you say?" asked Nazipha.

"Nothing. Just legends. The Cave."

Behold the Companions of the Cave, who had veils drawn over their ears for numberless centuries ... in order to rouse them, to test them. Some say they were five, and their dog the sixth. Others say seven. Only God knows their true number. We relate to you their story ...

"Sasha, even if we knew how to find it, how would we get there? The roads are all mined. The country is controlled by bandits. Hekmatyar's men would be all over the place. No. We should leave the country. Not in the jeep. It would be too obvious. But a horse, maybe. Ride into Pakistan. Leave everything behind."

"No."

"No? What do you mean, no? Why not?"

"I'm here for something."

"A mission. The OSNAZ speaks! What can you accomplish? What can any one person accomplish? Maybe we can live. Nothing more than that. Just live. Isn't that enough?"

Betake yourself to the Cave and behold the sun declining to the right, and when it set, turning away from the Companions to their left . . .

"North," said Belenko.

"What's north?"

"The cave mouth opens to the north. The Companions of the Cave are supposed to be asleep. On their backs. Facing the entrance. At least that's what the *Qur'an* says. Above a high valley."

"What on earth . . . ?"

"So the sun would rise on their right, decline to the south, and set to their left." He scratched a pattern in the dust at their feet. "The cave opens to the north. Above a valley. Someplace."

"A cave above a valley. Someplace." Nazipha shook her head. "That surely narrows things down. Listen, Sasha. Forget the bomb. Forget this place. Go home. I would if I had one left. You still do."

A cave above a valley, its mouth opening to the north

Nazipha was right. It narrowed the list of possibilities all right. From the ridiculous to the absurd. *Give up.* The voice whispered, insistent. *Give up.* The hairs rose on Belenko's forearms. *Give up.*

"We should give ourselves up to the Coalition," said Nazipha.

"No. We'll find a way." Belenko sounded more confident than he felt.

"Did OSNAZ teach you how to make miracles, too?"

"Miracles still happen. Look at you. After ten years. I thought you were dead." Belenko saw her tense up. "I thought of you each day. But here you are. Alive."

"For now." She looked out at the deepening gold of the afternoon light. The declining day.

"Now is enough." Belenko felt the words stick in his throat. "All those years buried. Down in the basement of the *les.* A crab with nothing to hold on to except a picture. You know I carried a picture of you? Ten years."

A tear glistened like a star on her cheek. "Why did you send me to Moscow? Why?"

"I had to. I knew . . . ," he stammered. "I saw what was coming. I had to get you out from underneath it. It was all falling down. I wanted you safe. In Moscow."

"You stayed."

"I was OSNAZ."

"No." She swiped her eye with the sleeve of her dark *chador.* "You *are* OSNAZ. You can't change by speaking Dari. By reading the *Qur'an.* By making love to an Afghan woman."

"We could start again. What's ten years? It would be just the same. We could leave the city. Find a place where nobody knows. Nobody asks."

She laughed, but it was short, bitter. "After what happened at the embassy? Think."

"For ten years I thought of you. Here you are."

"Don't be an idiot. You're an OSNAZ with a mission."

"I'm not one of them!"

"Aren't you?"

Belenko thought of Markelov's ghosts. Maybe he wasn't just hunting them. Perhaps he'd become one, too. A noise pricked his consciousness. He spun. A sudden crackle came from the pile of hay heaped on the back of the broken tonga cart.

"Who is there?" asked Nazipha.

"Just a mouse," said Belenko. "Listen. Maybe we can—"

Suddenly, another voice sounded out of the darkness. "A very frightened mouse, strangers," said a new voice, low and thick with the Kabul variant of Dari.

Belenko spun to face the dark corner where the voice had come from. His nerves surged with sudden adrenaline; his muscles knotted in anticipation of attack. His right hand had formed a hard, killing wedge entirely on its own. The brain could bury anything. But killing was something the body did not forget. "Who is there?"

"Even a mouse must live someplace," the voice replied with a cackle. "For God is great." The rustling grew louder. A dark form materialized from the broken tonga cart. *"Bikhuda,"* the man said as he slid off the wooden back, brushing off his *shalwar kameez,* "this mouse was afraid. With all your talk of strange things, of the Cave. I thought angels had come."

"You can see we aren't angels," said Belenko.

"I cannot," the man said with a shake of his head. He advanced into the thin light coming from the street. He was a short, round man with clothes several sizes too large, drawn in around the waist by a webbed army belt. Half his face was smooth and young, but the other was a mass of burn scars that had twisted and drawn tight across his bones in the healing. One sleeve of his loose shirt was empty. Hay still clung to his striped blouse. He walked up to Belenko until he was scarcely a foot from the tall Russian's face. He sniffed the air like a cautious dog. "You," he said, "are not an Afghan."

"He is a *khabarnega*," said Nazipha, using the rough Pashto word for journalist. She turned to Belenko. "Sasha," she whispered, "he's blind."

"Aye, I am," the maimed man replied. "God's truth. But I can smell and I can hear." He took a few steps to Nazipha, homing in on her breathing, his one arm before him. He stopped when his hand caressed her soft cheek. He took in a long, deep breath and shuddered. "The light cannot come into my head anymore. The Russians took it with them when they left. But tell me. You said you wish to visit the Shrine of the Cave. Is that so?"

"Yes," said Belenko.

"Then you are in great luck." He bowed. "I am Wali Ahmad Khan. I studied to become the caller of the mosque just outside. My father was master of this *serai* and owner of the finest horses in all Afghanistan. Please tell me, who possesses such a sweet voice?"

"Nazipha Popol."

"Popol. A good family. Very good."

"They're all dead."

"Who isn't? And you?" the blind man asked Belenko.

"Brown," he replied.

"An *Amrikan*." The young man turned to Nazipha. "Once my father owned the whole *serai*. The entire block! I was to climb the minaret and call the faithful to their prayers. And such horses. Our stables always held the best. *Qara* stood by *qirmiz*, and they all listened to my *shalaq* if they knew what was good. There were such fine horses!

But now? Except for one, they are all dead. Father. Mother. My whole family. The mosque, it was—"

"We saw it," said Belenko, impatient. "What do you know of the Cave?"

"What do I know?" The young man touched a scarred eye socket with a dirty finger. "Why, I have seen it."

"Seen it? Where!"

"When I could see, of course. Now I can only remember. A poor mouse hiding in a dark corner. Listening to strange tales. Caves. Mysteries—"

Belenko interrupted. "Wali, *where did you see the Cave of the Sleepers?*"

"Please." Khan drew back at the harshness of Belenko's tone. "Are you Moslem?"

"I'm a student of it."

"Then you should know the answer yourself," said Khan in a tone that was both lecturing and admonishing. "The Companions of the Cave sleep above the Valley of God. Where else?"

Belenko sighed. "The Valley of God." It was like saying it was everywhere. Nowhere. *Give up.* He glanced at Nazipha. She had the strangest expression on her face. Maybe she was right. Perhaps it was time to become practical. "Wali," he said to the blind man, "you said that there is one horse left?"

"Sasha . . . ," said Nazipha.

"My last *ablaq.*" It meant the horse was a piebald mare. "My favorite. The roan. The chestnut. They were just animals, but this *ablaq* I found wandering on the . . ." Wali stopped. "In the open."

"Sasha," Nazipha repeated, but Belenko looked at the tonga cart, its back heaped with hay. Would it be searched on their way out of the city? It might work. "Is the *ablaq* for sale?"

"Do you sell your families in *Amrika*?"

"*Sasha!*"

Both men turned to face her.

"The Valley of God," she said. "There *is* a place like that. A *real* place. Out beyond the end of the Bamian Valley."

"Of course it's real," said Wali. "Did I not say?"

"It's called," said Nazipha, "the Valley of the L'al."

"Yes. Yes," said Wali. "Everyone knows this."

Beyond Bamian, thought Belenko. He'd conducted OSNAZ missions in that country before. It was steep, remote, and utterly hostile to life. It was, in the end, a great place to have a war if you were the guerrilla. *The Valley of the L'al.* It was a long journey even in peacetime. Days. Weeks perhaps. How could he get there in time?

Belenko turned and watched the last of the light catch a million floating dust motes in its pale beam. Drifting. Flying across the column of light. *Of course!* "Wali," he said, "if you will not sell your horse, perhaps she can be rented for a short journey?"

"Perhaps."

"Sasha," said Nazipha, "this horse will not fly us to the Cave of the Sleepers."

"No. You're absolutely right. But I think I know who will."

14

—

THUNDER

"Flight? Tacco. We better turn around if we want to land with any light left," said Lieutenant Carranza as the *Galloping Grape* droned over the sere, lifeless landscape. The shadows were growing long as the sun neared the western horizon.

Harper looked off the nose. At Markelov's suggestion, they'd looped south, then west, avoiding the highest mountains. *Where would I hide a nuke?* she wondered. *Not out in the open.* She turned and watched the light fracture the Hindu Kush into gigantic prisms of light and shadow. That's where it had to be. Why did Markelov send them so far south? She hit the intercom. "Anything, Chief?"

"Negative. Not a goddamned thing." Svoboda tuned the Sniffer for maximum sensitivity, expanding the five horizontal lines on his screen until they were fat ropes. Markelov was leaning over the CRT display, the ominous metal case wedged between his legs. A spare headset was clamped to his ears.

In the P-3's purple nose, a thousand pencil-thin beams were electronically swept across the landscape. An equal number of receiving elements listened for a return. Svoboda watched and waited for an echo the computer would recognize as a nuclear weapon.

"You sure the nose is working right?" Harper asked.

"Affirmative."

"Sir?" she said. "Suppose we climb and take a quick peek to the north?"

"North?"

"Where the nose got a nibble this morning. Markelov's guesstimate sure hasn't panned out. Why not try something different?"

Donovan looked off to the right. The high mountains ramped up to the sky, the snow on their crests gold in sunset. "Kind of late for peeking, isn't it?"

"No, sir. It would be faster. We'd cut a corner and land at Kabul twenty minutes sooner. Even with the climb factored in."

"You really want to find that thing, don't you?"

"I don't want to fly home with an empty bucket, Commander. Not with my reputation. We both know this is my last chance."

Donovan nodded. "Okay. Let's take a look on our way back to Kabul. Your airplane."

"Coming north." Harper banked the *Galloping Grape* right until the Hindu Kush were centered off the nose. She ran her throttles forward. The patrol plane began to climb.

Donovan pressed the intercom button on the yoke. "Tacco? Svoboda? We're headed back. Keep your eyes open for threats."

"They're wide open, sir," said the chief.

"Such luck. We may never find it, I fear," Markelov said to Svoboda. He leaned over the nuclear detection gear operator, bracing himself on the upper switch panel. "What does this mean?" he asked, pointing to the flat lines.

The chief pulled his headphones off and looked up at the

sweating Russian civilian. He was supposed to be respectful to officers, and that was hard enough. But there was nothing in the rules about Russians. "It means keep your hands off my panel."

Markelov raised an eyebrow. "Where are we headed now?"

"Back."

Harper kept the *Galloping Grape* on a northerly heading. The mountains grew closer, higher. The Bamian Valley, the one they had searched that morning, appeared off to the right. They went right by it. Beyond the crest lay a maze of canyons that opened up to Afghanistan's mountainous heart. They topped the range and a new valley lay before them. The low sun beamed straight down its length from the west.

Harper banked the plane to the east.

"I'll be damned." Donovan leaned over and looked down. "Some kind of crops growing in that canyon. See it? One-thirty, two o'clock. Red fields."

Harper glanced down at the tiny swatch of color. "Roger. Poppy red."

"You think it's a—"

"Shoot! There's an old runway, too. Somebody lives down there after all. I wonder where they get the water for the crops?"

"Ice melt probably," said Donovan as he checked his chart. "I wonder why Markelov said nobody was around? Looks pretty busy down there for being uninhabited."

"I wonder that, too," said Harper.

Donovan folded up the map and watched the dirt airstrip pass under the *Grape*'s long wing. "Pretty short. I see some tire tracks, but who knows how old they could be. Better log it."

"Roger." Harper pressed the present-position function on

the *Grape*'s inertial navigation computer, storing the dirt runway against future need. When she was finished, she squinted down at the ground. "Sir? I see a plane down there. Far end of the strip. In with those boulders. Looks like some kind of twin, doesn't it? A big one. You want me to circle?"

"Go ahead, Lieutenant." Donovan peered down and caught sight of a cruciform shape in the midst of a jumble of boulders. "You've got sharp eyes, Hot Dog. It's a gooney bird. Looks like it's sat there quite a while."

Harper banked up steeply on a wing for a better look straight down. "It's a Douglas DC-3 all right. What do you think it's doing down there?"

Donovan shook his head. "Maybe an old wreck. Maybe fossilized for all I know. The wings look like they're covered with dirt."

"Tire tracks look pretty fresh for a fossil," Harper said, keeping the *Grape* on a tight tether, circling the remote airstrip. "My father and I used to dust cotton down by the Rio Grande every summer. We'd run across a little strip in the middle of nowhere every now and again, you know, no road, no ranch house, no visible reason for it to be there. Fly too close and the wings would come back peppered with birdshot. We'd just tape them over, mark up our map, and make sure we kept our distance the next run. Of course, marijuana isn't all pretty and red. Not like poppies."

"I read you loud and clear," said Donovan. "Only they probably pack something more lethal than birdshot down there."

"Probably."

Donovan pressed the intercom button on his yoke. "How about it, Chief? You sure the Sniffer's running?"

"I just ran another BIT test. I show a green board, Commander," said Svoboda. "There just ain't nothing out there."

"Keep looking. There's a little airport right below us." The maze of badlands down below was already in deep shadow. Donovan checked his map. He crossed out a square.

"No signal, sir."

"Airport?" asked Markelov. "Where are we?"

"I guess," said Donovan, "the Valley of the L'al is cold, after all."

"Target is still in range," called the operator of the ZSU-23. The twin-barreled antiaircraft cannon tracked the intruder as it circled. "They see the plane."

"Why are they right here?" The Baluchi squinted into the dusk as the silver plane droned overhead. The schedule had the Americans looking at Khadir. After they'd been convinced nothing was there, the weapon would be transferred. If need be, they could stay a step ahead of Satan that way. The Baluchi wondered, could the Americans see through rocks?

"Don't fire unless I say." He took his binoculars and scanned the airstrip below. The Lisunov had been covered with sand and dirt to match the sere ground. It would be hard to spot against the rocks. Still . . .

"Distance is opening!" called the Zeus gunner.

The Baluchi could hear how much the gunner would like to bring down the buzzing airplane. "Don't be so anxious," he said. He focused the binoculars on it again. What were those markings? He caught a flash: US NAVY.

"They look for us."

"No," said the Baluchi. "I don't think so." He watched as the plane moved off into the gathering dusk, its nose pointed east. To Kabul.

* * *

The shaft of light turned crimson, dimmed, and then gut-
tered out like a snuffed candle. In the dark stable, Belenko
and Nazipha were nearly as blind as their guide.

"We should get ready," said Belenko as he peered
through the cracked door at the deserted street outside. A
pale wash of dusk still filtered down from the sky, bouncing from the light stone of the ruined buildings all around.

Belenko turned. Wali was hitching his last horse to the
tonga cart. "You know, I may become a believer yet."

"In what?"

"Miracles. We have no money. Nothing to give Wali for
the use of his horse. No way to threaten him." The thin
wail of music filled the hot, dusty stable. It was a sad song,
a song of old days. Better days. "But there was the radio.
In the jeep. We gave music to a blind man. What better currency is there on earth? First you. Then this. Two miracles
in one day. Who knows? Where there are two, there may
be three."

"You will be safe as babies with me," said Wali as he
harnessed the horse to the tonga cart.

Nazipha turned to Belenko. "What will happen at the airport?"

"You said it was too far to walk to the Cave of the
Sleepers, that Hekmatyar's men were everywhere. We can
still get there, but we have to leap"—Belenko's hand flew
through the dark—"like an eagle. To the Valley of the L'al.
The Valley of God."

"Eagles have wings," said Nazipha.

"Almost finished." Wali hummed along with the music
wailing from the radio. A tabla drum softly beat time to the
sad voice of a harmonium. Wali sang happily. When he was
done, he patted the *ablaq*'s hindquarters. The horse barely

stirred. "Done," he told Belenko and Nazipha. "Are you both ready?"

Belenko helped Nazipha onto the back of the cart and hopped up himself. He pulled the hood of her *chador* up over her head and pinched it nearly closed in front of her face. "Keep the cloth over you," he said, "otherwise it will be hard to breathe." He gently pushed her flat to the rotten boards, covering her with a deep pile of dry hay, then covered himself. They were both as blind as Wali now. He heard the door to the stable creak open.

"Very well, very well," said Wali Ahmad Khan. The radio was wedged between his feet. He took up the *shalaq* and snapped it over the head of the mare.

The cart jerked once, then again as the mare backed up, her iron shoes clattering loud in the stillness of the night. With another backward lurch, the tonga rolled out onto the deserted Kabul street.

"To the airport," said Wali in a voice far too loud. "Fly, fly away we go!" The snap of the whip produced an infinitesimal acceleration. "Hai, hai!" Wali cried.

The horse began to trot. Belenko grimaced under the hay, wishing he had told the fool to keep his mouth shut.

Another tune came from the radio now, a song of war and of bravery, the refrain ending with the words *we are all mujahedin.* The blind driver began singing as the horse pulled them along, the cart bouncing hard over the uneven cobbles. Belenko reached under the hay, searching. He found Nazipha's hand as it burrowed its way toward his own. Their fingers clasped as the cart began to pick up speed. *I've been wrong so many times,* he thought, *this once, make me right.*

"Better get strapped in, sir," said Chief Svoboda to Markelov. "We'll be landing in a minute."

"What? Oh. Yes. Of course." *Damn him!* thought Markelov as he snapped the aluminum case closed. Belenko was supposed to put in a good effort, receive his pay, and go home quietly after convincing the Americans that the Russian side was earnest. Who better than an expert? An OSNAZ? Now, he would have to bring Belenko back in. One way or the other. He put one of the heavy green headphones to his ears and tapped Carranza on the shoulder. "I have a wavelength here," he said, passing a slip of paper to the tactical coordinator. "Can you dial it in?"

"You mean a frequency." Carranza nodded. "Not one we use, but we can do it. Who's on the other end?"

"Just dial it in," said Markelov with a frown. He wasn't used to underlings questioning his direct orders.

A new voice came over the intercom. "Where I come from," said Harper, "we get taught to ask nicely if we want something."

Carranza grinned, his fingers poised over the number two communications set.

"In the spirit of new thinking, of cooperation," said Markelov, each word a hard nugget, "please." Carranza dialed up the private embassy frequency and handed him a push-to-talk switch. Markelov seemed uneasy at being heard by the *Grape*'s entire crew, but then he shrugged, pressed the button, and sent a stream of fast Russian into the deepening dusk. A rapid-fire response deepened his frown as well. He handed the push-to-talk switch back to Carranza. "Thank you."

"No problem, sir. Find out what you wanted?"

"I found out what I found out."

"Crew," said Harper, "set condition five. We're starting our descent to Kabul."

Markelov sat down and snapped his belt, his mind racing ahead to what he would find back at the embassy. The damage could be written off to a rebel attack. But there was the matter of Belenko himself. *Where did that bastard go?* he wondered as the *Grape*'s engines throttled back for the approach.

Wali Ahmad Khan let the horse find its way through the maze of streets and piles of rubble. He was literally as blind as a bat, but he knew from the peculiar echoes of the horse's hooves on the stone buildings exactly where he was. The cart turned off the small street that held the stable, making for the river crossing to the north. He breathed in deeply, smelling the faint odor of the sluggish Kabul River. They were right on course. He reached down and turned up the volume on the radio, letting the sad song mingle with the steady clop of hooves and the clatter of the tonga's wheels on the cobblestone street.

The road was wider now, and the echoes were not so distinct, yet he trusted his horse to know the way. The smell of water was stronger now. Soon, he knew, they would pass the first checkpoint. It had been set up by the old regime. Another had been set up at the Kabul River bridge. They were both manned by Coalition soldiers now. Unless, of course, Hekmatyar's thugs had captured them. Who knew? God.

He felt the horse veer right and pick up its pace as it entered a wide space without the comforting echo of walls. He tugged the reins to slow the *ablaq*. This was no place to rush. Mines were thickly sown off the path, and Wali knew all too well that a horse could set one off even more easily than a man. Any moment now, some poor, miserable soldier would—

"Halt!" came the inevitable cry from the sentry. Wali heard the click of metal as rifles were caught up and brought to bear, clips of bullets rammed into place. He pulled back on the reins to slow them even more, leaned over, and clicked off the radio, pushing it under his *patou* blanket. Soldiers, of course, were all thieves.

"I said halt!"

The tonga cart jounced over a pile of loose rock and came to a stop.

"There's a curfew! Where are you going?" demanded the soldier as he came up cautiously beside Wali. "Who are you?" he bellowed.

"He's the blind one," someone called out from within the wooden sentry box. "He always comes this way for hay."

Wali Ahmad Khan smiled and nodded.

"He has hay," said someone else.

"So? You cannot eat it. Let him pass."

"Blessings, blessings," said Wali. "May your night be safe and your day lucky. Blessings."

"Get going," the soldier said, and with the flat of his hand, slapped the *ablaq* into a fast trot.

"Hai, hai," cried Wali Ahmad Khan as the cart jounced along. The whip cracked and the horse began to trot faster.

The street opened onto a broad plaza. Wali heard the echo of his tonga cart's rumble reflected off the far side. It drew nearer and stronger. The smell of water and sewage rose from the Kabul River as he neared its bank. The road bent, following the river north toward the bridge. On the opposite bank was the Rayon, the government district that had grown up under Soviet occupation. The stone bridge marked the beginning of Route 2, the Salang Highway. On its way it passed the airport, the big air base at Bagram, and then snaked through the Hindu Kush on its way north to the land of the invaders itself.

"Hai, hai!" Wali cried, and with another crack of his *shalaq*, the tonga hurried on toward the last checkpoint. *Char-dast!*

* * *

"Well," said Markelov as he stepped down from the *Galloping Grape*'s waist ladder. "All for nothing. I hope we do better tomorrow." He carried the heavy metal briefcase he had brought on board. He glanced up and saw a pair of headlights racing across the parking ramp. The sound of the Russian embassy's car grew louder. "My driver," he said to Harper alone. "Can I give you a lift?"

"We'll all take you up on that, sir," she said.

"A-firm on that one. I ain't hanging around another night," Svoboda said. "No way."

"Me, too," said Carranza.

"Well," said Markelov, "I suppose we all can squeeze in."

"Then I guess that's it," said Donovan. "We'll take on fuel in the morning and fly another sector. I hope your assistant came up with something for us to check out. Belenko, wasn't it?"

Markelov scowled. "I will know more when I return to the embassy."

Donovan looked up into the indigo sky. The sun had dropped behind the mountains to the west, leaving the airport in the center of a long, probing finger of black shadow. Except for the single pair of headlights drawing near, not a vehicle moved, not a light showed from the few undamaged buildings. Overhead the first stars burned through the pale wash of a high-desert sunset. The *Grape*'s hatch thumped closed and both Carranza and Svoboda hurried down the boarding ladder.

"The aircraft secure, Lieutenant?" Donovan asked Harper.

"Everything's bedded down for the night, sir," Harper replied as she stooped to check the security of the wheel chocks.

The Russian embassy car came up to them and stopped,

its engine-gunning nervously. "I think we should all get going before—" Markelov began, but his voice froze as a burst of orange light erupted from the flanks of the nearest line of hills. As he watched, his mind as mired as his feet, a second and a third joined the first, rising like a string of dazzling comets into the starry sky. The whistling scream of the first rocket's flight came a moment later.

"Incoming!" shouted Svoboda. He dived under the high wing of the P-3 and rolled up against the landing gear, knowing even as he did so that the thin aluminum above him would offer no protection.

Donovan stood in the open, his mouth wide, his neck back as though the display were a Fourth of July finale. "Jesus," he said. Harper grabbed him by his flightsuit and pulled him down to the ground. Markelov dived down beside the embassy Jeep, peering over its armored hood as the rockets smoked across the sky. He knew at a glance that their trajectory was taking them someplace else. Kabul was about to be hit.

The rocket stream scorched by overhead. Half a dozen orange exhausts winked out as the last propellant burned, leaving the heavy, finned warheads to coast invisibly toward Kabul. *Any moment now,* thought Markelov as he counted the seconds to detonation. *Any . . .*

"Halt!" shouted the *mujahed* at the river crossing.

Wali reined in the *ablaq.* Silence terrified him, but he knew how to deal with mere soldiers. He brought the tonga to a stop at the ramp leading to the old stone bridge.

"Where do you think you are going?" the Coalition soldier demanded. "Don't you know there's a curfew?"

Wali heard the squawk of a radio and the murmur of other voices. *How many were here tonight?* he wondered.

He turned his face in the direction of the sentry's voice. "Day and night are as one to me."

"They are the same in prison, too."

Uzbek, thought Wali as he quickly sized up the sentry's accent. That was not good news.

"Well? Are you deaf? Let me see your identity card!"

Wali Ahmad Khan hesitated. He remembered when the government had first passed out cards—Allah be praised—with his very own face pictured on it. It was a wonderful, miraculous thing at the time, sure evidence that the government could extract all manner of miracles from . . .

"Bring him over here," said another, more distant voice.

"Get down!" the sentry bellowed right into Wali's startled face.

He started to move, but suddenly a hand grabbed his *patou* and snatched him from the plank of wood that served as his seat, sending him sprawling onto the dust. The *ablaq* whinnied nervously and stamped her foot, pulling at the harness.

"Ay! Look what I have found!" the soldier crowed. A snap of a switch brought forth a stream of music. The radio.

"No!" Wali scrambled to his feet. The wooden stock of an AK assault rifle pushed him away as several other men laughed. Uzbeks! They all were thieves! "No! That was a present from my own father the night he died! I swear on the *Qur'an.*"

"That you are a thief!" said the soldier as he changed stations. "Be still and count yourself lucky."

"Get the horse, too," said someone. "She's a fat one." A general murmur of assent went through the assembled troops. One horse such as this could feed them for many days.

Belenko felt Nazipha's hand grip his tightly. His ears had

picked out five, perhaps six men. How many weapons? *Five AKs and a machine gun nearby,* he thought. *And only one path to run.* They were at a cleared zone, and the earth to either side would be mined. What were the chances?

"Where did you get this radio, thief?" asked a man with the sound of command in his voice.

Wali swung to face him. "Please, Captain," he said, guessing the man's rank, "I am only a poor hay man, not a thief."

The *ablaq* stepped backward and whinnied again as she was unhooked from the tonga cart's traces. She stamped a foot at the stranger's rough hand.

"Please! Not the horse! It is the only way a blind man can live! Is this the way you treat a wounded war veteran?" He stopped at the cackle of laughter that followed his plea.

"You don't need to work where you are going," said the sentry. "You are going to Pul-e-Charki!"

Nazipha squeezed Belenko's hand tight. The name of the infamous central prison galvanized him like a high-voltage charge. He pulled the Makarov from his belt and worked himself free of the hay. He peeked over the rotted wooden sideboard of the tonga. A blinding spotlight held Wali in its grip. Suddenly, there was a flicker of light. Not from the earth. But from the sky.

"Look out!" a soldier shouted.

What . . . ? Belenko wondered. A tremendous, soundless flash erupted off to one side, illuminating the entire scene with the horrible clarity of a false and deadly daylight. Belenko felt the heat wash over him even as he dived back down into the hay. A tremendous *crack* followed on its heels, loud enough to announce the end of the earth. Belenko was already flat to the tonga's boards when the concussion shoved his face into the wood. The horse screamed in the sudden silence that followed.

Belenko's eyes popped back open, his mind racing faster than thought itself. From somewhere deep in his OSNAZ training, Belenko knew that fate had offered him another chance. Another miracle. He shoved the pile of hay from Nazipha's body as another earsplitting scream sounded from the dark sky.

Ssss-crack! Five hundred pounds of high explosive blasted a hole in the muddy bed of the Kabul River. "Come on!" he shouted, pulling her to her feet. "Now!"

The third rocket landed in the shallows, throwing up a geyser of black water and sewage. Like a cloudburst from a clear sky, the filthy water drowned the generator that lit the checkpoint's spotlight in a shower of brilliant sparks.

The sudden darkness was cut by the distant whoosh of more projectiles inbound. A low groan came from an injured soldier. Belenko leaped from the tonga, Nazipha in tow.

"What are we—"

He heard the banshee wail grow loud as the rocket screamed down on them. *Ssss* . . . He grabbed the horse by a loose rein, yanked her so that she stood between them and the bridge, and pressed Nazipha to the warm flanks. The fourth warhead ricocheted from a stone caisson and detonated. The span shook under the blow. The *ablaq* reared and screamed as a hail of stone pellets shotgunned them. The sound of the next projectile was already growing in his ears.

Suddenly, Belenko knew. As the rocket's whoosh turned into a whistle, as the whistle became a screech, he picked Nazipha up off her feet and threw her across the mare's back. Dry, cracked reins in hand, he leaped up in front of her and pulled her head around until she faced the stone bridge.

"Go!" Nazipha screamed as she held on to him tight.

Belenko dug his heels into the *ablaq*'s bony flanks. *"Char-dast!"* he bellowed.

The *ablaq* seemed to leap straight up on all four legs, her eyes white with panic. But when her hooves struck the earth, they began a tattoo that built into thunder. The stone bridge was wreathed in acrid cordite smoke. Belenko dug his heels in again, and the horse charged straight into the cloud.

Wali Ahmad Khan crouched in a drainage culvert beside the road with two soldiers. Their breath came in sobs as they heard the rockets tip over and start their wailing fall. Wali heard his last horse pound off across the damaged bridge. *Ssssss* . . . He pushed the radio deeper into the folds of his *patou*. He switched it on. The same song was playing. Sad. Beautiful. "We are all *mujahedin* . . ." *Crack!*

At first he only felt the pressure. Then he felt the wetness; finally the sting from a hundred punctures ripped into his flesh by shrapnel. *Go with God,* he thought as a new darkness, deeper, softer than the one he knew, reached for his heart. *Go with God.*

"I think Charlie got tired," said Chief Svoboda. He unwrapped himself from the *Grape*'s landing gear. He could taste rubber in his mouth. Or fear.

Donovan listened for more rockets, but the night sky seemed innocent once again, hammered with brilliant stars. "Chief," he said as he slowly stood up, "Charlie was a long time ago."

"No, sir. When they got you dialed in, they're all Charlie."

"Maybe staying out here isn't such a bad idea," said Carranza as he dusted off his flightsuit. "They didn't lob any of those bastards at us last night. Just at the town." Carranza looked over at the glowing smoke from the bridge, and then at Svoboda. "I think I'll stay put for the night."

"You're sure, Lieutenant?" asked Donovan. "Chief?"

"I'm with Tacco. You can have Kabul."

"Sooner or later," said Markelov, "everyone comes to the same conclusion."

15

—

IRON

Markelov watched the glow of the rocket bursts fade to black. He smiled. Who wouldn't want to escape a place like this? He only hoped that the Americans would arrive at the same conclusion soon. But then a darker thought emerged from the swiftly shifting patterns inside his head. That pattern had a name: *Belenko*.

"We're ready if you are," said Donovan from the front seat of the Russian embassy Wagoneer.

"Yes." Markelov got into the back, shut the door, and moved close to Harper. Closer than he needed to. "Why don't you both come to the embassy for dinner? Kabul is such a lonely place and I'm sure you won't be here for very much longer."

"No, thanks," said Donovan from the front. "We aren't here to enjoy ourselves."

"A pity." Markelov inched closer to Harper, felt her leg. He patted it in a fatherly way. "We have women pilots in Russia, you know. The best."

"They fly combat?" She moved away, toward the window.

"Of course. They fly everything the men fly. MiGs.

219

Sukhois. Even the giant Antonovs. My own company has arranged letters of cooperation with other countries to demonstrate the quality of Russian airplanes."

"MAYAK?" said Donovan.

"Absolutely." Markelov smiled at Harper. "We could use a good pilot at MAYAK. On the demonstration team. Think of it. Geneva. Flying the most advanced jets in the world for a good salary. Plus many other incentives. Would you like that?"

"I have a job with the Navy, sir." But her eyes betrayed more than a little interest.

"Ah. Yes. Combat. Is that what you would like? To fight?" He moved in again, stroking a knee now.

"Not tonight." She took his hand and put it back on his own leg. She crossed her legs and placed the sole of her boot against Markelov's jeans. "How come the Russians are driving an American car?" she asked, changing the subject.

"It's safer." He moved away, brushing the dirt off.

They drove south along the deserted road toward Kabul, the powerful engine the only sound filling the plush, armored cabin.

"I sure hope your man comes up with something for us," said Donovan. "Belenko?"

"Yes," Markelov said distractedly. *Belenko,* he thought as he stared into the night. *How will I fix that?* He would have to speak with Brown. Put their heads together. It was too damned late for any of this. Belenko was the past. MAYAK was the future. And Markelov wasn't about to see it compromised by a fossil who refused to understand the ways of business. A ghost.

Donovan put his head back and closed his eyes. The hum of the tires and the fatigue of flying conspired together to lull him into a light sleep.

Route 2, the Salang Highway, had been a showpiece of engineering in its time, built by Americans and then reinforced by the Soviets to bear up under the weight of main battle tanks. To the south it ran from Kabul to Kandahar, then back up to Mazari Sharif; to the north it snaked by the mouth of the Panshair Valley, through the Hindu Kush, and on to the old Soviet border. Most of it was barely wide enough for two cars to shoulder by each other, but here, so close to the capital, it was a broad four-lane highway: a Potemkin turnpike. The divide had been planted with orchards and ornamental shrubs. Now, all that remained was the skeletal shapes of dead trees and burned-out military vehicles. Markelov sat quietly watching the charred remains go by.

"Black out there," said Harper as she watched the empty terrain flash by beyond the Wagoneer's headlights. "All the same, I wouldn't want to have a flat. It looks like a great place to get jumped."

Markelov's eyes went automatically to the two weapons cradled beneath the Jeep's dash, an RPK-74 machine gun and an SVD Dragunov sniper rifle mounting a starlight scope. "We're really quite safe," he said to her. "The tires are filled with foam and the ground is seeded with mines on both sides of Route Two. The Coalition patrols come out on a regular schedule each day. Of course nothing is certain in war," Markelov elaborated, "but it would be very difficult to travel across a minefield at night, even for a wood . . . a bandit."

"I don't see any patrols out there tonight," she replied.

"You're safe as in your father's arms," said Markelov. "Before, when the Soviets—" Suddenly the Wagoneer swerved, cutting off Markelov in midsentence and throwing him against the door.

"What is it?" Donovan was instantly awake.

"I saw someone!" shouted the driver as he brought the

car back into the center of the lane and slowed, looking off to his left at the center divide. "In the middle, by those trees! I thought . . ."

"So? Get moving then!" Markelov's pulse drummed in his temples even as a cold wash of fear ran down his neck.

The driver grabbed the handle to the small spotlight mounted on the roof of the car. He snapped the light on and a beam stabbed out into the darkness. As the car began to speed up, the beam swept across the blasted, blackened trunks of what had once been a row of almonds.

Markelov saw them. "Mother of . . ." he said beneath his breath.

"I see 'em!" said Harper. "Is that a horse with—"

"Stop!" Markelov screamed at the driver. "Give me the weapon!"

"Exactly so!" the man answered out of old military habit. He jammed on the brakes and unsnapped the light machine gun from under the dash. As the heavy Jeep slewed to a halt, the RPK was already in Markelov's hands. The Kabul MAYAK representative furiously cranked down his bullet-proof window.

"Who is—" Harper began.

"Turn around!" Markelov roared.

Belenko spurred the sweaty *ablaq* behind the stump of a dead almond and listened to the sound of the engine. He hadn't expected to encounter any traffic on the dark highway, at least none he couldn't hear or see well in advance. There wasn't much in the way of official traffic at night, and by the look of the burned wrecks littering the center divide, there was good cause for caution. Why didn't this lone vehicle know that?

Nazipha clung to Belenko's back. She turned, nearly slipping off the sweaty mare. "Did they   " She stopped when a finger of brilliant light shot out from the car's roof. It swung one way, then the other, then in a dazzling, burning flash, it caught them square in its beam.

"Hai!" Belenko kicked Wali's *ablaq* into action again, but after running flat out all the way from the rocketed bridge, she clearly had little more to give than a hard-breathing trot. Blood from a dozen tiny shrapnel wounds glistened on her side, and her breath was foamy and hot. "Come on!" He slapped his palm down hard against her steaming flanks.

"They're following!"

Belenko swung in his perch and saw that the car, who-ever it was, had reversed course. It was coming for them. "Hai!" he yelled, and dug his heels in again, yanking the reins around to dodge between the black trunks of the dead almond trees.

Belenko swung the *ablaq* to keep the trunk of a tree be-tween them and the car. He looked ahead. There was a burned-out truck of some sort, its wheels pointed skyward, like a dead insect. Beyond that only the blackness. He gal-loped them around the hulk and made for the next shield, a twenty-foot branchless snag dead ahead. But before he gained its lee, the light suddenly caught them, making the dead-white trunk come ablaze and destroying his night-adapted vision.

First came a gout of yellow muzzle flame; next the ham-mering of a dozen 5.45-mm rounds into dead wood. Only then came the distinctive high-speed buzz of an RPK ma-chine gun. Nazipha buried her head in his back as Belenko kicked them into a gallop and out from the spotlight's fo-cus.

Left! He yanked on the leather rein hard and jinked to one side of the snag as the stuttering light of the weapon erupted once again. *Right!* Would he dodge the machine gun or steer them into its field of fire? The high insect-whine of bullets passed over his head, followed by the crackle of automatic fire. *Left!* He leaned forward and took a double handful of the exhausted horse's mane. "You can do it!" he shouted into her ear. "You're the best horse in all Afghanistan! Hai!" She seemed to sense the mortal danger closing in from behind and ran faster. Belenko could tell from the wildness in her eyes and the unevenness of her gait that she was already into the last of her reserves.

The car's headlights now joined the spotlight, illuminating their path, making it easier to see but far too easy to be seen. They were silhouetted against the utter black of the deserted road. Belenko knew that on level ground, the race between the faithful *ablaq* and their pursuer could only end one way. The headlights grew brighter and the engine roared in Belenko's ears. They were galloping up a steady incline, one that seemed to lead directly into the starry sky. The beams of the embassy car burned into his back like lasers as they crested the small hill.

"Sasha!"

The road that split from the Salang Highway for the Kabul airport was visible ahead and to the left. It was impossibly far. They would never make it.

Belenko yanked the reins to the left, leaving the center divide, taking off at an angle across the blacktop. The *ablaq*'s hooves pounded like steel pistons. A flashing strobe came from behind as the embassy car slewed around to expose the gunner. A string of supersonic cracks blasted by at head level. The dark air was full of death. Hard little drops of death. Belenko clung tight to the horse's mane as the bullets stung the air.

The crumbling verge of the southbound roadbed came up on them fast. Beyond it was nothing but open country between them and the Kabul perimeter fence. The *ablaq* stumbled, nearly falling on the hard surface. She righted herself just as they came to the edge of the roadbed. Belenko kicked the mare back into a gallop.

"No!" screamed Nazipha. "Don't! Not . . . we can't! There are . . ."

But with a final leap into darkness, the horse left the hard surface behind and landed on the dusty earth beyond.

"Quick!" Markelov shouted. The driver gunned the Wagoneer across the unpaved divide and onto the south-bound lane.

"What in the name of God are you doing!" demanded Donovan as he was thrown against the door. "Who in hell are you shooting—"

"Almost!" Markelov leaned out the window, the RPK in his hand, taking aim on the target framed in their head-lights. He held the weapon as steady as he could and fired. The ripping noise of high-velocity slugs pouring from its muzzle was deafening. A stinging cloud of cordite filled the Wagoneer. "Yes!" The horse was riderless! "I . . ." He stopped when he saw that Belenko had merely ducked low. "Closer!" he ordered the driver. "We must get closer!"

The driver shot him a nervous look as they drew near to the edge of the road. Markelov was beyond noticing. He saw his target fleeing across the ground out ahead, the horse throwing up puffs of dust and leaving a yellow cloud behind.

Suddenly, the driver swerved and braked hard. The gal-loping horse and its riders went black as the headlights swung away. "What are you doing? Fool!" Markelov yelled. "Follow them!"

"I can't!" the driver replied, sweat pouring from his brow.

"What do you mean you can't!"

The driver nodded at the black terrain. "Mines."

"Fuck your mother." Markelov reached forward and unhooked the sniper rifle from beneath the dash. With a well-oiled click, he rammed the Dragunov's long barrel into its stock and checked that the big starlight scope was on.

Nazipha had her eyes tightly shut as they pounded across what she knew must be mine-sown ground. Each strike of hoof on dirt could well be the last. Did Belenko realize it? Not that it mattered now. She held him tightly around his waist, the heat rising from the exhausted *ablaq* a cocoon around them both, a magic shield. She looked up at the starry sky, wondering whether she would live to see the first light of dawn. The mare's breath now came fast. Sweat was flung back from her neck. If only this magnificent mare could fly them up into the heavens and . . .

Suddenly, a spasm tore through Belenko's body, an electric blast that transmitted straight into Nazipha's own flesh.

"No!" Belenko screamed, and twisted. The crack of a rifle came an instant later. He began to fall to the left even before Nazipha's brain registered what had just happened. A second round flew overhead. *Crack!*

The horse, no longer goaded by Belenko's heels, slowed, her breath coming hard, foam pouring from her flaring nostrils.

"Sasha!" Nazipha grabbed him, tilting him back upright, feeling the sudden, awful wetness on her cheek, a wetness that she knew was Belenko's blood. "Are you—"

A third *crack!* of a bullet sounded in her ears. Belenko leaned forward onto the *ablaq*'s mane as the horse came to a stop just twenty meters shy of the perimeter fence and in full view of the rifleman. He shook his head and slowly, painfully, bobbed back up, his long legs back down the horse's wet flanks.

"Sasha!" Nazipha cried, for even in the dark, the spreading stain on his jacket was visible.

Just a little more, he thought, the burning in his upper arm raging like a wildfire through dry brush. He fought back, encircling it, digging a moat filled with his own blood against it, controlling the pain. *Just a little more.* He formed the agony into a smaller and smaller package until it was a pinpoint jabbing him like a white-hot needle. He looked up and made out the glint of the fence against the stars. He turned back. The headlights of the embassy car were so very close, pointed off at an angle. *Single shot. An SVD with a starscope,* he thought. *They are invisible, but we are bright as . . .* He shook his head. He could catalogue it all later.

"Sasha! You're—"

"I know. I know, Nazichka. Don't worry." He noticed how much effort it took to make his voice sound normal. "Not much farther now. Stay low." He pushed her nearly flat to the *ablaq*'s back, turned, reining the horse to the right, testing whether the mare would respond.

The horse shuffled wearily in the direction Belenko wished, her flanks shuddering with fatigue. He took hold of the leather reins, measuring the distance to the fence. Belenko bent low. He whispered in her ear. "*Insh-Allah,* in the name of God," he said, gripping her flanks as tightly as he could, "one last thing I will ask, then you can rest and eat barley and drink cool water in paradise." Her ear twitched and she whinnied as Belenko whispered. "But for now, in the name of Allah, the merciful, the compassionate"—he gathered his voice, a powerful pressure building in his throat like a river dammed against a flood—"one last word." He put his mouth into her flattened ear and bellowed, *"Run!"*

The horse exploded into motion just as the fourth shot

whined by Belenko's ear. The crack of the Dragunov chased the streaking bullet across the night.

Ten meters. "Hold on tight!" he said as he dug his heels into the *ablaq*. "Haihaihai! *Char-dast!*" The horse screamed as she saw the fence loom suddenly from the darkness. "Hold on!" Another rifle shot sounded as the mare began to rear. "Now!" Belenko shouted, hauling back on the reins, and the mare leaped into the air.

At first Nazipha thought Belenko had been struck again. But the sound that filled the air was not human. The *ablaq* screamed as Nazipha had never heard an animal scream: a piercing wail of exhaustion and despair, the sound a cornered creature makes when surrounded on all sides by patient, hungry predators, or that most patient of all hunters, death.

Still the mare rose up into the air. Her forelegs cleared the highest strand of barbed wire, six feet above the dusty ground. Momentum pulled her body along behind. She began to fall, but the *ablaq* was no longer fearful, no longer overwhelmed by exhaustion. Her rear hooves tangled in the barbs, snapping metal poles and pulling the fence down behind her, but she felt nothing. It no longer mattered whether this last effort or the 7.62-mm high-velocity round from the deadly Dragunov had burst her heart. As she struck the earth, the scent of green grass and cool waters filled her nostrils. The *ablaq*, unlike her riders, had no more reason to run.

Chief Svoboda rolled the dice. They clattered out on the small table in the *Grape*'s aft cabin. Acey-deucey was as much a part of a naval aviator's existence as black coffee and boredom. He took an extra turn, driving Lieutenant Carranza's pieces from the board. The *Galloping Grape*'s cabin was awash with soft red nightlighting. Svoboda entered his win on a flight log form. "That's five straight. Jeez, Lieutenant, didn't they teach you how to play at Canoe U.?"

"We never played with round dice," Carranza said with a grimace. "And as for . . ." He stopped and swung his head forward. "You hear that?" A tiny pop, no more than a suggestion of a sound, had registered on Carranza's nerves.

Chief Svoboda heard it, too. He was already on his feet. "Sounded like a shot a ways off." He walked forward to the *Grape*'s main hatch and checked that it was securely locked. He listened. "Just one." A scurrying mouse fled beneath his boots. Svoboda kicked at it but the rodent was too swift. "Damn. Another one." They were coming up the boarding ladder in search of food. "They must think we're Noah's Ark or something."

"We are for them." Carranza had been shocked the night before when he played a flashlight across the tarmac below the P-3. A hundred red eyes had stared back up at him. "We ought to set some . . ." He stopped again. "There it is again."

Svoboda listened. "Two. Three." He closed his eyes. "Four."

"Better take a look." Carranza stood up and joined the chief. "Let's go dark." Svoboda hit the lights as Carranza undogged the hatch. It swung in and to one side. "Black out there."

The brilliant desert stars were bright enough to make out the boarding stairs leading down to the tarmac. Despite the dryness of the air, a heavy dew had formed on the metal rails of the ladder. Carranza swiped one dry, feeling the first hard traces of ice on the rails. How could that be? "Damn cold," he muttered. It had nearly topped a hundred degrees the previous afternoon; how could a place be ungodly hot and cold, all at the same time?

"See anything?"

"A-firm." Carranza could see a pair of lights in the distance, headlights, and they were moving. "Some kind of action outside the fence. I see a patrol moving out there." He listened hard, but the vehicle was too far away to hear its engine. All he could hear was a faint scuffling from below. *Damn rats.*

"Dog the hatch, Lieutenant."

Carranza lingered, watching the speeding headlights. "Why do you think everyone's so anxious to fight over this dump?" Carranza turned his back to the night. "I'll be happy when we're wheels up and out of here. I'd rather . . ." He stopped cold. The iron finger pressed against his spine was utterly unmistakable.

"You," whispered Naziphu, "follow me down. Now."

Carranza didn't move.

"Hey. Come on, L-T, the frigging rats are lining up for the inflight movie. Close the door before . . ." Svoboda peered at Carranza's odd posture. "What's with you?" The chief hit the night lights, flooding the *Galloping Grape*'s cabin with red. "Jesus."

"Both of you. Come down and help me." Naziphu's green eyes burned black from under her blood-smeared *chador.* "Now."

"Where the fuck did . . ."

The 9-mm's slide made the smallest of sounds as the trigger slack was taken up. But it was plenty loud to Carranza. "Chief," said Carranza. "Let's just do it, okay?"

"Roger that," said Svoboda.

"Slowly."

Carranza went first, wondering whether he should run for it once he got to the bottom. Could she see him in the starlight? Would the chief react the right way? How did she sneak up so quietly? He reached for the icy rail and moved slowly down, Svoboda two rungs higher. *The commander's gonna crucify us,* Carranza thought.

Nazipha came last, the muzzle of the black Makarov PM inches behind Svoboda's broad back. At the bottom, she motioned them to the right.

Carranza nearly tripped over Belenko before he saw him. "Chief," he whispered, although he didn't know why. He could shout for all it would do any good. "Chief!"

"I'm right with you, L-T," said Svoboda. "What—"

"Pick him up!" Nazipha commanded.

Carranza leaned over Belenko's prone body. One of his arms was slick with fresh blood. "He's hit! The guy's been shot! I think he's dead, Chief."

"Not yet. Both of you. Pick him up!"

Carranza looked up. If he ran one way and Svoboda ran the other, she probably couldn't aim . . .

Nazipha raised the pistol and fired. The flash strobed them into a portrait of shock and fear. The crack of the bullet as it flew overhead was convincing. Svoboda got under one arm, the lieutenant under the other.

"It's the fucking Russian," whispered Svoboda as they made their way back to the P-3's boarding ladder. A red glow spilled from the still-open hatch. As they climbed the cold stairs, the crimson light turned Belenko's blood to black. Svoboda saw that both his flightsuit and Carranza's were covered with it.

"Markelov?" said Carranza.

"No. The skinny one. Let's put this guy on the bunk," Svoboda said to Carranza. They lowered Belenko to the wide seat behind the *Galloping Grape*'s galley table.

"You have bandages?" asked Nazipha.

Carranza turned to face her. "Sure. Why don't you get it for us? It's right up beside . . ."

She pointed the weapon at Carranza and shook her head.

"Like I said," the lieutenant finished, "why don't I go get the medipak?"

Svoboda reached for a flashlight, noting that Nazipha did not react to his movement. *I'll try that again real fucking soon,* he thought. *But not with a flashlight.* He illuminated Belenko's upper body. "Don't look too bad," he said, pulling Belenko's jacket away. "Creased him is all."

Belenko moaned, his eyes still closed.

"Sasha!" cried Nazipha. "I'll never forgive myself!"

"He'll be all right." Svoboda ripped Belenko's sleeve away. It was already stiff with congealed blood. The wound in his upper arm was ragged; the Dragunov's bullet had been tumbling when it struck flesh, tearing an uneven passage through soft tissue and sinew before exiting. It looked more like a bite than a bullet's work.

"My God. Will he be all right?" she asked, biting her lower lip.

"Why don't you ask me some other time?" said Svoboda acidly. "Like when you aren't holding a fucking pistol at my head. Guns are dangerous, lady." He pressed hard against the gaping tear. *Direct pressure,* he thought. The wound wouldn't kill the man, but loss of blood might. He looked up as Carranza returned with the emergency first-aid kit. He caught a look from the lieutenant that told him Carranza had managed to retrieve more than bandages and tourniquets. Svoboda nodded. *Good boy,* he thought. *You may live to be a real sailor yet.* He took a sterile bandage and closed it tight over Belenko's wound.

"He should be in a hospital. It's got to be . . ." Carranza stopped and looked back at the *Grape's* open hatch. The sound of an engine was growing loud. He shot a glance to Svoboda. *Now?*

The chief nodded.

Carranza cleared his throat, trying to seem unconcerned, eyeing the heavy gun in the hands of the small woman standing next to him. At the bottom of the medipak was Carranza's .45-caliber service revolver. "I think we need a bigger bandage on that, Chief. There should be one in here somewhere. Check around."

"Good idea, lad," said Svoboda. The sound of the engine now was unmistakable. A squeal of brakes came from right beneath the boarding ladder. He dug into the medicines and gauzes. The hard shape of the automatic was right there. *Now,* thought Svoboda as he shoved the bandages aside and reached for the pistol. *Or never.*

16

—

THE CONFEDERATE TRIBES

"WHAT MAKES YOU THINK THEY'RE HEADED THIS WAY?" Donovan demanded as they braked to a stop right under the long wing of the *Galloping Grape*.

"Because I know him," said Markelov. "Belenko's a very troubled man. Ever since he left this place. I must say, there were rumors."

"What kind?" asked Harper.

"Drugs," Markelov said. "It is always a risk in a place like Kabul. A person identifies too closely with an alien land. He loses his anchor. His stability. Anything is possible."

"Why were you shooting at him?" asked Harper.

"I'll show you what he did to the embassy when we get back. He attacked it."

"Attacked?"

"With a tank. We must be very careful." The embassy driver shut down the engine. He looked up at the looming shape of the American patrol plane. Starlight glinted off its aluminum skin, and dull red light glowed softly from the portholes. "Wait for us here, Vasily," Markelov said. The driver nodded and snapped a new magazine into the RPK.

Markelov turned to Donovan. "Shall we check in on your men?"

"Not *we*, Markelov. *I* will. And another thing," said Donovan as he swung open the back door. "There will be no gunfire around my aircraft. In fact, I don't want you anywhere near it. Understood?"

"I don't think you realize what kind of man Belenko—"

"Lieutenant," Donovan said to Harper, "kindly keep our two Russian friends company. I'll call down if I need any more bodies."

"Yes, sir," she said, getting out and standing between the ominously quiet *Galloping Grape* and the parked car.

Markelov watched Donovan walk to the boarding ladder. He still had ten rounds left in the SVD Dragunov. A thin curl of smoke issued from the long snout of the sniper rifle. "He doesn't know Belenko. He's a very dangerous man. By training. And also by habit. Very dangerous."

"The commander knows what he's doing."

"Nevertheless, I think it would be better if we came along. The night is full of bandits. Vasily?" The two Russians got out of the car and quietly closed the doors.

"Cover me," said Markelov. The driver took up a position behind the Wagoneer, the RPK resting on the armored roof. Markelov smiled and walked up to Harper. Her arms were crossed over her chest. She didn't move.

"You're a lovely woman. Now, get out of my way."

"Sir, the commander gave you your orders. You will step back from the aircraft," she said defiantly. "And point that damned thing away." She nodded at the SVD.

Markelov swung the rifle's muzzle off to one side. "Come now," he said, "we are merely—"

Harper jabbed her finger hard into Markelov's chest. "Listen up: you stay right where you are, buster, and not one step farther. No jokes."

Markelov heard the driver chuckle. He smiled patronizingly at Harper and made a move to grab her shoulder and shove her to one side, but in a blur of motion she stepped inside him, wrapped a leg behind one knee, and gave a sudden push on the opposite arm. Markelov squalled as he toppled backward, the SVD dropping to the ground with a clatter even as his fall came to a stop with his head a few inches from the tarmac. Harper held him suspended by his leather jacket as she kicked the rifle out of his reach. His mouth moved, but he was too stunned to speak.

"Sorry, sir," she said with a smile as she slowly let him down. "But orders are orders."

"Lieutenant?" called Donovan. He had turned at the sound of the scuffle, but it was already over. *Good going,* he thought.

"Everything seems to be in hand, sir," she replied, letting go of Markelov.

The embassy driver set the RPK down on the roof of the Wagoneer and rushed over to help Markelov to his feet. The driver turned to Harper, but Markelov shot a blistering stream of Russian at him and he stopped, a strange smile on his face.

"Chief? Lieutenant?" Donovan called up the ladder. *Why do they have the hatch open?* Donovan wondered. The red night lights were on, but no sounds were coming from the open hatch. Were they asleep? Both of them? He stepped up onto the fourth rung of the boarding ladder. The metal side-rails were cold as ice and wet with . . . He stopped and looked at his hands, holding them up to the light coming from the hatch. It was black and sticky. *Oil?* He rubbed his fingers together and smelled a mixture of damp soil, copper, and rust. *Jesus.*

He took the stairs two at a time, bursting into the cabin even as his brain registered the fact that it was a foolish thing to do unarmed. His momentum carried him right into the center of the aisle that ran down the P-3's fuselage. He swung his head left, then right. *Where is everyone?* The door to the head was closed. Beyond it the dinette and galley were empty, but the *Galloping Grape*'s medipak was strewn across the table, an opened bandage roll sopping up fresh blood from the deck. The cabin was as quiet as a tomb, yet where had all that blood come from? Donovan's neck crawled with icy premonition.

"Chief!" He turned left and made his way forward. The Sniffer station as well as Carranza's electronic cubicle were deserted. The hairs on his arms began to rise. "Tacco!" He pushed aside the curtains to the cockpit and stepped in, reached overhead, and snapped on the white floodlights.

"Commander?" called Harper from the bottom of the boarding ladder.

"Get up here!" he replied. Suddenly, a loud thump came from behind him. Before he could do more than sense the disturbance, two sharp reports from outside the plane were followed by the ripping explosion of the RPK being fired on full automatic. Donovan froze, his boots rooted in place until a *tick!* opened a perfect round hole in the *Grape*'s cockpit wall. He spun, and there, through a haze of cordite smoke, he saw Harper standing in the center aisle. She was not alone.

Belenko pointed Carranza's .45 away from Harper and at Donovan. He had one boot jammed against the bottom of the door to the head. One of his arms was wrapped in a blood-soaked battle dressing. "You are just in time to join us."

"Sir," she said, her voice quavering, "I didn't see . . ."

Just then Markelov appeared in the hatch, his arms above his head. Nazipha held the RPK in a one-handed grip. She prodded him forward. The machine gun was still hot. Its owner lay on the cold concrete beside the embassy car.

Belenko nodded appreciatively. "Pavel Ill'ch. MAYAK must really pay you well to get you out on a night like this. Bandits are everywhere."

"You don't know what you're saying."

"Don't I? I can begin with opium. Money talks, nobody walks. I think you would do well to talk."

"What's going on?" Donovan demanded.

Markelov ignored him. His Russian was low, full of warning. Dangerous. "You'll wish you had never come up from your hole, Belenko. After this there will be nowhere for you to go. No safety anywhere. Brown and I—"

"Ah, Brown," Belenko said with a thin smile. "I thought as much. After all, there isn't enough hard currency in all of Moscow to pay for all the poison you've put away at the embassy."

"Bastard. You'll lose, Belenko. Trust me to know. This time you have gone over the line. Murder of a Russian citizen!"

"What do you call your profession?"

"Business is business." Markelov looked away. He switched to English. It carried the same ominous tone. "And you," he snarled at Harper. "You see what you have done?"

"Where are my men?" Donovan inched closer to Harper. There was pounding on the door to the head. "In here!"

"Chief?"

"Yeah," came the muffled voice of Chief Svoboda. "We're both okay."

Belenko nodded behind him. "I am afraid they will have to remain where they are for now. And please, Commander"—he cocked the .45's hammer and placed the muzzle behind Harper's head—"don't come any closer. These are desperate times we live in. And as Pavel here will attest, my thinking is not always predictable."

Harper's eyes were closed as she waited for the explosion.

"All right," said Donovan, his hands opening and closing, his jaw tight in his anger and his frustration. He saw a fresh welling of blood stain Belenko's bandage. Could he wait him out, hoping the wound would drain him? "What is it you want?"

"We are going to fly," Nazipha answered, her voice strong and clear. She glanced at Belenko.

"Pavel," Belenko said. "You mentioned a technical matter to me. A detonating device. I don't suppose you have it with you, do you?"

"Once an OSNAZ," Markelov sneered, "always an OSNAZ." He turned to Nazipha. "You see? He's even using you to perform his sacred patriotic duties. But there's still time if we—"

"Shut your mouth," said Belenko, pointing the cocked .45 at him. "Or I might choose to perform my sacred patriotic duty right here and right now. You are a smuggler, Pavel. Brown would have your share and only addicts would mourn you. I would not. And MAYAK? Perhaps they will dedicate a plaque."

Markelov's face drained as he stared down the black hole of the gun barrel. He clamped his mouth shut and glowered.

"Now, about the detonator? You were going to bring it with you when you flew with your good friends the Americans. Where is it?"

Markelov's eyes flicked out the open hatch and back at Belenko.

"Very good. Nazipha, the first one to move, shoot."

Belenko turned to face the closed door to the head. "And the first one who tries to come out will be the one who kills your commander. Think about that." He waited, listening.

"Commander Donovan?" called Carranza.

"He's not joshing, Tacco," Donovan replied.

"Sasha, listen to me," Markelov said quickly. "You've gone around the bend. You need help. Stop this while you can. The material you saw was part of an operation to—"

Belenko shoved the .45 into Markelov's side. "One bullet, Pavel. It would be no bigger than your little finger, and I would love to do it. Really. I would. Do you believe me?"

"Fuck your mother. You're crazy."

"Everyone seems to think so. Move."

Nazipha leveled the RPK at Donovan's chest as the two men descended the boarding ladder.

"What does he think he's going to do?" As Donovan spoke, he rocked forward on the balls of his feet. "We can't just fly around and drop you off someplace. This whole thing is nuts."

Nazipha kept quiet, the weapon at the ready in her hands.

"He doesn't need to do this," Harper said. "If he knows where that damned thing is, we'll go—"

"Be still!" Nazipha snapped, bringing her weapon up and snapping back the bolt.

"Get that thing out of my face," Harper snarled, "or I'll make you eat it."

Nazipha backed away two steps.

Markelov reappeared in the hatch with the heavy aluminum electronics case in his hands. Belenko was right behind him. "Commander Donovan, I presume you have a map that shows the Valley of the L'al?"

Harper's ears pricked. "Forget it," she said. "We've already rigged it. We went up and down that valley this afternoon. Better come up with something better."

A look of doubt flitted across Belenko's face. "You have . . . you've been there?"

Donovan saw in Belenko's expression the first signs of a break in his resolve. "Look, if you want to go take that nuke out, fine. There's no need to hijack us to do it. Give us what you know and we'll look anyplace you think is worth looking. That's why we showed up in this hole, remember? And Belenko," Donovan said, "I'd say you need a little medical attention."

Belenko glanced at his upper arm. The bandage was beginning to drip onto the deck. "No, I don't believe you. We will go to the place Nazipha was told . . ." He gritted his jaw tight and shook his head. "Why do I bother explaining? We will do as I say."

"What if we decide not to listen?" Harper challenged.

"An excellent question. If I must, I will shoot one of you and then another. Eventually somebody will change his mind. It usually works."

"I don't think you get it, Belenko," said Donovan. "We're a team, and we work together or we don't work at all. This is a mighty big airplane as it is for a small crew to handle. You subtract even one of us and it's not going to happen. Period."

"Fuckin' aye," said Chief Svoboda from behind the door.

Belenko raised his one white eyebrow. "Very well. If I cannot subtract, I can at least divide." He stepped back and snatched a fat roll of medical tape from the kit, his eyes never wavering from Donovan's. He shoved Markelov down into a seat. "For your comfort and safety," he said to him as he wrapped the bandages round and round, mummy-fashion, pinning him. When he was done and Markelov could barely breathe, he looked up. "Nazipha, you watch the woman." He nodded at Harper. "Shoot her if you need to, or if the other two so much as lean on that door. Is that clear, gentlemen?" When there was no answer, he pounded on the door to the head.

"We hear you," said Svoboda.

"Shall we?" Belenko said to Donovan.

"No, sir," said Donovan, his arms crossed over his barrel chest. "That's not going to work at all. I'll say it again. Either we fly as a crew or we stay right here. And that"—he nodded at the .45 in Belenko's hand—"is not going to change the situation one bit. You can blow us all to hell, but it won't move your ass one foot off the runway. You want to fly? Then I call the shots. Otherwise, you might as well start flapping your arms. It's your choice."

Markelov strained out a smile. "You are checkmated," he croaked. "Fool."

Belenko's face suddenly looked very pale. He was sweating despite the cool night air. *Not much time,* he thought. "Very well, Commander." He swiped his brow with his sleeve. "You have made your point." He walked beyond Donovan. "Order your men out."

"Sasha!" said Nazipha. "If you—"

"Don't worry."

"Tacco! Chief!" called Donovan. "Come on out."

"Slowly," Belenko added. The door to the head cracked open, then swung wide.

Lieutenant Carranza was first. "I'm sorry, Commander. I thought that fucker was out cold. We were wrapping a bandage on the bastard when—"

"Don't sweat it, Tacco," said Donovan. "Chief? Let's play it the way Mr. Belenko here says."

"Very good. I'll be with you in the cockpit," Belenko said to Donovan. "Nazipha will stay behind to make sure your crew carries out your very wise orders. And Pavel, it would be most unwise to test her. I don't think she likes you very much at all. I wonder why?"

"You think I care what a woodchip thinks?"

"No, but I think you might care what a woodchip with an RPK might decide to do." Belenko weaved over to the open hatch and kicked the boarding ladder off. It smashed to the tarmac twenty feet below. "The door, please," he said to Svoboda.

"Button us up, Chief," said Donovan. The hatch swung out and latched tight with a spin of its handle. The chief seemed ready to take a bite out of anyone who came too close.

Donovan saw the tension in Svoboda's neck. He was like a spring-loaded device ready to snap. "Take it easy, Chief. We're going on a little flight, then we all walk."

Svoboda glared at Belenko. "Right."

"Come on, Lieutenant," Donovan said to Harper.

"Right behind you, sir," she replied, following Donovan forward. She walked by Belenko. She caught him looking down and away, a strange glazed expression plastered on his pallid skin. *Time may just be on our side,* she thought.

Suddenly, he looked up, his eyes widening, then coming back into focus. "Move." Belenko herded Carranza and Svoboda behind the two pilots to their stations. When they were both seated, he went aft to retrieve Markelov's detonator case.

"You will die," Markelov announced with a sad shake of his head.

"Probably," Belenko replied, and took the detonator forward. He placed it on Svoboda's console and opened it. "I understand you can sense the presence of nuclear weapons at some distance?"

"Me? No," said Svoboda. "I'm just the cook."

"Tell me, cook, can you operate this?"

"That? I made better boxes in high school, pal."

"No doubt you did. Show me."

Donovan settled into the front left seat. Harper took the right. She looked behind to be sure Belenko was out of earshot. "You think there's something to what Belenko said? About drugs?"

"All I know is I have a bunch of armed crazies running around my aircraft," said Donovan. "The rest kind of pales by comparison."

"Belenko says the nuke's up at the head of the Bamian Valley. We really gonna run up there again?"

"How's our fuel? We didn't top off after we recovered this afternoon."

"Enough," she whispered as she buckled into her restraint harness. "We have the fuel for an out and back, but not if we have to go anywhere else. It's dark out there, Commander. We go fooling around some unlit pea patch, we might roll this thing up in a big ball. Either way, we'll need to fly a max conserve profile. And what then? Where will he want to go afterwards?"

Donovan looked behind and lowered his voice. "Don't sweat it. We aren't getting that far. He's bleeding pretty good. How long do you think—"

"Probably long enough, but sir?" Harper pointed at the control panel overhead. Her polished fingernail tapped the cabin pressure wheel. It established the oxygen content of the *Grape*'s cabin while flying at high altitude.

Donovan nodded. "Just what I was thinking." His eyes went to the oxygen mask hanging on the rear cockpit bulkhead. He glanced back and saw Belenko standing just aft of

Svoboda's Sniffer station. "I think a slow cabin bleed at altitude would do it," he whispered.

"No probs, sir," said Harper with a grin. But it quickly faded. "Commander?" she asked as Donovan tightened up his shoulder belts. "What if the thing is really out there?"

"What thing?"

"The nuke. Suppose Belenko is right?"

"Lieutenant, I had an old track coach who gave me some good advice about a hundred years ago: *take the hurdles one at a time.* That's how we're all going to make it tonight. One jump at a time, okay?"

"Well?" demanded Belenko. The pistol was in his hands as he pushed his way through the cockpit curtains. He turned and saw both Carranza and Svoboda, each in their seats, glaring back at him. He raised the gun for emphasis and let the curtains fall closed. "What is the delay?"

"Relax," said Harper with a scowl. "You want us to rush and forget something?"

Belenko grabbed the spare headset and held it up to one ear, nodding for Donovan to begin.

"Turn 'em up, Lieutenant," said Donovan. "We have an anxious passenger."

She clicked the cabin intercom to life. "Crew, comm check."

"We're with you, Hot Dog," said Svoboda. "You got that sneaky bastard up there? He wants me to blow the nuke if I get a twitch. What do I do?"

"We're working on it, Chief. And be advised the bastard is on the party line. How about it, Tacco?"

"I'm here," he said sullenly.

"Check is complete." Harper's fingers brought on the auxiliary power unit. The APU whined beneath the flightdeck, its sound building to a roar. "Is that embassy car clear?" she asked, looking over Donovan and down to the ramp.

"Clear," said Donovan. "The driver—"

"Is dead. Starting one." Harper toggled on the main power bus and hit the autolite for the first engine. Soon, all four were spinning up at idle. She switched on the red anticollision beacon high atop the *Grape*'s vertical stabilizer.

Belenko belted himself into the jump seat behind the two pilots, watching the red light sweep the ramp below. "Can you hear me?" he said into the boom mike.

"We hear you," said Donovan.

"Then listen to me. One of you will fly, and the other will point on the map where we are. I warn you, I am very good with maps. If something doesn't look right, the least little thing, I will be most unhappy. Is that clear?"

"Clear," said Donovan. "Lieutenant," he said to Harper, "once we're airborne, you keep a running nav log for our guest here. But Belenko, if I need her, she does what I say. Understood?"

Belenko nodded. "I think we understand each other quite well, Commander." *Just a little longer,* he thought. *Just a little bit longer.*

The Baluchi stood at the mouth of the Cave of the Sleepers, staring up at the summer constellations. Just over the line of mountains on the far side of the valley, the Scorpion clawed its way into the velvet sky, its stinger down below the eastern horizon, embedded in Kabul. The Cave was a splendid hideout. He regretted their having to move. But a U.S. Navy airplane droning directly overhead was not a good sign. The ruined fort at Khadir, left over from the time of Alexander the Great, would be safer now. The Russian had seen to it.

The stars seemed like hot sparks rising from a campfire, some silver, some gold, others hard, cold blue. There was a purity here above the Valley of the L'al, one he would miss in Kabul. Did the Prophet Himself spend such nights on the Arabian desert, looking up, wishing that the angels had never come?

A cool wind fell from the high crags, disturbing the rotors on the three helicopters parked near the Cave's mouth. He could hear the voices of their pilots as they prepared the machines for the dawn run to Khadir.

"What a beautiful night God has given to us. So peaceful."

The Baluchi turned. It was Gulbuddin Hekmatyar, the leader of the radical *Hezb*. The darkness softened his stringy, chiseled features. But his eyes glittered like splinters of ice, quick, appraising. Hungry. "The weapon?" asked the Baluchi.

"Resting with the mummies," said Hekmatyar.

"You mean the Companions of the Cave."

"Well, they look like mummies, don't they? Wrapped in cloth and stacked like wood. Even the dog." Hekmatyar's laugh was high and strange. Down in the valley, a wild dog yipped and howled.

"Respect their power, if not their truth," the Baluchi said as he took the PNV-57 low-light goggles from beneath his robe, switched them on, and peered through them. The landscape became a strange, alien green. The starlight was intensified by the Soviet-made gear, clearly showing the ZSU antiaircraft guns and their crews. He faced the helicopters. The two Mi-24 gunships seemed like giant black cats poised to leap at prey. They would guard the smaller troopship that would transport the bomb to Khadir. "The misbelievers say that all of history is the work of accident. But look how events have transpired. What better proof of the hand of God? It's so peaceful tonight."

Hekmatyar smiled. His teeth glistened. "The world will not see another like it for a long time."

"Insh'Allah," the Baluchi agreed. "God willing."

17

—

THE DISASTER

"Through ten thousand," said Harper. She eyed the cabin pressure controller. She tapped the gauge. "Sir?" she said to Donovan. "Pressure's not holding. I think we have some holes in the skin."

"Probably a bunch of them," said Donovan, remembering the burst of gunfire on the Kabul ramp. "We'll have to go to masks above twelve if it doesn't stop." *Damn,* he thought. *We can't put our passengers to sleep if we're all wearing masks.*

"I'll run it up full and see if it balances out." Her worried look told Donovan that she had reached the same conclusion. If the crew had to don oxygen masks, then so would Belenko and the woman.

"There is some problem?" said Belenko.

"Not yet," Donovan answered.

Belenko squinted at the chart unfolded on Harper's lap, then out the window, then back again. "I don't see any mountains," he said suspiciously. Carranza's .45 automatic was cradled in his lap. His face was slick with sweat despite the chilly cockpit.

"Count your blessings, Belenko," said Harper.

The cockpit windows seemed coated with thick, black paint as they climbed toward the mountains. Only by craning her neck and peering straight up through the eyebrow windows could she see the stars. "Through eleven." Harper's flight display showed them climbing strongly to the west. *Thank God,* she thought. The firefight hadn't hit anything vital. It was a miracle.

To the right of the engine display, the ground-mapping radar showed a God's-eye view. They were closing in on the high mountains of the Ghowerband Range.

"Dark," said Donovan nervously. He leaned far forward and looked up. The stars blazed supernaturally bright overhead, but the sudden motion of his head gave him a cold, premonitory feeling of vertigo. With the black ground and the star-powdered sky, it was as if they were flying inverted over a great, lit city.

"Through twelve," she said. They were already over the outlying bulwarks of the Ghowerbands. In the distance, a milky white cone appeared: the fifteen-thousand-foot summit of the range. She inched her throttles forward as an invisible downdraft ate into their climb.

"Cabin altitude is holding, sir," she said, pointing at the overhead gauge. The leakage through the bulletholes puncturing the *Grape*'s skin was now balanced by the rush of pressurized air from the four engines.

"Is the . . . device ready?" Belenko said, his words sounding slightly slurred.

"I'll check." Harper pressed the intercom button on her yoke. "Chief, how goes it?"

"I show a green board on the nose and a green board on my weapons panel, Flight," Svoboda replied.

"No, the detonator," Belenko said, shaking his head to clear it. "The box. Markelov's box."

"Stand by. Through fourteen thousand," said Harper, eyeing an ice-clad mountain loom out of the inky black. She hit the intercom again. "Chief, our passenger wants to know about the detonator."

"Tell him to come play with it himself. I have the Russian box patched in to a transmit jack," said Svoboda. "It's some kind of a burst transmitter, but mega-crude. It uses a tape reel, if you can believe it."

"Will it work?" asked Donovan.

"I didn't build the sucker. I . . . wait a minute!" Svoboda suddenly stopped. "Flight!" he said, his voice full of surprise. "You aren't gonna believe this. I'm picking up a signal out ahead. Max range."

"What kind?"

"Damn! I think the nose is onto something! Stand by. It's still on the outer range ring. Let me clear it. . . . I'll be damned. Hard target! Vector two six zero. Range is about one twenty. I'll nail it in a minute."

Belenko heard the interchange. "How far to the L'al Valley?"

"Another hundred miles." Harper checked their ground speed. "We'll overfly it in about fifteen minutes."

Belenko listened. "Time enough." He unstrapped himself from the jump seat. "You want to destroy the bomb?"

"Yes," said Donovan.

"Good. So do I. Don't turn around while I am in the back."

"Don't worry, Belenko," said Donovan. "I told you the truth. We're here to find that weapon, too. You didn't need to hijack us to . . ."

Belenko slowly stood. "I know you wouldn't want any harm to come to your crew. And I promise you. If you turn, something might happen. Markelov told you I was crazy?"

"He did."

"Believe him," said Belenko as he pushed open the cockpit curtain and staggered aft.

Svoboda was head down over his CRT. The big display showed seven horizontal lines; but the eighth was no longer flat. A small, steep hill had appeared. The printer began to chatter. Svoboda tore off the message. A grin spread across his face as he read it. "Flight? We got it, sir. And it's a big mutha. Range is down to ninety."

Markelov's detonator was at Svoboda's feet. A coaxial cable plugged it into a spare transmit receptacle on the nuclear detection gear's console. Belenko walked aft.

"Belenko!" shouted Markelov. "Get me out of this thing!" He was still fastened tight to his seat with bandages. His normally sallow face looked red and tight, a balloon about to burst. "We can still work something out. You and me."

Nazipha stood back from him, the machine gun still in her hands.

"How do you feel?" he asked her.

"I can do what I have to."

"What about it, Aleks?" Markelov prompted. "Can we strike a bargain? A deal? There's time."

"Certainly," said Belenko. "How about this one: you make sure the detonator is functioning properly, and I don't kill you. Interested?"

"Go fuck yourself." Markelov looked away, a haughty disdain on his face. "You can't afford to kill me. I'm your ticket home."

"Home. Where is that?" said Belenko. "You know I cannot return to Kabul. And Russia? Even worse. Who would believe a rogue OSNAZ against the word of the esteemed MAYAK representative?"

"You need help, Aleks. Mine." Markelov glanced up. Hopeful.

"Perhaps. But tell me. I'm confused. We are close to the bomb. You know it. I know it. You don't seem very happy. Why?"

"Tied up with a woodchip holding a machine gun? You want happiness?"

"Still. I wonder," said Belenko, moving close. "Could it be that destroying the bomb will not make you a hero at MAYAK? That arranging for an old OSNAZ to come, to fail, to go through the motions of making an earnest effort, that all of that will now come undone if we actually succeed?" He searched Markelov's face.

"You have no idea what you have done."

"You tell me."

Markelov looked as if he were being forced to lecture a dull child. "You're the Islamic expert. Answer your own question. You want the world to be eaten up by chaos? A hundred little countries splitting, resplitting themselves like germs? You want that? You said it yourself in Moscow. We need a glue. One man. One voice that speaks for all the Moslem lands. *That* we can live with. Do business with. Not chaos."

Suddenly, there it was. "You sold the weapon to them."

Markelov shook his head sadly. "What if we did? Look, we can still come to an agreement. Consider it, Sasha. A job. Comfort. Your life. Who will offer you that much again?"

Belenko stared down at Markelov. "Lenin was right. People like you. Like your MAYAK. They'll sell the hangman a new rope, even with one foot on the gallows."

"We could work together. In Geneva. On a number of—"

"No thanks, Pavel. I'm old-fashioned. And I already have a job to do. Now, about the destruct device. Is it functional? Or just a sham?"

"Go fuck yourself. You're so smart. You go push the

button. Live with yourself if you can." Markelov turned to face away from him.

"I will, Pavel Ivanovich," said Belenko, "because I can."

The Baluchi watched the helicopter crews prepare their machines for the flight to the remote hideout at Khadir. Four guards stood watch over the bomb container at the mouth of the cave. Even from here, the Baluchi could see the red light on its case winking. A spotlight played across the helicopter landing pad. The yawning mouth of the Cave of the Sleepers was wreathed in shadow, a black backdrop against which the three helicopters stood out in stark contrast. The Mi-8 seemed squat, a partridge nestled in between the two gunship hawks.

The Baluchi turned away. He could hear the voices of the men at the two ZSU-23 antiaircraft guns. A match flared, revealing a face, then died away. The guns were pointed up into the empty sky, but he could hear the excitement in their voices. He squinted into the yellow flood of the spotlight. He suddenly turned, listening. The voices of the guards echoed from the rock walls around them. What was that? He listened. "Silence!" he shouted. The voices fell away, one by one.

"Aircraft!" screamed one of the ZSU-23 gunners. "Aircraft!"

"Range twenty," said Svoboda. "The nose is getting a tight fix, sir," he said to Donovan. "Come right to two niner zero. Showing a hundred-and-fifty-KT boomer."

"Two niner zero," Donovan repeated. "What about weapons effects?"

"Like the biggest Fourth of July you ever saw, sir. Mountains will break up the fireball. Shock wave will be unpredictable, too. But we should be safe outside ten miles and headed away. We'd be even safer home in bed."

"Amen," said Carranza. "I show a whole bunch of nasty terrain up ahead."

"I don't see a damned thing out there," said Harper, her nose nearly pressed to the windscreen glass.

"If the chief is right, and Markelov's box works," said Donovan, "it's gonna get hot around here in a few minutes."

"Flight, Tacco here. The valley heads due west." Carranza watched the outlines of the high mountains shift on his big scope. "That puts our target up in the hills. We have high terrain in all quadrants. We'll be inside small-arms range if we don't climb."

"Roger, Tacco," Donovan said as he banked the big patrol plane away from the walls of the Valley of the L'al. The wings fell through thirty degrees, then forty, before Donovan caught them and brought the *Grape* back into a standard-rate turn.

"Take it easy with those maneuvers," warned Harper. "There are some serious mountains off the nose."

"I'm glad you're flying with me, Hot Dog."

"Remember? One hurdle at a time."

"I know." Donovan wiped his brow dry with the back of his flightsuit sleeve. "Be ready to take it. It's goddamned black out there and my instrument scan's rusty as hell. Just keep your eye on things and backstop me, okay?"

"No sweat, sir," she said with a nod. "You're doing just fine."

"Range ten."

"Ah, Flight?" said Svoboda. "Nose here. If we're really gonna set this thing off, we don't want to be this close."

"That's a roger," said Tacco. "We'll probably get zapped with EMP if we're near enough for that Russian detonator to work, too." The electromagnetic pulse could shut down the P-3's electronics. It would make the bolt of lightning that had struck them over Japan seem like static cling.

"He's right." Harper saw the fuel display turn a warning amber. "Fuel's going to be critical, too. One pass is all we get. We should be on the ground at Kabul right now."

"Understood," said Donovan. "One pass overhead to confirm, then we'll circle back at max power. I want to be headed away from it when Belenko pushes his button. You sure he'll wait until we give the word?"

"If he values his ass, he will," said Harper.

"That's what worries me. Chief? I want you to shut everything down on my signal. I just hope the EMP pulse doesn't fry us."

"You got it, sir," said Svoboda. Belenko sat next to him in the spare Sniffer operator's seat. Nazipha stood to one side, the RPK still in her grip. "We're going in," Svoboda told the Russian. "You keep your finger off that damned button until I say so, unless you want to wind up crispy-crittered."

Donovan pushed back from the yoke, signaling for Harper to take over. He'd felt tendrils of vertigo seeping into his brain, corroding his confidence.

"I have the airplane," said Harper as she scanned the instruments. "Sir, if that thing is really down there, they may not be so damned pleased with us cruising on by."

"What do you suggest, Lieutenant?"

"The nose says we have a hit. Markelov says we have to be inside ten klicks—"

"That's six nautical miles, give or take," said Donovan. "So?"

"So I say, let's bend south and keep a safe distance from the Sniffer's datum. Then we can circle back at high speed, just like you said, and hit the button at max range, eastbound. Why give them a target to shoot at?"

Donovan nodded. "You're right." She banked the patrol plane left.

"Flight, Nose here. Steer three zero five for an overhead pass."

"Negative, Chief. This isn't a rigging run," said Donovan. "It's for real. We're going to keep our distance." He stared off in the direction Svoboda had just suggested. *What?* A pinpoint of yellow light flickered slightly right of their course. "Look!" he said, tapping Harper on the shoulder.

She saw it, a star removed from its brethren and set against the walls of the L'al Valley.

"Flight, Tacco here. I may be picking up some structures out there, too." Carranza manipulated the controls on his radar. Something was offering a better, stronger return than merely rock. "Maybe some trucks, or vehicles of some kind. Passing off the wing."

"Damn!" Svoboda shouted. He retuned the Sniffer sensitivity. "I'm losing it!"

Belenko went to the porthole behind Carranza's cubicle and watched the tiny light march by off to their right. As he watched, the light suddenly winked out. "Where . . . ?"

"Radar range eight miles," said Carranza. "Passing off our three o'clock. Flight, the valley necks down out ahead. I'm painting steep terrain at twelve o'clock for fifteen. It's going to be a tight turn."

Harper hit the intercom button. "Chief, is our ESM up and running?"

"Roger, Hot Dog," he said, taking his eyes from the Sniffer display and checking over the defensive systems. "ESM is sweet. Chaff and flares are on auto, IR optics are armed, and my weapons show a ready board. But the target's faded out. I'm resetting the Sniffer—" He suddenly stopped. "Warning! Radar emissions at four o'clock! X-band! Gun directors!"

Belenko moved behind Svoboda, holding on to the back of his seat as he saw a multitude of red lights flash on the defensive system panel. "What has—"

"Shut up!" Svoboda hollered. "Flight! X-band radar has a lock! It's a Zeus! I say again—"

"Hang on!" Harper shoved all four throttles forward. The *Galloping Grape* surged ahead, her airspeed building through 250 knots as she dived into the narrowing valley. "Come on, Chief, jam that sucker!" Two loud thumps echoed through the cabin.

"ESM is dropping chaff!" shouted Svoboda as the plane jinked hard right. The computerized defensive systems were attempting to confuse the hostile radar with clouds of aluminum strands. "Jammer is on search mode!"

"Harper!" Donovan yelled as they dropped through eleven thousand. "Watch your altitude!"

"I've got it, I've got it." Harper put her tail to the threat and dived, the speed stiffening the Orion's controls as she sought to mix the *Grape*'s radar return with that of the far side of the valley's rim.

Suddenly, the sky was filled with a stream of fat green meteors. They seemed to rise at a leisurely pace, but by the time they blasted by, the globes had elongated into streaks of light. The shells corrected as they pursued the *Grape* down.

"Chief!" Donovan shouted. "Jam that Zeus!"

"I'm trying!" Svoboda's hands flew over his console, looking for the right combination of signals.

"Triple A is correcting! Look out! We're gonna get hit!"

Belenko saw the flash of the exploding shells brighten in Svoboda's porthole. It was now or never. He grabbed the detonator box, switched it on. A green light glowed. His finger poised above the button that would transmit the de-struct code.

Svoboda saw the motion from the corner of his eye. The Sniffer had lost the bomb, but he knew it was close. Too close. *Shit!* "No!" he yelled as he yanked the antenna lead out of the jack just as Belenko jammed his thumb down on the button. He gave the Russian a shove, forcing him back against the cabin bulkhead.

"Chief!" cried Harper as she jinked away from the fire. They were running out of altitude.

"That asshole almost—"

The stream of fire suddenly stopped.

"Jammer's got a lock!" Svoboda crowed. "We broke the bastard! We busted his chops, Hot Dog. That Russian tried to blow us away!"

The sounds of scuffling came over the intercom.

"Flight!" screamed Carranza. "Mountains at twelve o'clock! Turn! I mean, *climb!*"

Harper saw the red light blink on the radar altimeter even as the cliffs swept in on them from dead ahead. The digits held them at fifty feet over the rocks; forty, then thirty.

"It's a box canyon!" Carranza shouted.

"Hang on, everybody!" Harper jammed all four throttles to the stops and hauled back on the yoke. The *Grape* streaked skyward.

"Oh, Jesus," said Donovan as they went vertical.

The radar altimeter froze at twenty feet, then slowly it began to rise. Using the tremendous reserve of energy accu-mulated in their dive, Harper flew them up, up, and over, through the vertical and beyond. *Almost, almost.* As she felt the weight begin to shift, as her shoulder harness began to bite into her, she rolled the big patrol plane upright with a swift, sure motion. They were now heading directly at the Cave.

"Flight . . . was . . . that . . ." stammered Carranza. "Did we . . . did we just . . ."

"Chief, you okay back there?" asked Harper.

"Christ, Hot Dog!" Svoboda said. "You just rolled us . . . hang on. We have a problem back here. Our passengers got bounced around some. I think . . . stand by. That son of a bitch tried to . . . never mind. They're all back in the tail in a furball. You want I should crack the hatch and toss their asses out?"

"Negative! You still have the detonator?"

"Bet your ass I do. I don't have a lock, but I stored the last datum. Range to the nuke is nine miles." Svoboda replugged the antenna lead back into the transmit jack. "We're set. Nobody's pushing anything but me."

"Hang on to it, Chief," Harper said as she roared in low and fast toward the stolen Russian warhead. "When I say so, I want you to punch that detonator good and hard." She shoved all four throttles to the stops. "We're gonna burn those bastards down."

"You got it, Hot Dog. Range six." Svoboda looked aft toward the tail. The two hijackers had been thrown hard against the aft wall and knocked out. Markelov was still in his seat, saved by the swaddling bandages that kept him pinned in place. Was that someone's arm moving? Svoboda was about to hit the intercom to tell Harper when an alarm went off on the defensive panel. *Oh, shit.* "Flight! I have radar again." He threw a switch and listened hard, analyzing the pattern of sound coming through his headset. "This one's different. Not X-band. More like a terrain-mapping set. And we are passing four miles to the datum."

"Okay, Chief," said Harper. "We should be far enough out of gun range on this pass. Keep—"

"Flight!" Tacco broke in. "Aerial target eleven o'clock and three miles, maneuvering!"

"Maneuvering?" Harper swept the dark terrain, but there was no way to pick out anything.

"Bogey at eleven for twelve! We have one target, range two and level. Repeat: we have a bogey out there. He's slow, but he's flying."

"The old DC-3?" said Donovan. "Maybe they're running for it."

"With the nuke on board?"

"Target confirmed! Making two hundred over the ground," said Carranza.

"We're looking," said Harper. The night was unbroken by any light except the arching dome of stars. A bright flash appeared slightly to their left. *Gunfire?*

Suddenly, a sharp clanging alarm bell vibrated through the *Grape*, loud enough to be heard through Harper's headset.

"Missile in the air!" shouted Svoboda. "Missile in the air!" The ESM computer, moving at the speed of light, had already catalogued it: on Svoboda's console, the letters *IR* glowed. "Chaff's away! Flares away!" The infrared deceiving optics mounted above and below each engine were now trying to confuse the heat-seeking missile bearing down on them. "Still tracking!"

"I see it!" Harper saw the brilliant white dot of sparking light curve up at her from nearly dead ahead. She yanked the yoke and the *Galloping Grape* banked up hard on her right wing. Two dazzling flashes erupted from behind as the magnesium flares began to burn.

"Mile and a half. Still guiding." *Come on,* Svoboda urged the defensive system. *One more time.* The *OBL* light flickered on his panel, then went off. "Come on. Come on."

The supersonic AA-8 burned in, seemingly oblivious to

the seductive whisper of the heat prisms or the distracting dazzle of the flares. Against the cold night sky, the *Galloping Grape*'s thermal image was large and strong. As the range closed, all eight heat prisms turned their attention on the AA-8's glass eye.

"It's starting to turn!" yelled Svoboda.

The *OBL* light came on and stayed on.

"Here it comes," said Donovan, bracing himself once more. "It's gonna be—"

The AA-8's warhead detonated with a stroboscopic flash, fifty feet under the *Grape*'s left wing. A watch-spring cloud of debris exploded outward, rattling the *Grape* with a hail of metal fragments. A red light came on underneath the turbine-temperature display for the outboard engine as the fuselage bucked through the turbulence. The interturbine temperature kept right on climbing.

"Damage to one!"

"Shut it down!" Harper commanded.

Donovan reached overhead, pulled the leftmost fire handle, and hit the autofeather switch. The huge paddle blades on the outboard engine began to slow, and the temperature stopped its dangerous rise and began to ebb. The red warning light blinked out.

"God damn you," Harper cursed their invisible attacker. "Chief! Master Arm on! Give me the Snakes!"

"Master Arm is on, your control. Missiles are hot."

"Harper!" said Donovan. "You can't fight us out of here! We're still faster than he is. Even on three engines. Let's get the—"

"The hell I can't. That bandit just flipped a missile at us. I don't think it was a real friendly thing to do." Harper could hear the growl of the seeker head over her headset. The Sidewinder's tone suddenly shifted, becoming louder, more insistent. She reached over to the center console, flipped up the trigger guard, and selected the starboard Snake. *Do it,* she said by way of a prayer, and punched the launch button twice.

The starboard Sidewinder kicked free of its rail out on the right wing and ignited in a flash of heat and smoke. It lanced out and dropped, curving slightly as it went. The bright exhaust diminished to a hot point of light as it guided itself toward their attacker.

Harper watched, mesmerized by the flight of the Sidewinder through the night sky. "Now that," she said, "is poetry in motion."

"And we're passing abeam the last stored datum of the nuke," said Svoboda as he shot a quick look at the Sniffer display. It still was blank. Had something failed?

"Overlap!" shouted Carranza.

In the sky ahead, a fatal flash erupted into an angry orange sphere of burning jet fuel. The stricken craft arced down like a comet trailing flaming fuel. It struck in a second detonation, this one lanced with the white streamers of exploding munitions.

"Splash one," said Harper. "Chief, stand by on that box. We're getting the hell out—"

"Look out! Missile in the air!"

The gunship had fired a second AA-8 an instant before it died. From the heart of the cloud of debris, a small dot of light was growing brighter.

"Block it!" Harper shouted as she banked away. "Come on, Chief. You can do it." Two flashes came from behind them, then a third, a fourth, as the flares dropped away.

Svoboda's hands danced across the defensive systems panel. The starboard heat prisms were dark! "Turn to one eight zero! We gotta unmask the port prisms!"

Harper yanked them into a savage turn to the south.

Svoboda jammed his palm down on the flare release. "Flares away! Chaff's away!"

It was coming too fast. The turn was too late. The bright spark was coming right at them, faster, faster. "Here it comes," said Harper. "Hold on . . ."

The AA-8's proximity fuse detonated ten feet under the *Grape*'s left wing, midway between the two engines. The hot fragments pierced her fuel tanks. The fire was almost instantaneous.

"Fire! Fire!" shouted Carranza. His porthole was lit with the yellow flames of burning kerosene.

"Emergency handle!"

Donovan reached up and pulled the shutdown control to the remaining engine on the crippled left wing and a moment later punched the Halon gas release. "Bottles away!"

"Not gonna do it," Harper said. The fire continued, fed not by the turning engines but by the thousands of punctures in the fuel tank. Already they were settling toward the invisible ground. There was no more what if. A crash was as preordained as sunrise. She hit the ditching bell. "Crew! Prepare to ditch!" It mattered not one bit that the nearest ocean was a thousand miles away. The *Galloping Grape*, streaming a banner of fire, was going down.

"Give me lights!" she said, ramming forward the two throttles that still controlled undamaged engines. The *Grape* slewed drunkenly under the imbalanced power, but Harper's boots shot out and ruddered them back straight. "Commander!" she repeated. "Get the gear and the lights!"

"What?" Had Donovan heard her right? He was stunned, his face already hot with the reflected fire burning up their left wing.

"Gear and lights! Landing lights!" When he didn't react, she yanked the landing gear handle out and down. As the wheels dropped free of the wells, she hit the landing lights.

They were already low; horribly low. The terrain streaked by not fifty feet under their nose. A rock garden of boulders and dry gulches whizzed past. She knew they would never survive a collision with them. They would bounce, cartwheel, and it would be over. "Flaps!"

"Coming down," said Donovan, finally free enough of his shock to act. The *Grape* ballooned up as the big flaps dropped and locked.

"Look!" There was a flat area at the very edge of the landing light's beam. The *Grape* swept over a braided maze of dry gulches, and then, square in their beam, the tail of an airplane. She hauled back on the yoke, trading her meager store of airspeed for one last bit of altitude.

"It's the gooney bird!" Donovan saw the start of the rough runway just beyond. "Hold it! Hold it! Just a little bit more! Hold it!"

"Engines! Shut 'em down!" she called. "Power off! Everyone lock in tight! We're gonna—"

There was one shriek of protest, one metallic scream of tortured metal before the impact collapsed the left main gear. The damaged wing scraped the ground, bending up, then snapping off the entire structure from the outermost engine to the tip. The flaming debris arced overhead, tumbling, tumbling, pursuing the fuselage down the dirt airstrip. Both engines broke free of their mounts, and streaming fire in their wake, bounced down ahead of the disintegrating patrol plane.

The Orion began to swing sideways, snapping off the nose gear, dropping the cockpit to the ground, furrowing the dust with the *Grape*'s proud purple nose. The windshield shattered, showering Donovan and Harper with glass and admitting a choking cloud of fine grit. A boulder field hurtled out of the darkness. She shot her arm out to keep Donovan from flying forward, only to discover his own.

They linked arms, then hands, as the fire-lit rocks suddenly rushed them.

Still moving at over thirty knots, the crumpled fuselage smashed into a boulder, nosed under, and tumbled onto its back.

The *Galloping Grape* was dead.

"You see?" said the Baluchi as he trained his night goggles on the flaming trail of wreckage below. "As I said. What is there left now to fear?"

"They killed one of the helicopters," said Hekmatyar. "The Americans are full of surprises. I don't like surprises. What if they send more planes to look for this one?"

"We will be elsewhere." The Baluchi turned, a smile of such intensity on his face that the guerrilla commander could hardly imagine what he was thinking. The fiery destruction of the intruder seemed to give him an almost sexual pleasure. "Come," he said, "and let us go down and see what new gifts God has brought."

18

THE SPOILS

It was cold; he could hear his heart now. It was strangely, strangely loud, and terribly fast. And then he heard a voice.

". . . on, sir. We have to get out." Harper tugged at him gently. She played a flashlight across his face.

The flash made him open one eye. "Where . . ." he started, his iris constricting to a black pinpoint against the beam.

"Thank God," said Harper. "Come on. I can't move you by myself."

Donovan stirred. He looked around at the hanging wires, the shattered glass. Where the devil was he? He tried to move himself, but his right arm refused to obey. He was looking up, but wasn't that a rudder pedal? Why was the floor above him? He rolled his eye back down. Two shattered eyebrow windows reflected Harper's flashlight.

"Commander!" The voice carried an unmistakable authority. "We have to get free of the wreck! Move it!"

Wreck? "Who wrecked? What do . . ." He stopped. Then it all came back, hurtling through Donovan's memory like a tidal wave. "Jesus," he muttered, and then tried to move. "I'm hooked on something. Harper? Is that . . . ?"

"Come on, Commander. It's time to start walking. There's an airplane parked at the far end of the strip and I plan to fly it. We have to skedaddle before anybody comes looking for us."

"I can't move my arm."

"That's because your weight is on it." She turned and looked behind to where the cockpit curtain used to be. Where Carranza and Svoboda had had their consoles there was now only black sky, stars, and flickering fire-light.

Donovan reached up with his free hand and grabbed a fistful of wires. He pulled himself off his right side, slithered out from under the deformed seat, and fell onto the cockpit ceiling. He struck the padding, but oddly he felt no pain, just a dull, general ache as though his body had been caught in heavy surf, tumbled end for end, and spit out onto the beach. The stink of kerosene was everywhere, biting and sharp as the icy air.

Harper wedged her boots under the instrument panel and hauled him to his feet. He swayed, dizzy, and then steadied. "Okay," she said. "We're going to get down off this damned rock and see about my crew. Then we're gonna take that gooney bird out of here."

"Gooney bird?"

"I'll explain later. You're in shock. Come on." Walking on the cockpit ceiling, she led him like a blind man to the lip of an eight-foot drop. The cockpit had cracked off the end of the P-3's fuselage, leaving the main cabin on its belly.

"Easy," she said as he teetered on what had been the fuselage joint between the cockpit and the cabin.

Three orange bonfires lit up the night, glinting ruby off

the crumpled metal of the *Galloping Grape*'s cabin. They marked the final resting place of three of the P-3's four engines. "Svoboda," Donovan said under his breath as his eyes followed the twisted aluminum to the tail. Then he heard it. The heavy *thump thump thump* of a helicopter.

"Commander!" Harper called. A stab of white light arrowed down from the helicopter's searchlight, playing across the gash left in the earth by the P-3's crash.

She looked back along the wreck to the emergency hatch. It was closed. The aft cabin was intact. The *Grape*'s proud tail was whole, although the vertical stabilizer leaned at an unfamiliar angle with the elevators resting on the ground. The energy of the crash had all been absorbed by the forward cabin.

She flashed a light back into the cabin. "Chief?" she called. "Carranza?" Her voice was swallowed by the incredible jumble of wires and metal panels filling the wrecked cabin. A scratching sound came from somewhere in the heart of the mess. She pulled away a seat that had been ripped from its rails. There he was. "Chief!"

"Hey," said Svoboda with a weak smile that quickly faded into a grimace of pain. His legs were pinned beneath the collapsed Sniffer console. "Suckered us, Hot Dog. I'm . . . I'm real sorry. I did my best. I did . . ."

"Hang in there, Chief," she said, yanking the broken seat away by its roots and tossing it out of the cabin. "We're gonna get out of this hole."

The whine of the helicopter was growing loud as, together, Donovan and Harper levered up the console, allowing Svoboda to crawl out to freedom.

"Thanks," he said. "I busted something, I think." The

searchlight swung nearer, the machine sidestepping its way closer, closer.

"Carranza!" Donovan called into the wrecked cabin. There was no reply. He pulled at the fallen insulation, the spaghetti of tangled wires, working his way deeper into the fuselage. He saw a swatch of green Nomex under a bent fuselage frame. "Carranza!" He cut his hand on a jagged end of metal, but Donovan didn't feel it. He pulled at it, bending it back and forth, back and forth, until it snapped off. "Give me a light!" he called back.

Harper looked up at the helicopter's searchlight.

"Lieutenant!"

Harper moved up behind Donovan, handing him her flashlight.

"Christ," said Donovan softly as he held the beam on Lieutenant Carranza's hand. By reaching down into the opening he had cleared, he could just touch Carranza's skin. "Christ," he said again. There was no pulse.

"Commander," said Harper. "We don't have much time. Is he . . . ?"

"Dead," said Donovan, backing out of the cleared space. "Carranza's gone. We better get a move on ourselves."

"Hey, Hot Dog," called Svoboda. "You better come on out here quick." The helicopter was close. "If we're going someplace, I think it better be damned quick. And I hope we're flyin'. 'Cause I ain't walkin'.'"

The roar of the helicopter now left no doubt about where it was headed. There was little time left. Less.

Then there was none.

A flash of white light flooded the scene, freezing them in its hot beam. A hurricane of rotor wind blasted down out of the sky.

The two pilots stood next to Svoboda as the helicopter came to a thunderous hover not twenty feet away, its searchlight a blazing sun in their eyes. Donovan took Harper by the shoulders as a cloud of dust washed over them. "If you want to make a break for it, now's the time."

"No way, Commander. No way at all."

"So," said the Baluchi as the Mi-8 came to a hover above the crash site, "you see what we have caught?" He manipulated the spotlight's control, sweeping it across the broken fuselage. The focus of the beam came to rest on the words US NAVY. The wind kicked up by the chopper swung an open hatch back on its hinges, tearing it off and sending it flying through the air.

"I told you. It's an American airplane," said Hekmatyar. "I thought the fat Russian was going to—"

"It seems he failed us." The Baluchi shrugged. "Americans. Russians. What is the difference to us now? If it were the angel Gabriel himself, have we not destroyed it?" He pounded on the cockpit wall. "Land!"

The Mi-8 bumped down on one skid, then both. The Baluchi threw open the sliding hatch and motioned to the guards. Four armed *mujahedin* leaped out and hit the ground, their assault rifles leading the way. The two leaders stepped out of the idling Hip, ducked low beneath the slashing rotor blades, and followed the chopper's searchlight to the downed airmen.

Three guards held Donovan and Harper under their muzzles. Svoboda still sat on the edge of the broken cabin. He leaned back, his face gray in the white light.

"Search the front!" Hekmatyar ordered.

A guard checked out the shattered cockpit. "Empty!" he called back to the Baluchi, and then moved to search the cabin, running back to the hole where the emergency hatch had been and climbing up and inside. A shout came from within. Then another. The *mujahed* appeared at the open hatch. "Someone's alive!" he called out. Then like a prairie dog diving for cover, his head disappeared. In its place came another.

It was Markelov.

"Well," said Hekmatyar. "Were we not just speaking of this one?"

Markelov, pinned to the seat by bandages, had not suffered so much as a cut. He climbed up and out of the shattered cabin, the guard prodding him from behind.

"It would seem our arrangement with the Russian no longer holds," said the Baluchi as the guard herded Markelov to them.

"We didn't think you'd return so soon, Markelov," said Hekmatyar.

"Thank God!" said Markelov, brushing dirt off his leather jacket. "I thought I would be burned alive in there!"

"An interesting idea," said Hekmatyar. "It can yet be arranged. Why have you brought the Americans here?"

"What do you mean? I was a *prisoner*!" He turned to the guard who had found him. "Tell them! How did you find me?"

The guerrilla nodded. "He was tied to a seat."

Markelov turned back to face the crumpled tail. "Belenko is still in there!"

"The *rus* probably tied himself," said Hekmatyar suspiciously. "Who else could have told the Americans to look here? I tell you. He led them to us."

"Belenko!" Markelov cried. "It was Belenko and his whore!"

Hekmatyar nodded at the guerrilla standing by Markelov. "It seems the *rus* has made a new alliance. Silence him." A long blade flashed red in the firelight.

"No!" Markelov twisted away from the point of the

knife. "Nazipha Popol! She lived. Don't you understand? She lived! *And they are still inside the airplane!*"

The Baluchi and Hekmatyar exchanged quick glances.

"Wait!" the guerrilla leader ordered. "Let him live a while longer." He turned. "Put them all in the helicopter and then search the plane again. And then burn it."

The Baluchi watched as magnesium flares were broken out from the helicopter. With all the kerosene around, they would incinerate the wreckage, along with anyone unfortunate enough to be trapped inside. "The Russian might speak the truth," he said.

"The world is full of surprises."

"He has been helpful before."

"We paid him."

"It costs us nothing to find out."

Hekmatyar considered this. "True. And I know how it will be done," said Hekmatyar with a smile. He faced the terrified Russian. "Very well, Markelov. We will extend you our hospitality. Your tale could be amusing." He nodded at the fighter guarding the Russian. "Let him go." Markelov moved away from the flashing knife and stood next to the Baluchi.

A commotion came from the shattered stub of the plane's fuselage.

"Get away from me, you camel-humping—"

"Chief!" called Harper.

The *mujahed* motioned for Svoboda to stand.

"Sorry, Ahmed," said the chief. "I have a busted mainmount." He pointed to his knee. The guard prodded Svoboda in the ribs with the rifle for emphasis. The chief made a sudden grab for the gun, and he very nearly got it before the surprised guard stepped back and away. "Mind your popgun, or you're gonna lose it."

"He's injured!" Donovan called back. "Don't you understand? He can't walk!"

The Baluchi walked up to Svoboda. He saw the swelling underneath the torn flightsuit. "Kill him."

The guard slipped the AK onto single fire.

"Yeah?" sneered the chief. "What now? You want to play hide the—"

The guard shot him in the head from a distance of three feet.

"Chief!" Harper screamed. With the gun still at her back, she broke free and made a break for Svoboda, but she ran straight into one of the guards. He dropped his AK and grabbed her in a bear hug. His shock at her sudden motion turned to a different sort of surprise altogether as he felt her soft breasts against his chest. "*Bi-khuda!* This one is—"

He didn't get to finish the sentence. Harper rammed a knee up hard into his groin, and the guard's words dissolved into an explosive gasp. She shoved him away and spun, looking for an opening to run through. There was no place to go. The other guards had collected the dropped rifle and had formed a solid ring of steel around them. She turned to the nearest one, looking ready to take him apart.

"What is it?" asked Hekmatyar as he walked into the circle.

"This one . . ." gasped the man holding his groin, "this one is not . . . not a man."

The guerrilla chief's gaunt face split into a toothy grin. "Truly," he said as he walked straight up to Harper.

"No!" shouted Donovan as a *mujahed* grabbed Harper and pushed her to Hekmatyar. Brown's words burned like a brand into his memory: *You'll be the lucky one. They won't let her go to waste.*

"Do the *Amrikans* use young boys now in their airplanes?" Hekmatyar asked. He nodded to the guard. "Or are you something else?"

"No!" Donovan lunged, but one of the guards brought the stock of his AK up and delivered a hard blow to his stomach. It was enough to send him to his knees.

"This one is female," Markelov said. "Her name is Harper. She's a pilot."

"Son of a bitch," Donovan gasped. He looked at the Russian. "You know these people! You—" A second blow sent him sprawling to the dust.

"Commander!" Harper made a move, but one of the guards was faster. A kick to the back of one knee dropped her next to Donovan.

"A woman pilot?" asked Hekmatyar. Markelov nodded. "Let us see what you are," said Hekmatyar as he hauled her to her feet. He gave the order to the guard she had injured.

The *mujahed* smiled a vicious little smile and grabbed the neck of her flightsuit. But before he could rip it, Harper suddenly moved away from him, pulling his outstretched arm as she went. One of her arms formed a fulcrum at his elbow, the other smashed down hard on his wrist. Once again his AK-74 went flying. The guard's forearm bent backward and snapped with a loud, dry crack. He toppled with a bellow of shock and pain. Harper made a grab for the guard's fallen Kalashnikov. Her hand had closed around the stock when Hekmatyar's boot came down hard on her fingers. Someone grabbed her, yanking her hands behind her back. An assault rifle was jabbed into her neck.

The Baluchi stepped up. Svoboda's watch gleamed from his wrist. "What have you found?"

"A she-devil," said Hekmatyar. His eyes were glazed, hard and dangerous. "See for yourself."

The mullah stepped in front of her, his face inches from hers. "Let us see what sort of creature you are."

"I'm gonna see you dead," said Harper. "And you can take that to the bank."

In a flash of motion, the Baluchi reached up and yanked her flightsuit's zipper down, tearing the fastener free of the Nomex fabric and exposing her bra. Her chest rose and fell as her breathing came fast. Hekmatyar watched, silent at first, but then he began to laugh. "Perhaps Markelov will enjoy his stay with us tonight," he said, glancing at the Russian.

"So you are a female after all. I once knew one like you," said the mullah, knowing that his Dari was incomprehensible to the woman. "I called her Little Bird. She thought she could fly, but in the end, all she could do was fall. And so"—he swept his robed arm at the wreck of the *Galloping Grape*—"have you done any better?"

"Don't . . . don't let . . ." Donovan said between breaths.

"Put them in the helicopter," Hekmatyar ordered the guards. "And then set fire to the wreckage. Leave nothing for anyone to see." He gave a final lingering look in Harper's direction. He turned to Markelov. "Would you like her?"

Markelov's fear began to evaporate.

"Tell us everything," said Hekmatyar, "and she is yours."

Markelov nodded. It was only right. She had gotten in the way back at the airport. She had let Belenko hijack them here. He could be dead! It was only right. He turned to face the crumpled wreck of the patrol plane. "Be sure you burn it well. Burn it so not even a ghost might find his way out."

Hekmatyar pointed to the Mi-8 "Go. I have business to

attend to first. You!" he said to the injured guard. "Wait a moment."

"Markelov's in with these bandits," Donovan whispered to Harper as they were marched to the helicopter. She shook her head. Her hands were clasped to her neck, holding the torn flightsuit together. Donovan saw she was shaking. A soft *pop* came from behind them. Donovan stopped and turned. Before the guard behind shoved him along, he saw Hekmatyar standing over the body of the guerrilla with the broken arm, a wisp of gunsmoke dissipating.

Just then a hot white flare erupted from the crumpled fuselage. Burning fuel boiled up in an orange fireball.

"There she goes," Donovan whispered as the flames took hold. He was pushed up into the hatch after Harper.

Markelov climbed in next. He paused at the lip of the hatch; he turned toward the burning patrol plane. *Good-bye, Aleks,* he thought. *Good-bye.*

Finally, Hekmatyar appeared at the open hatch. He nodded at the three prisoners sitting on the floor of the Mi-8's cargo deck, the weapons of their guards at the ready. He turned to the black-robed mullah. "There are your devils. An old man, a frightened girl, and a Russian who will sell his soul to live another hour."

"We are in no position to keep hostages," the Baluchi observed as the turbines began to scream. The helicopter danced on its skids and lifted off.

"Hostages?" said Hekmatyar. He stared at Harper. "I prefer to think of them as the spoils of war."

Belenko watched as the helicopter's brilliant beam swept across the burning wreckage one last time and then winked out. He touched the cool metal of the detonator once more, just to reassure himself that it was still there.

The heavy pounding of the Hip's rotors fell away as the machine climbed, leaving only the sound of the wind whistling through jagged metal, the crackle of hot flames.

"It might not be safe here," warned Nazipha. "The weapon is large. One hundred and fifty kilotons."

"Safe?" The crash had spread the tail section by the most whimsical of chances. They had survived so much already. Now, alone with the means of achieving his mission, Belenko was not about to let a rogue atomic weapon stand in the way. He clicked the detonator's master switch on. The built-in battery powered a small green light.

"The burnout zone will be . . . ," she began, but Belenko stopped her with a gentle touch to her arm.

"Please." He glanced at the dark splotch still spreading across his upper arm from the gunshot wound. Her eyes followed his. "How far will I be able to walk? God is great, Nazichka. He has been very free with miracles today. I don't think we can expect another." She didn't answer. "Besides, however unsafe it is here," he said as he eased from behind a large boulder, watching the helicopter's upward progress, "up there it will be far more so." He smiled as the helicopter rose up the side of the valley. He felt along the detonator's face for the transmit button, the control that would send the suicidal code to the nearby nuclear warhead.

"Sasha?"

"Yes?"

"I knew you'd come back. I knew."

"Yes," he said, his finger poised over the command button. He saw the helicopter slow, come to a hover, and land halfway to the top of the valley's rim. "We all find our way home. It may take ten years. But we come back."

"Sasha . . ."

"Look away, Na:ipha," he warned her. "And stay behind the rock."

"Sasha," she said as she clung to him. "I love you."

He turned and faced her, taking her chin in one hand and bringing her face level with his. As they kissed, he pressed the button and held it down. A series of dissonant musical chirps sounded. "I love you, too."

19

THE CHAMBERS

"WHAT IS THIS PLACE?" ASKED HARPER AS THEY WERE PROD-
ded toward the open mouth of the cave. The Mi-8's engines
wound down behind them, its rotors kicking up clouds of
dust.

"I don't know," said Donovan. Ahead, the man in the
dark robes stood at the entrance to the cave. Hekmatyar
swayed from one foot to the other next to him, impatient
and eager.

Arrayed across the landing zone were two dozen armed
mujahedin, each carrying an assault rifle. Donovan slowly
turned his head as he walked, noting the second attack helicopter and the antiaircraft emplacements surrounding the
landing pad. He heard the drone of a heavy diesel generator.

"Sir," Harper whispered, "look." She nodded at a long,
low stone wall lit by a brilliant spotlight. Iron rings hung
from it on short lengths of chain. The rock was covered in
red stains. She didn't think it was rust.

"Stay close, Lieutenant. Don't let them split us up."

"Say the words," said Hekmatyar to the priest.

The Baluchi nodded, and a candle was thrust into his

hands. He lit it, then held it up and behind him, casting a dim light into the interior. The flickering light revealed the dull gray container of the stolen Russian weapon, its red internal power indicator winking on, then off, on then off.

"Behold," the Baluchi said to them in Pashto. "The power of God brought to earth. Satan has plotted to give this power to the misbelievers, the House of War. But God is a far better plotter than Satan, for now it belongs to the *Dar al Islam*, the House of Belief. You," he said, pointing to the captured fliers, "you have used this power to destroy. But we will use it to create."

"What's he yammering about?" whispered Harper.

"Quiet!" Hekmatyar admonished her.

The Baluchi continued, "In the name of evil, of misbelief, you have come to steal this power. But evil's time is over, and misbelief shall be annihilated by the Word and the Law. Contemplate your errors while you can, for at first light, you shall explain them to God Himself." He turned to Donovan. "Why have the *Amrikans* sent you?"

Donovan shook his head. He didn't understand Pashto.

"He asks why you were sent," Markelov translated.

Donovan looked at the Russian with utter contempt. "I was running behind on taking vacation days. I heard Kabul was a hot liberty town."

"He refuses," Markelov relayed.

"We will find out before this night is done." The Baluchi nodded and two guards pulled Donovan away.

The mullah's attentions turned to Harper. "Little bird, the pagans pray to females just as they pray to Satan. It is no wonder that the devil sends you to do his work. But Allah has said, 'A curse on Satan.' " He spat to the dusty ground. "We are bound to respect a woman of the faith. God demands no less, just as we are forbidden a woman in her time. But this she-devil is not a believer, thus, she is lawful

to any man who wishes to take her." He turned to Markelov. "Tell her this, and ask her who else knows of our existence here in the Valley of the L'al."

"Go fuck yourself," Harper answered after the Russian
had translated the mullah's words.

"I think she needs persuading," said Markelov. He
turned, smiling. "You should have accepted my invitation
to dinner," he whispered to her.

"Take her inside," Hekmatyar ordered.

"No!" Donovan yelled when four guards moved up behind Harper.

"Get your mitts off me!" she snarled. They prodded her
forward, careful to keep out of her reach. They'd already
heard what had happened down in the valley below.

"Harper!" Donovan called. "Lieutenant! One jump at a
time! Remember!" The nearest guard grabbed him as he
tensed to make a move. He twisted out of the grasp and
turned around swinging, his fist connecting with the guard's
jaw, snapping his head back, sending the guard's cap flying.
The next thing he knew he was on the ground, his mouth
filled with dust.

"Perhaps I misjudged," said the Baluchi. He nodded toward Donovan. "Put this one on the wall."

"What happened?" Nazipha looked over the curve of the
boulder at the wall of the valley. "It didn't . . ."

"I know," Belenko answered, jabbing his finger down on
the destruct button again and again. The only result was the
same chorus of tiny electronic tones. "Made in the fucking
Soviet Union," he seethed, then got his anger under control.
"Maybe we are out of range. How should I know? You're
the electronics expert. You tell me." Belenko pressed the
button again, imagining the valley erupting in the dazzle of
a nuclear fireball.

"If the weapon is inside the cave, then . . ."

"Yes. I must bring the device closer."

"Sasha," she said, knowing what was going through his mind, "you are in no condition to climb mountains. In the name of God, you have been *shot*. Let me."

He shook his head. "Markelov told me something. In Moscow, people stand in lines with no work. No hope. Nothing. He said uselessness was worse than being hungry. And you know? He was right."

"So?"

"I have come to do something."

"Stop the OSNAZ talk!" she snapped. "It might take hours to get up there on foot. The trail is probably watched. There were guards—"

"Sssh. I know." He snapped off the power to the transmitter. The green light went out. He shut the case.

"You can't go," she said firmly. "It is not your fight. And what if you found it? You would be right next to it when it exploded!"

"True. Wait for me down here. If I can't blow it up, maybe I can disable it somehow. Push it off a cliff, who knows? If I'm not back by sunrise—"

"No. You aren't going up there by yourself."

He stood up, swaying slightly as his balance slowly returned.

"Sasha," she said, standing right beside him. "I helped them steal the cursed thing. They killed my brother. They nearly killed me. I have come here to do something," she said, repeating Belenko's words. "And I will do it, too."

"Nazichka . . ." Belenko began to protest.

"I lost you once," she said quietly.

He sighed. "When could I ever say no to you?"

The scattered wreckage still burned in places, casting enough light for them to find the trail. It led from the airstrip toward the base of the valley wall. Holding the aluminum case, the two figures slowly merged with the darkness beyond the orange glow. In a moment, they were gone.

They took no chances. Five guards marched Harper down a long, low corridor of stone. Weak bulbs hung from bare wires strung along its length. Oil-burning torches stood ready should there be a power failure. She could smell the sweet aroma of kerosene coming from them. It was a familiar smell. Jet fuel. Home.

They came to a branch in the passage. The guards prodded her to the right. The underground gloom deepened, the very air taking on the weight of the mountain overhead. Twenty feet in, they came to a low, arched opening covered by a rough *patou* blanket. It masked a small chamber beyond. The blanket was swept aside. In the dim light of a low-watt bulb, she made out a skeletal black iron cot. A stained green blanket was thrown across it. *No. Not . . .*

"In!"

When she hesitated, four pairs of hands threw her down onto the cot as one stayed back at a safe distance, covering her with his rifle. They tied Harper's hands tightly behind her and shoved her face flat. The iron bedframe was bolted solidly to the stone floor. The rough army blanket smelled acid in her flaring nostrils. She rolled slightly to watch them take another length of rope and knot her feet together just above her boots. She glanced around the cell.

Deep within the cave, the small room had been cut from living rock. There were no openings except for the one they had pushed her through. The light came from a single bulb in the far corner. She'd wanted to fly combat. This was the nightmare, the reason combat had been denied her. Could she hack it?

She felt them tug at her boots. With a snick of a knife,

they cut the laces free and pulled them off her feet, throwing them into the corner of the chamber. The air felt cold on her toes as they moved the leg hobbles down to her ankles. "Nice and tight," she said to them. *I can handle this,* she said to herself. *I can handle this.*

The guard looked at her and pulled the hobbles until they bit into her flesh. He turned and smiled at the other three, saying something to them in quick, excited tones. They laughed.

She wiggled her feet. There was no slack in the bindings. *Idiot,* she thought. *They can't even get that right.* If they tied her legs together, they sure as hell weren't going to get them apart, and if one of them cut her loose, he'd only have himself to blame. She vowed to take the nearest two down. One way or the other.

One of the men shoved her face flat to the blanket again, and then a band of heavy plastic cut into her neck. "Hey!" she protested, straining against the neck loop. The binding was looped under the metal frame of the bed. *This is gonna make it tough to . . .*

Then someone grabbed the collar of her flightsuit. The sharp point of a knife scribed down her back, accompanied by ripping fabric. Now her back felt the chill of the cave's cold. They pulled her flightsuit off, cutting it away at her shoulders, and tossed it next to her boots. The knife returned, and her bra followed the flightsuit. She felt the waistband of her panties pull tight. The one with the knife said something else, and the other guards laughed again. The thin fabric cut like tissue under the blade. *I can handle this,* she said to herself again and again. *I can handle this.*

A rough hand thrust between her legs, but one of the other guards barked an order, and the hand went away. With a low murmur and a snicker, all five turned and left her to wait.

She listened as their footsteps receded. A final laugh echoed from rock to rock, and then it was silent. She shivered as the cold settled onto her naked back. She closed her eyes. *I can handle this,* she prayed. *I can handle this.*

At first she thought it was the wind. But then she heard voices. Whispers. She tensed and listened as they grew closer. *I can handle this.*

Nazipha put her arm out and stopped Belenko short. "Over there," she whispered. They had gone two-thirds of the way up the path from the valley without so much as hearing a patrol. The bright lights of the helicopter landing zone still burned at the entrance to the cave, almost enough to see by. The growl of a generator throbbed from above.

"Facing north. Just as I thought." Belenko calmed his breath, emptied his mind of everything but silence. He eased himself forward and listened. Up ahead, from behind a massive boulder, he could hear low voices. *Two.*

"Sasha, they might be . . ."

He put a finger to his lips and moved toward the guardpost, each step deliberate, silent. *How are they armed?* he wondered as he approached. *Probably AKs and night goggles,* he thought. An orange light flared from a cigarette lighter. *Forget the night goggles.* Then he smelled it: the unmistakable odor of *anasha.* The wild hemp grew throughout Afghanistan. *Idiots.* These troops were as bad as Russian conscripts! A giggle came from behind the rock, and another waft washed downhill to Belenko. He waited for them to start whispering again, then took another step. But before he could take another, a clatter of weapons sounded, followed by the heavy tread of unconcerned feet. Belenko froze.

Suddenly, a figure rose to full height from behind the boulder. *If he is looking this way . . .* Another flare of orange light, another giggle, and Belenko saw that the guard was facing uphill. The man put aside a glowing pipe and staggered out from behind the boulder. He took a long, looping step, lurched to the right, and stopped. The splash of urine on stone masked Belenko's final approach.

You'd never make an OSNAZ, thought Belenko, his hand tensing as he crept up directly behind the unsuspecting *mujahed.* He caught the doomed man's head in one hand, wrapped his other tight around his throat, and snapped his neck back onto itself so quickly the urine stream was unbroken.

The man was already dead as he sagged to the cold ground, a long, final breath escaping, sending warm steam into the air. *Never piss uphill.* He searched the *mujahed.* Belenko found a dagger strapped to his belt, but no firearms. He tested the blade. It was rusty and dull. *Figures.*

"Wakil?" came a voice from behind the rock.

Belenko grunted a reply as he stripped the *mujahed* of his *kaffiyeh* bandanna. He wrapped it over and around his head, leaving only his eyes exposed. The knife in hand, he staggered back to the guardpost. He stumbled by two AK-47s as he rounded the rock.

"Almost midnight. It's your turn to—"

"Yes," said Belenko, whipping out the knife.

"Who . . . ?"

Belenko leaped onto him, shoving the surprised *mujahed* flat to the rocks. "Your doom," Belenko said as his arm swung in a high arc, burying the knife in the guard's throat. He misjudged, and he heard steel grind bone. But with a twist, it was done. He let the man drop and turned back downhill, whistling softly. Nazipha materialized out of the dark, her *chador* blending perfectly with the night, her footsteps utterly silent. She carried the bright aluminum detonator box beneath her robe.

"Here." He handed her one of the guards' rifles, keeping the other for himself. He looked uphill to the brazen white light streaming from the cave. "There should be twice as many checkpoints. Patrols. Ambush sites."

"They are Hekmatyar's men, not real *mujahedin*. They never had to do battle. They got others to do the fighting, and the dying."

"Not tonight." Belenko motioned for her to follow.

They reached the lip of the broad helicopter landing area without encountering another guard. Belenko saw two antiaircraft gun emplacements to either side, and voices coming from behind their shields told him they were manned. A strong light played across the flat area, focused on a low rock wall. He counted the number of fighters, his eyes passing over the separate cluster of pilots standing near the two helicopters. *Sixteen*. Foolish and overconfident though they might be, there were still a lot of them.

Nazipha seemed to read his mind. "How will we get inside?"

"Maybe we won't have to." He watched the gunners at their ZSU-23s with avid interest. These were potent antiaircraft weapons; they could be even more deadly against mere men.

"If the weapon is deep inside, then it won't hear the signal," she whispered. She saw the Mi-8 troop chopper parked next to the Gorbach gunship and drew in her breath. The last time she had seen that craft, it was flying against a deep blue sky, and she had been falling, falling. She grabbed Belenko's arm.

"What is it?"

Nazipha shook her head. "Look," she whispered, nodding beyond the parked helicopters. One figure stood alone and isolated against the wall of rough-hewn rock. It was Donovan.

Belenko squinted, then shrugged. "Nobody made the Americans come." He turned to Nazipha and held out his hands for the detonator case. She shouldered out of her assault rifle and gave it to him.

"There is still time. I could wait while you—"

"I am with you," she said simply, and moved close beside him.

He nodded and slowly, quietly, opened the case. A turn of the master switch brought the green light back on. He closed his eyes. Before he could reconsider, before anything could intervene, his finger jammed down on the transmit button, and the same string of musical notes sounded. *How quick will it be?* he wondered. He opened his eyes. "I guess," he said as he switched off the detonator and closed the box, "we shall have to get even closer."

"We are already right on top of them."

"Listen," he said, looking at the cave's black mouth and then over at the nearest ZSU gun. "Have you ever fired one of those?"

She looked deeply offended. "Sasha, am I not an Afghan?"

The candles flickered in the central chamber of the cave, illuminating an intricate wooden screen just at the edge of the light. It separated the vaulted space from a smaller anteroom. The bundled shapes of the five Sleepers could be seen stacked like old wood against the anteroom wall. A smaller bundle lay at their feet. Joining the five was a sixth: the dull gray warhead case, its status light winking red like a beckoning beacon. A fine dust filtered down on a cold draft from overhead.

"As God is my judge," said Hekmatyar, "I believe you speak the truth. You are certain the Americans will not come looking for their own?"

"They will accommodate themselves to the new reality," said Markelov. "The Coalition in Kabul is doomed. A new wind is blowing. Washington knows it. Moscow knows it. They won't stand in the way. Trust me. I know."

"What does MAYAK know?"

"Frankly," said Markelov, "we are at the beginning of a long and fruitful relationship. You are a fist. But MAYAK can be your arm. What is one without the other?"

"The Americans fight harder than I suspected."

Markelov shook his head. "The woman is a special case."

"I hope so," said the guerrilla commander. "Go. Enjoy her. Then give her to the guards. They'll know what to do."

"And tomorrow?"

"We leave for Khadir at first light. We'll send you back to Kabul. A survivor of a terrible wreck with a cautionary story to tell the Americans. And Markelov . . . ?"

"Yes?"

"You were lucky tonight. Don't ask anything more of God. He's going to be very busy in the next few days."

"At your service."

Donovan strained against the iron rings, but they held fast. His arms were outstretched, hanging from the chains. They weren't long enough to permit him to sit. He watched the *mujahedin* load the helicopters. They were getting ready to leave. He doubted he would be invited to join them.

Think! There had to be a way. Something to use. A tool. He hunted in the light of the bonfire for something. Anything. The earth at his feet was stained dark. His boot came across something loose in the dust. He worked at it, kicking it with his toe until he saw what it was: a shard of bone. He felt his last hope dissolve as he stared at the fragment.

* * *

"Get out of here!" Markelov said to the guards loitering outside the room. "Don't worry. I'll leave her alive for you. . . . You! Give me a knife." The *mujahed* handed him a curved blade, bright and sharp. The guards moved away from the arched entry. Markelov pulled the dividing curtain aside and saw Harper's naked back on his bed.

So *small*, he thought, letting his eyes linger on her body. *So small*. He walked up to the bed, wary, watchful. Still she didn't move; not so much as a muscle flinched. He explored carefully. He had seen her break the arm of the guard down in the valley. He had no wish to ask God for luck. He let the tip of the knife run across the backs of her well-muscled legs. A sound, a voice, made him turn to the entry. "I said get out!" he roared. He heard another whisper, then silence.

"Well, fatboy," said Harper. "I guess it's just you and me."

He jumped at her words. "Don't call me that," he said, flustered. "Don't ever call me that again. You will be quiet or you will join the others at the wall."

"Don't you like to be called fatboy?"

"I said quiet!" Markelov placed the knife on the floor and pulled off his leather jacket and tossed it to the rock floor. "You are playful. But two can play. I am in control."

She strained against the neck band and felt it give slightly. She'd been stretching it out over the course of an hour. Maybe more. "Why don't you untie me, then? Like you said, fatboy, you're holding all the cards." She heard the voices outside again.

"I said quiet!" Markelov slapped Harper's naked back, leaving a red imprint of his hand. "That's better." He pulled his shirt off, then worked his pants down over his erection and stepped out of them, letting them drop to the ground. He wagged his penis close to Harper's face. Its engorged tip barely showed from beneath the folds of his gut. "This is what you will get," he said, his voice nearly choked in his excitement. "I will break you apart."

"Wake me when it's over, Tinkertoy," she said, straining at the band around her neck again. It gave a fraction of an inch more. *I can handle this. I can . . .*

"Maybe you'd rather have the knife, bitch," he cursed. He grabbed a handful of her blond hair and pulled her up against the strap holding her neck. It stretched, almost snapped.

One more of those, thought Harper as the band pulled tighter, then slackened, giving her more room to work.

"I know what whores like you want," he said, running a hand from the tie at her neck over her firm buttocks, lingering there, watching her muscles tense and twitch. "Fear gives you your pleasure, doesn't it? What will happen next? Will it be flesh, or blade? Which?" He thrust a hand between her knees and tried to push them apart, making doubly sure she could not rise against him. When he was satisfied, he eased himself on top of her, his knees digging with all his weight into the backs of her thighs. "I will make you fear me."

I can handle this, she prayed as his hand groped for her. The whispers came back. Was there a guard watching? How many? It didn't matter. Like Donovan said. She'd take them one at a time. *I can handle this.* She tensed her legs together, tight. "Looking for something?" she asked, only a tiny quaver betraying her real fears.

"This," he spat. He spread her cheeks with one hand while guiding himself with the other. She tensed again, hard as stone. He pressed against her once, again, but he could find no entry. "Don't fight. It will be over sooner if you don't fight."

"Sorry," she said between clenched teeth. "I must be nervous."

"Open yourself! Open!" he said, and slapped her again. "Open!" He reached up and yanked her hard against the neck band, then let her head flop back down. He tried forcing her legs slightly apart, but they were bound too tightly together. He heard voices from behind. He swung his sweaty head, but there was nobody. Whispers.

"What's the matter? Can't do it, *fatboy*?" Harper taunted.

"I'll kill you."

"Not with that little thing you won't."

"Shut up!" He got off her and yanked the ropes binding her ankles together. He found an end and pulled. "Now," he said as he climbed back on her.

I can do it. I can do it. I can do it! Harper cleared her mind of fear, cleared her mind of the sweaty, panting weight on her, cleared her mind of everything except one burning thought: *I'm gonna take you apart.* She breathed in deeply. Markelov forced her thighs apart. He was shoving, imbalanced, grunting like an impatient hog. *First the neck.* She gathered all her power, imagining the band around her neck snapping like ribbon. The whispers came again, but she didn't have the time to wonder. *Now!*

"I said—" Markelov began, but the next thing he knew he was sailing through the air in a wholly unexplainable fashion. A look of utter confusion on his sweaty face, he struck the cold floor, driving the breath out of his chest. He blinked. When he opened his eyes, Harper was *above* him, her hands still tied behind her. Her bare foot was coming down! "Guar—" he screamed, but it was cut off as she smashed his windpipe with her heel. His head bounced up once. She did it again, feeling the vertebrae snap.

She squatted and snatched the knife up behind her back,

cutting both her hand and the rope in two quick slices. She didn't feel the pain.

She spun again to face Pavel Markelov. He was dying.

His face went from red to purple as she watched. He clawed at his throat. He was strangling himself with his swelling neck tissues. His breath went from a gasp to a heave to a high, terminal whistle.

She leaned down as his face turned the shade of a ripe eggplant. "Don't take it personally," she said as his eyes glazed, "but a lady likes to be asked."

She left him and grabbed his leather jacket from the ground, then the blue jeans. They swallowed her. She tied off the belt so that she could move and with knife in hand, moved to the door and eased open the curtain to the corridor.

It was empty. A yellow glow illuminated the cave's main corridor. A cool breeze flowed in. Silently, padding on bare feet, she walked down the black hall of stone, the knife in her hands. *I can handle it,* she said to herself. She smiled and felt a wash of victory flow through her like a powerful electric charge. The blade felt good, its weight a confirmation of her abilities. She fully planned to use it. The image of the Baluchi ordering Svoboda to be shot played in her memory as she neared the main hall.

Harper froze. She heard voices coming from around the bend. *Chief,* she thought as she flattened herself against the wall, silent, waiting, *the Russian was mine. But the next one's for you.* She tensed her knife arm, all her power, her energy flowing into its sharp point. A lightning rod begging to be struck.

The footsteps grew louder. Suddenly, from around the bend, the spotlight outside the mouth of the cave shattered. Then came the heavy stutter of a big gun. A single green meteor streaked down the corridor, sparking as it bounced from rock wall to rock wall, spalling chips of stone as it came. The guards shouted and ran out, away from her. She fell flat to the ground as a second shell flashed by, detonating deep inside the cave with a *crack!* She low-crawled back to the main corridor. A hot orange glare erupted, brighter than noon.

As Harper looked down toward the cave's entrance, a rolling cloud of live fire was coming her way.

Nazipha swiveled the ZSU from the burning Mi-24 and fired a long burst right above the heads of the guards defending the cave. The searchlight was out, Belenko had made sure of that, but she could see well enough by the flames of the burning gunship. The defenders were sheltered behind large rocks, their return fire now a steady yellow wink of AKs; but it was no protection from the ZSU. She squeezed the firing handles. The 23-mm shells struck the rocks and exploded, showering the *mujahedin* with shrapnel from above and behind. Their return fire faltered. These were not hard-bitten guerrillas, after all; they were Hekmatyar's men, more used to ambush than being ambushed. She pumped out another string of shells, the green tracers flashing and caroming off the rocks.

Men were running now, some screaming for mercy, leaving their weapons behind, their figures casting long, frantic shadows.

She wheeled the ZSU around to face the intact Mi-8. The burning gunship blew up as the fires reached its ammunition. White-hot fragments laced the night, mowing down two *mujahedin* caught in the open. A rattle of metal struck the ZSU's metal shield, then a round spanged off, followed by a second, then a third. She ignored the return fire as she blipped the azimuth controller so that both barrels were pointed at the Mi-8's open hatch. *Little bird,* the voice came back to her as she took hold of the firing handles, *fly!* The Baluchi's face swam up from her nightmare, his mirrored sunglasses glinting. The phantom's face wrinkled into a laugh. She closed her eyes and squeezed the firing handles, and the gun pumped and rocked.

She fired a full tray—fifty rounds—of 23-mm projectiles into the Mi-8. A tremendous rolling detonation washed over her, silencing the ragged popcorn report of the defenders' rifles. When she opened her eyes, the helicopter was gone, and in its place a yellow cloud boiled up toward the stars.

She reached down and hauled up another coil of 23-mm rounds and fed it into the waiting tray. No return fire came from the cave; the silence was broken only by the moaning of the wounded. She let go of the firing handles and eased off the ZSU's seat. *Now,* she thought once more of the Baluchi, *for you.*

Taking her own RPK machine gun, Nazipha stalked across the killing ground like an avenging spirit and made for the entry to the cave.

Firelight streamed in from the landing area outside the cave. It was bright enough to see that the two men Harper had planned to kill were already dead, burned by flaming gases the explosion had injected into the corridor. She listened, but the firefight had stopped as quickly as it had started. *Donovan,* she thought. The air was sweet with the stink of flaming jet fuel and roasted flesh as she moved silently toward the mouth of the cave.

She sensed the presence of another person, a softening of sound, a faint edging outline of heat against the cold stone. She spun, the blade coming up, but it was too late.

"Markelov!" Belenko kicked her legs out from under her and snatched the knife from her grip, throwing it aside. He was on her in a flash, a knife of his own pressed to her throat. She felt the blade push at her skin, then its tip broke through. She was paralyzed by the certainty of death. She closed her eyes. *Oh, God,* she thought, *oh, God* . . . Then the pressure relented. A trickle of hot blood streamed down her neck onto the rock. The knife was plucked away.

"You?" Belenko said, incredulous. "You? I thought it was . . . but . . ."

She opened her eyes and saw Belenko, a *kaffiyeh* wrapped around his head.

"What are you doing here?" he said. "I thought . . ." He released her, moving back toward the crevice he had hidden in. He retrieved a bright aluminum case.

"You have . . . ," she croaked, her voice coming back, "you brought . . ."

"Yes." A slight sound came from behind. He turned and whistled. A whistle came back, the soft warbling of a little bird.

Nazipha padded up, her dark *chador* black against the backdrop of the fires outside. "Ready," she said.

"Come on," he whispered to her, ignoring Harper completely. They walked by her, but then Belenko stopped. Almost as an afterthought, he turned and spoke. "This is not your fight. There is a trail down the mountain just beyond the helicopters. Get out and run as far and as fast as you can." He held up the detonator case, turned, and disappeared with Nazipha into the heart of the cave.

Harper got to her feet, feeling the puncture wound at her throat. *Donovan,* she thought. Her hand fell away. She stepped over the bodies of the two men caught in the fireball and made her way outside.

It was a vision of hell. The landing area was scattered with burning wreckage from the two helicopters; the heat seared her skin as she held up a hand against it. The air was punctuated by the moans of the wounded. She kicked a rifle, then stooped to pick it up. *Oh, Jesus, don't let him be dead,* she prayed as she bent low, keeping behind the cover of rocks, working her way to the last place she had seen him.

"Markelov?" Donovan croaked, his voice a hoarse whisper. No. Was he hallucinating again? Had he just seen . . . Yes! "Lieutenant?" He was hanging from the iron rings fastened around his hands, his arms stiffened over his head.

Harper stepped up from the darkness. "Commander! I'll get you down in a flash." She put down the rifle and examined the iron bands. Fastened with a heavy catch, they had bitten deep into Donovan's wrists. "I'll bust you out in a second."

"I thought . . . I thought you were . . ."

She jammed the barrel of the AK into a link in the chain and twisted. The iron snapped. She broke the band holding his other arm, catching his fall as the metal yielded, letting him down to the ground, his arms still extended over his head.

"I can't . . . ," he said, "I can't move them."

"Sir, he's got it with him. He's in there. The detonator, I mean, Belenko. He and the woman are in the cave."

"What?"

"He said there was a trail down to the airstrip." She looked and saw the cut in the rocks beyond the landing area. "Over there. We've got to get down and away. He's gonna blow that damned thing!" She heard a voice, then another. She spun. Whispers.

Donovan forced one arm down to his side, feeling the rip of tendon and tissue. He cried out as he commanded the other arm down as well. "Okay . . . Lieutenant. Okay." He moved his boots under his body, and Harper helped him to his feet. "Your flightsuit . . ." he said, noticing the strange outfit she wore. Markelov's leather jacket was open, her breasts smudged by soot and dust. The jeans were as loose as an Afghan *shalwar kameez*. "Where . . ." He looked away. "Markelov . . ."

"Won't be coming along. It's a long story. Let's get moving. I hope I get to tell it to you sometime."

As they penetrated deeper into the cave, the firelight streaming in from the mouth dimmed and finally, around a bend, went utterly black.

Nazipha held her hands out before her as they moved along the wall, feeling their way in. "Sasha, it could be anywhere. Maybe you should try it from here."

"No. We will come—" Suddenly, a blinding white flash erupted not fifteen feet away, and the bright spark of a bullet whined by Belenko's head. The muzzle flash had illuminated for an instant a dark, robed figure standing in the corridor.

Nazipha knew who it was. Firing from the hip, she sent a stream of RPK fire right at the ghostly form, but when the noise died away, she could hear him laughing.

"Little Bird," said the Baluchi as he turned up his low-light goggles to full, "you have flown a long, long way." The goggles gave him a perfectly clear view of the two figures. They were tight to the wall, a bright case at their feet. He knew he was completely invisible. He saw Nazipha raise the rifle and ducked into a crevice. The shots spanged away and he laughed again. "What have you brought me in that box?" he said as he squeezed off a shot.

A chip of flying rock sliced across Nazipha's brow. "How can he see us?"

"By the Faith," the Baluchi said, and laughed. He watched the two intruders, waiting for the right moment, then turned and hurried deeper into the cave. "By the Faith!" he called out.

His words and his laughter echoed after him.

20

VICTORY

THE DARKNESS WAS COMPLETE; THE SILENCE WAS AS HEAVY AS dense fog as Belenko eased along the rough wall of the cave, with Nazipha right behind him. *That bastard could be anywhere,* he thought as he moved, one step at a time. How did that black-robed bastard see? There was no telling which step was safe, and which would be fatal. Then Belenko realized. *Of course. He's using PNVs. He could be ...* His hand brushed against something soft and he sucked in his breath.

"What ... ?"

"Quiet," he whispered. He grabbed hold of the object. It was a rolled piece of cloth. He put it to his nose. *Kerosene?*

"What is it?"

"A torch of some kind. I think ..." He froze. Someone was up ahead in the dark!

"Who are they?" asked Nazipha.

He listened. The voices were inaudible. Yet somehow they seemed close. Whispers. But coming from where? Inside his head?

"Sasha, how can he see us?"

300

"Infrared goggles. PNV-57s probably. Standard Red Army issue. MAYAK again. Money talks."

"Then what can we do? How far does this cave go?"

"Why ask me? You're the one who knows so much about the Cave of the Sleepers. Remember?"

"It's just an old story!"

"Apparently not." He laughed softly.

"What's so funny?"

"Here we are doing our best to find the one thing that will surely kill us. People really are crazy."

"Listen!"

The whispers were back. Louder.

"I have an idea." Belenko sniffed the kerosene again. He reached into his breast pocket. He was long out of Primas, but the matches were still there. "I think I know how we can catch him," he said, holding up the oily cloth. It was as dark as the back of the moon, but still, Belenko had an idea by the throat. "He sees in infrared. With this we can overload the goggles for a few seconds. He might be confused for an instant and freeze. You might get a shot before he reacts."

"But first we have to find him."

"I have another idea." Belenko took hold of the aluminum detonator case and began to scrape it against the rock wall.

The Baluchi froze and turned, swinging his head from side to side to survey the tunnel behind. *Where are they?* They were fools to follow him. *And how did that woman live?* He stopped, a snarl forming on his lips as he heard the scraping of feet. They had ruined years of careful planning. If both helicopters had been damaged then . . . it would be a disaster unless . . . He stopped, listening to the steady *scrape scrape scrape*. His fist formed into a gnarled ball. He could see. They could not. He brought the Makarov up to the lenses of his goggles and checked. There were plenty of bullets left. He began to walk toward the sound.

The walls of the cave were bright green as he retraced his steps back. The tunnel took a slight bend. The sound was stronger now. His view was perfect. He waited, but where were they? He moved closer to the bend in the corridor. Yes! There was no doubt! They were right around the edge. Close. A meter. Half.

He inched closer, his body flat to the wall. He came to the turn, his fingers feeling the rounded edge of the stone, the other holding the 9-mm at the ready. Silent as a shadow, like a spirit, like the hand of God Himself moving unseen upon the world, he moved out into the open and turned. A ragged smile broke out as his goggles revealed both of them not ten feet distant! They were huddled together. His smile became a disdainful sneer. *One bullet,* he thought, bringing the Makarov level, *will kill them both.*

Belenko's nerves extended like a piano-wire net cast before him. His head felt ready to explode. He held the oily cloth in one hand, a match ready to strike in the other. He heard a noise, a warning. Then silence. *Easy. . . .* Another twinge, almost subliminal, almost imaginary, vibrated his taut nerves. It was as faint as the falling of a single snowflake, but for Belenko, it was enough. He stopped short and gave Nazipha the sign. She put down the case and leveled the RPK.

When it came, the click of the Makarov's firing mechanism was as loud as a fire alarm. "Now!" he screamed, striking the match and setting the oily cloth alight just as the crack of the shot split the air. A solid blow struck Belenko's head, doubling his vision. He nearly dropped the flaring cloth but did not. He could not. He felt a wild strength course through him; a steadying, reassuring strength.

Nazipha aimed and fired at the Baluchi's black robe. The Kalashnikov's muzzle blasted yellow as the Baluchi twisted away behind a bend in the corridor.

Wearily, Belenko sagged to the ground, blood streaming from a gash at his temple.

"Sasha!"

"Help me stand. I think"—he shook his head to clear his wandering vision—"I think you hit him."

The Baluchi's side boiled in waves of agony. He touched the wound and nearly fainted from the pain. *That woman,* he seethed. His hate gave him back his strength. *That woman.* His robe was already wet, soaked through with his blood. He pushed away the hurt and clamped down hard on the bloody hole, biting his lip to keep from screaming out loud. Nevertheless, a moan escaped his dry lips as he held his gut.

He turned the insect eye of his goggles down the corridor. The white flare of the fire was guttering out. A fresh jab rose from his torn flesh. He staggered to his feet and retreated deeper into the cave, leaving bright drops of blood to mark his passage. *I must . . .* He stopped, listening. All he could hear was the frantic beating of his heart. *I must get to it . . . they cannot be allowed. Not allowed.* He hurried, leaving a clear crimson trail as he went, heading straight for the shrine at the very heart of the Cave of the Sleepers.

The path down the mountain rounded out onto the valley floor. There below them, the embers of the *Galloping Grape* glowed softly under the stars. "At the other end," she said to Donovan, pointing to the east. "We flew right over it when I . . . when we crashed."

Donovan noticed the bloodstains at Harper's neck. A rivulet ran down between her breasts. "You're cut, Lieutenant. How did it . . . I mean, did that . . ."

"Don't worry. I handled it." She zipped up Markelov's leather jacket. "Remember, sir? One jump at a time."

Donovan turned. The sky to the east was alight with the faintest wash of the coming dawn, outlining the mountains as black, constricting walls to the north and south. "Markelov. The Russian was working with them."

"Was."

Donovan stopped and stared at her.

"He won't be coming out, sir. I saw Belenko go in. With the detonator."

"I see. Then we'd better hurry."

"Yes, sir. We'd better."

The Baluchi was sweating in the cold air of the cave. He swiped his face, forgetting he still wore the night goggles, and sent them skittering to the floor. To his utter amazement, the darkness was far from complete. Ahead, a gold light beckoned from the cave's central chamber. *Be praised,* he thought, *the bomb is still guarded.* His feet crunched the ruined night goggles as he stumbled to the light.

The light grew stronger as he neared the low arched entry to the central room. Suddenly, a fleeting shape rocketed out of the passage. The Baluchi stared in utter horror as a small dog ran by him. The Cave of the Sleepers was one of Islam's most holy places! Dogs were unclean! In his fury he forgot his wound, his pain. "Who has befouled this shrine with a dog?" The beast scampered off into the darkness. He would see to it that the responsible party was punished! Punished! He walked to the doorway, summoning up his reserves of energy, bent his head low, and entered.

The bomb case was there. The red eye on its status board winked on, then off, on then off.

Where was Hekmatyar? He should be here! The Baluchi slowly, painfully turned. A multitude of candles burned, their flames flickering under the breath of an unseen draft. Then he looked at the old wooden screen, the one dividing the chamber off from the resting place of the five Sleepers. Mummies, as Hekmatyar had called them. Dried husks of men who probably wandered up here and died a natural . . . the Baluchi's mouth dropped open.

They were gone.

He turned again, trembling now. Who had robbed the cave? Who had defiled it with a dog? The Baluchi's thoughts struck a solid, inescapable wall. *Some say they were three, their dog the fourth among them. Others say five . . . only my Lord knoweth best their true number. . . .*

"No," was all the Baluchi could say. "No."

Whom God leaves to stray, for him no protector shall show him to the Right Way.

Just then, a sound came from behind him.

The Baluchi saw the flames of Belenko's torch appear in the entryway. He raised the black Makarov, but try as he might, the weight of it bore his arm back to his side. His heart began to beat faster and faster. He raised it again when Belenko's face appeared, and once again his arm sagged back down. Impotent. Nazipha's face joined Belenko's as they peered into the chamber. His heart was ready to burst from his chest, stumbling over its own chattering rhythms as her eyes locked onto his.

"Snake," she said, pushing Belenko aside. "You have run out of places to hide." She pointed the RPK at his chest.

"Nazipha, no," said Belenko. "It doesn't matter now."

"It matters to me. For my brother. For me. For the country you have betrayed with your holy lies. For everyone you have ever deceived with your poison. In the name of the true believers, your sentence is death."

"No," said Belenko, pushing the barrel of the RPK down.

She swatted him away and aimed the machine gun again. "Pray that God is forgiving." She tightened her finger on the trigger. "Because I am not."

"No!" Belenko screamed as the muzzle blast flamed yellow.

The Baluchi's black robe erupted with a hundred tiny, terrible plucks. The rifle's roar echoed in his ears as he fell. The rock floor felt warm, yielding, as though it were made of softest carpet instead of bare stone. But as he surrendered to it, as death reached a comforting hand to his heart, something happened. Something stopped. A looming shadow fell across him as he lay. A presence.

Agony, like storm surf, washed over him in waves, piling higher and higher, hotter, fiercer. He was drowning in it. He prayed for release. But he could not die. *Stop it!* he screamed, though nothing escaped the bloody froth at his lips. All he heard in reply was whispers. *Stop it!* But the agony doubled, then doubled again. From the depth of the ghostly shadow he heard a sound: it was laughter.

"Nazipha."

When the full clip had been fired, a musical tinkling echoed as brass casings came to rest on the hard floor.

A voice came from behind Belenko. He spun, but there was nothing. It came again. The words, the whispers. Belenko knew what to do.

He snapped open the detonator case and touched the master switch; the green light already glowed.

Belenko reached out and touched Nazipha's warm hand.

She looked up at him, the fear receding at his touch, at his reassuring smile. "The Sleepers are gone," she said.

"Maybe they were never here."

"Where will we go?"

"Who knows? But we'll go there together. Did I not promise?" He had no doubt that the bomb would hear this final summons. The sixth Sleeper would soon wake.

They came to the abandoned Lisunov, its tail black against the milky aura of early sunrise. Donovan squinted at it. It was both odd and familiar. It *looked* like a DC-3 with its tail low and its cockpit way up high. It had the same two radial engines, the same fat cigar of a fuselage, and a long, stout wing that defied age. But . . .

"Sir?" Harper had found the hatch to its cabin unlocked. "Belenko means to blow the device. I don't know how far away we have to be, but . . ."

"Hawaii," he said as he climbed up into the open hatch. "But I don't"—he saw she was already gone—"think this is a gooney bird."

"Doesn't matter," said Harper, looking around the oddly designed interior. The floor tilted up toward the high cockpit. She pulled the hatch closed and dogged it down tight.

He followed her forward. It was like walking up a long inclined ramp. At the end of the aft cabin, they came to a door. On the other side, the smell of an old airplane cockpit wafted by them. The stink of sweat, rotted leather padding, old wiring, and spilled hydraulic fluid was unmistakable. Home.

"I hope this works," she said. She automatically settled into the left seat. The pilot's seat. *I can handle this, too.*

As Donovan eased down into the right, he saw her peering at the instruments.

"Damn, this thing is all in Russian." She checked the

overhead switch panel. A snapped switch brought on dim cockpit lights. "It's all wrong! How can we—"

"Take it easy, Hot Dog. It must be a copy. Their version of the old gooney. I used to fly SNBs. This won't be that different. I'll talk you through it, but you've got to do the flying."

"But, I mean, how can I fly this without . . ."

"It's the only set of wings we have, Lieutenant," he reassured her. "You could fly the *Grape* by ear, couldn't you?"

"That was different."

"Come on, Hot Dog, you haven't scared me yet. If it's a good copy"—Donovan nodded at the far subpanel—"the starters will be over there. Port side first. Prime 'em, clear 'em, and crank 'em over, and let's get the hell out of here."

"Not much battery left," she said, nodding at the dim lights.

"Then it better be enough. Fuel levers on, left and right. Go ahead."

"Yes, sir." She unlocked the manual primer knob and gave the first engine a shot of raw fuel.

"Crank one, mags off. Count four blades and switches hot."

"Cranking one." The starter whined and the big blade thumped once, twice, three times. On the fourth pass she swung the magneto lever. The Lisunov stumbled, snorted, and finally, with a clank and a shudder of cold pistons, kicked over.

"Yep," said Donovan as he listened to the ancient, familiar rumble of a radial engine. "It may be a copy, but that sound is pure Pratt and Whitney. Now"—he nodded at the controls for the other engine—"do it again."

Harper got the second mill turning with greater aplomb.

"Go ahead and taxi us," he directed. "Better take the

edge of the runway. We tore up the middle coming in with the *Grape*."

"Roger." Harper goosed the throttles and swung the old Lisunov out onto the runway. She slewed them over to the far edge. "Sir, I've never—"

"Hot Dog, I trust you. Let's get headed east, okay? One jump at a time."

"Yes, sir." She swept both throttles full forward and the old transport began to rumble down the runway. She glanced at the instruments, but they were all measured in strange units. Liters of borscht. She listened instead, and when the old bird sounded ready, she hauled back on the yoke.

They were flying!

She banked them around until the heavy glass windscreen was filled with the delicate light of dawn. She kept the throttles in full, letting the Lisunov climb at its own pace.

The terrain fell away below as the sky ahead turned from gray to red. To her left, a few guttering fires still burned before the mouth of the cave. "You know the old saying, sir?"

"Which one, Lieutenant?"

"About it being better to be on the ground, wishing you were flying, instead of the other way around?"

"What about it?"

"They were wrong."

"Maybe. I just hope this thing . . ." Donovan didn't finish his sentence. The right engine blew its last wisps of oil overboard. With a shudder, the ancient pistons seized, then released, then seized again, the metal spot-welding itself into a useless lump. The RPM dial staggered down, dying, as the old plane yawed, on the edge of a spin.

"Feather it!" Harper shouted.

Donovan's hand went to where the propeller feather con-

trol was in a real DC-3 and punched a big red button. As
the pistons glowed white hot, as smoke trailed from the exhausts, the pitted prop slowed, slowed, and stopped. An instant later, the engine froze with a terrible, terminal clank.

"Jesus," she said as she stood on one rudder pedal bare-
foot and banked into the dead engine. Donovan's boots
were jammed down on his own pedals, helping her. They
could just hold altitude. The pass into the lower Bamian
Valley was dead ahead. The old Li-2 was flying like a balanced broomstick. Anything, a gust, a moment's lapse in
her concentration, and they'd do a wingover straight into
the rocks. The pass looked black, backlit by the red wash
of sunrise. How long would the good engine hold?

"Low country dead off the nose," said Donovan.

"It better be." She risked a look at Donovan. "You're
getting pretty good at feathering engines."

"You're giving me a lot of practice." He glanced at the
instrument panel. "We're still flying. I think."

"Yes, sir," she said, sweat breaking out on her forehead
as they rumbled toward the pass. "We are."

Right engine dead, the left putting out everything it had,
they entered the twisting hall of stone.

"It's time."

"I know," Nazipha replied.

"You know what?" said Belenko.

"You said it was time."

"Did I? Maybe I did." He squeezed Nazipha's hand.

"What about Hekmatyar? I think he escaped."

"Forget him," said Belenko. "Without the bomb, history
will, too."

"God damn!" Harper whooped as the last twist in the
canyon's passage revealed the opening flatlands of the

Bamian Valley. She glanced out at the howling engine. "Thank God and Pratt and Whitney!"

"And the Russians who copied it," said Donovan.

She edged the left engine's throttle back, then a little more. They began to lose altitude, but now they could afford to. The high country receded behind them.

"To think," said Donovan, "we almost let the Air Force have you."

"Ready?" asked Belenko.

"With you."

Belenko pressed the detonator button. The same series of musical notes sounded. But this time they were different. They'd sounded discordant before. Unconnected. Not this time. This time they were music.

A hot sliver of sun broke the eastern horizon, lasering a brilliant beam straight down the Bamian Valley. It grew from a fragment into a perfect golden crescent. "Pretty," said Harper. Her leg was stiff from holding full rudder pressure against the dead engine. The plane was still descending, though as the wings bit into denser air, their rate of fall was slowing. If they didn't need to climb between here and Kabul, they would make it.

She looked at the terrain outside the oily windscreen. "If I remember that mountain, we should be fifty miles out of Kabul. How are your arms?"

"About like your leg."

"We make a great team."

"That we do." Donovan felt the warmth of the sun bring life back to his skin. He looked at her and smiled.

Suddenly, a brilliant flash lit the very tops of the mountains, turning them blinding white, dousing the sun itself. Then it was gone. Harper twisted in her seat and saw an angry sphere boil up from the other side of the high pass. From the Valley of the L'al.

Purple and orange flashed from the sphere's circumference, turning yellow as it rose higher, higher. It paled as it rocketed upward. As it veiled the crescent moon, it was thin as gauze. A spherical shock wave crashed against the unyielding granite walls of the valley, reflecting back and forth, dying away. In the lee of the pass, the Li-2 never felt a bump.

"I guess that's it," Donovan said. "We did it."

"Belenko did it." Harper pulled off a touch of power to the left engine, letting the Lisunov descend again. The mouth of the Bamian Valley opened onto the Kabul plain. Dead ahead. She faced Donovan. "There's another thing, sir. My reassignment."

"Don't worry, Lieutenant. Fly as well as you do, you're staying put. You are one impressive young lady. I mean that."

"After crashing one airplane and losing—"

"Carranza and Svoboda were doing what they loved, Harper. They were lucky that way. Most people never get that chance."

She nodded. "But that's just it. I want my chance."

"Done. I'm supposed to head up this new training wing at NAS Barbers Point. How would you like to take on teaching those wet-eared kids how to fly P-3s and survive?"

"Commander, I'm honored that you'd ask me that, and it isn't that it wouldn't be a good idea, even though the Navy would have a fit—"

"I'll take care of the Navy."

"Even if you could, I mean, it *is* a good idea. They ought to know how to be more than a clay pigeon. But I want . . ."

"Fighters?" Donovan filled in.

"Sir, Commander, I learned something in that cave. I

have fighters in me. I really want them. And I can handle it. Combat, I mean. Both sides of it. I know it. Not that teaching someone how to roll a P-3 wouldn't be fun, but it feels like another dead end. You said most people don't get their chance. Well, I want mine." The mouth of the valley opened below them. Kabul appeared off their right wing. She released some of the heavy rudder pressure, letting the plane naturally bank itself into the dead engine. The long runway appeared at the foot of the low, dusty city.

"They wouldn't let you fly in combat. The Navy won't change that much."

"Who knows?" she said with a sly grin. "Remember. One jump at a time." She pulled back power and angled down toward the airport. "Well? What do you say? I'm ready if the Navy is ready."

"Hot Dog, all I have to say is, they'd better be."

"Gear," she called. The runway was dead ahead. Close.

"Coming down." As Donovan reached over and pulled the lever out and down, Afghanistan rose to meet them.